We step and do not step into the same river,
we are and we are not.

Heraclitus

PENGUIN BOOKS

Spilt Milk

Praise for *22 Britannia Road*:

'So convincing, completely gripping, admirable'
Daily Mail

werful, stark and beautiful. Alive to the compromises, deceptions and passions that traumatic situations can demand'
Marie Claire

'An affecting story, extremely well told'
The Times

'A moving, powerful account of the day-to-day struggle for survival'
Sunday Times

'A most accomplished first novel. Powerful story-telling and entirely convincing in its evocation of post-war England' Penelope Lively

'Gripping . . . a deeply felt debut' Helen Simonson

rrowing, terrifying, heartbreaking, incredibly moving. Prepare to be left teary-eyed more than once'
Stylist

'A riv ing historical novel, set in post-WWII England . . . crimes of love and war'
Oprah.com

'Convincing, touching'
Independent on Sunday

'A haunting debut'
Easy Living

'A moving WWII debut'
Grazia

'Readable and engaging throughout'
Financial Times

ABOUT THE AUTHOR

Amanda Hodgkinson was born in Burnham-on-Sea in Somerset and grew up in Essex and Suffolk. She currently lives in south-west France with her husband. Her first novel, *22 Britannia Road*, is available in Penguin.

Spilt Milk

AMANDA HODGKINSON

PENGUIN BOOKS

PENGUIN BOOKS

Published by the Penguin Group
Penguin Books Ltd, 80 Strand, London WC2R 0RL, England
Penguin Group (USA) Inc., 375 Hudson Street, New York, New York 10014, USA
Penguin Group (Canada), 90 Eglinton Avenue East, Suite 700, Toronto, Ontario,
Canada M4P 2Y3 (a division of Pearson Penguin Canada Inc.)
Penguin Ireland, 25 St Stephen's Green, Dublin 2, Ireland
(a division of Penguin Books Ltd)
Penguin Group (Australia), 707 Collins Street, Melbourne,
Victoria 3008, Australia (a division of Pearson Australia Group Pty Ltd)
Penguin Books India Pvt Ltd, 11 Community Centre,
Panchsheel Park, New Delhi – 110 017, India
Penguin Group (NZ), 67 Apollo Drive, Rosedale, Auckland 0632,
New Zealand (a division of Pearson New Zealand Ltd)
Penguin Books (South Africa) (Pty) Ltd, Block D, Rosebank Office Park,
181 Jan Smuts Avenue, Parktown North, Gauteng 2193, South Africa

Penguin Books Ltd, Registered Offices: 80 Strand, London WC2R 0RL, England

www.penguin.com

First published 2014
001

Typeset in 11/13pt Dante MT Std by Palimpsest Book Production Ltd, Falkirk, Stirlingshire
Printed in Great Britain by Clays Ltd, St Ives plc

PAPERBACK ISBN: 978–1–905–49071–4
TRADE PAPERBACK ISBN: 978–0–241–00435–7

www.greenpenguin.co.uk

For Little Pan and Kitty, with love.

They were a mend-and-make-do kind of family and you had to love them for it. For their patchwork quilt of births, deaths and marriages, the mistakes and foolish regrets, and all the pretty little silken scraps of good things too. They had come together for a family picnic that day. Nellie sat in her deckchair in the shade of summer-green willows, watching them arrive.

The slow procession of men, women and children made their way down to the riverbank, stepping through long grass, one after the other, their hands drifting through the day's fragile bloom of field poppies, all the newborn crimson petals falling at their touch.

The murmur of voices, the greetings and talk turned to seasons remembered, harvests and ploughing, the days of childhood. They discussed winters long ago gone, whose legendary harshness was in retrospect to be marvelled at and even doubted a little, particularly this deep in the year when the barley fields were pale gold and in the distance the village with its church spire and the tarmac roads beyond shimmered into the vagueness of a heat haze.

Black and white farm dogs lay low, eyeing the Tupperware boxes of sandwiches and sausage rolls. The transistor radio announced cricket scores. A tartan rug was spread out by the bulrushes, and the baby in its frilly white knickers and matching bonnet wriggled and laughed while the women cooed over her. Sunburnt men sprawled in the grass with bottled beers, straw hats tipped low across their brows.

Resemblances were strong among them, and Nellie often thought the missing ones, those who were absent today, would be no different. They would no doubt have inherited the stubborn streak that ran in the family, the same tendency to freckle in the sun, the same deep eyes and perhaps the overfull upper lip that must have come from her mother originally and had somehow found its way through generations of faces, so that some of the family shared what they called the 'Marsh sisters' look'.

Oh, heavens, Nellie thought, eyeing the new baby. And how did I get to be so old?

She looked at the river, its cool waters running through the fields. She longed to take off her shoes and stockings and dip her feet in its currents once again. A frog croaked and leapt in the reeds. As a young girl Nellie had known love by this river and too much sorrow to speak of. She knew its heart and what it guarded there, down where fish the colour of stones lurked like secrets in its dark and silted bed.

A boat was pushed out onto the water. The oars splashed. Nellie listened to the talk around her, the baby babbling, the creak of the poplar trees. She could feel the earth gathering itself under her feet. The low buzz of things growing. The river that would run on into the future. She remembered the young woman she had once been. Go on, she urged her memories. Go on. Swim!

PART ONE

One

Their eyes were the colour of the river. Grey as rain-swelled waters. It was how you knew the three of them were related. Nellie, Vivian and Rose Marsh.

They lived miles outside the village, down by the river which curved like the blade of a hay sickle around their home. No children needed loving or scolding in their two-up, two-down thatched cottage, no men needed breakfasts cooked or work clothes mended, but there was still plenty to occupy the women.

Rose believed in the glory of work and each morning the sisters left their beds as though their names had been called, rising to their chores before dawn. There was the rustle of skirts, the rough sound of boots on wooden floors, a chorus of coughing, sleep still thick in their lungs. The stove door slammed, water boiled. Chamber pots were emptied, the clank of the ash bucket handle ringing out in the silence that hung over meadows and woodland.

Nellie rinsed the chamber pots under the water pump by the garden gate. This morning she had a feeling something was going to happen, and she wasn't sure whether it was good or bad. She hoped it wasn't bad luck stirring in the March wind. She would go in soon and tell Rose and Vivian what she felt. They'd probably roll their eyes. Rose might say she was a farm worker, not a fortune-teller.

She touched the rabbit's paw in her pocket and decided it would be good luck. They deserved a change in fortune. Rose was in poor health again. The potato clamp was nearly empty, and mice had got at the flour bin last week when Vivian left the lid off.

She was about to go in when she heard footsteps and in the dim light saw a man walking along the grassy track towards the cottage. He had a knapsack on his back, his hat pulled low over his ears, his collar turned up. He walked quickly, as though he might be carrying news. With sudden excitement Nellie imagined him stopping at the cottage. Perhaps he was a distant relative. Another family member long forgotten, come to change their lives and fortunes? She waited, watching. He had come for a reason, surely?

He took the path down to the river away from the cottage, past the handsome black poplar trees which gave their cottage its name. As he walked away, Nellie felt a sense of disappointment that was so deep, it was as though she had suffered a great loss. She knew there was no sense in it – nobody ever visited them – yet she had been sure he was going to speak to her. He walked on, past the small wooden jetty where fishermen tied punts and boats in the summer months. Nellie loved to swim there, a place where the river bed dropped down into deeper water. Even in winter, she braved its heart-stopping coldness.

A flock of starlings shook themselves noisily out of the trees, streaming upwards into the turquoise sky. When she looked again, the man was gone and her sisters were at the door, calling her inside.

All through breakfast there was much talk and discussion. It dispelled Nellie's earlier low spirits, replacing them with a feeling of purpose. She had been the one who had seen the man. It felt like an important claim to make.

'Was he tall?' asked Vivian, pouring honey on her porridge and licking a drop of spilt sweetness from her finger.

'Not terribly.'

'Short then?'

Nellie shook her head.

'He was whistling. Though I didn't recognize the tune.'

'A whistler and a crowing hen will bring the devil from his den,' said Rose briskly. 'We should lock the door today.'

Rose didn't like a stranger coming so close to the cottage. She opened a newspaper and began searching for stories of escaped convicts or drunken soldiers absconding from barracks. Single men looked for wives around here. A woman could be bought for seven shillings and sixpence, the cost of a marriage licence. A married man got himself a better wage on a farm than a single one.

Rose looked at Vivian eating porridge, twenty-three years old, her blonde hair swept into a bun. Nellie, fifteen months younger, sat beside her. Her shoulder-length dark brown hair was plaited in a tight style that pulled at the corners of her eyes. She was strong-looking. Moon-faced with the smooth features of a carved saint. She was the one who most closely resembled Mother.

When their father died, Rose and Mother had lived in this cottage with the new baby Nellie and toddling Vivian. It had been a brief time of perfect happiness after the misery of losing Father. And then, just after Nellie's second birthday, Mother caught diphtheria, brought to their East Anglian village by city children come from London to holiday at Hymes Court, the big estate fifteen miles away. Rose was seventeen when Mother died, just a child herself. The sense of abandonment burned within her even now, so many years later. There had been anger too, at the unfairness of being left to raise the girls alone. In those early years of bringing them up, working at the Langhams' farm, struggling to keep them fed and clothed, Rose's dreams had been filled with ways of losing the children. She'd imagined forests where she might leave them. She'd dreamed of market-day crowds, the girls in their straw hats, neat pinafores and button-up boots, motionless as pale stones, and she hurrying away from them, fast as rainwater rushing down a drain.

Some nights when Rose had longed for sleep, after a day's work at the Langhams' farm, when the little girls suffered from illness and would not settle, she remembered the story of Moses. He was floated downriver by his mother and found by the Pharaoh's daughter who then unknowingly employed the mother to care for the boy. As the children's coughing and crying filled Rose's exhausted hours, the story made more and more sense to her. She would float them down the river in the hope that some rich lady might find them.

In the light of morning though, she always changed her mind. How could Moses' mother have abandoned the child, knowing the river might take him for itself?

'I suppose I am stuck with you,' she told the girls. She remembered how their grey eyes had stared anxiously up at her. How they had clung to her skirts.

Seasons came and went and came again, until one day Rose looked at the sisters and was shocked. They were young women, just as she had once been. Her fears over raising them were replaced by another fear. That they might leave her. So she had decided they would be spinsters, all three of them, and live here for the rest of their lives, together. Quietly. Hidden away from the world.

Rose ran her finger across the newspaper pages, turning them carefully.

'There's nothing here about escaped prisoners or soldiers absconding. This man had a knapsack, you say?'

'That's right. And a black billycock hat.'

'I'll ask Mr Langham,' said Rose, closing up the newspaper. 'I believe he was taking on a new man at the stack yard. Maybe that's who your stranger is. Just a nobody.'

Nellie watched Rose scanning the newspaper. Her elder sister wasn't interested in the latest stories of suffragettes and Lloyd George's hatred of them. Rose didn't want to read about Home Rule in Ireland or polar explorers in lands of snow and ice. The sinking of the *Titanic* the year before, in 1912, meant nothing to her. Ships can do two things, she said. They can float or they can sink. Where's the news in that?

Rose loved stories closer to home. Reports of vagrants stealing food from honest tables, their knapsacks bulging with other people's belongings. The local gazette was her preferred reading. It was full of dreadful stories that made them lock their door at night and fear the creaking sounds of the isolated house.

Since childhood, Rose had regaled Nellie and Vivian with other scandalous tales of commercial travellers preying on young women. Men who stole kisses and more from ignorant country girls hankering after romance and feathers for their hats. According to Rose, these men courted lonely countrywomen, offering love like a sleight of hand, a card trick, a gift they gave and took back, leaving behind bitter husbands and unwanted children who looked nothing like anybody else and grew up with roving ways. The stories were meant to frighten Nellie and Vivian, but secretly they were thrilled by them.

Nellie longed to glimpse the salesmen who brought their hand carts into the village, their footsteps quiet as falling snow. The sisters' cottage was too far from the village for them to come calling. She wanted to be sold ribbons and dainties and pills for ailments. To be persuaded to buy miracle cures for disorders of women, for rickets and palpitations of the heart.

Nellie watched Rose close up the newspaper and fold it neatly, adding it to the pile on the dresser. Had their elder sister been their carer all these years, or their gaoler?

'He didn't look dangerous to me,' she said.

'They never do,' replied Rose.

Nellie glanced at the sky through the small kitchen window. It was going to rain. That's what she had felt earlier. Not luck. Just a change in the weather. The disappointment she'd felt when the man turned away from the cottage settled on her once more.

It poured for three days, curtains of rain that shut down the landscape. Rose went to work in the Langhams' farm kitchens and came home at night with news that the river had flooded in the next village. The mystery of the man was solved. He was a hired hand come to take the place of a lad who'd been kicked by a carthorse a few weeks earlier.

Nellie and Vivian exchanged disappointed glances. They had discussed him at night in their shared bed, another one of their sweet, mad, whispered conversations. They'd imagined him as a rich man, then a poor man, or a travelling magician pulling rabbits from his hat.

Vivian, who read as many romance novels as she could persuade the vicar's wife to lend her, had decided he was a man betrayed by his sweetheart. Nellie, always warm-hearted, imagining his sorrow, said he must be walking the length of Britain to forget her. By the time he got to Scotland, she was sure he would not be able to recall her name.

'Oh no,' Vivian had said, pressing her hand to her breast. She was the kind of girl who tended to brood on things. 'Oh no, you're completely wrong, Nellie.'

He would remember his sweetheart for ever. For eternity. True love was like that. It could never be forgotten in a lifetime.

'A farmhand?' Nellie asked Rose. 'You are sure it was him?'

'That's right. A hired hand.'

Nellie and Vivian pulled glum faces. There was nothing remotely interesting about a farmhand.

On the fourth day the rain hadn't stopped and Rose asked Nellie to dig out the ditches by the house. Rose coughed and spat a bloom of redness into a handkerchief. 'Mr Langham will be sending a farm boy over with sandbags. Put them across the door.'

'Don't go,' said Vivian. 'Stay home today, Rose. You should rest.'

Rose breathed in, a wheezing sound. She waved her hand to bat Vivian away. 'Don't fuss over me. I'm staying at the farm tonight as Mrs Langham's son has been taken poorly. I'll be back tomorrow.'

Nellie fetched a clean cambric hanky for her. Lavender scented, its edges rolled and stitched by Vivian. Rose was worn down by work and ill health but she would not rest. Vivian wrapped a scarf around Rose's neck and stood on tiptoe to kiss her cheek.

They watched her go along the riverbank. Always the same in her old black coat and short-brimmed hat. Today she had a grain sack around her shoulders, a small protection against the driving rain. She was as tall as a man and bony, with hunched shoulders. She disappeared into the storm with the funny stiff-legged gait she had, her wispy plait the colour of bonfire smoke. What colour her hair had once been was unknown. Blonde, perhaps? She was a private woman who rejected any gestures of affection between them. Rose was loyal and yet unknowable, a mystery just as much as a fixture in Nellie's life.

All morning, Nellie dug ditches. Rainwater dripped in her eyes and off the end of her nose. Her hat flapped wetly against her face, and her skirt clung to her legs. By the afternoon, as the wind slanted the rain sideways, she was tired and shivering. She climbed out of the ditch and went inside.

'I've prepared a bath for you,' said Vivian, hurrying her in, helping her out of her wet clothes, undoing the hooks and eyes on her dress, the laces on her hobnail boots.

Nellie lowered herself into the steaming tin bath in front of the stove. Vivian's love and kindnesses were as warm as the hip bath she sat in. She admired her sister. Vivian was a romantic soul, unaware of the hard toil that farmwork was for Nellie and Rose. She kept their home, and was gentle and gay, and good with the names of plants and wild flowers that grew around the cottage. She was a great reader and there was always the feeling that, with better luck, she might have been a schoolteacher instead of a washerwoman.

'I'm coming in too,' Vivian announced. She undressed, letting her slack black pinafore drop to the ground, clambering over her sister, who complained but laughed, pushing her with her hands.

They were a muddle of legs and arms, slippery buttocks and bellies until they finally sat facing each other, legs dangling out of the tub, water slopping onto the floor.

Nellie watched Vivian washing. Her naked body was always a surprise, no matter how many times she saw it. With her clothes on, Vivian looked like a pale little moth, fluttering from one chore to the next. Naked, she was a secret revealed. Something private and delicate. Watching her was like peeling back the petals from a flower and seeing the stamen hidden inside.

'You are a rare beauty, Vivian.'

'And you are splendid, Nell.'

'I'm like Rose,' said Nellie, passing her sister the block of soap. 'Too tall and I have shoulders like a man.' She stretched a long leg out of the water, revealing a scar across her thigh, a farming accident when she had been a girl. 'And look at that,' she said. 'It's lucky for me I don't need to worry about finding a husband.'

Vivian laughed, a rich, rippling sound, unguarded and loud. She lathered up the block of yellow soap in her hands. 'You are handsome and fine, with very pretty ankles, and that's what counts for a man, isn't it? You are my splendid twin and I would marry you tomorrow.'

Nellie laughed. They were not twins. They both knew they were not. But long ago, as children left alone with nothing but their imagination to entertain them, they had created this story for themselves and still liked its fantastic qualities. They'd decided Vivian had fallen out of her mother's womb early on account of her small size, while Nellie had grown extra large to take up Vivian's place. So though they had been born a good fifteen months apart, they were still twins. Nellie knew this was not possible, but she and Vivian had told the story to each other so many times, the truth of it was unimportant.

And what did truth have to do with stories, anyway? The truth as far as the villagers saw it was that Rose, Nellie and Vivian were unfortunate spinsters, forgotten and dull, hidden away from the world. In fact, they had chosen not to marry. Truth was always different, depending on whether you were the listener or the teller of a story.

Nellie's favourite childhood tale was about two little girls found in a pit in the woods nearby. Nobody could ever say if it was true or not. The wild girls had green skin and spoke a language unintelligible to others. The girls smelled like fox cubs and ate only fruit. The villagers sold them to a travelling showman. He made them eat meat and would not let them be together, and soon the sisters died of sorrow and stomach pains.

Who cared about the veracity of that village tale? Nellie still, even now as a 22-year-old woman, felt angry the girls had been separated. And there was the truth of the story, if it needed one. The way it made her feel like her heart was swollen and raw with love for Vivian.

Vivian reached a wet hand over to the table where she picked up a small bundle of burnt matches. With a match she drew a soft black line carefully across both her lids, close to the lashes. She opened her eyes. The black made them shine and appear luminous, like the eyes of music-hall stars on cigarette cards. She handed the match to Nellie.

'Your turn.'

Nellie took it just as someone rapped on the window.

A male voice called out, 'Hello? Anyone in there?'

Nellie dropped the match in alarm and the two women began to struggle to get out of the bath, water sloshing across the hard earth floor.

'I saw a face!' cried Vivian. 'It's those boys again.'

A shadow passed by the window, and Nellie hurled the bar of soap at it.

'Get out of here!'

Vivian was crawling on the floor, trying to reach her dress on the back of the chair.

Nellie stood naked, her long limbs dripping soapy water.

'Take a bloomin' good look at us, would you?' she yelled. 'I'll put the wind up you. I'll tell your mothers what you were doing. I know who you are!'

'Nellie, sshhh! Don't shout!'

'Why not? They need telling.'

Nellie felt her face darken with shame. This was what being a spinster meant. No village lad would dare spy on a married woman. He'd get horsewhipped for his trouble. But she and Vivian were fair game for rowdy boys.

'They'll be calling us witches next,' she said. 'Like poor old Anna Moats.'

Vivian was already dressed. She pulled on her boots.

'She *is* a witch.'

'She is not.'

There was a knock at the door. And again.

'I've got sandbags from Mr Langham. I can leave them here. Are you all right in there? Mrs Langham said to see you were safe. The river's rising fast.'

The sisters looked at each other in panic.

'You go upstairs,' whispered Vivian. 'I'll answer the door.'

In her bedroom Nellie fell onto her knees, pressing an eye to a hole in the floorboards. Vivian opened the door to a man wearing wet-weather clothes, a big black rubberized cape, and a hat that covered his face.

'Good day, Miss,' he said, taking his hat off and shaking the rain from it. He had high cheekbones. Dark hair. 'I've sandbags for you. Terrible weather, isn't it? If this goes on much longer we'll all be turning into fish. I nearly had to swim here myself.'

He told Vivian that Rose was ill. Mrs Langham had called the doctor and Rose would not be coming home tonight. Nellie could see Vivian holding her hand to her face, trying to hide her black-lined eyes.

Nellie crossed to the window and watched the man leave, hunched against the weather. It was the man she had seen walking. Her stranger. The farmhand. Rain splattered against the window and she finished dressing. When she looked out of the window again, he was standing by the river, looking back at the cottage. She slipped away, afraid he might see her staring.

Vivian mopped up the spilt bathwater and Nellie made Rose's bed, tucking in the blankets extra tight. Neat corners, a blanket turned down properly, pleased Rose, and Nellie liked to please her. A black-bound Bible sat on a chair in her room. In it was a photograph taken at a village fete to celebrate Queen Victoria's Diamond Jubilee in 1897. Rose, with a very young Nellie and Vivian, stood by a flower arch away from the crowds. She had on a wide-brimmed hat decorated with flowers. The three of them held hands. Rose looked young and hopeful.

Rose didn't look young or hopeful these days. The time was coming when she would be unable to work. Then they would care for her here. She'd lie in this bed until the end came for her, and what would become of Nellie and Vivian then?

Nellie held the photograph up to the light. She had no memory of it being taken. She loved the way they held hands so tightly, like paper-cut maids in a row. Or maybe she loved the wonder of a recorded image from another time, like the magic lantern shows she'd seen as a child in the Parish Rooms, all the brightly coloured, faraway foreign lands that had astonished her innocent eyes.

The next morning Nellie was collecting eggs in the hen house and was the first to see the flood water coming across the fields. She ran through the orchard and found the front gardens flooded. Despite the sandbags against the door, the parlour was already ankle deep in water. A knot of shining eels flickered on the scullery floor. Vivian was trying to scoop them into a bucket.

Nellie carried Rose's newspapers to safety. As she came back downstairs she heard a sharp cracking sound, then the front door creaking and groaning on its hinges. The flood waters were pressing against it. The thin wooden panels of the front door gave way. They split and broke, and a gushing wave of dirty brown water exploded through the door. Riding on it, a monster burst into the kitchen. A three-foot-long fish with clouded eyes. It came through the broken slats, fat and fast as tarnished coins tumbling from a ripped purse.

Vivian screamed. Nellie tried to take the thrashing beast into her arms. It was an omen. A sign of luck. An antique creature come from the depths of the river.

'We should put it back,' Nellie yelled. 'Free it. It's a sign of good luck.'

Vivian climbed onto the kitchen table. 'For heaven's sake! Do you think it's going to grant you three wishes? Get away from it, Nellie, before it hurts you.'

'It belongs to the river,' Nellie insisted.

The pike bucked and flapped at her feet. It was a muscular creature and solid; it flexed and panicked like a carthorse trying to free itself from deep mud. They were never going to be able to save it. In desperation, Nellie took an iron poker and ended its suffering with a blow to the head.

'I'm going to get herbs to cook it with,' she said in the silence that followed.

Vivian climbed off the table and gave Nellie a hug. 'It's not magic. It's just a fish,' she whispered, and turned her attentions to catching the pots and kettles floating around her knees.

Nellie waded through the garden. The rain was softer now but still persistent. The fields were covered in pale lakes of water. The cottage was an island, a place where monsters could wash up and yet, not far away, the modern world hurried along. There was a daily omnibus service to neighbouring villages. It stopped outside the post office in the village, from where telegrams could be sent all over the world, so the postmistress claimed. A railway station too, where you could ride a train all the way to London. New factories had sprung up, miles downriver. On still days their hooters could be heard, telling the workers it was time to go home. The young twentieth century was all around her. It was just that their lives were not a part of it.

Three wishes, Vivian had said. One for each sister.

Good health for Rose. Ostrich feathers for Vivian and sherbet for her sweet tooth. Nellie didn't know what she'd wish for. A train ticket or a boat ride to other lands. Maybe just an end to the long winters when she froze her hands blue, harvesting turnips out of the frosted mud.

What happened next stayed in Nellie's mind for a long time. A boat rowed into view. In it were two men. The one standing, the one without the oars in his hands, was her stranger.

'We're to take you to the farm,' he called. 'Mrs Langham sent us. Your sister's very ill.'

'No, thank you,' called Nellie. She heard Rose's voice in her head, telling her to send the men away. 'No, we don't need help, thank you. We'll walk there.'

Then Vivian appeared at the broken door. She had her hat and coat on; the pike, wrapped in brown paper, lay in her arms.

'We'll come with you.'

Nellie could see her lip tremble a little. Vivian rarely left the cottage.

'Bring the boat up to the door, please.'

The two women sat with the pike lying across their laps. Nellie held a black umbrella over their heads. The boat rocked gently on the flood waters. The rain was softly falling, leaving misted jewels of raindrops on their clothes.

'And that pike just came in through the door?' the stranger asked, wiping his face with his sleeve. Nellie tried to imagine his name. Was he a Tom, a Dick or a Harry?

'Now that's a poacher's excuse if ever I heard one. The local policeman would laugh till his socks fell down if you tried that one on him.'

'It is a gift for Mrs Langham,' Nellie said, glancing up from under the brim of the umbrella. She noticed his eyes were dark brown, dark as winter plough. 'There are no poachers in our family. We do not take what does not belong to us.'

She looked down again and the rest of the journey passed in silence. When the boat slid onto dry land up by the farmhouse, Nellie shook out the umbrella and closed it. Vivian held the pike, struggling slightly under its weight. The sisters stood up, readying to get out. The rower took the fish from Vivian and the stranger held out his hand.

'Here, let me help you ladies out.'

Vivian ignored him. Nellie hesitated and then put out her hand.

'That's a good girl,' he said, and grasped her fingers in his.

His hand was warm, hard and muscular. There was a pulse in his thumb that she felt as he pressed it against the flesh of her palm. Had she ever held a man's hand before? But yes. How could she have forgotten? There had been the incident that had scandalized them all. She remembered and stumbled, nearly falling over the lip of the boat. Heat flushed her face and she laughed nervously, pulling her hand away, stepping quickly away from the man.

'Come on, Joe, leave off playing the gent and give us a hand,' said the rower as Nellie and Vivian carried the fish towards the farmhouse. 'We're to drag the boat up to the stables.'

Joe. His name was *Joe*. She whispered it to herself as they trudged through the mud, the word as round and smooth as a river pebble in her mouth.

'The doctor has been,' said Mrs Langham, folding her solid arms across her chest. The woman was a great one for misery. She had brown hair as fine as darning wool, eyes that glittered with the thrill of impending disaster, a high colour in her round cheeks. 'He came for my son, who was taken bad the other day, and he heard your sister coughing and didn't like the sound of it. She had a shocking bad night, I'm afraid. The doctor thinks she should go to hospital.'

'Oh no,' said Vivian. 'Rose wouldn't want that.'

'Rose has been like this before, Mrs Langham,' said Nellie. 'We'll get her home and nurse her ourselves.'

Mrs Langham shook her head.

'It's a time of waiting, my dears. You'll just have to see what her fever does.'

'She would prefer to be at home with us,' insisted Vivian.

'You can't move her now. Go and sit with her. Be with her in her last hours. Take the vigil. Poor old Rose, she's not had much of a life.'

Rose lay in a single bed, a pale grey blanket covering her, sweat dampening her brow.

'Take me home.'

'We will,' whispered Vivian. 'Tomorrow.'

Rose closed her eyes. She seemed to sink lower into her pillows. 'Together you will be safe. You must promise me you'll always be together.'

The sisters promised easily. Of course they would stay together. Hadn't they always?

'The morphine has calmed her,' said Vivian after a time. The two of them were settled in chairs, blankets over their knees. The lamp had been put out and the room was in darkness. The sound of their sister's breathing washed back and forth.

'Joe is a fine name, don't you think?' whispered Nellie. 'The man in the billycock hat? His name is Joe.'

'Sshh. Don't wake Rose.'

'She's sleeping. Joe must be short for Joseph, I suppose?'

'I have no idea, Nell. And you should stay away from him. You know what Rose says. Don't forget what happened to you.'

Nellie hadn't forgotten. Rose and Vivian would never let her. It had sealed the sisters' fate.

Some years ago, when Nellie was seventeen, one of the Langhams' hired hands had said hello to her, leaning over a farm gate as she passed by. Rose insisted they mustn't speak to strangers, but Nellie had ignored her rules. She was full of good feelings that day. What harm could it do to say hello?

He was an ugly little fellow with bowed legs and a fleshy smile. He showed her his wallet, which contained three locks of hair.

'This is my wife's chestnut hair, this buttery curl is the baby and this brown lock our son.'

Nellie was touched by his tender words. He told her he hoped she would make a good wife one day. Nellie nodded. Rose had never spoken of their future back then, but she and Vivian talked secretly of the husbands they might have.

He picked yellow-hearted field daisies for her, and Nellie sat until late into the night, listening to his talk. She wished she was his wife so he could have spoken as gently of her as he did of the woman whose lock of hair lay in his hand.

There seemed some heroic quality in a woman loving a man as ugly as this one, and Nellie at seventeen thought she would be equal to the task. When he asked if he could have a curl of her hair as a keepsafe, she agreed readily.

'Oh, but you're beautiful,' he told her, his breath damp on her neck. Night had fallen and insects spun around them, drawn by the flame of the hurricane lamp he lit. His fingers stroked her long neck. 'A peach you are, my dear. A cherry, a sweet blossom in God's garden.'

Nellie closed her eyes as the scissors flashed in his hand. He left her with cropped hair as short as the hogged mane on Mr Langham's bay cob. The man slid her severed plaits into his knapsack and told her to get on home before the bogeyman got her.

Rose rocked Nellie in her arms when she returned to the cottage in tears. Hadn't she warned her about strangers? Had he done anything else? Oh, but Nellie was so young to be ruined by a man. Nellie tried to explain that he had not even kissed her, but Rose didn't seem to believe her. Beside them Vivian cried heartily as if she were the one whose hair had been stolen.

Anna Moats the midwife came to the cottage soon after. She'd heard the village gossip.

'The hair will grow,' she told Nellie. 'It's your heart we need to protect, my dear.'

Rose sent Anna Moats away. Doctors cured illness; policemen and courts punished badness. Everything else between birth, love and death was in God's hands. Anna Moats was a fraud. Hadn't her husband died of illness even though she said her remedies could cure all? The woman was a drunkard without a seed of sense in her head. That woman couldn't cure a ham hock for Christmas, let alone a gullible girl taken in by a man who sold hair to wig makers.

Nellie had thought differently. She crept to Anna's house and asked for a cure. Anna's daughter, Louisa, invited her in, showing her a pale pink ostrich feather fan she had been given by a travelling showman she'd met. Wasn't it beautiful? She flapped the fan and danced around the room while Nellie ignored her, trying not to breathe in the sour smells that made her eyes water and her gorge rise. Herbs hung in bunches from the ceiling, and dried animal bones tied together with twine dangled like marionettes.

'Is she really a witch?'

Louisa laughed lazily and threw herself onto the couch, smoothing her darned skirts.

'Witches don't exist. Not in real life. My mother just pretends they do.'

'I don't pretend anything,' said her mother, coming into the room. She was as solid as a birthing sow, with a stiff-hipped gait. 'I help where I can, that's all.'

Anna filled a blue glass bottle with pins, mare's urine and a snip of Nellie's hair. She corked the bottle, and together they went to the river and threw it in. Nellie couldn't say why, but when she saw the bottle float away, relief flooded through her.

When she got home, Rose was waiting for her. She took Nellie's hand and kissed her cheek. Sometimes things happened for a reason, she said. Even bad things.

'There are stories about you now. Nasty gossip. Some villagers say you sold your hair. Some say you lay down with that man and you cut your own hair off because you were ashamed of what you'd done. People like to talk, and they like best of all the kind of story that brings shame on the innocent. I won't let them shame you, dear. Mother always said that talk and lies cannot touch us if we're deaf to the sound of them.'

The sisters would be spinsters. Rose's fingers squeezed Nellie's hand. Their mother's wedding ring, which Rose wore, cut into Nellie's skin. She tried to pull her hand away, but Rose had her tight in her grip.

'My darling girl. We will turn our backs on them all. It is better this way.'

Rose coughed harshly once or twice. Was she crying? But no. She had long been consumptive and it was the disease making her eyes teary.

'I love you,' said Rose. 'Sisterly love goes beyond the dangerous infatuation that men can provoke in women. We must dedicate ourselves to sibling love and in this we will be pure. Safe and bonded together for ever, even beyond death. We will be happy, you'll see. I chose to forgo marriage when you were babies. I was just a seventeen-year-old girl like you, Nellie. I have never regretted dedicating my life to you. You will not regret dedicating yours to us.'

Nellie heard a mouse hurry across the wooden floorboards. Rainwater dripped in the gutters outside the window. She listened to Rose lying in the bed beside them, the rasp of her breath. What a weight Rose's particular brand of love was. Nellie pressed her cold feet together and tucked her blanket tighter around herself. If Rose got better, she would stop her silly dreaming. A fish was not an omen. It was just a fish. A man appearing out of the blue was just a man. It was as simple as that.

Mrs Langham shook her awake just before dawn.

'Wake up,' she cried. 'Wake up. Here you are sleeping like babes and your sister has slipped away.'

Nellie and Vivian got to their feet, going to Rose's side in a flurry of panic.

Mrs Langham busied herself, putting out the fire in the hearth, turning mirrors to the wall, opening windows to let Rose's soul fly free. Nellie and Vivian crouched over the body, unable to move away, saying Rose's name over and over, as if they could call her back to them. How could she have left them while they were sleeping? It was not possible, and yet the dead woman lying in the bed, her cheeks as cold as frost, was already not Rose. Their sister had gone, and in her place was the worn body of a 37-year-old woman. A thin, fragile-looking stranger.

Rose's words, spoken so long ago, tumbled over and over in Nellie's head. That love endured, even beyond death. She held Vivian's hand. They had been orphaned as children when their parents died, and now, as women, they felt orphaned again.

'What are we to do?' asked Vivian. 'How will we live?'

'We have not lost everything,' Nellie whispered. 'We still have each other.'

'We *only* have each other,' answered Vivian, and began to cry.

Two

The cottage was different without Rose. The sisters were different. They felt lost and uncertain. Rose had been in charge of every aspect of their lives. She alone had wound their father's clock on the mantelpiece and opened and closed the curtains at the beginning and ending of each day, as if she controlled time itself. Without her, Nellie and Vivian let the clock run down. Rose had kept the pantry locked, and Vivian opened its doors wide. She took out jars of cherries and made a blancmange with their juices. They ate the sweet sticky fruit with their fingers until their mouths were stained red and their bellies ached.

When they ran out of food in the cupboards and went hungry, growing thin-cheeked and listless, Mrs Langham sent over food parcels and they accepted them without fear of hurting Rose's pride. The vicar's wife offered them charity from the paupers' fund, giving them money to tide them over until they felt they could work again. Mr Langham brought planks of wood and mended the broken front door.

For months after the funeral, the sisters wept. All through March and April they clung to their home and to each other. They slept late in the mornings and refused to leave the cottage. The rooms were humid and full of the smell of the river, but they didn't care. They became immune to the rotten stink of river-weed and the cloying perfume of balsam flowers opening in the heat of spring. When frogs squatted in the butler sink in the scullery, belching loudly on the windowsill, Nellie lifted them, dry and cool in her hands, and took them back to the river. Green newts shimmied in under the cracks in the door. Vivian put them outside but they came back, like messengers from the river, reminding them of its closeness. The cooking range rusted. Even the light through the thin glass windows seemed damp and watery. And still the sisters cried, adding their own salt tears to the wet little riverside cottage.

May brought hot weather. Day after day, the glaring sun scorched the land. The cottage was a waterless ship then, beached and cracking in the drying afternoons. Bedding hung from open windows like windless sails; the door and window frames shrank ever more crooked. Finally the sisters had no more tears. They, too, were dried out.

'If you're willing to work,' Mrs Langham said when she called to see the sisters, 'we need women to take picnics to the labourers in the fields.'

'We'll do it,' said Nellie, her lips stained red with cherry juice. 'We'd be glad to.'

They collected jugs of tea and parcels of bread and cheese from the kitchens, crossing the water meadows, following a group of other women with their arms full of picnics. All along the river where the men were working, yellow buttercups smothered the green banks. Church bells for a wedding pealed in the distant village, the sound drifting across the fields.

The labourers coppicing the willows had put down billhooks and saws and settled themselves under oak trees where it was shady. Swallows – the first of the season – darted across the sky. They brought a new summer on their wingtips. Vivian marched on ahead, catching up with the other women handing out picnics. Nellie stopped to watch the birds. They swept towards the river where a man waded in the shallows, a bundle of canes on his shoulder. It was him. *Joe*.

He heaved the canes onto the shoreline and climbed the bank, grabbing at bushes to pull himself up. It looked to Nellie as though the river was reluctant to let go of him. Finally he stood on the bank. When he turned his head in her direction she stumbled forwards, horrified to be caught staring, treading on her skirts, nearly dropping the jug she was carrying.

He waved and called loudly to her.

'Do you have a drink there for me, Miss?'

'Cold tea,' Nellie called back, lifting the jug, liquid spilling down her arm. She cursed her clumsiness. Now she had no choice but to go to him. Perhaps it was the hot sun that made her feel slow or the way he stared so openly at her, but Nellie stumbled again as she walked. Sunlight dropped through gauzy clouds. She offered him the tea and his face lit in a slow smile. She could smell the river on him, a familiar odour of green weeds, mud and washed stones. Nellie found herself lifting her face to breathe in his watery scent.

'Hello, Poacher,' he said. 'Stolen any more fish lately?'

The day was murderously hot. A curl stuck to her face. She had forgotten to brush her hair that morning and her long plait was coming undone. She laughed, her cheeks reddening. 'We didn't steal it. Honestly, I told you, it came through the door.'

He took the picnic she offered him and said he'd take her word for it. He settled himself on the ground, cross-legged, eating hungrily.

'The name's Joe Ferier. Sit down with me.' His request sounded cheerful, ordinary. 'Keep me company for a minute or two. That can't do any harm, can it?'

'I'll just wait for the jug and be on my way, thank you.'

She stood stiffly, watching the swallows dipping to drink in the river.

'All the way from Africa,' Joe said, pointing at them. 'Imagine that. A whole winter spent on another continent and then they find their way home. We humans would need a map or a compass, but those birds don't have either.'

'Swallows don't go to Africa,' Nellie said. This she knew for a fact. Anna Moats had told her. 'In winter they sleep in leaf mould in forests. They wake up again for the summer, just like hedgehogs.'

He laughed and pulled a small book from his knapsack. 'Is that right? Tell me, can you read?'

Nellie looked at the book's title.

'*Birds of the British Isles*.'

'Good. Take it and read it. Swallows do not hibernate in leaf mould. Now, will you sit down with me, seeing as you have borrowed my book?'

'All right,' she said, grinning, finding a place among the buttercups and thistles. She put the book in her pocket. 'But not for long. I have work to do.'

'Not for long suits me fine,' he said, smiling at her.

Joe liked to talk. He said words never cost anybody anything. He was a traveller. Passing through on foot, looking for work. He came from a place in the north. A seaside town with brightly painted houses and so many seagulls the air was filled night and day with their calls.

'They sound like crying babies,' he said. 'A terrible sound. Crying babies. I couldn't get away from there quick enough.'

He'd been a traveller since he left home aged fourteen. It was a good enough life. There were many like him on the road. He pointed to the earth track worn by the cows who wandered the same way each day, up to the farm to be milked and then back out to graze. He never wanted to walk the same road twice. Time wore out your shoe leather no matter what, and a travelling life was better than one spent walking over the same paths, the same fields, until the day you died.

Nellie stole a look at him. His trousers were too short, his thin ankles poking out of them. His shirt was mended and neatly patched at the elbows. She would have liked to ask who had done the mending for him. His face was tanned and fresh with youth, his nose straight, a well-shaped mouth with a moustache hiding his top lip. His dark hair receded at the temples. A black felt hat was on the grass beside him. It had a collection of blue jay feathers stuck in the band. She reached out and touched the feathers, hoping he wouldn't notice her curiosity.

'This is a fine meal,' he said, peeling a hard-boiled egg. 'Last farm I worked at we got what the pigs refused to eat. They gave us bread you'd break a tooth on.'

'Everybody likes Mrs Langham's picnics. Old Hang'em – I mean Mr Langham – is the meanest beggar you ever clapped eyes on, but she's a decent sort. She'd give away Langham's boots if she thought somebody needed them more than him.'

'Sounds like he needs to watch where he leaves them then,' said Joe, and Nellie laughed. She was surprised by how pleasurable their conversation was.

In his knapsack was a sketchbook and a roll of papers. He was a self-taught artist, making a record of the countryside as he travelled. He unrolled a watercolour of a big house surrounded by trees. It was a place not far away. Hymes Court. Nellie knew it vaguely.

'I've plenty left to learn,' he said, studying his painting closely, poring over it. 'And you, Miss?' he looked up. 'What about you? What do you like to do?'

She cleared her throat. 'My name is Eleanor Marsh. My sister calls me Nellie. I'm a good worker, ask Mr Langham.'

'I'm sure you are. But what do you like to do? Do you have a pastime, a passion?'

'A *passion*?'

She was not sure she had ever spoken that word out loud. She told him she loved to swim. It was the finest feeling she knew.

A breeze picked up and rustled the leaves in the poplar trees. Nellie felt cool air against her face and saw the hairs rising on Joe's wrists. The day was golden with sunlight. Was it possible she was in love? Could it happen this fast? But Vivian's romance novels were full of people who met at the top of a page and were in love a paragraph later. Why shouldn't she fall in love the same way?

Joe smiled and got to his feet, brushing eggshell off his waistcoat. His glance journeyed over her shoulder, and Nellie turned her head.

Vivian, with the small hands and feet of a woman not made for farm work, hurried towards them. A heat haze blurred in front of her. There were pale sweat marks on her blouse. Her heart-shaped face was pink and flushed under the wide brim of her straw hat. Her blonde hair curled around her cheeks, and her eyes were wary.

Nellie looked again at Joe. He was watching Vivian, studying her the same way he looked at his painting, as if there was more to discover. She thanked God that Rose wasn't here to see this.

'Is that your sister? What's her name?'

'Vivian,' said Nellie, her throat too dry to say any more.

Louisa Moats, the old midwife's daughter, had stood beside Vivian when she first arrived at the riverbank, telling her about the dance in town. After the annual horse fair, a group of horse dealers had paid some musicians to set up a band and play all night in the beer gardens of the Rose and Crown. She'd danced until the heel of her boot had fallen off.

'So I took them off and carried on barefoot.' She lifted her skirt to show off a dance step. 'You should have come. They have a gramophone with stacks of recordings. You should have some fun while you can.'

Vivian could imagine Louisa throwing off her shoes. At school, she'd been a slow-witted girl, always barefoot, dirty necked. Now she was a woman, unmarried, and still slovenly.

'I was right as a mailer that night. Couldn't stop dancing, even danced on the way home.'

'You use such odd expressions,' said Vivian, and knew she sounded stuck-up, like she thought she was a grand lady. It wasn't such a strange expression either. Rose used to say the same thing.

As prompt as the mail, as right as a delivered letter; satisfied and timely. That was all the expression meant.

'Look at her,' said Louisa, nudging Vivian, acting as if she hadn't heard her. 'The wheelwright's wife. What a sight.'

Vivian stared, though she knew she shouldn't. The wheelwright's wife sat leaning against a tree, a baby at her exposed breast. Milk glistened on the infant's chin and spilled from the corner of his red mouth. Field flies drifted around the baby's sticky cheeks, the mother batting them away with her hand. Such a sleek and plump infant. He gazed at his mother with open adulation, as if she was everything he would ever desire in life.

Vivian wondered what it might be like to be so very loved by an infant. To have those dark-lashed eyes look at you that way, like you were sweeter than all the plum cake and honey in the world.

'Is that your sister over there?' Louisa tipped her chin towards the river. 'Do you see her, sitting alone with a man? I didn't know she was courting.'

Vivian turned reluctantly away from the sight of the baby. She looked back across the field, startled by the sight of Nellie in conversation with a man.

'She's got her heart set on that one,' said Louisa, nudging Vivian in the ribs. 'And he looks pretty happy too.'

Vivian didn't answer her. She hurried towards Nellie, all thoughts of the baby quite forgotten.

'Hello again, Miss,' said Joe as she arrived. 'Joe Ferier. You remember me? I came in a boat and rescued you in the floods.'

Had he rescued them? She didn't remember it that way. He lifted his hat. His eyes seemed to have sunlight in them, small flecks of gold in the brown. He reached out and shook hands with her, gripping her fingers firmly, the way Vivian imagined a man might take a girl's hand to lead her into a dance. Then he let go and stepped back, smiling at both women, looking from one to the other, a hand shading his face from the fierce sunlight.

'It's the eyes. You've got the exact same eyes. There's the resemblance. You wouldn't know you were sisters unless you looked at your eyes.'

He was studying them openly and Vivian felt irritated by him. A helpless sense of dislike rose up in her and made her cheeks burn. She knew how he saw them. Spinsters. Sad old maids to be pitied and laughed at. No doubt they looked as sombre to him as the shadows the trees threw over the river. He saw right into the heart of them. The flimsy romance novel she carried in her pocket, the frog's bone and lucky rabbit's foot in Nellie's purse.

'We have to collect the jugs,' she said. 'So if you have finished, Mr Ferier, then we'll leave you to get back to your work.'

She grabbed her sister's arm, but Nellie was staring as if the man might turn into something else at any moment, something extraordinary, a feathered fish or a fur-covered snake.

'Nellie?' Vivian raised her voice. 'Come on. We must go.'

By the time they joined the gang of women returning to the farm with empty jugs and baskets, and Vivian looked again, the men were all cutting willow canes and she couldn't make out which one Joe was.

A week later, Vivian and Nellie stood in the garden together. Nellie heaved armfuls of the vicarage sheets into the washtub, her face calm and steady.

'I saw him again.'

Vivian scrubbed at a sheet. She, too, had seen him.

'Who?'

'Joe Ferier. I saw him in the hay fields.'

Vivian had seen his tent pitched half a mile down the river. He liked to stand beside it, painting, with an easel set up. Whoever heard of a hired hand painting watercolours?

Rainbows appeared in the soap bubbles that rose up and floated around them. Nellie caught one in her hand and popped it. Vivian put the paddle down.

'I'll make a blancmange for tomorrow,' she said, wanting to change the subject. She stamped on a bubble as it landed on the ground beside her. Nellie giggled. She whipped up the soap suds with her hands, sending more bubbles flying around them.

The sisters danced round the washtub, their clothes soaked by their splashing, a strange kind of excitement taking them over. Nellie shrieked and stamped her feet. Vivian scooped handfuls of soapy water from the tub and launched them at her. She ran towards the orchard, Nellie chasing her. They ran until they sank to their knees in the long grass.

Vivian looked up at the sky, catching her breath, blades of green tickling her face. She turned her head to stare into Nellie's grey eyes, so like her own. Her sister's good, strong face was starred with brown freckles. Vivian would have the same freckles too if she didn't use a chemist's cream to make them fade.

Nellie threw her arms back, revealing the sweat-marked pits of her blouse, and Vivian breathed in the familiar musky scent of her.

'I had the strangest feeling when we met Joe Ferier the other day,' Nellie said. 'I thought I might fall in love with him.'

Vivian sat up. 'Oh, Nellie. No. Be careful. And not him. He's uncouth. We know nothing of his family, his parents.'

'We don't know our parents either.'

'We know they were good people.'

'Don't go getting in a bother about it. It was just a feeling, that's all. It went away as fast as it came.' Nellie turned on her side, a thoughtful look on her face. 'Do you know where swallows go in winter?'

'Swallows? They migrate to Africa. Why?'

She fell back into the long grass. 'I just wondered.'

'I'll make a blancmange,' Vivian said again. She was glad Nellie was talking of other things now. 'I'll make enough for tea and for breakfast too. We can eat it in bed together if you like.'

She picked a dandelion and squeezed the milky stickiness from its hollow stem. The harvest would be over soon enough. Joe Ferier would be gone for good, and she and Nellie need never think about him again.

Three

Yellow butterflies drifted in the late afternoon light and the air was heavy and hot. Nellie walked along the riverbank. She was going to swim and wash off the dust that clung to her from a day spent turning hay. She stopped and undressed under the willows, slipping into her swimming clothes. She had stitched lead weights into the hem of a cotton farm smock to keep it from lifting up in the water, and wore two pairs of black stockings for modesty's sake.

Nellie loved the Little River. It was shallow at its banks but, according to village legends, deep enough in its slow-running centre that a heavily laden hay wain pulled by two horses had once fallen in and was never seen again. Nellie hoped one day to find the sunken cart.

All year round she swam. In spring and summer, she pushed through clouds of midges and bobbing ducks. In winter, she broke the ice and dived in, coming up with mud on her nose, red mottled skin and an unexpected grin on her face. Rose had always disapproved. Only labourers, farm dogs and water rats swam in the river. Nellie could still remember teaching herself to swim as a child, Vivian standing on the riverbank, her hands holding tight the rope they'd tied around Nellie's waist, ready to pull her out if she went under for too long.

Up by the oak trees that same afternoon, Vivian stood watching Joe Ferier's tent. She swayed back and forth, as if building momentum to set off across the field. He had probably forgotten Nellie altogether. He was camping by the river, minding his own business, and did not need a silly woman asking him if his intentions towards her sister were honourable. And how would she explain it to Nellie? She would be struck down with embarrassment. *This will not do*, she told herself.

Joe Ferier was a handsome man. There was no denying that. One day he would marry and have handsome children with a wife who would fuss over them. But that wife would not be Nellie. Vivian turned round and hurried home, hoping nobody had seen her under the trees, wishing she had never thought to go there.

In the hay fields on the other side of the river, Louisa Moats lay back in a flattened bed of grass. She felt the rough earth under her buttocks, the sun warming her face. A ladybird crawled onto her cheek and she let it, feeling the slight tickle of it. Rowley Livet, the village wheelwright, told her she was a fine woman but an expensive one. He held out a tightly woven gold straw hat with a band of white feathers that turned into small wings on the crown. Did she know how much it cost him? And his wife at home with milk fever wanting money to pay the doctor.

'She doesn't need the doctor. All she need do is soak a few cabbage leaves in milk and slap them on her titties,' Louisa said. She took the hat, laid it carefully beside her and slung her arms around his neck. Could she bring herself to kiss this man who had breath like raw onions and a smell of turpentine in his hair? For a new bicycle she might. A nice black one with a basket. She fancied her pretty hat was just the thing to wear for bicycle riding.

The wheelwright's hands, dry as kilned oak, slid up her thigh. He would get her a bicycle. Anything for his darling Lou-Lou. Across the fields, Louisa saw a woman standing alone. She looked familiar.

'Wait up,' she said, pushing him away. What was Vivian Marsh doing? Then she saw what the woman was staring at. A brown tent by the river.

Vivian Marsh, that mousy, shy little woman, was lovesick. She had fallen for the new farmhand. The one who gave himself airs. She'd seen him reading heavy-looking books in front of the other men like he was educated or something. Louisa laughed. Two sisters after the same man? This would be interesting.

'You all right?' asked the wheelwright.

'Never better. Right as a mailer, my love,' she replied, and kissed him.

Nellie climbed down into the water. She swam on her back, floating slowly with the current.

'Who's this?' a voice called out. 'Ophelia splashing in the reeds, is it? Or a mermaid come to enchant me?'

Joe Ferier was sitting by his tent. He wore long johns and his hat, a needle and thread in his hand, darning a shirt.

'I have your book,' she said shyly. 'The one on birds. I can go and get it. I left it on the bank.'

He thanked her, took off his hat and said he thought he'd swim too if she didn't mind sharing her river with him. Nellie turned away so he wouldn't see her grinning.

She was quicker than Joe in the water. She knew she would be, but still he tried to race her. From the weeping willow upstream to the row of elders at the widening bend of the river, they swam together. Nellie dived underwater, air bubbles bursting from her lips, a sense of daring enveloping her. After the long winter and the flood and losing Rose, an awful sadness had weighed her down for months. She could feel the water washing it away. The sun threw its dazzling white light across the water, and Nellie turned and twisted in its warmth. This moment, the river, this man. They seemed to belong just to her.

A Sunday evening in June, Nellie sat beside Joe, unlacing her boots. Behind them in the meadow, brown cows gathered like an audience, heads low, watching them with mild eyes.

'I have something for you,' she said. She took a stone from her pocket. Vivian had found it when she was weeding Langham's fields. Her sister always found things. Toffee-coloured flints shaped like arrow heads, black stones she called devil's toenails. She had a sharp eye and a collector's desire to hoard. She kept empty birds' nests and discarded eggshells. She pressed wild flowers and knew the names of every orchid, admiring them all, even the ones which stank like billy goats.

'It's a hagstone,' Nellie said. She was not in the habit of giving gifts, and felt foolish. 'You can thread a string through the hole in it and wear it on your belt. It brings good luck.'

'I'll need a bit of luck,' said Joe, holding the stone up to the light and squinting at it. 'I'll be leaving soon.'

She looked over her shoulder at him, trying to keep her voice light.

'Leaving?'

He showed her an advertisement for the America Line sailing company. A picture of a big steamship in still waters with a blue sky and lots of white clouds puffing around the ship's tall smokestacks. Joe was going to sail to America. He set up a fishing rod and settled himself on the bank. He was sure he could be a serious artist in America. A painter. No master to work for but himself.

Nellie watched the reeds moving back and forth at the water's edge. She had not thought of him leaving.

The fishing line twitched and wriggled, and Joe reeled in a small trout. He whooped and yelled and stamped his feet in triumph. Nellie leapt up too, caught in his good humour, stamping her bare feet, pointing her toes, doing a step back and forth, a jig she and Vivian had made up.

Joe grabbed her by the hand and swung her round in a waltz.

'You dance like a man, Nellie. I bet you've only ever danced with other women.'

'With my sister, yes.'

'You have to let me lead. Follow me. There you are. You see?'

He waltzed her round and round, and she let herself drift in his arms until she felt dizzy. Then suddenly he kissed her hard on the mouth, pressing his body against her, his hands holding her tightly. She pushed him away in horror and he let go, an amused look on his face.

'Will you build the fire or gut the fish?' he asked, stepping away from her as if nothing had happened. She said she'd build the fire, hurrying to gather wood, her fingers touching her mouth where her lips felt bruised, tears of confusion pricking her eyes.

They cooked the trout and ate the moist pink flesh with their fingers. Fish scales glittered on Joe's bare arms and several stuck to his face, small winking discs of light on his stubbled chin. He was talking, full of opinions about the world. She and Joe were the same age, and yet she felt like a child in his presence. She knew so little. He talked politics. Farmers were not taking on union men, so they could avoid the minimum wages recently set for workers. There were strikes in the north of England. Nellie knew nothing of any of it. He read to her a book of poetry by someone called Pound. She didn't like the verses at all and only pretended to listen, sucking fish juices from her fingers, imagining herself on the deck of a steamship, watching the coast of England slipping from view.

When she got home, Vivian was sitting up, a candle burning low beside her. She was mending a skirt, her fingers sewing quick stitches. The needle flashed silver as Vivian stabbed the fabric with it, pulling it out, stabbing it into the cloth, over and over.

'Did you enjoy your swim?'

Nellie fetched a glass of lemonade from the jug in the pantry. She wished Vivian had been asleep in bed so that she could have avoided this confrontation.

'It was refreshing, yes.'

'You never swam at night before. I wonder why you do now. You are rarely at home these days.'

'The evenings are so hot,' said Nellie. She turned her back on her sister, her face burning.

Vivian stopped sewing. 'It's unladylike the way you run out of the house after our evening meal. You're like a farm dog after a rabbit. What makes you so keen to leave me behind, I wonder?'

'You sound like Rose.'

'That's because she would have said the same thing.'

'I'm going up to bed now,' said Nellie, finishing her drink. 'Will you come soon, Vivie?'

'Is it him you swim with?'

Nellie could not bear this conversation.

'He likes to swim and so do I,' she said, and went up to bed, not waiting for a reply.

Vivian stopped sewing. Nellie was going to marry Joe Ferier and leave her. She was sure of it. Alone, Vivian could not keep the cottage and earn enough to live on. She'd have to go into domestic service or move to town and work in a factory. Joe Ferier was ruining everything between the sisters. She got up, tidying away her work. She locked the front door and closed the curtains. The worst thing was, she was jealous. Horribly jealous that he had chosen Nellie instead of her.

At the Home and Colonial Stores in town, Nellie bought a cardboard suitcase, a packet of hooks and eyes (in case they were hard to come by in America), a new girdle, and felt violets to sew onto her winter hat. If Joe wouldn't stay, then she and Vivian would go with him. She enquired into the price of train tickets to Southampton and found a shipping agency by the docks who told her she could buy her passage to America through them.

'I'll want a double berth, for my sister and myself,' she explained. 'I'd like to reserve the berth and I'll pay for it in the next few weeks.'

'You can go with whomever you want, Miss,' said the man at the desk, yawning. 'Take my sister too, if you want. I wish you would. But you have to pay up front.'

She didn't have the money.

'Then I'll come back later,' she told him.

Nellie vowed she and Vivian would wear ostrich feathers in

their hats when they left. A barrel organ played a jaunty tune outside the railway station, and in a moment of madness she tossed her last shiny shilling into the black cap of the small monkey that sat upon it, thinking it might bring her luck. The monkey chattered noisily and ran to its owner, holding up the shilling. Nellie suddenly wished she could retrieve the coin. She would need all the money she could get in order to leave, and here she was giving it away like a lady with a heart set on charity.

The sun was low by the time she walked along the dusty road towards home, her shadow with its suitcase a dark giant walking in front of her. Nellie felt defiant and sure. Joe said the world was there for the making. It was shapeless until you formed it your own way. He said you just had to stand up and start walking in the right direction. Nellie lifted her head. He was right. She was ready to walk. All she had to do was persuade Vivian to join her. She prayed her sister would agree to leave the cottage; Nellie would not leave without her. She would find the right time to talk to Vivian, and she'd understand it would be an adventure. Next week, when Joe was leaving. It was best not to give Vivian too much time to think about it.

Vivian lay beside Nellie in bed in the dark under their lace curtain tent. She was sweating, the heat of their two bodies making her feel weak. These were the dog days of early summer, and the night was sultry with heat. The window was open in the hope of finding a breeze, the room quiet but for their breathing and the sound of mosquitoes whining. She had discovered the suitcase a few days ago, packed and hidden under the bed.

Vivian felt Nellie touch her hand under the covers, and rolled against her. Nellie may have a quick temper, her feet might be cold in bed all year round, she might hate darning and always sew a crooked seam, but Vivian could not bear to think of life without her. To lose Nellie would be to lose a part of herself.

'Don't you ever long for another life?' whispered Nellie.

Vivian closed her eyes. Of course she did. The wheelwright's wife feeding her baby came into her mind. There was the scent of the river in the room. And something else. Woodsmoke in Nellie's damp hair. Fish scales and waterweeds, the nicotine perfume of pipe tobacco on her skin.

She wrinkled her nostrils, pushing Nellie away, pulling the sheets up to her chin.

'You and I don't need to stay here for ever,' said Nellie. 'Not now it's just the two of us.'

'This is our *home*,' Vivian replied. How could they possibly leave here? They were meant to be here. They were sisters. She hated Joe Ferier with a passion that shocked her. She could picture him perfectly. His dark eyes, his scarf loose around his throat, revealing the soft dip of collarbone. She would drown herself in the river rather than let Nellie leave her.

A day later, Vivian saw Joe walking across the fields. He was easy to spot, even at a distance. With his arrogant loping gait and black hat, he looked more like a landowner than a hired hand.

Vivian left the cottage. She would talk to him. Ask him to explain to Nellie that he could not take her with him. The sisters would not be separated. She would make sense of all this, as she always tried to make sense of everything.

As a child, Vivian thought she had been chosen by God to understand the connections He had made in the world. She had believed He wanted her to become a schoolteacher one day. She'd counted the number of fine fronds that made up an owl's wing feather, noting in an exercise book that the dry hollow stem of the feather and the tiny elements of it all were part of a whole pattern of connecting things. Everything was God's secret. A feather might be as soft as a girl's cheek, but it was also as dry as a corn stalk, strong enough to carry a bird in flight and as light as a whisper. It was all those things. A river could be no more than a snake of silver in the grass, or it could be wide enough to hold the whole sky in its reflections, but it was all water, tiny drops of cold that filled rain butts and church fonts alike. A man could be handsome and given to walking with a swagger, and yet hold the key to everything without even knowing it.

When she saw him, she pretended to be surprised.

'Not working?' she asked. 'I hear Langham is worried about the harvest this year because of the drought.'

'Well, I've worked my hours in any case,' said Joe. 'I'm not labouring for Langham now, so he can't hire or fire me as he chooses.'

He wished her well, tipped his hat and began to walk away. Vivian called his name. She asked if he was a believer. He looked surprised.

'In what? God, you mean? I suppose so. I think I doubt everything I believe in, and believe in everything I doubt. That suits me fine.'

Vivian said doubt was not a pleasant feeling. She preferred to be sure of things. She and her sister were fortunate. They never doubted each other. They were bound together by love, like a good woven cloth made of the warp and weft of shared blood and history, the way family ought to be.

He laughed, pushing his hat to the back of his head.

'Is that right? And which way are you walking, Miss Marsh?'

A drift of swans flew overhead and landed on the river, beating snowy wings, tiny curled feathers dislodging themselves, floating in the air. Vivian watched the birds arching their long necks, settling their pure-white plumage, pretty as china ornaments. Nellie always said if you saw a swan flying against the wind, no matter how bright the day, a bad storm would follow.

'I'm going this way,' she said, walking in the direction the swans had taken upriver. 'Which way are you going?'

'The same way as you,' he replied, and fell into step with her.

At the bend in the river where willows overhung the water, Joe suggested they sit down. Vivian agreed. She wanted to tell him she would lay down her life for Nellie. That she would never let him steal her away.

'How long do you intend to wear black?' he asked her. 'It's so Victorian to be dressed in widow's weeds for months on end. Heavens, we're in the twentieth century now, Vivian, or hadn't you noticed?'

'I am well aware of that. I am grieving my sister Rose. And besides, we have always worn black to honour our parents' memories.'

'I would like to see you dressed in colours. Something to show off your pretty blonde hair.' Joe began unpacking pencils and paper from his knapsack. 'Can I draw you?' He unrolled a piece of blue velvet which held reams of paper. 'I've drawn your sister Nellie several times, but she fidgets. Just lift your head a little higher, could you? Beautiful. Thank you.'

Vivian was surprised at her own obedience. She kept very still, just as he said. Beautiful? Only Nellie had ever called her beautiful. She wanted to see the drawing but he had the paper angled away from her.

'So, you are leaving soon?' she said after they had sat in silence for a while.

'Yes, I'll be on my way in a day or two.'

The air was hot and sticky, and crickets buzzed in the long grass. The sound of his pencil strokes on paper was pleasant. Who would have thought such pleasure could be derived from being looked at by somebody?

There was a loud splash in the river, and Vivian jumped. A quick flicker of silver hovered in the air above the water. A fish breaking the surface. It flashed like a secret catching the light, a shard of mirror that dazzled the eye and was gone, leaving ripples behind it. Vivian remembered why she was there. She took off her hat and wiped her face with a handkerchief.

'She won't go with you.'

'Who?'

'Nellie. She won't go away with you.'

'Go where?'

Vivian felt the sun burning her face. She had never spoken so frankly. She could hear the shrillness in her voice. 'Are you pretending you didn't ask Nellie to go with you? Tell me, do you love all women like this? Do you promise them things and then leave? Is that it?'

Joe said he hadn't promised anything. And as for love, he certainly never promised that to anybody.

'So you don't love her?'

Joe put down his pencil. 'What do you know of love, Vivian? I've seen you watching me while I'm working in the fields. Standing under the trees near my tent. I've seen the way you look at me.' His voice slowed. 'I like to look at you too. I was sure you knew that when you met me this afternoon, pretending it was by chance.'

Vivian snatched up the drawing. He had paid more attention to the fine execution of her mended boots and patched skirts than to her face, which was softly shaded and indistinct, her eyes downcast under her tatty straw boater.

'How can you be so heartless? You've made me look like a pauper.'

'What you choose to see is what you want to find. Keep the drawing. Throw it in the river if it displeases you. To me it's a portrait of simple beauty. You are beautiful as you are, but you don't see it.

'Wait,' he said, catching hold of her arm as she got up to leave. 'Stay. I'm a careless oaf. I didn't mean to hurt your feelings. You are lovely. You're so very lovely. Please, just stay. Really, you're beautiful, Vivian.'

Did she hate him? And if she did, why did she let him kiss her? She was horrified by her inability to refuse him. By the desire that overtook her. Hidden under a curtain of leaves, Vivian gave herself to him like a confession, a truth that could no longer be denied. Her fingers, her lips, her eyes swarmed towards the sweetness of his body. She could not stop herself. She took his face in her hands and pressed her lips to his mouth and it was hot, his tongue thick against hers.

She didn't know if she was doing this to keep her sister or because she desired Joe so badly she would do anything to have him. Or perhaps she wanted to prove to Nellie that she was right: that Joe was rotten through and through, and hatred was what burned inside her.

He came to the cottage the next day, walking up the path minutes after Nellie had left to work on the Langhams' farm. They lay down in the orchard all through the quiet hours of the day. Vivian breathed in the smell of him, tobacco and herbs in the dip of his collarbone and something else, peppery as watercress, a pungent earthiness like river mud in winter: the scent of her sister. Was she really saving Nellie or destroying her? Joe would belong to neither sister, but they would share him as they had always shared everything.

There was no cake baked that day and the housework went undone. Supper was cold potatoes, a tin of sardines from the store cupboard and a badly washed salad full of grit, hastily prepared while Nellie sat waiting at the table. Vivian couldn't eat a thing. Nellie said she must be coming down with something. She looked feverish. Her pupils were dilated. Her skin flushed.

'You have a rash on your face. Should we call the doctor?' asked Nellie.

Vivian touched her cheeks. Joe's stubble when he'd kissed her had reddened her tender skin.

'Nettle rash,' she said, and cleared the table.

'It's the heat, perhaps,' said Nellie.

'And you will be swimming I suppose?' Vivian cleared the plates. 'I think I'll lie down. You go. Enjoy the water.'

She watched Nellie running towards the river and knew she was meeting Joe. She knew it, but she could not say a word. And if Nellie did leave with him, Vivian felt she deserved to be left behind for what she had done. She deserved only punishment.

Joe came to the cottage again on Friday morning, and this time they were pulling at each other's clothes before he had even removed his hat. Vivian took him up to her bedroom, where they made love greedily. Afterwards they lay naked in each other's arms and slept. When she woke she listened to his breathing, watching his chest rise and fall, studying the slant of his hips, the curling dark hair between his legs, his pale genitals. This was how husbands and wives must be together. Able to stare at each other. She had a man in her bed. Nellie was the only other person she had ever slept beside.

They were sorry creatures, she and Nellie. Sorry, lonely women. And she was the sorriest. Treacherous and cruel. Taking the one thing she knew her little sister desired. The thought of Nellie made her leap from the bed, gathering up her discarded clothes, waking Joe, asking him to dress.

'Let's go to the river,' he said casually, pulling on his boots. 'We can lie together under the willows.'

At the end of the day, they sat by the water. A factory hooter sounded, miles away, at the guncotton works. Pigeons chorused in the trees. Joe said he was leaving. He could not stay. He was a traveller. Always moving on. He would not forget her, but it was time for him to leave.

'Don't cry,' he said, kissing her forehead. 'My pretty Vivian. Maybe I'll come back for you one day.'

He walked away, whistling a tune she recognized. 'The Song of the Lark'. She committed to memory the cut of his jacket, the easy way his arms hung at his sides as he walked. He never once looked back.

On the ground beside her was the velvet he had wrapped his paper and pencils in. She picked it up and in its folds was a small brown hagstone. She held it in her palm and rubbed its smooth surface. It was the one she had given Nellie.

The barley fields were thick with blood-red poppies as she walked home through the fields. The ears of barley crackled as Vivian's skirts brushed against them. Stalks were crushed under her feet; petals stained her skin and clothes. She hoped she would not be seen by anybody with her hat askew, blonde hair loose around her shoulders, her cotton blouse dusted with pollen.

Nellie met her at the cottage door, holding a black hat in her hands. Joe's hat.

'I found this,' she said, her eyes filled with tears. She looked defeated, as if all the storm of her character had blown out of her. 'I found it in our bed.'

Vivian went past her into the shade of the kitchen and put the hagstone on the table. She turned and took Nellie's hands.

'Don't cry. He's gone now. It's just us. The two of us. How it is meant to be. Look at me. We can forget him now.'

'Gone?'

'Yes. He's gone and we are together, just as Rose said we should be.'

That night Vivian dreamed she saw Nellie standing by the window, in her black winter coat despite the heat of the summer night. She held her suitcase in her hand. She dreamed Nellie was asking her questions, over and over.

Why did you do it? Why, why?

Nellie's face swam back and forth, so full of hurt she could have made a stone cry with the pity of it. A watery light moved in the room, like a candle seen through thick tears. The dream was as slow as weeds in a river; it pressed down on Vivian like water. She was drowning in regret. She gasped for air. Slowly she turned and dragged the bed sheet across her face. *Go away*, she pleaded. *Go away*. The white linen covered her. She closed her eyes tight.

When Vivian woke in the morning, a breeze drifted in through the open window, carrying the noise of insects and birdsong. Nellie's side of the bed was empty. The brown hagstone was on her pillow. Vivian got up, hurriedly straightened her clothes, splashed her face with cold water from the bowl on the dresser and went downstairs. The door stood open and light poured into the shadows of the room.

All day Vivian hoped Nellie might return. She imagined her coming in from the garden with a bowl of raspberries, complaining about the birds eating all the best ones. Or appearing barefoot at the gate, her hair and clothes damp, her boots in her arms. She knew in her heart that Nellie had gone. She had taken her suitcase and left the village.

Vivian had never thought much of the world beyond the village. She remembered a trip organized by Mrs Langham for the farm workers. A trip to the seaside in a charabanc. Vivian had stood on the beach and watched the tide go out. Nellie teased her because she had not wondered where it went. She'd accepted the bowing out of the water just as she accepted its coming back later in the day. Had her whole life been like that until now? An acceptance of everything?

She began to sing a hymn Rose liked, 'Thy Will I All Thy Sins Forgive', her voice weak and faltering. Nellie's chickens came running to the door, thinking they were being called, expecting to be fed. Vivian shooed them away.

For months afterwards, waking or sleeping, she felt the weight of what she had done. She was sick with regret, and her headaches lasted for weeks at a time. She lost her appetite and lay in bed thinking of Joe. It shamed her to feel the ache in her body when she thought of him, but she relived the days she had with him again and again.

Sometimes she wondered if, with time and distance between them, Nellie might manage to think of her with less than hatred in her heart. Joe had said there was no wrongness in love, and she clung to that idea. After all, she loved Nellie and Joe both. *You are shameful*, the voice of Rose whispered to her as she passed her dead sister's bedroom.

When Vivian collected the laundry from the vicarage, the vicar's wife asked after Nellie. Vivian said she was away visiting relatives. She made it sound so convincing, she almost believed her lies.

Slowly Vivian's sickness left her. Her hair began to shine and her appetite increased. She filled out, her cheeks rounded, her eyes shone. She tied her corset tighter every day against her swelling body. When she passed Rose's bedroom she put her fingers in her ears, but still there was the accusing voice of her sister's ghost.

A late summer storm woke her and she stood watching yellow lightning illuminating the river. The wind shook the black poplar trees, making their ancient limbs groan and murmur. They sounded like a choir of voices. Like gossips chattering, recounting a scandalous tale. *I hear them too*, she heard Rose say, her voice rattling the window frames.

Harvests were brought in and the land ploughed into stiff clay furrows. Still Nellie did not come back. The bees in the orchard swarmed and disappeared, leaving their hives to be squatted by woodlice and earwigs. The trees bent to the ground, their limbs heavy with fruit. Overripe apples scented the air, and mornings turned damp and misty.

Louisa came to gather windfalls with her mother, Anna Moats. The two of them remarked upon Vivian's changing looks. They told her she must be a late bloomer. Even Vivian could see it. In the small hand mirror the sisters owned, she saw how her eyes shone. Her face had filled out and softened. Her blonde hair was thick and lustrous.

Vivian should find herself a husband, Louisa teased.

Vivian believed she deserved nothing of the sort. If they knew what she had done, they would have banished her from their company.

'My sister Nellie will be home soon,' she told them, as if this was more important than any talk of husbands.

At Christmas, the vicar dropped off a package from his wife. A blood-red paisley-patterned dress, and a soft woollen shawl, slightly holed by moths.

'It's blue,' said Vivian, holding the shawl up.

'You have worn black long enough now, Vivian. We hope to see you at church with your sister when she returns.'

Vivian wore the shawl and it was a comfort to her. She sat upstairs in her bedroom, letting out her waistbands and sewing extra seams in her blouses. Every night she dreamed of Joe Ferier coming to her bed. She woke in the mornings lonelier and hungrier than ever.

Four

When Vivian had put the hagstone on the table and the sisters had stared at Joe's hat, retrieved from their bed, Nellie had wanted to hurt Vivian. Instead she had gone to the river to swim. When she got back she dressed in her best clothes and stood for a long time in their bedroom, watching Vivian sleeping, standing over her, listening to her breathing. Nellie put the hagstone on her pillow, picked up her suitcase and tiptoed downstairs. She could never harm Vivian but she could not stay with her either.

All through the night as she walked, she heard Rose's voice, recounting stories of criminals and murderers. Though she told herself she was not afraid, she didn't risk stopping to sleep in a haystack or barn. She was not given to this kind of fear, but then, she concluded, she had been innocent before. Only those who had known or witnessed bad things knew the kind of treachery the night hid.

She reached the town at dawn, just as the factory workers were crowding the streets on their way to work. She sat down on a bench by the corn exchange and slept. In the afternoon the sound of a barrel organ woke her. The monkey she had given money to just days before came and sat beside her, offering a slice of apple. She took the fruit gratefully, and the man turning the barrel said he remembered her.

'You're our lucky shilling lady. Yes, I remember you. The name's Eddie Samson. You all right, Miss?'

'Not really,' said Nellie. She was too tired to be shy. 'What's the monkey's name?'

'This is Delilah. Do you get it? Samson and Delilah. Quite the couple we make, me as bald as a baby's you-know-what and her all covered in black hair like a heathen. Delilah is fussy about who she likes, but I can see she's taken a shine to you. If Delilah likes you, then so do I.'

He offered Nellie a sandwich, and she let Delilah sit on her knee and pull felt violets from her hat while she ate.

At the end of the day, when he packed up his barrel organ, Eddie said he could not leave a lonely damsel in distress. He would help her in any way he could. The best start, he said, was to have a drink.

At the docks, the pub was full of noise and crowds. Nellie and Eddie sat in a room with black-painted floorboards, drinking gin and playing dominoes. She had never been in a bar before. The heat of the room and the crowded faces stunned Nellie. All the voices rising up sounded to her like the croaking madness of frogs in spring rain.

The first drink made her dizzy, and she was so busy watching the people, she lost one game of dominoes after another. The next drink loosened her tongue. She laughed and cracked jokes like a man, her elbows splayed, hair falling over her eyes, her mouth hanging open, trying to stop the thoughts of Vivian and Joe that came to her, washing back and forth in her mind.

A woman with a mouth like a spoonful of red jam bent over Eddie, lifted his soft cap and kissed him on the head. He grabbed her around the waist and plunged his face against her chest. Then she pushed him away and stumbled on to another table, collapsing into the lap of another man.

'Look at you, you dear girl!' Eddie said to Nellie. 'Frightened witless! You're surely too old for such innocence? You got a strict father who's hidden you away all these years, is that what it is?'

'I have not got a father,' she slurred. 'I have a sister.'

'Mother Superior's kept you under lock and key, has she? I'll look after you, dearie. What you need is a plate of fish and chips and another drink.'

They ate and drank, and Nellie explained how the river had

brought Joe Ferier to her. It had brought him to her, and then her sister had fallen in love with him.

'Ah, love.' Eddie leaned his elbows on the table, his face sorrowful. 'Love's a tricky so-and-so. I'd give up on this Joe chappie. Forget him. He sounds like the sort who likes to break hearts.'

'No,' said Nellie. 'No, it wasn't him. It was my sister. She stole him.'

'But did he ever belong to you in the first place, my dear? Did she steal him or did he steal her? Seems to me they both treated you badly. You lost out both ways, didn't you? Have another drink, why don't you.'

In the noise and crush of drinkers, Eddie said he had a feather bed. Big as a boat it was, and so deep you thought you'd never stop falling into it. 'Closest you'll get to heaven,' he said, and stroked her arm. 'Aren't I the fool, spending all my money on you and then offering you my bed too.'

Nellie stood by the door of the bar while Eddie bought a jug of beer to take away. The monkey climbed on Nellie's shoulder. Outside, the ships in the docks loomed like black mountains. Was Joe Ferier camped out in his canvas tent? She wanted to see him. To ask, had it been him or Vivian who'd sought the other out? She looked back at Eddie, who had his arms around the woman with the red mouth.

Nellie sat down on the roadside, resting her head against the wall of the bar. She was so tired. A feather bed did sound like heaven. Her own bed at home would be even better.

The next thing she knew, someone was wafting smelling salts under her nose. A green glass bottle waved in front of her, and she coughed and spluttered.

'Come on now,' said a woman's voice. 'You can't sleep out here, love. The police will take you away.'

It was the woman who had kissed Eddie. She wore a wide-brimmed hat and a soft gauzy scarf around her narrow shoulders.

Her black coat reached to her ankles, her bosom was lifted high, her waist small and waspish.

'Your mouth is the colour of raspberry jam,' said Nellie.

'She's dead drunk. Leave her. She'll be all right.'

'Eddie, have a heart. You got her in this state. You can't just leave her.'

Nellie felt Eddie and the woman lift her up. They walked her down the street. She tripped up a step and went through a door. Then they lay her down on a bed. It was hard and lumpy, but she was tired and she closed her eyes with relief.

When she woke the next morning, she was on a threadbare settee with a coat over her. She lay there, unsure of what to do. Just as she thought she should get up and leave, the woman from the night before came in wearing a pale pink dressing gown, her hair loose in waves around her shoulders. She handed Nellie a cup of tea.

'I'm Jane. Eddie's wife. Don't look so frightened, dear.'

It was on and off between her and Eddie, she explained. She wanted to know how long Nellie had known him.

'I gave the monkey a shilling last week. Then I saw them again yesterday.'

'That's what Eddie says. You're not his type anyway. He tells me you're down on your luck. Is that the truth of it?'

Nellie's head ached and she felt sick. She told her everything. She was aware as she talked that her openness was not expected. Had she said too much? Rose always said other people should never know your business.

'So you're quite alone?'

Nellie nodded. She could not go home. She needed a job. A room and a job. She was a hard worker.

'I've got a friend who might help you. Her brother's looking for a woman to work for him. You get yourself ready.'

Jane gave Nellie a jug of water and a bowl to wash in. When she was ready, she took her to a café to meet a friend called Trixie.

Then she left her, telling her in future to stay away from other women's husbands.

'You been causing trouble?' asked Trixie. 'You a husband stealer?'

'Never,' said Nellie, affronted by the accusation. She looked at the woman's lined face. She had the feeling Jane had left her here to get rid of her and that there was no job.

'On your own, are you? Me too. I lost my husband ten years ago, sorry little widow that I am.'

Nellie said she felt she had lost enough to qualify as a kind of widow too.

Trixie knew what it was like to fall on hard times. Her husband had died owing money, and she'd lost her home and was living with her old mother and working as a draper's assistant.

She pressed a handkerchief to her eyes. 'I've been ruined by marriage. He took my best years, and all the time he was spending every penny we had. The best I can do is try again. Get married, I mean. Good or bad, every woman needs a husband. I've found myself a better candidate this time. A very good man.' She smiled, and nudged Nellie in the ribs. 'He's dependable, sensible, and as boring as a closed-up pub on a Sunday.'

He was a draper whose wife had died a year ago, and she felt he was ready to marry her. The trouble was he didn't want to move in with Trixie and her mother, and Trixie didn't want to move into the flat above his shop.

'Her spirit's there. His dead wife. I feel like I'm going to suffocate in her curtains and soft furnishings. I'm trying to persuade him to sell the flat and get a new house. There are some lovely new villas out on the London Road. Gardens front and back.'

It rained all morning and the two women sat slowly sipping their tea in the café, next to the window, watching the umbrellas of hurrying passers-by.

'Well,' said Trixie when the rain stopped and the waitress had asked if they were going to buy another pot of tea. 'We can't sit here all day. We should go and see about this job for you.'

The sun shone a dirty yellow through grey clouds. Everything – windows, shopfronts, trees, hat brims – dripped water. Nellie's suitcase was falling apart. It wouldn't last another night homeless, and neither would she.

Trixie took her to a green-tiled shopfront with pig carcasses hanging from hooks in the window. A great row of them dangled like giant sugar mice, waxy and pink and bright with raindrops. To enter the shop and stand in its cold interior with its smell of meat and pine sawdust, Nellie had to lower her head and walk under a bower of dripping pigs' trotters.

Trixie's brother, Nathan Rumsby, wore a spotless striped apron. He was a bland-looking man with small eyes, close set and framed by thick lashes, so it was hard to tell what colour they were. With his butcher's cap on his head he came up to Nellie's shoulder. When he took it off, revealing a head of fine blond hair, he was an inch shorter.

The butcher said he hadn't heard of any Joe Ferier, but he had a room she could have if she worked hard. He couldn't pay her much, but she could start right away. He'd feed her and she'd have lodgings for free.

'Hard work rewards itself,' said Nellie, thanking him. She was surprised to hear Rose's favourite phrase slip so easily from her lips.

As the weeks passed, Nellie became immune to the loneliness within her. The work wasn't so bad here. It was blood she scrubbed out from under her fingernails these days rather than earth. Not what she had imagined, perhaps, but she clung to her new life, believing that this was what she needed, this solitude, a chance to see what fate had in mind for her.

She saw Eddie again by chance, walking by the docks, but he looked straight past her, as if he didn't know her, and she decided it was better that way. He was a married man. It made her blush to think of his invitation to share his feather bed.

One night in October when the moon shone through her curtainless windows, she woke and saw the butcher standing in the room. He was naked, his skin as bloodless as uncooked tripe. There was a curved thickness to his thighs, his belly round and solid. She heard him go away, the door closing behind him. Nellie pulled her blankets around herself.

The next day Rumsby acted as if nothing had happened. His eyes, which she finally worked out were a dirty moss colour, were as restless as ever, flicking over her and then away to the carcasses he was cutting up. The next night he was there again, at the foot of her bed. And the night after that. After a while, Nellie slept through his visits, only waking to hear him make a small groaning sound, his naked feet slapping the bare floorboards as he hurriedly left the room.

Winter wound its scarf of frost around the town. The bacon in the butcher's shop carried diamond-sharp ice crystals in its thick bands of fat. Nellie worked 6 a.m. to 6 p.m., six days a week. Her days off she spent looking for Joe. She often went down to the docks. She thought he might be there, thinking of finding a ship to sail to Southampton, where the steamers left for America. She liked the docks and stood on the quay, watching the trading ships and the barges heavy with cargo. They drifted low in the water, loaded with coal, coke, malt, lime and bricks. It was amazing to see how this stretch of their river, so many miles away from home, was solid with traffic. To think of the isolated stretch of river her own cottage sat on.

On Sundays, she tidied the flat and the butcher visited his mother, taking meat pies and parcels of pork for her. Rumsby dressed up then, a good hat and a thick wool coat, his boots polished, his beard trimmed. He rubbed lard into his fingers to make them soft because he said his mother liked to hold his hand. Nellie couldn't imagine anybody would want to hold his hands if they knew what he did in her room at night.

At Christmas, he invited Nellie to accompany him. His mother lived in a house near the park. Nellie sat on an upholstered chair with the stuffing coming out of it. The striped wallpaper on the walls was faded and falling down in places. Trixie served candied fruits and mince pies on a tray.

'She doesn't hear,' said Trixie when Nellie spoke to her mother. 'Deaf, dearie. She can't see too well neither, and her waterworks have sprung a leak. If I had the money I'd pay a nurse to look after her. I'm worn out by the old bird.'

The butcher sat on the sofa by the gas fire, holding his mother's hand. Nellie ate nothing, said very little and felt out of place. She realized she missed her home and the comfort of Vivian's company.

'Cold meats,' said Rumsby as Trixie ushered them into the dining room where she lit the gas lamps. 'We'll have cold meats and bread and butter with a glass of cider.'

Nellie sat at the table with the mother. Through the open door, she heard Trixie talking to her brother in the hallway. She was praising Nellie. Saying what a hard worker she was and he wouldn't find better. Nellie leaned slightly towards the door. A look of fear passed over the butcher's mother's face. The old woman clutched her throat and gave a small cry of alarm. A puddle of yellow urine steamed around her shoes.

'We'll move Mother into your rooms,' Trixie was saying. 'Nellie will look after her. I've already a buyer for the house. We have to act fast or he'll find another property and we'll have lost our chance.'

'What if Nellie won't do it?' Nathan said.

'You must *make* her marry you. For goodness' sake, Mother will only sell this place if you have a wife. She says you need her here until you have a wife to look after you. You know that. We must get a move on. We both need money, Nathan, and we're not going to get it with Mother holding on to the house.'

Trixie said Nellie was no spring chicken, but Nathan wasn't exactly young himself and she was sure Nellie would accept a marriage proposal.

'She's too tall.'

'She's the best Jane could find. I just hope this one will stay and not disappear in the middle of the night like the last one.'

'She'll stay,' Nathan Rumsby replied gruffly. 'She's got nowhere else to go.'

When they returned to the flat above the shop that night, Nellie went to her room. She took a chair and wedged it under the door handle. She would find another place to live, but for the moment, with the winter so hard and so little money in her pocket, she had no choice but to stay where she was. For a week she put the chair against the door, and for a week the butcher left her alone.

'If you pay me five shillings more, I'll leave my door open,' Nellie said to him one morning. She might be a countrywoman, but she didn't have straw for brains. She was catching on to how people were with you when you were on your own. Well, she could play the game too.

He put his hands in his apron pockets and his eyes flickered over her slowly.

'How much for marrying me?' he asked. 'You'd keep your room. We can have a long engagement. As long as you like.'

Nellie didn't answer him. She thought that kind of decision might cost more than money.

A grey, misty morning in February, Nellie and the butcher's mother walked through the crowds on the docks, stopping to watch the fishing boats that had sailed in on the tide. Huge baskets of fish were being unloaded, stacked high on the cobblestones. Trixie had married her draper and moved away, and the butcher's mother lived with them now. Nellie and the butcher were engaged. That was to say, if the old woman ever asked, she showed her a ring Rumsby had got from Woolworths.

Seagulls screamed and Nellie thought of Joe, of the town he had come from in the north where the birds sounded like crying children. A seabird dived low over one of the fishermen, its yellow beak slicing the air close to his ear. The fisherman swung his head down, lost his footing and upturned the basket of fish he was carrying, spilling mackerel everywhere, a flickering silver dance at his feet.

Other seabirds swooped down. The noise of the birds frightened a herd of cattle being driven through the thoroughfare and they began to barge and push each other, knocking into the piled baskets of fish on the quay, spilling more of them. Children and stray dogs came out of alleys and mossy passageways just as fast as the seabirds descended. Men and women, too, fought for space among gulls and urchins, cramming fish into their pockets and shopping baskets. All around, the seagulls screamed and the fishermen yelled.

Anna Moats heard the commotion as she limped out of the Jug and Bottle. She saw the fish thick on the ground, the gleaners bent to their task, policemen and a few soldiers running, and the cattle stampeding. She decided to get a fish for her supper. The cattle veered towards her. Anna pulled a toad's bone from her bag and held it out. The cattle cantered past, not one of them touching her.

It had once been common knowledge that Anna had something cunning about her. She had been proud of her reputation. If you wanted a neighbour's cows to stop giving milk and their hens to stop laying, then Anna Moats was the woman to call on. She could help if you were the one whose cattle had been cursed or the butter kept curdling. A runaway herd of cows on the docks held no fear for her, and anyone who had known her as a young woman would not have been surprised to see the way the animals parted around her.

She tried to grab a fish, but her gnarled fingers couldn't hold on to it. The fish were everywhere, slick and bright and smelling of the sea. A pain in her hip took her breath away. She looked at the harbour waters and tried to step away from them, but the crowds pushed and shoved her. If the cattle had been afraid of her, the people were not. Anna was old in her bones. She was too often seen drinking to be taken seriously. A man bowled past her and nearly knocked her flying into the water.

By now, more people were coming to gather fish. The butcher himself had heard the commotion and brought a basket to fill. Rumsby's mother complained about the smell of fish guts in the air. Nellie told her to hold her handkerchief tighter over her nose. The old woman coughed and spluttered and said she wished she were back in her own home again.

'Shut up, will you?' snarled Rumsby. 'You smell worse than a load of fish yourself.'

Nellie carried the basket into the crowds. The cattle had been driven off towards the market square, but people were still on their hands and knees on the quay, pulling fish from pools of cow shit. There was an old woman far too close to the water's edge.

'Be careful,' called Nellie. When she got close, she realized she knew her.

'Mrs Moats?' she said, taking her arm. 'It's me. Nellie Marsh. Come away from the edge.'

'Nellie Marsh?' said Anna. 'What're you doing here? Your sister said you was visiting relatives. Let me look at you. You came to me years ago and I cured you. Didn't I?'

Nellie said she had.

'People like you believe in what I do. These days all anybody wants is motor cars and machines. Men and women are slaves to 'em. They don't care, do they? They have their picture houses and trips to the seaside and the old ways are being lost. If I had book learning I might have written books so nobody could forget how things were. I know just as much as doctors, and probably a damn sight more. I might not be able to read words, but I can read a face.'

Anna pointed a finger at Rumsby. 'That one, for example. I can read his face all right. He thinks he owns you. You should stay away from that man. He's got blood on his hands.'

'Pig's blood, Anna. He's a pork butcher.'

'Not how I see it. You'll have no life with that one, I assure you. Get away as quick as you can.'

'I've nowhere to go,' said Nellie.

'Nowhere to go? But of course you do. You come on home with me.'

Nellie glanced at Rumsby and his mother. They looked back expectantly, like large birds waiting to be fed.

'All right,' she said. 'I'll come with you. Just for a few days.'

Five

Vivian had no idea how the child would be born, but she loved it already. Some days she lay on her bed for hours, a hand on her belly, feeling the movements it made. How would it find its way out of her? Her ignorance shamed her. She'd heard Nellie talk of lambing. Of the afterbirth and the importance of it not being left in the ewes. She supposed a human birth would be similar. She'd read all their housekeeping books and found only passing references to childbirth. Water needed to be boiled and a layette should be prepared. She should have seen a dentist, one book said. Pregnancy loosened women's teeth. Another book recommended that after the birth the mother should stay in bed for three weeks without moving. Then she could get up and wash herself. But how could she do that alone?

Vivian looked at the clothes she had sewn, the small nighties and cotton caps, and hoped they would do. Everything was prepared as best it could be. She'd told the vicar's wife she could not wash their linen any more, blaming the cold of winter, saying her fingers were rheumatic. She still wore a girdle tightly bound to hide her swelling shape, but in the cottage she risked undoing it, relieved to be able to breathe a little easier. She never took it off completely, thinking that if anybody came to visit her she'd have time to pull the girdle's restricting laces tight again before opening the door.

Without any income now, she had to rely on her own stores to eat. She had stocked up on tinned foods before her money had run out. She'd bought flour, lard, sugar and salt, raisins and tea. All through the summer months she preserved fruit and made jams and pickles with this moment in mind. Jars of beans and tomatoes and cases of apples filled a shelf in the pantry. By being careful she'd had plenty to eat over the winter and enough to last to springtime.

She gathered sticks and branches and made a log pile taller than herself. In the orchard, clumps of waxy snowdrops bloomed and Vivian picked bunches of them, filling the cottage. Jars and old tin cans filled with white flowers lined the stairs, the shelves and windowsills. They gleamed like hundreds of tiny candles. Dressed in the red robe the vicar's wife had given her, Vivian prepared her home for the child.

When her time came, she screamed because she thought someone might hear her and come to help. When nobody came, she fell silent. Nellie's hagstone hung from a string over the mantelpiece, a charm to protect her. She had piled wood by the fire and brought in the last of the coal. Vivian laid out Rose's old newspapers on the floor and fed the stove until the kitchen was so heated, sweat ran down her face. The windows steamed as though a hundred faces were pressed against them, watching her solitary endeavours.

'That baby was cold as winter,' Anna was saying, sitting by the fire in her cottage, holding court, regaling Nellie with her tales of birthing local women. 'I can assure you, the child's mother saw it was gone from us. She was crying like a cat stuck down a well. I cannot tell you what wholly occurred that day, but I rubbed the little thing with my hands, standing over the fire with it, massaging it till it coughed and spat and took a breath. I put it to its mother's breast and it sucked so hard the mother fainted.'

'Is that really true?' asked Nellie. She was stirring a pot of soup on the cooking range. Anna was full of stories and Nellie doubted most of them, but they drew her in nevertheless.

'Do I look like a liar?' said Anna. 'I en't got no tall-tale blisters on my tongue. I only speak the truth, and if I don't like the truth then I don't speak it. So there.'

Nellie nodded. She'd heard Anna say that many times. She had been living with Anna and her daughter Louisa for a month now.

Several times she'd walked up to her old home, thinking she might speak to Vivian. Once she had been standing behind the elder trees, hidden from view, and Vivian came out of the cottage to feed the hens. Her sister's face was dreamy-looking, her eyes shining with a peacefulness Nellie did not recognize. Was Joe Ferier in the cottage? It stopped her heart to think of them together. But no. She was sure Vivian was alone. Her sister moved slowly through the long grass of the orchard, lazily, like someone who did not know they were being watched. She wore a red dress and a pretty blue shawl. Her blonde hair cascaded around her shoulders. Vivian had been skinny before, but she looked womanly now. It hurt to see Vivian looking so content. To realize that living alone suited her well.

The hens – Nellie's jolly red hens – followed Vivian across the garden, chasing after her skirts like fond children. Vivian was talking to them. She went indoors singing an old hymn Rose used to sing, the cottage door banging shut behind her, the hens settling on the doorstep to wait for her. Nellie turned away. Her sister did not need her.

It was surprising to find there were still women in the village who called upon Anna Moats to deliver their babies. Nellie had gone with her to two confinements. It had been alarming to see women lumbering like wounded cattle through the pain of childbirth. Nellie felt useless. She did not know how to help. Their cries frightened her. 'There's no romance in childbirth,' said Anna at the bedside of a labouring mother. 'You hold her hand and tell her she's a bloody marvel,' she instructed Nellie as the woman's face twisted in pain on the pillow. Nellie did as she was told. Such a small gesture, the clasping of another's hand in your own. The woman clung to her. 'Thank you,' she whispered. 'Thank you. Thank you.'

The same day, Nellie and Anna did a tooth extraction. The old soldier in the village had a rotten tooth. He was in agony, a gin sweat pouring off him. Cheek like a cooking apple, green with infection, shiny, round and swollen. Nellie got the tooth in a good grip with the pliers, her knee on the man's chest, and then exclaimed loudly that the smell was too much to bear. She'd almost vomited over him, and Anna, gin-soaked herself, pushed her aside and pulled the blackened tooth, promising them all a tot of drink when it was over.

'So will you deliver this baby?' Anna asked Nellie and Louisa. 'Mrs Thomas will be labouring with her sixth child, but I can't walk there with my bad legs. She's a strong woman and it'll be an easy birth.'

'I can't,' said Nellie. 'Not without you. I'm afraid of what might go wrong. I think she should get a nurse.'

Anna scowled. 'A so-called qualified midwife wants fifteen shillings to do what I do for eight. Three months' training these women get, and I've more years' experience than I care to remember. A doctor costs one pound. All well and good if your husband's working, but Mr Thomas hasn't had full-time work in months.'

'We'll do it, Mother,' said Louisa roughly. 'No need to take on.'

'Can you manage a bowl of soup, Anna?' asked Nellie. The old lady thanked her and Nellie turned to ask Louisa, but she was putting on her coat, saying she was going out. It was a dark afternoon and snow was beginning to fall. Nobody would want to walk anywhere in this, except Louisa had told Nellie she was meeting the wheelwright, who had asked her to go away with him if he could get at his savings without his wife knowing.

'I'll be back before you know it,' said Louisa, and gave Nellie a wink.

'You think you might go and see your sister soon?' asked Anna as Nellie ate soup. 'You and Vivian were so close. It's a sad thing to see you apart. A man, was it?

'Usually a man involved when women fall out,' Anna said when Nellie didn't reply. 'Well, don't leave it too long. It takes courage to go and make things better. You're a brave girl, Nellie.'

'I don't think I am,' said Nellie, and watched snow falling against the window.

Anna Moats thought she would miss Nellie when she was gone. She was sure Nellie would go back to the sister she loved. That was obvious. Nellie was stubborn and acted tough and distant with folk, but it was plain to see the woman had a heart as tender as a naked heel in a new boot.

After Louisa left, Anna sat back in her chair and told Nellie she had been the midwife who'd delivered both her and Vivian. What a laugh to see the girl's astonished face! Of course Rose had never told her.

'You were our mother's midwife?' asked Nellie.

'For both of you. I brought you into the world, my dear. Your afterbirth is buried in the same place as your sister's. Right under one of the apple trees in your orchard.

'A slip of a thing Vivian was, born early and quickly. You were another story, Nellie. A long labour and a breech birth. You came feet first into the world, which is no way to arrive. An awkward birth makes for an awkward child, you know. Baby girls who make their mothers suffer at birth grow up contrary in later life, thinking themselves too good to get down on their knees and scrub a kitchen floor.'

'Well, I'm not like that,' said Nellie.

'No, you're not. Not at all. An exception, you are, Nellie Marsh. I'll have a bowl of that soup now, if I may?'

Anna sat by the fire, sipping from the bowl Nellie put in front of her. She wouldn't say it, but Nellie's mother had nearly died of exhaustion. All the long hours of labour she'd sat on the bed, back rounded, her white cotton nightdress bunched over her thighs, legs pulled up, her hands holding them apart, trying to look over the vast curve of her belly, crying as if she was calling the child out of her. Cursing the father of it and Anna too, for her inability to make the pain go away. Poor Rose Marsh. And so young. Rose's mother had been a saint, claiming the children were her own daughters, and her husband going along with it. Oh yes, people said an awkward birth made an awkward person. But surely in this case it was the mother, Rose Marsh, unmarried, already shamed with one little bastard daughter, who had been turned awkward and hardened by Nellie's birth?

Six

Vivian held her baby girl in her arms, bundled up in a piece of blue velvet, pressed against her heart and the warmth of her chest, the way shepherds carried lambs, knowing the beating of their own hearts might just work miracles. She took the path along the river. The wind rushed over the water, running fast ripples across its surface. Ahead she saw a woman bent against the wind. She was in the arms of a man, and the two of them went away across the fields. For a moment Vivian thought of Joe and felt a sharp stab of envy. The passion of the couple stirred the lovesickness she still suffered with.

Outside Anna Moat's cottage, Vivian hesitated. She had never been here before. But Anna Moats would be able to help her. She'd know how to make her baby strong. She crept to the window and peered inside.

What she saw nearly made Vivian drop the baby. Nellie was there, standing at the stove, candlelight illuminating her back. She was stirring a pot, and she stopped suddenly and turned her head towards the window. All this time Vivian had suffered alone and Nellie was at Anna Moats's house?

She heard footsteps. Louisa Moats and a man talking together. That was who was on the riverbank. That ragbag woman and the wheelwright. Vivian felt herself chastised all over again. Nellie was here, punishing her still; but surely, after what she had endured alone, she deserved to be forgiven? She turned and hurried back to the cottage, tears stinging her eyes.

At home she lay in her bed with the child. The fire had gone out. The stove was cold. She had no coal left and no strength to get in wood.

'Nellie will come,' she whispered, drawing the baby closer. 'Nellie has to come back now.'

'I'm swollen up,' said Mrs Thomas. 'I can't even get my shoes on. I need a doctor, but my husband says he's drunk in the pub and won't come out. You'd better know what you're doing, you two.'

Mrs Thomas's five children stared out from their seats beside the open hearth. Baby clothes were airing by the fire.

'This is an infusion of blackthorn leaves,' said Nellie, handing a bottle to Mrs Thomas. 'From Anna, for your pains.' Nellie took gloves from her pocket. 'Can we boil some water? I need these to be as clean as possible.'

'What is she going to do with another brat?' whispered Louisa as Nellie boiled the gloves. 'Don't look like she can manage the ones she's got. Do you reckon I should tell her how there are ways you can bring off a cure in the early months? Just in case she falls pregnant again after this one? Means you can keep your husband happy and yourself in a decent state too.'

'You children should go and play,' said Nellie loudly, though she knew it was far too cold for them to be outside. She wished Louisa would stop talking like this.

'You should know too. Every woman should,' whispered Louisa. Nellie coloured darkly. Louisa talked of purges and cures, pennyroyal and Epsom salts, castor oil, bitter aloes, a bit of gunpowder on a dab of margarine.

'When I was a littl'un,' Louisa said, fishing the gloves out of the water with a pair of wooden tongs, 'there was always women wanting help, coming up our garden path. Coins in their hands and problems in their bellies. I helped me ma and I never looked away. Not once. I've seen stuff would have you on the floor in a dead faint.'

'I don't doubt it,' said Nellie, and wondered if she didn't feel faint right now.

*

Anna Moats had been right. Mrs Thomas knew what she was doing. The baby was born quickly and without fuss. Nellie wrapped it in a clean sheet, trying not to notice the swollen genitals, scarlet as boiled beetroot. She set about tying off the cord with a shoelace as Anna had showed her.

'This one's called Christopher,' said Mrs Thomas, lying back on the pillow. 'Handsome little chap, en't he? My lovely boy. Christopher Thomas. He'll go far, when he grows up. I got a good feeling for him.'

Nellie thought he was anything but handsome. She handed him to Louisa, who dangled him upside down and slapped his buttocks. The older children stood in the doorway, scratching their heads, laughing when the baby screamed. Mrs Thomas was seedy with lice too. Nellie had seen them moving through her hair as she wiped sweat from her brow.

Outside in the cold night, Nellie stood with a spade in her hand. Snow was still falling. She had blood on her apron and her hands were shaking. She kicked the spade into the ground, making a hole. The frozen earth didn't want to yield and she grew warm, chipping away at the soil. She bent to pick up the bucket and tipped it, pouring the afterbirth into the hole, kicking the earth back over it and stamping the ground down. Anna Moats said it was important to bury it deep. That way the child would never stray far from home. Like having your roots in the ground, Anna reckoned. You might go away, but you'd always come home because that's where your beginnings were.

Nellie had been surprised when Anna had told her that her beginnings were in the orchard by the cottage. Vivian's too. And if Anna had been their mother's midwife, then why had Rose always disliked the old woman so?

Nellie gathered flat stones and laid them on top of the compacted soil to keep foxes away. She heard footsteps and stopped. It was Louisa.

'The husband has turned up. I don't think they need us any more. I forgot to say, I saw your sister earlier. She was outside the house. Ran off like the devil was after her. It en't none of my business, but I reckon you should go and see her.'

Nellie felt snow melt on her eyelashes. She tasted the icy flakes on her lips. Yes. She would go and see Vivian. It was time.

'I'll come with you, shall I?' asked Louisa.

Nellie hesitated. She dropped a last stone down on the turned earth.

'If you like.'

She realized she would be glad of the company.

All around, white flakes of snow flew. Nellie and Louisa pushed through a gap in a hedge, crossed a wooden bridge over a ditch and continued down a track enclosed by trees. The wind picked up, tunnelling along the alley of trees, and the snow fell faster. As they came to the end of the track, the land rose slightly and there was the cottage.

The door was ajar. Nellie stepped into a room no warmer than the outside. She reached instinctively to the table and found a lamp and a box of matches beside it. She lit the lamp and looked at her old home like she was seeing it for the first time. Smoke from the cooking range had blackened the ceiling. A sampler stitched with red lettering and green leaves entwined around them hung on the wall. *God bless our mother*, the stitching spelled out. A small brown stone with a hole in it dangled from a length of string over the mantelpiece. Nellie recognized it. The hagstone.

There were footsteps on the stairs and Vivian came down, calling her name, a candle in her hand. Her feet were bare. Her hair hung matted around her shoulders. Nellie was shocked by her sister's appearance, but she tried to smile. To make the moment seem less strange.

'You came,' cried Vivian, and dropped the candle, which flared and went out. She threw her arms around Nellie's neck. 'She's upstairs. My baby is upstairs. I don't know what to do. I've been waiting for you. I've been so afraid, but I knew you'd come home.'

Nellie pushed her sister away. What was she talking about? Had she taken in an orphan child?

'No. It's my baby. Joe's daughter. Come and see her. Bring the lamp.'

Vivian led them upstairs, her bare heels black with dirt, stepping over jam jars and tins filled with dead snowdrops.

The lamp lit the room softly and the ceiling looked low, the walls dark and indistinct. Vivian drew back the bedclothes where a baby lay on the pillow, swaddled in a blue velvet cloth. It was nothing like the newborn they'd just delivered, who had swung his fists like a fighter and was pink as a fresh boiled shrimp. This baby's skin had a yellow tint. Louisa lifted the lamp towards the child to see it better. She sucked air in through her teeth, like a farmhand looking over a horse, assessing it for its usefulness.

'A little girl, is it?'

'This is Josephine.'

Nellie's mind was full of memories of Mrs Thomas's overheated little house, the children and the rudely healthy baby boy.

'Who helped you, Vivian? Who birthed this child?'

'I did it alone. I thought I might die. I wanted to but then there she was, my own little baby, and I was glad I was alive. Do you want to hold her, Nellie?'

Nellie shook her head. She felt Joe's betrayal all over again, and she saw he had betrayed Vivian too. She remembered the day she had found Joe's hat in this bed. The hatred she had felt for her sister. 'We must get the fire lit,' she said, struggling to know what to do. 'We need to warm you both up. This place is freezing. A baby needs to be kept warm.'

She went downstairs and busied herself lighting the stove, relieved to have something to do. She told Louisa to fill the kettle, and Vivian came and sat with the baby by the stove.

'I'm waiting for Joe to come back,' she said. 'I want him to see his daughter. And then we'll all live here, together. All of us, Nellie. We'll be happy, won't we?'

Nellie didn't answer her. Her heart had turned, in a matter of moments, to a cold damp stone, heavy and incapable of feelings. She would never live with Joe. How could Vivian even speak of him? She became practical and quiet, ignoring Vivian's nervous chatter. She found some woollen socks and put them on her sister's cold feet. She draped a blanket around Vivian's shoulders too and blew on her icy fingers to warm them.

'Get a blanket for the baby,' she said to Louisa, who was also busying herself, tidying the kitchen, winding the clock that had not been wound since Rose died. Nellie brought logs in and managed to scrape a little coal from the stores. She saw she would have to chop more wood tomorrow. She went outside to get eggs, and Louisa followed her across the snow. Nellie opened the door to the hen house and felt cautiously inside until she touched the dry, warm feathers of a hen.

'That baby's ill,' Louisa said. 'I've seen them like that before. I've heard Ma say you've got to get the urine of the child and put it in a clean bottle. You put that bottle facing upstream in the river so the current runs over it, and as it clears so the baby's yellow colour goes. But even Ma says she en't sure that is a real cure. She always says there's nothing you can do except wait and see with a yellow baby. We could take her up to the vicarage and knock on the door and leave her on their front step for them to take in. Thing is, that baby don't want to be dying on us when nobody knows we got it here.'

Nellie didn't reply. She buried her hand under the hen and took the warm egg she found there. Joe Ferier had done more than separate the sisters. He had ruined them.

They drank tea and ate fried eggs and potatoes. The baby lay in the crook of Vivian's arm and Vivian held her fork in her other hand, cutting the egg with the edge of it. It looked an awkward way of eating.

'Give her to me,' Nellie said. 'Give me the baby while you eat.'

Nellie took the sleeping baby and cradled it. She looked like Vivian. You could already see she was her child. The soft abandon of its limbs and the heaviness of the child's head troubled her. Nellie could feel a tight pain in her lungs, an ache in her breast, some deep emotion pulling at her guts.

'She's ours, Nell,' said Vivian, smiling. 'Yours and mine.'

'Don't go loving her,' warned Louisa. 'She's sick, poor creature.'

'I'll fetch the doctor,' said Nellie, panic making her hand the child to Louisa. She reached for her coat. 'I'll get him out of the pub even if I have to carry him. He'll have medicine to make her better.'

Louisa shook her head.

'You en't going.'

Louisa thought it was likely the doctor would call out the hygiene inspector. He might take the baby away to a hospital and then they'd never get it back. An unmarried woman giving birth on her own? Vivian could end up in the lunatic asylum, because surely only madwomen brought this kind of shame on themselves. And she'd never hold her head up in the village. The shame of it would be too much. She'd lose her job as laundress at the vicarage. She'd have no money and end up giving up the child in any case. The Langhams might throw her out of the cottage too.

So Nellie didn't go. The fire crackled and spat, and the room began to warm. The three of them sat together, Vivian singing to the baby, the clock ticking loudly. Outside, the wind whistled and moaned. The poplar trees by the river were creaking and groaning as if they might be felled by the snow blizzard. The baby's breathing was shallow. There was a deep anxiety between the sisters, a pulsing fear in each other's eyes.

They were countrywomen and knew when death had entered

a house. They felt it settling on the child, the dreadful sorrow of it pressing against their own fast-beating hearts. When late that night the baby died, Nellie and Louisa stood over Vivian, watching her grieve, unable to take the pain from her. In the hours before dawn, Vivian took her baby and washed and dried her. Then she dressed her in clean clothes and wrapped her in the blue velvet.

'Joe Ferier has to be found,' Nellie said. 'He has to see what he's done.'

'You can't tell anyone,' insisted Louisa. 'We've got to keep things quiet. Things will be right as a mailer if you don't let on.'

Louisa took charge. She began organizing, planning, deciding what to do. The baby must remain a secret. The police would want to know what had happened here. Vivian had hidden her pregnancy. She had given birth alone and the child had died. The police might say Vivian had killed her baby to be rid of the shame of it.

Vivian stirred then, crying out and protesting that she would never harm a child. She loved her baby. But Louisa would not be swayed. Vivian would have suspicion cast upon her if anybody knew about this. She'd have to prove her innocence. It was hard and it was unfair, but that was how things were and they had to understand that. Everything would be fine if they kept this secret.

Vivian insisted her baby must be baptized and buried in the churchyard. Louisa said it was impossible. The two women argued back and forth. Nellie watched the brown hagstone hanging from a length of string. It spun slightly in the breeze that Louisa made as she marched up and down the room, arguing with Vivian. Nellie remembered giving it to Joe, last summer, sitting by the river. She took it down and slipped it in her pocket.

'We'll go to the river,' she said, reaching for her coat. 'I'll do it,' she told Vivian. 'I'll make sure she has a proper burial.'

*

Vivian stumbled. Ahead of her, Nellie's hat tipped forwards against the east wind, her back straight, her footfalls as sure as ever. Vivian's coat was wet and heavy with snow against her legs. She fell and the ground was hard and stony. She remembered Nellie as a child. She had been the fastest runner at school, with or without her hobnail boots. The best crow-scarer among all the children in the village too. Vivian had a memory of her sister. Black crows and jackdaws swooping down onto the flowering bean fields, and Nellie aged eight, undoing her long plaits, shaking her brown hair loose, running up and down the fields, arms outstretched, hollering and yelling, jumping into the air. She'd always been the brave one.

Nellie lifted her, telling her she would be all right, putting her arms under Vivian's and helping her forwards.

'Oh, heavens,' said Vivian, fighting tears. 'I'm sorry, Nellie. You're so brave. And here I am falling down. Will Josephine go to heaven? Babies go to heaven, don't they? I know we are all sinners in the eyes of God, but I cannot think of a baby being born guilty of anything. Me, yes, I'm guilty. Guilty of hurting you. But not Josephine.'

'Her soul has gone right up with the angels,' said Nellie. 'This is just her body and she doesn't need it any more. You keep going a little longer, Vivian. Just a bit further.'

At the riverbank, Louisa gathered stones to weigh the velvet bundle down. Nellie was bent over, pulling off her boots.

'You can mourn her here whenever you want. Vivian, you can come down here and she'll be with the fishes. Swimming in the reeds with them. You hear me? Come the summer, you'll be able to stand here in the sunshine and look at the water. All the things you see alive in there? Well, Josephine will be right there with them. We'll come and sit here together. We'll come here to see her, for the rest of our lives. Until we're old, and then we'll join her one day.'

'You promise?'

'Of course I do. I promise.'

Vivian nodded. Her sister was always the brave one.

'If I'd had a doctor—'

'You did what you could, Vivian. I should never have left you.'

The snow stopped falling. Nellie took the bundle in her arms and walked down into the river. Vivian strained to see into the darkness. Nellie's white undergarments shone for a moment and then were gone.

Nellie waded into the black waters. She felt the cold pressing her lungs, filling her with confusion. The river wanted to take her for itself. It was surprised, no doubt, by the heat of her body and, wanting it, it sucked the air from her lungs. She was burning in the icy water. The last time she had swum here had been in the summer, with Joe. Back then the river had wrapped itself around her like a lover.

She forced her arms to move and struck out towards the centre of the river. She knew it would have been no good throwing the bundle into the water in the dark. The stones might rip the velvet and the body might float up. The only way to do it was to dive and lay her burden down upon the river bed. And there, the creatures in these waters would take it and keep it. Vivian would be able to mourn her then. Nellie thought of the fish, the monster washed up on their kitchen floor. They'd taken the sorry creature from the river and now here she was giving their own sorrow back to the waters. And this was the only choice. Better than the churchyard, where an illegitimate baby would be judged and unwanted. The water would baptize her and take her to its heart.

There was a papery crust of ice on the surface of the water. It crunched and cracked as she swam through it. By tomorrow morning the river would be frozen. Villagers might skate on it, as they often did in a cold snap. Her limbs went weak. She began to feel cold and afraid. If she died in these waters, they would not find her until the thaw.

In the middle of the broad sweep of icy water, her courage came back. Nellie owned this river. She knew its currents, its gravel bed. She would not be taken by it now.

She dived and the pain in her skull was terrible. Her teeth froze and her jaw turned brittle. She touched the river bed. She could not go down any further. She dropped her bundle. The baby was safe now. Delivered to its grave. She had done what she set out to do, giving it over to the care of the river. She pushed up to the surface, gasping for breath, the cold slowing her movements. For a moment she was lost. Which way to go? Which bank to swim for? On one side were Vivian and Louisa with her clothes. On the other side were snow and open fields. If she got it wrong, she would die of cold. She kicked and swam off towards what she thought was the right bank. And then she heard something. Vivian calling her name over the wind. She turned, and this time she heard her sister's voice again. She knew she would make it back. The river would not take her, only the secret she had given to it.

Seven

Nellie sat on the window seat in the cottage, watching the lapwings flying over the fields. It was 1917, the country was still at war, and Vivian had been gone for nearly three years. The longer Nellie stared at the birds, the more she doubted those fragile shapes were blood and feather and bone. Against the pale sky they looked like rags; strips of black fabric dancing back and forth. She looked down at her hands resting in her linen skirt. Her sewing box sat beside her, a pile of mending untouched. She was no good at darning in any case. Vivian had always done it. Since she had lived alone, Nellie's darning and mending had not improved at all.

Of course Vivian had left. Every time it rained she had rushed to the window, watching for any change in the water level of the river. Any sign of it rising made her anxious. She'd been afraid of what flood waters might deliver back to them. Nellie had tried to reassure her. She'd put the brown hagstone in a cotton bag and told Vivian that as long as one of them had the stone then the river would not give up its secret. It would not betray them or the baby.

Nellie got up from the window seat and put on her hat and coat. Outside, the lapwings gathered into a black knot in the sky. They moved away until they were a pencil line, and then a dot, and then gone. She cycled into the village, glad to be in the fresh air. It was a wonderful thing, a bicycle. Louisa had left it to her as a gift when she eloped with the wheelwright.

Should Nellie marry, like Vivian had? Even if she was open to the idea, and she wasn't sure she was, there was no one left. In one day back in 1914, the village had lost all its men. They'd marched off to the train station, off to war, chummy and triumphant, their arms around each other's shoulders, like work gangs swaggering across the barley fields at the start of the harvest.

She thought of Vivian and her married life often. It was still a regret that she had missed the wedding. Nellie had bought Vivian a bale of damask table linen as a present, and the day of the wedding Nellie had left the house with it under her arm, in plenty of time to catch the train. Shoes polished, gloves in hand, she had wandered down to the river. Standing under the willow tree, she tried to work out how her life and Vivian's had changed so drastically. She'd lost track of the hour, mesmerized by the waters and the fish gliding in the depths. By the time she walked hurriedly the six miles to the station, she'd missed the train, and Vivian, in a county town miles away, was married without her sister there to be glad for her. She had tried to explain several times to Vivian what had happened, but she was sure her sister did not believe her and thought instead her non-appearance had been a way of punishing her for leaving. Perhaps there was a little truth in that too.

At the Parish Rooms up by the church, Nellie stepped into the warmth of the wooden hall. On a trestle table were plates of boiled tongue sandwiches and slices of walnut cake. The vicar's wife was serving tea from a big metal urn.

'Ah, Nellie.' She handed her a cup of tea. 'We missed you at Red Cross classes. We were bandage rolling. You didn't call for the laundry either. Have you been ill, my dear? Really, you must say if you can't manage to take in washing any more.'

Nellie muttered her apologies and accepted a sandwich. She'd not eaten all day.

The vicar was showing newsreels of the war. The film flickered and jumped. Men in uniforms, smiling and dazed-looking, marched in unison across the big white sheet stretched over a wall of Sunday-school Bible pictures. Some of the men had bandages around their heads like turbans. They pointed at themselves and laughed, giving the thumbs up to the camera. It was hard not to smile back. She watched the long rambling lines of them in heavy uniforms, scanning their faces, looking for Joe Ferier.

'This is rather old footage,' announced the vicar, breaking Nellie's thoughts. She blinked as the gas lights were lit, and glanced at the film tin beside her.

'September 1916,' the vicar said. 'A whole year out of date.'

'The main thing is to see our boys overseas,' said his wife. She smacked the hand of a child trying to take a sandwich. 'We must try to be informed about what is going on.'

'And how is Vivian? Is her husband still doing warden duty?'

'As far as I know.'

'Poor you,' said the vicar's wife. 'You must miss your sister terribly.'

Nellie took another sandwich and nodded. She wondered if Nathan Rumsby had found himself a wife. Perhaps she should go and see if he would still consider her. She had to do something. She couldn't rely on free sandwiches to feed herself much longer. Farm work was sporadic since Langham had retired and a new tenant had taken on the farm. Recently she'd got a letter in the post saying a rent collector was going to be calling to inspect the cottage. The new tenant couldn't let her have the cottage rent-free any more.

The vicar's wife had moved on to another conversation.

'They are prisoners, let us not forget.'

'Conscientious objectors . . .' the vicar said. 'What do you think, Nellie? We have prisoners in our village and just one guard with them. I find this a very dangerous situation.'

Nellie swayed away towards the door.

'It's a patriotic duty to join up,' the vicar said. 'Our young men willingly give themselves to defend the Empire. It is our duty to serve God, King and country. Nellie, do say hello to your sister if you see her.'

She took another sandwich from a tray and left the hall, taking a path into the trees to see if conscientious objectors were really working in the woods. She found them quickly, a group of long-faced men with dark beards and the martyred look of the misunderstood, dressed in prison garb, thin and gaunt, chopping logs and clearing undergrowth. A guard stood smoking, watching them from a distance.

Not one of the men lifted his head from his work when she strolled past along the sawdust-strewn track. They hid their faces from her, and she wondered if they thought she might be there to offer them white feathers for their cowardice.

There was the sound of arguing behind her, voices raised in anger, and she turned to see a group of soldiers talking to the prisoners. One soldier had his head bandaged. Another walked with a stick. A third had his shoulder and arm bandaged and wore an eye patch. Nellie had to pass them to get back out onto the road.

'You should be in France, fighting like real men,' said the soldier with the eye patch. 'You're a bunch of cowards. Worse than the bloody enemy.'

The other soldiers were pulling him away.

'Curb your language, man. Look, there's a lady present.'

'Don't hold back on my account,' said Nellie. Her hat had slipped sideways and she tried to organize it back into place. 'But you should think on a bit. These pacifists are scrimshankers and shirkers, but I do believe they might be right. If every man in the country refused to fight, the generals would have to do it themselves. In which case the war would be over by now.'

Nellie hadn't meant to be so outspoken. She felt cheered by the look of surprise she received, and walked away with a spring in her step, a triumphant smile creasing her face.

As she cycled home past the Parish Rooms, the vicar called out to her. An army chap had come by looking for a cook for a military hospital. The wages would be good. They needed somebody straight away.

'You could attend an interview today. I think you might know the house. A place not far from here called Hymes Court.'

It was September and the cold weather was already setting in. A season working indoors would be better than harvesting sugar beet. She would go there now. For the first time in many months, Nellie felt good fortune coming her way. A sense that something might happen. That luck might be on her side for once.

Vivian opened her eyes. The eiderdown felt silky against her skin. She could hear Frank snoring in the other bed. Birds sang at the window and there were street noises outside, voices, cars, horses and carts.

She got out of bed and dressed behind a screen, putting on her roll-on corset, a slip and a flowered tea dress in crêpe de Chine. Soft wool stockings and red leather T-bar shoes with a small heel.

In the bathroom down the hall, she washed and checked her appearance in the mirror. She still marvelled at the indoor bathroom with its ceramic bath and a sink with shiny metal taps for hot and cold water. In the mirror her eyes looked calm. Pale grey with a thin blue rim to them. Her hair had recently been salon-waved. She drew a sweep of blonde across her forehead and fixed it with a hair clasp. She did not look like a countrywoman any more, and she was glad.

Vivian tucked a stray curl behind her ear and powdered her nose. It had been a sensible decision to marry Frank. She was fond of him, but she didn't love him. If she didn't love him, she was sure he could never break her heart. She applied red lipstick and blotted it with a tissue, just as she had read how to in a magazine. She used a little block of coloured wax and a small brush to paint her eyes. Another magazine article on feminine beauty, written by a man, had said it was off-putting to see women too brightly painted. Vivian read avidly these days, borrowing books from the town library. Books on manners and etiquette, housekeeping and homemaking. *The Young Woman's Friend, A Wife's Companion, Good Manners for All Occasions, How to Care for a Husband.* She was teaching herself to speak correctly too, as if she could cast off every memory of her past life with every ragged country vowel she refused to utter.

She went down the staircase with its faded red Indian runner and stopped on the landing where the guest bedrooms led off a corridor. Four rooms, two either side.

On the landing was a large brass spittoon, something Frank had brought back years ago from India when he'd worked out there as a young man. Vivian had filled the dimpled brass pot with peacock feathers. Nellie would have been horrified to see such unlucky feathers in a house. Vivian stopped to arrange the feathers, glancing out of the window onto the grounds at the back of the house. There was a scrubby rose garden, and a small vegetable patch which had been lawn before the war. Beyond were stables, where Frank's automobile was parked and a green-painted pony trap gathered dust. An apple tree stood tall over one of the stables. All this was hers.

It was hard to think she had once believed so fervently in a spinster's life. She had read the other day that a husband was the most important element in a woman's life. Above children and other family members. Granted, it was another article written by a man – why were so many articles aimed at women written by men? But he'd made a convincing argument. It made a kind of sense to think that married women should treat their husbands as both the masters of the home and eternally needy children. Women were natural carers, after all.

Frank came downstairs. He wore a baggy charcoal suit, and his round-rimmed glasses had smears of fingerprints on them. He was rather elderly, but he had a good head of grey hair and thick white eyebrows that hung over his glasses in a comic fashion. His face was soft and good-humoured. He checked his watch and smiled.

'Am I late this morning?'

'No, dear,' she said, enjoying the sound of the familiarity in her words. 'I was waiting for you.'

He held out his arm to her and they walked downstairs. On the ground floor was a hallway with a set of doors going off to the right and a small reception desk. A drooping fern in a glazed green pot sat on the desk, along with a brass bell, and a gong was suspended from a dark wooden frame. A carved cuckoo clock on the wall loudly tick-tocked.

At the reception desk, Vivian let go of his arm.

'Kippers this morning, please, Mrs Stewart,' said Frank breezily, and disappeared into the dining room. Vivian went into the kitchens and put on an apron.

Frank liked his kippers poached in milk and then set on a plate with a knob of butter and slices of dry toast. The cook, Mrs Dunn, was making breakfast for the guests: two farmers in town for the livestock market. Vivian said good morning.

'It's raining,' said Mrs Dunn. And then, 'Don't forget he likes brown toast.'

'Thank you,' said Vivian. She knew the cook didn't like her. Every time she entered the kitchen she felt she was trespassing. Frank had laughed it off when she told him.

'She doesn't have to like you,' he said. 'You don't have to like her either.'

Despite the hurt she felt at his short reply, she had been glad he explained things to her. It stated clearly in one of her household management books that a distance must be kept between staff and members of a household. Kindness and distance. She flipped the kippers onto a warmed plate and congratulated Mrs Dunn on the newly washed floor. For a moment she heard Rose's voice in hers, the sureness of it, the way she always knew how to be correct. Nellie used to say Rose was an ogre, but that was unfair. It must have been hard for Rose raising her sisters alone.

Vivian wrote regularly to Nellie. She still felt guilty for leaving her alone. Poor Nellie. Vivian hoped one day to be able to ask Frank if her sister might come and live with them.

In the dining room, Frank was discussing the war with his friend Bernard Harding. Dr Harding was a balding man in a starched white collar and dark tweed suit. 'Stewart,' he called her husband, as if it were his first name. He and Frank had gone to school together. These days, both of them being too old to join up, they did warden duty, guarding the railway yards and urging people to keep their lights dimmed and curtains closed in case of Zeppelin raids. Frank, ever cautious, had asked Vivian to put up black paper on the windows to hide the lights at night.

Dr Harding ran a surgery in the centre of town. He was a man devoted to society and the improvement of it. He'd been mentioned in the local newspaper just the other day for giving a talk to a ladies' club. He'd lectured a full hall on the importance of eliminating weakness in the offspring of the working classes. Good breeding, he'd been quoted as saying, was vital for the future of the British Empire.

When she'd first met him she'd thought he might be a possible husband for Nellie. He was a lifelong bachelor. 'Everybody's uncle,' as Frank jovially called him. Vivian could not understand a man wanting to be a bachelor all his life. She didn't believe anyone really wanted to live alone. Frank had been a bachelor too, but one in need of looking after when his mother died. He said Vivian was his angel sent from above.

'Would you like more tea?' she asked the doctor as she put the kippers down in front of her husband.

'Bless you,' he said. 'Mrs Stewart, that would be wonderful.'

Frank gave Vivian a mild smile. He had the same way of looking at her when he watched her getting into bed at night. Fondly. It was nothing like the way Joe Ferier had looked at her. She shivered thinking of Joe, a light stirring of the hairs on her arms. She touched her sleeve, smoothing her skin back to dullness. There was no passion in Frank's gaze and she was glad.

She'd met Frank by chance. He had been the answer to her problems just as she had been the answer to his. She and Nellie had been walking one afternoon in late summer.

'It's going to rain,' Nellie had said. She always had an uncanny ability to predict the weather. Vivian had thought of the river and felt the familiar panic rise within her. The fear that her baby's watery grave might be disturbed. It was always unbearable to imagine that.

It had been humid for days and there was a sudden drenching downpour. The sisters walked slowly through it, a long way from home. Vivian heard a noise like a threshing machine's engine and turned to see a small black motor car bounce around the corner, shiny as a beetle. It braked heavily and skidded, its front wheel mudguard knocking Nellie over onto the grass verge.

The more Nellie insisted she was all right, the more Frank insisted he should drive the women home, or to a doctor's surgery. It was Vivian who took charge. She wanted to get dry. Yes, she yelled, bent against the rain and wind, one hand holding her soggy hat down to stop it getting blown away. Yes, they would accept a ride.

Frank turned up at the cottage the following week carrying a bouquet of goldenrod and purple irises. He liked to drive in the country on Sundays, he said, and thought he'd stop to see if Nellie was recovering.

Vivian found a tablecloth in the dresser drawer, one of their mother's. She spread it over the table and invited Frank in. She served him tea in their best teapot. Nellie did not come home, though Vivian was sure she had caught sight of her heading across the fields away from the house. She doubted she would return until Frank's motor car was gone from the track outside. Nellie had become more like Rose since they had started living together again, avoiding the gaze of others, being reclusive and shy, talking of the dangers of the outside world, just as Rose had.

'Next time you come,' she said to Frank, because already it seemed that he was a man of routine, 'I'll have fresh scones baked.'

He had a small guest house in a town forty miles away. His mother had owned it, and when she died her housekeeper continued to run it. Now the housekeeper had died too, and a man simply couldn't run a guest house. He needed a woman to do it.

Frank visited on Sundays and always with a bunch of flowers in his plump hand. Each time they heard his car approaching, Nellie set off across the fields, announcing she had things to do, though what these things might be, she never said.

'Perhaps your sister doesn't like flowers?' Frank asked when Nellie had been late leaving and they could both see her running through the orchard.

'Don't mind her,' said Vivian. 'She's awkward. I like flowers very much.'

He stayed for hours, without need of conversation, hands folded over his stout belly, drinking tea and eating cake, happy to watch her mending clothes or doing her chores. He seemed to grow more comfortable in the chair the longer he sat there. Some days he stayed until it got dark and Vivian had to ask him to leave for fear Nellie was sat outside, waiting to come inside.

'Why does he keep coming?' asked Nellie a couple of months later. She brushed a hand across the yellow chrysanthemums arranged in a stone jar on the table. 'He drinks all our tea and takes our sugar.'

'He has asked me to marry him,' said Vivian. She had been waiting to tell Nellie. Hoping she would understand she could not bear her life here any more. So much had happened. She longed to be away from this cottage, where every room was filled with memories of her daughter.

'Marry you? But you can't marry him. We're sisters. We promised Rose we'd never marry.'

'I have said yes.'

'But he's so old.'

'He needs a housekeeper.' Vivian avoided her sister's hard stare. 'Forgive me, Nellie. Living here I feel like the river is watching me, waiting to catch me out. I cannot stay any longer. I hope you will come with me. I shall explain to Frank.'

'No,' said Nellie. She had lived away from home for those months after Joe left and she always liked to suggest she had learned a great deal about human nature during that time. 'If he marries you, he will expect you to give me up. You are leaving me.'

'I would never do that. I shall insist you must come with me.'

But Nellie had been right. Frank had said they'd wait and see about her sister joining them.

Vivian and Frank's honeymoon was a night at a hotel by the sea. A favourite place Frank had been coming to since he was a child with his brothers and parents and then with his widowed mother until she passed away. A grey stone hotel perched among rockery gardens of pink heather.

'Vivian,' said Frank that first night. 'Come to bed. There's nothing to be afraid of.'

It was touching to hear the gentleness in his voice. He thought her innocent and afraid. She felt knowing instead. She had already been Joe's wife. Not in name perhaps, but she had been the mother of his child.

She woke the next morning and expected to see her sister beside her, the wooden crucifix that hung on the lumpy limewashed wall of their room. Then she heard Frank snoring and remembered. She was married. She whispered her new name under her breath. *Vivian Stewart.*

She had thought Frank would give her what she desired more than anything, but in the time they had been married there had not yet been any children.

Vivian brought another pot of tea and a jug of cold milk to the table for the doctor.

'Isn't she a treasure?' Frank said, beaming.

Dr Harding agreed heartily. 'Your mother would have adored her,' he said, and added another sugar to his tea.

Eight

Hymes Court sat in a valley, a long tree-lined driveway leading to it. There were circular steps to the front door, stone pillars and a yellow rose climbing them. Inside, nurses in starched white uniforms bustled back and forth across parquet floors. A wide sweeping staircase led the eye upwards, and framed oil paintings hung on the walls up the stairway.

'You want the side entrance,' a soldier told her. 'Kitchen staff don't use this door.'

Nellie liked the work. The nurses said her rice pudding cheered even the weakest of the men. She baked bread and made health-giving jellies. Eggs in aspic, beef tea, calves' foot broth, stewed rabbit in milk. Her heart went out to those poor wounded boys that came and went in their temporary hospital rooms. She would have spoon-fed any one of them if she'd been asked to.

The owner of the house, a military man called Williams, was away fighting and his mother and sister had moved to Switzerland for the duration of the war. His wife and six-year-old daughter had stayed behind. They lived in the east wing, away from the wounded soldiers who cried in the night. Away from the smell of iodine and mustard plasters.

Nellie saw the little girl coming and going with her mother. Her name was Dorothy. She had blue eyes and a pleasing face. Dorothy waved at her each time she saw her, and Nellie felt flattered by the child's attentions.

'You remind me of my sister,' Nellie told her, when the girl's mother brought her into the kitchens one day.

'Is she six like me?'

Nellie laughed.

She was a loveable child. Nellie couldn't help feeling Vivian's little one might have been like her had she lived.

What Dorothy liked best, her mother said, was a Victoria sponge with plum jam in the middle. Their old cook used to make them.

'My sister was the cake maker in our house,' Nellie said. 'But I'll have a try.'

The next day more casualties arrived and there was no time to be baking cakes. She worked long hours, chopping vegetables and pushing pots and pans back and forth, steam filling the kitchen, her face red and flushed. The nurses were rushed off their feet too, and nobody had time to stop and talk or to walk in the gardens where red tulips and wallflowers coloured the unsettled spring weather.

'Dorothy's gone,' said a nurse when Nellie finally took a sponge cake up to the east wing.

'Gone where?'

'Abroad. Her mother was worried they might catch tuberculosis from the soldiers. They've gone to Switzerland. Some people get all the luck. I wish I was out of it.'

Coming downstairs, Nellie studied the oil paintings that lined the staircase. The richness of the depth of paint made her want to reach out and press a finger to the canvases. There was a painting of the present family. Dorothy stood between her mother and her father in his army uniform, a ribbon in her blonde hair.

Nellie supposed that one day when the war was over and Dorothy grew up, there might be an oil painting of her with her own children here, along with the others. The thought pleased Nellie, though she couldn't say why. Perhaps she felt glad that in all this chaos there might be a life that could be lived simply and happily.

Nellie took the cake to the soldiers' mess rooms. A newspaper was spread on the table and a name caught her eye. *Langham*. She read on. The two Langham boys had died in action. Poor Mrs Langham and old Hang'em. She picked up the paper to take it away with her. A picture of Nathan Rumsby was on the front page, next to news about the possible end of the war. He'd been found guilty of murdering his mother. Nellie dropped the paper.

A soldier picked it up and handed it to her.

'Hello,' he said. 'I remember you. You had a plan to end the war. A good one, I'd say.'

Scarring covered the right side of his face. He wore an eye patch. His cheekbone, the unscarred one, was high and smooth, his hair combed and glossy with hair oil.

She moved away, thinking of getting back to the kitchens.

'Ah, but you don't remember me? Why should you? One wounded soldier looks much like another.'

Nellie clasped the newspaper to her. 'Perhaps I do know you. I have to go, excuse me.'

He said he was the soldier who'd got into an argument with some pacifists one day last year in her village. 'Let the generals fight it out. That's what you told us. Wonderful!'

Nellie still didn't remember. She thought she might fall down if she didn't get outside and breathe fresh air, and yet something made her stay. He seemed so desperate to talk. He'd got himself blown up in the Somme, had a stint in a hospital in Dorset, and now found himself back at Hymes Court, where he'd been invalided back on a Blighty One. That was shorthand for any wound bad enough to get you sent home. Once he was discharged from here, he really was home for good. Demobbed. Pensioned off. No more running like a rabbit out of the line of fire. Well out of it all.

'It's very good to see a friendly face at any rate,' he said. 'Let me introduce myself. Sergeant Henry Farr. Single so far, the lads like to call me.'

Nellie held out her hand.

'Eleanor Marsh. Nellie. And I really have to get back to work now.'

'Damned good cake,' she heard him say as she hurried away.

At the end of the day he came to the kitchens to find her. He leaned an arm against the door frame and smoked a cigarette.

'I can't abide children. I have these blasted night terrors, you see. Noise can set them off. The sound of children crying sends me off in a spin.'

'I don't have any children,' she said, taking off her apron and shaking it out. 'And I don't want any either.'

They spent her days off together. She met him off the omnibus and took him home to the cottage, where they walked in the orchard. On sunny days they sat by the river.

Henry Farr had been an army man all his life, and now he was finishing his career as a company sergeant. It was over. He was fagged out, used up and useless. With the shrapnel wound he'd got in his groin, and he hoped she'd pardon his French, he couldn't even piss straight.

He described the French villages he'd seen, all bombed and ruined. He told tales of wounded men and the dead horses that lay where they had fallen. He spoke like the other soldiers in the wards spoke to each other, a bantering rough language full of slang and filth and hard jokes.

He was nothing like Joe Ferier. Henry was not interested in travel. It seemed a noble thing to him, to walk the same path every day. Sticking to something was what was important. Nellie said she agreed. He wanted to know all about her life. About her sisters. The types of apple trees in the orchard. How to force rhubarb and blanch dandelions. Nobody had ever asked her so much about herself.

They walked through the gardens of Hymes Court, where other soldiers strolled or stood around smoking, looking out over the fields, contemplating the horizon of sky and woodland. Henry thought they were probably composing poetry because war seemed to do that to some men. Either it made them bloody-minded cynics or it made them weep like women and take up writing verse.

'And do you write poetry?'

'No, no. I'm the bloody-minded cynic, I'm afraid.' But if he was honest, and he said it seemed an easy thing to be honest with her, he did weep. Sometimes he laughed too, though he didn't know why. 'Fucked up royally,' he said, laughing. 'Done over by those cunts we call officers. Oh, but we did it all for glory, heh?'

'Ah,' said Nellie, thinking of Rose and her belief in the glory of work. 'Ah, yes, glory.' She told him she had known an artist who had read poems to her. She hadn't liked them much. 'He's probably in France now. Joe Ferier, does the name mean anything to you?'

'Not at all.' Henry stopped walking. 'Does it mean anything to you?'

'He was a friend of my sister,' she said lightly.

Beyond the kitchen gardens were abandoned glasshouses, and they sat on a bench in the shelter of one, the sun filtering through the frames and colouring the glass with rainbow prisms. Henry hoped he didn't shock her with his coarse language. He was too used to the company of soldiers.

'I don't mind a bit of swearing,' Nellie said, lifting her face to the sun and closing her eyes. He didn't have to mind his Ps and Qs with her. She liked him just as he was.

Henry picked flowering lilac for Nellie, woody branches of it, but she refused to take it indoors because lilac in the house was bad luck. She had a list of plants he should never bring indoors. Blackthorn, bluebells, may blossom, ivy. White flowers of any kind. She was full of old wives' tales and fears that would have made him laugh if he hadn't heard the same kinds of superstitions in the trenches. He and his men had all of them relied on charms and omens to keep the shells away. Counting broken trees, finding meaning in the foolhardy way a bird might fly across the shell-torn sky, seeing another day's grace in the sudden sprouting of mushrooms in the grassy fields of no-man's-land: all of it the base of calculations they made on staying alive. Coming from Nellie, though, such beliefs seemed charming and innocent.

'This is the tree of the heart, the hawthorn,' she said, putting a green bud on his tongue, telling him locals called it bread and cheese. When they were children, she and her sister had loved picnicking on the sweet buds. He ate, wondering whether he might die of poisoning and not minding too much if he did.

'What do you want from this wretched world?' he asked Nellie as they walked through the village. They were going to watch newsreels at the Parish Rooms.

'Company,' she replied, and their hands brushed together for a moment.

In the Parish Rooms the vicar shook Henry's hand and said it was an honour to have a veteran come by. He apologized profusely for the footage. Six months out of date, but what could you do?

The newsreel turned and flickered. Soldiers marched in fields of mud. Henry felt hot. He started to sway. Somebody moved beside him and he tried to apologize for his shaking.

'Got to get out,' he whispered to Nellie.

She took his arm and led him outside. He gulped the air. The sky was darkening to dusk. He shivered and shook. Children gathered, curious to see a grown man falling to the ground.

When he stopped shaking, Nellie was there, talking to him. Her words came and went in his ears. She was explaining about the birds she liked to watch, how they flew in the wind like rags. How she felt like that herself sometimes, all ragged and lost. She put her hands on his shoulders. They sat in the damp shadow of evening, holding each other.

*

Nellie drummed her fingers on her kitchen table. She blushed deeply. Henry was saying she must think about the consequences of marrying him. He coughed and cleared his throat and went outside and came back into the cottage and went out again, wiping his boots on the doormat so many times Nellie told him he'd wear it out if he didn't stop.

'You don't have to do this,' she told Henry, but he bolted the door of her cottage and said he had to show her what she was getting into, marrying him. It would be a marriage without children. They were agreed on that. Friendship and companionship were what they would have, but still, Henry felt there were things to be discussed. There were things he simply could not give her. Physical relations were out of the question.

'But I don't want them,' she insisted, her hands covering her face.

It was impossible to talk of these things, she told Henry. Her heart, she said, was a terrible dry thing. She did not say that it had been hurt so badly by Joe and by Vivian that she did not dare expose it a third time. That, he did not need to know.

'I'm a rotten old codger who's past his prime. I want you to see what you're buying before you sign the cheque.'

He took off his shirt and unwound his puttees, laying them out on the table. He unbuckled his brown leather belt. Nellie glanced at the door. She hoped nobody would call at the house. She fanned her face. It felt very hot in the room.

'Henry, really, you've got nothing I haven't seen before . . .'

'Too late, old girl, here I am.'

Henry stood naked in front of her, except for his socks and his eye patch.

'This,' he said, pointing to his thigh and groin, 'was shrapnel. An eight-inch shell burst alongside me in the trenches. And here,' he pointed to his chest, 'was where a shell came in through the top of my shoulder and out just here by the collarbone. So. What do you think? You can tell me honestly. I don't want charity. We can call it all off. Just say the word. I am no good to a woman who thinks her husband has certain duties to perform, because I'm not up to that kind of thing. I can't do what a man should do in a marriage bed, and I haven't the heart for it either.'

Nellie lifted her skirts and pulled down her stocking, showing him a curved purple scar on her right thigh.

'A stone flew up from the threshing machine. It had a line of flint in it. Went clean through to the bone. Blood everywhere. I couldn't walk for a while. They had to stitch it and I wouldn't let the doctor near me. I was ten years old. My sister Rose threatened to hit me over the head with a hammer if I didn't sit still. She would have done it too. She was the one who stitched it up. The doctor said I was too much trouble. I'm after company, Henry. Nothing more than that.'

In Rose's old bedroom – because Nellie had never been able to sleep in her old room since Vivian left – they lay down together and held hands. Henry was naked under the coverlet; Nellie lay on top of it, fully dressed. They slept for a few hours. When they woke, they agreed they would marry as soon as possible.

Nellie and Henry married in a register office in town on 12 November 1918, the day after the war ended. Their local town was splendid with celebrations and there was dancing outside the corn exchange, but they avoided the crowds in case the noise set off Henry's nerves. Vivian sent a pair of white lace gloves for Nellie and apologies for not being able to attend the ceremony. Frank had bronchitis again. He'd come out of hospital now and she was nursing him. Henry's brother George, who ran a public house in London, sent them two crystal tumblers and a little Union Jack flag. The vicar and his wife sent a hamper. Nellie opened it and found jars of chutney, pickled walnuts, a bottle of cider and a box of fancy cakes, little squares of sponge iced in bright colours.

'Now that is a splendid gift,' said Henry, standing behind her, putting his arms around her waist. 'They must think a lot of you. Just as I do.'

'I suppose so,' said Nellie. She was still thinking about Vivian. She'd been surprised when her sister had written to say she could not come to their wedding. Had she been paying Nellie back for not attending hers? Nellie took the old brown teapot down from the shelf and set about making tea. A memory of Rose drifted into her mind. Her sister's grey hair scraped back into a tight bun, her worn hands reaching for the same teapot. How disappointed Rose would be to know the sisters had separated. There was a space on the dresser next to it where their mother's best teapot had been. Vivian had taken it when she left.

She didn't care about teapots, but there were shadows between her and Vivian she couldn't get rid of. She still woke some nights thinking of the river. How cold the water had been, that moment when she hadn't known which bank to swim to. She had not swum again in the river since that night. The baby owned it now. Every time she stood on the riverbank and considered swimming, she knew she could not.

Nellie made tea and buttered a few slices of bread. Henry liked sugar sprinkled on his. She set two plates down on the table and put out the teapot and a jug of milk and poured the tea. On the wooden dresser their wedding photo sat in a metal frame.

The photo had been taken in a studio. Nellie seated on a wicker chair, white lilies and trailing ivy in her hand, Henry standing behind her in his army uniform. A pair of fluted wooden pillars towered behind them.

'Corinthian,' said the photographer when Henry asked. 'Don't move. No smiling. Very good. Thank you.' Behind the pillars was a richly painted screen. Ragged children playing in an olive grove. Blue skies. A glaring sun. 'Ancient Greece,' the photographer had told them.

Mrs Henry Farr. Friendship seemed to shine out of that name

like a lamp lit in the dark. Joe had said she would never leave the village and he had made it sound like a failing in her. He was right, but so what?

Here she was in a photo, getting married in ancient Greece. Wherever Joe was now, she would bet he had never been to ancient Greece.

She took the lid off the sugar bowl and spooned sugar onto Henry's bread. She was sure they could be happy here, the two of them. A muscle twitched in Henry's cheek. She reached out her hand very slowly so as not to frighten him, and stroked his face.

Nine

Vivian sat at her sewing machine, putting the finishing touches to a dress. She had thought she would never wear black again. Especially now when the war had been over for months and everybody seemed to want colour around them. Even the trees had held on to their autumn hues longer this winter and green shoots and catkins were coming through, shivering in the March days while the old leaves still clung to the branches.

In the high street, red, white and blue flags waved and snapped back and forth like wet washing in the breeze. Coloured bunting dangled in front of shops and buildings, tangled up in windows and wrapped around lamp posts. Fireworks still went off at the weekends, and the church bells rang out at all times of the day. On the trams the women conductors sang 'It's a Long Way to Tipperary' and let soldiers ride for free.

Vivian had decorated the guest-house façade with bright flags and bunting too; Mrs Dunn's son Stan, a limping man who had not fought in the war due to his poor posture, had got a ladder up and done it for her. Then, in respect for Frank, she had asked him to take them down. She'd hung a black silk bow on the door knocker to show she was in mourning for her husband.

At the funeral she sat next to Dr Harding, Frank's two brothers and their wives. Vivian looked behind her to where Nellie and her husband, Henry, sat together on a pew nearest the door. Henry was a tall man with a battered, scarred face and, Vivian thought, a rather caustic way of speaking, as if he thought he was a lot cleverer than anybody else. When she looked back later, as they stood to sing hymns, Nellie and Henry had gone.

After the service Dr Harding talked to one of the brother's wives while Vivian sat quietly, relieved to be left alone for a moment. She listened to their whispered discussion about the tragedy of the war. The loss of a generation of young men. The woman's sons had been lucky and were returning home. She hoped they might settle into jobs and find decent women to marry, the need for family being greater than ever.

'The Empire,' sighed Dr Harding, as if it were a shimmering thing he saw in front of him.

As the mourners left the church, Vivian saw Nellie standing with Henry among the gravestones, the wind whipping their coats. She hurried across to them.

'There you are, Nellie.'

'Sorry about that,' said Henry. 'I get a bit bothered in crowds.'

'That's all right. I was worried you'd gone.'

'We're so sorry,' said Nellie. She hadn't stopped saying this since she had arrived. The way she said 'we' annoyed Vivian. She wanted Nellie to speak to her as a sister, not as somebody's wife.

Vivian had thought to link arms with Nellie, but as they walked back to the guest house Nellie slowed to allow her husband to keep up with her and Vivian was obliged to walk in front of them. Henry carried a cane, his stride stiff and careful. It occurred to Vivian that perhaps the sour look on his face was due to pain from his war wounds. She was surprised to see how gentle Nellie was with him. As if the man was breakable.

At the guest house Mrs Dunn provided sandwiches and glasses of sherry and fruit cake with royal icing, all laid out on white tablecloths. Vivian was relieved to see the old woman had put on a clean apron to serve the guests. Vases of lily of the valley were on the tables, filling the room with their sweet scent. She could see Frank's brothers were impressed. She'd had long conversations with the undertaker about the style and ways of doing these things and had taken his advice freely. 'Fashions change,

Mrs Stewart,' the man had said, straightening a brilliant-white cuff. 'But good taste must prevail.' It was he who told her lily of the valley was the most fashionable flower for funerals this year. 'I'll have them then,' said Vivian, and when he said they'd be out of season and costly, didn't even ask the price.

Frank's two brothers said she'd done a very good job of the funeral. They were aged, balding, short-statured men. They had the same mild, apologetic look about them that Frank had had, and both were fat like him. Edward was an insurance agent; Clifford, a post-office clerk. Vivian served them sherry and they agreed Frank's death from influenza was an absolute tragedy.

'He never actually told us he had married,' said Edward. 'He was always devoted to Mother.'

'He worshipped our mother,' added Clifford, raising his eyes to the ceiling. 'We didn't think he'd ever marry.'

'She might have left the house to the three of us, but of course Frank was her favourite and got the lot.'

'Isn't Mrs Stewart a marvel, Edward?' said Dr Harding, stepping into the conversation. He gave Vivian a pat on the arm. 'I never saw Frank as happy as when he met and married this dear woman.'

Thank goodness Dr Harding was there to support her. It seemed every time Vivian was at a loss for words, he was beside her, at her elbow.

'I'll get another plate of fruit cake,' Vivian said, and escaped thankfully into the kitchen. She stood at the back door, smoking a cigarette, looking out over the muddy gardens.

'There you are. I've been searching for you.'

She turned. Nellie stood there, her pale grey eyes studying her. 'Your hair suits you short.'

Vivian touched her head. She thought her new cut a touch too daring really, but her hairdresser had encouraged her to have it done. He'd said it showed off her neck. He'd been the one to suggest she wear a shorter hemline too.

Nellie still had her long hair pinned up in a top knot, pre-war style. She held a pair of gloves in her hand, and she wore the old black coat she'd had for years. Vivian could see the inexpert mending Nellie had done to the shoulder where the seam had come undone.

'I didn't know you smoked.'

Vivian smiled and threw the cigarette outside. 'Frank got me into the habit. I rather like it, though I don't smoke in public.'

'If Rose could see us now,' said Nellie. 'You with your cigarettes and your big house. Me married to a soldier. She'd be scandalized. Do you remember how she liked to find newspaper stories about drunken soldiers?'

Vivian laughed. She felt the warmth of Nellie's voice. They knew each other again. They were sisters once more. Girls who had grown up sharing a bed. Vivian could feel them both stepping back into the place where they shared thoughts and sentences, all the secrets of their sisterly hearts. It was, she discovered, all she wanted. If she could walk away from the guest house and back to the cottage with Nellie to live as spinsters once again, she would have done so without a second thought.

'I'm hiding from Frank's brothers. Frank has left everything to me in his will and they're furious about it. He had life assurance too, so it turns out I'm worth a pretty penny. Apparently it was Edward who urged Frank to take out the policy. He must have thought the money would go to him.'

'Blimey, Vivian the heiress,' said Nellie. 'A rich widow. I'm shocked.'

'It's not an awful lot, but I will be comfortable and I own the house. When I think how poor we were, growing up, and yet we were happy together, weren't we?'

'We were always happy together, Vivie.'

'And you're happy now, I suppose?'

'With Henry? Yes. He is a kind man.'

'I'm glad to hear that.'

They sat at the kitchen table. Vivian fetched her sewing box and mended Nellie's coat while her sister made tea. She sewed a last stitch and broke the cotton with her teeth.

'That's better. Try it now. Good as new.'

'Thank you. I always knew you were meant for a life like this. You were never a farm girl.'

'Only because you and Rose wanted me to keep house. I might have been good working in the fields.' She could have thrown her arms around Nellie, but she didn't move. 'I thought you might like to live with me here, now that I am alone. I have plenty of room. I thought that if you and Henry have children one day . . .'

'Children?' Nellie shook her head. 'I don't want children. Babies are too fragile. I'd be so afraid . . . After what happened to Josephine. And the thing is, Henry can't—'

'Josephine?'

They turned to see Henry in the doorway looking restless, his raked shoulders slumped as he leaned on his cane.

'A friend of ours,' said Vivian smoothly. 'I was just mending Nellie's coat.'

'But did I hear you discussing children? Can't stand them. Nellie doesn't like 'em either.'

Vivian had been sure there would be children in Nellie's marriage. She had already imagined them, their soft faces around this table.

'But you're married. And the Empire?' she said, Dr Harding's words coming back to her. 'The continuation of the British Empire depends upon us all. It's your patriotic duty to have children. Dr Harding says—'

Nellie reached across the table and took her hand, stopping her outburst. 'The Empire? What's that to do with me?'

'Nell, we should be getting along,' said Henry. 'I do apologize, Vivian, but we have a train to catch.'

Nellie stood up. 'Yes. We really should go now. The train takes an age and then we have to walk back to the cottage.'

'What she means is she has to dawdle alongside me.' Henry waved his cane at Nellie. 'An old cripple like me takes a bloody age to get anywhere. Luckily your sister has the patience of a stone. I'm a lucky man to have her.'

To have her? But of course he did. Nellie was his wife.

'So you are,' said Vivian. 'Very lucky.'

'Are you ready to go home, Mrs Farr?' asked Henry cheerfully.

Nellie stepped forwards and hugged Vivian.

'Look after yourself. You've got everything you need now. Money. A house. I'm glad,' she said, and pushed something into Vivian's hand, whispering into her ear. 'You keep it safe now.'

Vivian felt something cool and hard in her palm. The hagstone.

'Goodbye, my sweet sister,' Nellie whispered.

Vivian slipped the stone into her skirt pocket.

She saw them to the door and watched them walk away down the cobblestone road. She waved, but neither looked back. They were already thinking of other things, she supposed. The journey back home to the cottage. Their life together there.

After Mrs Dunn had washed up and gone home, Dr Harding settled in Frank's worn old armchair by the fire and Vivian stood by the window, studying the marks sticky tape had made on the glass where she'd had taken down the blackout paper Frank insisted they put up. She could feel the stone, a small weight in her skirt pocket. Her daughter would be five years old now, had she lived. Nellie had loved her too, so how could she suggest she did not want any children? Was it the memory of that night by the frozen river, or simply her soldier husband's wish that she remain barren? Vivian rubbed at the glass with her finger and looked out. Perhaps Henry thought the world too awful a place to bring children into.

The street lamps glowed, and rain sparkled in their light. Even now, months after the war had ended, there were still soldiers making their way home. Joe Ferier might be among them, walking somewhere, or sitting in a railway carriage, pencils and paintbrushes in his kit bag. Perhaps he was thinking of her. Of that summer by the river. 'I love you,' he had said.

She closed the curtains, busying herself, lighting the lamps in the room. She topped up the doctor's glass, listening to him talk about Frank, imagining Nellie and her soldier husband riding the train home, the dark walk back to the cottage, the sound of the poplar trees by the river. Perhaps it was the long day, the people, the sadness of missing Frank, but she felt tears coming. Or perhaps, she thought, it was homesickness that gripped her. The desire to be back with Nellie, living together in the riverside cottage, when that was now impossible and they both had their own lives to lead.

Nellie sold her furniture and donated what cutlery and china she didn't need to the paupers' fund in the village. In her old bedroom, Henry stored his trunk with his uniform and ceremonial sword and black boots. A pleasing smell of tobacco, mothballs and boot polish filled the room. Sometimes she went in there just to stand and look at his belongings. Now she helped Henry carry them all downstairs to the waiting cart. There was nothing much left in the room afterwards. Just memories of Vivian. She piled the toys they had had as children into a box. The oak apples and the marbles, the shells and pencils, little patchwork silks, whistles and odds and ends, scraps of wool and cotton reels. A headless porcelain doll bore testament to a particularly fiery row, though what the argument between her and Vivian had been about she could not remember, only the rage with which she had flung the doll against the bedroom wall. Nellie threw the valueless items into the orange flames of the bonfire that Henry was tending in the garden. It could all go, all of it.

'It's the local housing authority's fault,' Mr Westfield had explained when Nellie first received the letter stating the cottage was unfit for human habitation. 'I've said I'll make good the repair work, but they won't budge.'

'We'll go to my brother's public house,' Henry said when they discussed what to do. Nellie suggested they live with Vivian, but Henry didn't think it a good idea. He didn't want to share a home with a stranger. It was a shock to hear Vivian described as a stranger, but perhaps he was right. She and Vivian were not close any more.

At Liverpool Street Station, Nellie was startled by the crowds. She had never seen so many people. She felt stupid, standing on the sooty platform with no idea which way to go. She wanted to go straight back home again. She wasn't sure what she had expected from the city. Women in fancy clothes and big motor cars, she supposed. There were plenty of smartly dressed people. And plenty dressed in filthy rags. What she noticed most were the pigeons. Clouds of them descending onto the smoke-filled platform like they were landing in ripe bean fields, and no scarecrows to put them off. More than anything, she thought, London was full of pigeons.

'Bloody creatures. Worse than rats,' Henry said, waving his cane at them. 'Filthy things.'

Nellie liked them. They landed around her and she felt they were gathering in welcome. As they left the station she saw a flower seller. A woman with a hand cart crammed solid with rich-petalled blooms. Orange and red hothouse flowers, white lilies and exotic plants she didn't recognize, boxes of violets and bright little spring posies. Colours that shone in the grimy station entrance. For a moment she wished Vivian was beside her, so they could point and stare together.

The car jumped over every pothole, and Vivian twice hit her head on the roof.

'All right?' asked Dr Harding as she rubbed her forehead. He was bent forwards, obviously delighted to be driving Frank's car. She thought of her late husband and imagined the horror he'd feel, knowing she had let Bernard Harding loose behind the wheel. She really should have been brave enough to drive herself. Frank had given her plenty of lessons.

The hagstone was in her pocket and she touched it. She was sure she had only love for Nellie in her heart. That and a desire to undo certain things, to smooth out the knot of family ties that bound them so awkwardly. Husband or not, it made no sense that Nellie had not responded to her letter.

Dear Nellie, Vivian had written. *I have been thinking and I would like to offer you and Henry a home with me . . .* It had taken many attempts to get the tone right. She had already suggested to Nellie at the funeral that they could live together. In her letter she had repeated the offer, stating clearly that Nellie and Henry would have their own rooms and would in no way need to spend their time with her. She'd put the letter in an envelope, addressed it, got her hat, coat and handbag and went to catch the last post. When she received no return letter, she decided to go and see her sister in person.

'Turn right here,' she told Dr Harding as they spun through the village, frightening the ducks around the pond. 'And then take the next left after the church. It's a few miles along the road.

Vivian stared at the rows of houses, the well-tended vegetable gardens. Gypsies were camped in painted wooden wagons just outside the village, their horses tethered beside them. When finally she caught a glimpse of the river, her heart quickened and she realized she still thought of this as home.

'That's it,' she said. 'Right ahead. Careful of potholes. Turn right here.'

They came to a stop by an overgrown hedgerow. Vivian got out of the car and looked up at the ruins of the cottage. A honeysuckle clambered into a broken window and came out on the roof. The thatch had slipped under the weight of green moss, leaving gaping holes. Several other windows hung open, their panes covered in what looked like thrown white paint but was, Vivian could see as she stepped closer, bird droppings.

'Surely they don't live here?' said Bernard. 'It's a hovel.'

Vivian pulled the garden gate open, yanking the bindweed and sticky goosegrass from its handle, the feel of lichen rough under her glove. Finches rose up out of the hedgerow, chattering loudly at having their peace disturbed. A pheasant called in the overgrown orchard.

'Shall we go?' said Bernard, getting out of the car and lighting a cigarette. Vivian shook her head. It annoyed her to have to share this moment with Bernard. It would have been better to have come alone. She left him smoking, playing with the iron water pump, splashing water at his feet, and took the track down to the river.

Here, nothing had changed. The black poplar trees swayed and the willow branches dangled in the water. She had loved Joe Ferier under those willows. There was the quick movement of fish as they darted back and forth in the river weeds. What was it Nellie had said? That they would be able to come here and know little Josephine was resting in peace. That they would come here for the rest of their lives.

She took the stone from her pocket. Nellie had promised that as long as they had the stone, the secret of the baby would remain with them. But that had been when they were together. She held the stone out over the water. It was over. All of it. Her baby and Nellie were lost to her.

And yet.

Vivian put the stone back in her pocket. The sisters might be together again one day. The stone might keep her daughter's grave safe and undisturbed. That's what she told herself as she walked back to the motor car.

'I'll drive back,' she told Bernard, lighting up a cigarette. She blew a smoke ring and was pleased to see the scandalized look on Bernard's face. 'It's my car, after all,' she said, and realized something had hardened inside her. She was no longer afraid of being alone.

When she returned home, there was post waiting for her. Bills and her own letter to Nellie, which had been returned by the post office. Among them was a small pale blue envelope, the address written in her sister's careful handwriting. She ripped it open. Inside was a short note. Nellie apologized for not having written sooner. She'd had so much to do. She had moved to London and was living and working in Henry's brother's public house.

Vivian could not imagine Nellie in a city. They had a biscuit tin once with a picture of the Changing of the Guard on it, the only image of London she knew. She imagined Nellie standing there in the crowds, wearing the farmer's smock that acted as a bathing suit, her old straw hat perched on the back of her head, her bare feet planted apart. Nellie looking beautiful and straight-backed, chewing on a bit of hay. It was enough to make her smile.

Weeks later Vivian sat in Frank's button-back velvet chair. Life was easier without Frank fussing over things, but still she missed him. She hadn't realized she had grown so fond of him. Frank had sat in this chair for so many hours at a time, slumped here with his hands clasped in his lap, turning one thumb over the other, smiling that soft, grateful smile of his as she brought him tea and cake. His mother would have approved of her, he liked to say.

The door swung open and Bernard came into the room with a tray of tea things.

'You sit there and rest your feet,' he said, putting the tray down and pouring her a cup of tea. 'A date and walnut slice?'

Vivian shook her head.

'The thing is,' he said, taking a slice of cake and seating himself on the little footstool beside Vivian, 'I have something very personal I want to ask you.'

Bernard smiled. He was clean-shaven, his cheeks raw-looking. Vivian had an image of him standing in front of a shaving mirror with a razor in his hand, like Frank used to. The careful movements he would make. The towel on his shoulder, his braces loose around his trouser belt. She imagined sitting in the bedroom brushing her hair and having a view of him in the bathroom. Dr and Mrs Harding. She had a certain standing in the town now. People greeted her cordially. The baker gave her the freshest loaves when she shopped, and the butcher always sold her a decent cut of meat. Her status gave her privacy and respectability, she had learned. People accepted her readily as a widow. A doctor's wife, though, would be another step up. A doctor's wife would be served first in the butcher's queue, all the other women – lowering their eyes, looking into their wicker baskets – accepting this fact in good grace.

'We've been friends for a long time now,' he said.

Was this going to be a marriage proposal? Could she forgive him his dainty size and bald pate covered in tiny freckles and moles? Bernard balanced the cake on his knee and took her hand in his.

'This is difficult to say, but well, here goes. There is a girl, a poor young thing – and she has got herself into trouble.'

'A girl?' She looked down at the sight of her slim fingers encased in his hands. 'What are you talking about? What have you done, Bernard?'

'Me? No, no! I've done nothing, Vivian. It's not what you think. Good Lord, no.'

The girl was not even known to him. Her parents were set on her making a good marriage in the coming year and, naturally, no man would dream of marrying her if he knew she had already had a child. A girl's virginity might be of slightly less importance today, in these modern times, than in years before, but there were some standards that hadn't changed, thank God. He hoped the young woman, who came from a good family, a civil servant's daughter, in fact, could stay with Vivian for her confinement so that she could hide her predicament from her social set.

'It would be an act of kindness that would be very well remunerated. I only ask because I believe you to be so full of good heart. I know you could help this young woman.'

'And afterwards?'

'The baby will be adopted and two lives will have been saved. You'll be paid well for having her here. Think of it as giving a woman and a baby a new start in life. I know you are not made of stone, Vivian. I know your days might be lonely without Frank and that you regret never having had children. I know your sister has lost contact with you. Speaking as your doctor, I feel this kind of work would suit you. This poor girl will be in need of motherly care. You could be so much help to her.'

'And I could adopt the baby? I could bring it up?'

Bernard shook his head. He let go of her hand and finished the slice of cake, dusting away the crumbs on his trouser leg with a napkin. Of course Vivian couldn't adopt it. A woman on her own bringing up a child? No, no. He fully expected Vivian would remarry, given a little time to let the passing of Frank settle. Then she could adopt a small tribe if she wanted. A married woman without children was of course a great tragedy. As was the shame of an unmarried woman who had borne children. Personally he liked a house full of merry little infants. He gave Vivian's hand a squeeze, and she took it as a sign of encouragement. Was he suggesting they might marry? Surely that was what he meant?

'I would be delighted to see you as a mother,' said Bernard Harding. 'And already you can be a mother to this poor girl from a good family who needs your help.'

When he left, Vivian thought things through. If she married Bernard, she could have children. That was surely what he was offering in his indirect, muddled way. She would help the girl. Of course she would. Her heart went out to her. Vivian had been a mother herself. Nobody could take that away from her. If Joe ever came back, and she knew it was a fantasy she should not entertain, then she would tell him how she had helped this girl and he would think her not just the mother of his child but a mother to others too.

Ten

The pub was a two-storey building beside soot-blackened railway arches. Its glass-panelled front doors were engraved with swirling white letters amid flowers and intertwining vines: *Superior Porter Stout and Ales. Old Irish Whiskey.* The place was dusty-looking; its brown windows needed a good wash. Only the brass door handles had been made bright by the many hands that took hold of them every day. Inside was a world of dark wood, sawdust on the floor, brass and gleaming mirrors behind the bar. Nellie turned around, looking at the sepia photographs on the walls. Boxing rings and whiskered men in leotards, crowds gathered around them.

'That's George twenty-five years ago,' said Henry. 'He was a middleweight boxer in his youth.'

'In my youth, indeed!' George bustled into the bar, his arms stretched wide in welcome. 'Plenty of life still in me!'

He grasped Nellie's hand in his, and she gripped his hand right back. He had brown eyes that had a sparkle to them, raised-looking knuckles on his square hands, a scar above one eye and a cauliflower ear gone purple years ago.

'She's got a grip!' he yelled, pretending Nellie had hurt his hand. He wore a signet ring on his little finger. He showed it to Nellie. A slab of silver and gold with a B engraved upon it. 'Bertha,' he said, waving his little finger at her. 'Our dear mother, God rest her. Got to look after family, haven't you? I'm heartily glad to see you both.' He patted Henry on the back. 'Who'd have thought an army man like you would marry? Let's get you a drink, both of you. I'll show you where you're going to be living. It's not much, Nellie, Henry will tell you, but I call it home.'

There was a kitchen at the back of the pub. That's where they would eat their meals. It smelled of mice, Nellie thought. Up a flight of dark wooden stairs, thirteen in all, were three bedrooms and a bathroom with a bath on claw feet that wasn't plumbed in. 'There is a box room too,' George said, opening a door to reveal a narrow staircase and a soft blade of light coming from a window above.

In the kitchen a long table was covered in newspapers and pots and pans. The cooking range was thick with grease. 'The cleaning lady doesn't like cleaning,' said George apologetically. 'Our sister, Lydia – oh, I told her you were coming, Henry, so beware of visits from her – says I should sack the woman.'

Henry laughed. He told Nellie his dreadful, overbearing sister might just be right for once in her life.

The big square sink under a dirty-paned window faced a yard out back. In the backyard was an elder tree. A tree of luck. In the country, every house had one in the garden. Its branches were black as coal, its leaves grimy and limp. It was as soot-covered as the railway arches outside. Nellie thought she might like to wash its leaves clean so she could see its greenery.

'I'm busiest on Fridays and Saturdays,' George said. 'I lost a lot of our customers to the King's shilling, but they're coming back now, poor beggars. I've got their wives as customers too. The war brought them out on their own, and I say it's all to the good. Women should be allowed to get out once in a while, hey? And don't they love a sing-song. I play a bit of piano and do some of the old songs. Weekdays when it's quiet, I offer a pinch of snuff and a look at the *Sporting Life* with every drink. That's for the gents. But you'll see. You'll get used to the work. And having our very own Mrs Farr behind the bar will bring a touch of class. Oh yes, you'll be very good for business, Nellie. I do hope you'll like it here, both of you.'

There was a loud rumbling sound and the dresser against the wall began to shake. Henry grabbed the edge of the table with both hands. Nellie moved towards him as he threw his arms over his head, dropping to the floor.

'That's a train going past,' said George, pretending to hold a wall up with his hand. 'You'll get used to it.'

The noise died away and the china on the dresser ceased its rattling. Nellie breathed in and then out slowly, as if testing the air. Henry was rocking quietly beside her. Sunlight broke through the clouds outside, and light filled the windows. A look passed between Nellie and George as they helped Henry into a chair. She could see George hadn't expected his brother to be in such poor shape.

'My dear brother, it seems you've got yourself an angel here,' George said, his brown eyes bright with conviction.

Her first night in London, Nellie hardly slept. She lay in her new bedroom, staring at the window. In the bedroom next door, her husband's brother lay in bed. She could hear him snoring. In the room across the hall, Henry was stretched out. She hoped his sleep was dreamless. She heard a group of men and women walking loudly under her window, their voices rising in laughter. They sounded carefree. That's how she would be from now on. No more back-breaking farm work to wear her down. She had moved to the city.

She rose early the next morning, as was her habit, and at dawn in the backyard watched the city make itself solid, coming out of the darkness, its skyline firm against the spreading grey light. Henry limped outside and sat on a stack of beer barrels, his walking stick across his knees. Sunlight fell across dirty cobblestones. Dandelions flowered hopefully in dark corners. It wasn't quite the Garden of Eden, Henry said, picking one of the small flowers and handing it to Nellie. But it was going to be home for them from now on.

Nellie put the flower in her hair. Vivian would have laughed to see her. 'Wet-the-beds' they used to call the ragged yellow weeds.

She was glad to be far away from her sister. She loved her but the weight of the past pulled at that love, making it awkward and complicated. The river burial still haunted Nellie, and she wanted to forget. Every time she saw Vivian it brought back thoughts of the baby. Joe Ferier's baby. A creature born out of a betrayal; a secret to be hidden. Rose had brought Vivian and Nellie up as spinsters, not as potential wives and mothers. No wonder poor Josephine had died. They did not have the right maternal instincts, she suspected, either of them. She picked a dandelion, shook the soot from its petals and put it in Henry's lapel. She bent again and picked one for George.

Right off, Nellie loved the pub. The first few weeks serving drinks the customers laughed at her country accent and made her feel shy and stupid, but George told her to ignore them. His clientele were all a rum lot of foreigners and cockneys anyway. Her country accent was just one more to add to the mix. 'You be yourself, Nellie,' he said as he closed up for the night. He bolted the door and lifted his fists, dancing across the room towards her. 'And if anybody gives you trouble, give me the nod and I'll sort them out for you.'

George poured them both a drink. A tot of rum for him; a glass of milk stout for her. 'A respectable lady's drink,' he said. 'Yes, you just be yourself,' he said again, and she smiled at him, feeling a blush come to her cheeks. *A lady*. That's just how he made her feel. He held her gaze for a moment before she looked away. The gas lights had been dimmed, and in the flickering golden light the mirrors behind the bar sparkled. She watched George shake a bucket of sawdust out on the floor. Its smell reminded Nellie of the pine trees back home. She breathed in the scent.

'We wandered in the shadow of the pines, my love and I,' sang George, and they both began laughing as he threw the sawdust up in the air and tap-danced through the falling dust.

*

Henry insisted George take Nellie sightseeing. Just because his nerves meant he couldn't go riding on buses and trams didn't mean she had to stay home. George took her to music halls and theatres, fairgrounds and boxing matches. Big department stores, with mirrors everywhere and shining marble floors, delighted her. She thought of her childhood and her youth spent in the cottage, the quietness of her life. All that time, there had existed this city, utterly unknown to her.

On George's urgings she bought a pot of face powder, a lipstick and a white ostrich-feather scarf that she draped around her shoulders. And still, wearing all her new clothes, she walked, as Henry said fondly one night, like a farm worker coming over rough ground, hoping to get home before dusk.

George took Nellie to cafés and market-stall vendors. She tasted foods she had never tried before. Jellied eels, hot salt beef, Dutch herrings and penny bagels, faggots and mash, doughnuts and cream cakes. Bright orange salmon eggs.

'Our little country peasant,' said George fondly. 'I like a woman who eats well. Let's go and have an Italian ice cream. I bet you've never tried pistachio before.'

In bed at night, Nellie closed her eyes, a hand on her full belly, indigestion and wind making her draw her knees up. She dreamed vividly. There were people everywhere, swarming shapes of crowds, fast and fluid as grain pouring from a torn sack. She and Henry and George were pushing their way through city streets, the three of them linking arms. Then they were in the pub kitchen and she was preparing a mutton stew, explaining how her sister Rose had taught her to cook. Vivian appeared with a child in her arms and said it was Nellie's. Henry said it couldn't be. George laughed at the thought of it, his hand stroking Nellie's cheek, offering her salmon eggs on a small silver spoon. The others disappeared and there were just her and George. He fed her and stroked her hair. He poured the eggs into her mouth on the tip of a spoon and they popped on her tongue, silky, watery, and full of the memories of wide rivers. When she woke before dawn, she opened her eyes and lay in a sleepy state, trying to recapture her dreams.

By Christmas they had become a tight little unit. No need for words a lot of the time. In the empty hours when the pub was closed up, Nellie cooked meals, conjuring up good things from scraps and leftovers. Henry poured gin. George tinkered on the piano and sang old music-hall numbers.

When Henry was ill and his melancholic moods kept him in bed, hallucinating and ranting, Nellie and George cared for him together. They were resolute that no doctors should be called. There would be no hospitals or mental wards for Henry. That, Nellie had promised him long ago.

'George is a good man,' Henry said when he went down with bronchitis again, his lungs forever weakened by the wartime gas. 'He'll look after you, Nell. I can't. George's got a soft spot for you. Fallen for your country charms, like I did. If I die I don't mind because I'll have ended my days here with you.'

'Get along with you,' she scolded. 'You should be on the stage.'

'I am serious. You must marry George when I'm gone.'

'Now that is ridiculous!' she said, pulling his bedcovers straight. 'What melodramatic nonsense you come out with, Henry Farr.'

More and more, Henry had become self-pitying, and she wasn't sure how to treat him so she was brisk with him, hoping that was right. She wiped his brow and bent to kiss his cheek. There were tears at the corners of his tight-closed eyes.

On Sundays when the pub was closed, George and Nellie went to the cinema. Afterwards they acted out the films for Henry. Charlie Chaplin's film *The Immigrant* had them all in stitches.

'You're the best tramp I've ever seen,' said Henry from his chair by the fireplace. He was in good spirits again. Robust in his humour. Quick-witted, as she liked him to be. He adjusted the blanket over his knee. 'George, show me the penny trick again.'

George put some music on the gramophone. A new American tune he loved, 'Shine on, Harvest Moon'. He grabbed a bowler hat from the hat stand and explained he was the little tramp in the story, finding a penny, giving it away, getting it back again. He shook his trouser leg and opened his eyes wide, dropping a coin on the tiled floor. He picked the coin up and dropped it again and lost it to Nellie, who was playing both the waiter and the girl in the film. She laughed too much and forgot which character she was.

'And does he get the girl?' Henry asked.

'Of *course* he gets the girl,' said George. He swung his arms around Nellie and spun her towards Henry. 'It's a hard job getting to kiss the leading lady,' he laughed, letting go of her.

'That's my job,' said Henry. Nellie leaned over him and pressed her lips to his forehead. The music rolled over them and when the record ended they played it again, none of them wanting the moment to end. 'Shine on,' George sang in a deep, bass voice, taking Nellie in his arms and dancing her around the room. The three of them sang lustily together. 'Shine on, harvest moon, for me and my gal.'

One night in the spring, Nellie woke with a start. She got up, tiptoeing downstairs in her nightdress, her long hair in plaits. It was pleasant to go out into the backyard and stand barefoot on the cobbles, watching the city sky. She liked the smog and the pale yellow bowl of light that hung over the buildings. It made her feel she was part of something vast and constantly changing. Fog licked around her ankles, and her flannel nightie clung to her body. Noise moved differently in the night. A girl's high-pitched laughter might come from the house next door or from far over the dirty Thames river. The creak and groan of machinery could be near or miles away. How her life had changed. She could hardly remember the woman she had been when she first arrived in London, a silent creature, shocked by the dense stirrings of a city. She still remembered nights by the river, so empty and silent the papery flutter of a bat's wing had made her flinch; the click of her boots on a country lane when she walked in moonlight, the loneliest sound she knew.

Candlelight flickered in the kitchen window. The kitchen door opened. In the rim of a beer barrel, the reflection of a gold signet ring caught her eye, the flash of it like a winking star.

'Can't sleep?'

'I hope I didn't wake you.'

'I heard you pass by my door. We're a nice little family, you, me and Henry. But, well, I confess I don't know what to do. You've got me thinking things I oughtn't be thinking, Nellie. I'm an honest man and Henry is too. Me and him have had a talk.'

'You've talked about me?'

'Nellie, I won't lie to you. I've had my share of romances. I'm not going to pretend I haven't. But I've come a cropper with you. So, yes, me and my brother have had a chat.'

'And?'

'Henry wants you to be happy. He knows he can't give you what a wife should have. I think you might be fond of me too. We can find a way to make this work, the three of us. If you're willing.'

Nellie swayed beside him. She held her breath.

'Darling girl,' he said as a train rattled past. 'It'll be all right. Me and Henry, we'll look after you.'

Nellie was twenty-nine years old. Ever since Joe kissed her seven years ago, when he destroyed her trusting nature, she had refused to think about how it might feel to lie in a man's arms. From the lewd chit-chat of women in the pub she had an idea of what sex might be about, though those women who winked and giggled and laughed like crows made it sound as rowdy as a village tug-of-war or a wrestling match carried out in the dark. Sex was something men wanted and women tried to wriggle out of.

And yet Vivian had not made it sound like that. She'd said she had been undone by her own desires. That she had been controlled by them. Nellie thought she understood that now. Her body ached for George.

And wasn't it true that a tree could stand straight for years even as the soil under its roots might be ebbing away? When it fell, and who knew what would start that chain of events off, it fell heavily, suddenly, all its tons of weight and years of growth keeling over in a heartbeat.

George stroked the back of her hand with his fingertip. Nellie moved closer. In this new city, in this new peacetime, anything seemed possible.

It was a very small baby that arrived in May 1921, a month earlier than the doctor had said it would. The child had tufted red hair and a wrinkled, ancient look to her. She cried, a hiccuping sound, damp as a rain-filled gutter. She had a mouth that puckered and pouted, caught between a smile and a fluid tearfulness. Such a tiny scrap of a thing, and reliant on Nellie to care for her. 'Don't cry,' Nellie whispered. 'Please don't cry.' The baby's arms and legs were skinny as wishbones. Nellie feared they might snap in her trembling hands. 'I'm a bit clumsy,' she told the baby. 'I'm no good with fragile things.'

They called her Bertha after Henry and George's mother, but the baby was so small, a fledgling creature, that George nicknamed her Birdie and it stuck.

'She's a dear thing,' said George, peering at her in her Moses basket. 'If you were the only girl in the world,' he sang. Nellie heard Henry moving about in his room upstairs. 'Sshh,' she said, pressing a finger to George's lips. It didn't seem right to flaunt their joy over the child.

'Am I your legal husband?' Henry had asked Nellie when she first broke the news to him. George stood leaning against the sink in the kitchen. Henry sat at the table. Nellie stood by the door, wringing her hands, chastened and tearful. She was already five months pregnant and could not hide it any longer.

'Yes, you are.'

'So if I am your husband, this child will be mine whether I like it or not?'

'Well, yes, but . . .'

'I encouraged this,' he said, and his face was hard and sombre. 'I let it happen. It's all right, Nellie. People will just think there's still a bit of fire in the old wreck of a husband you have. When it's born you'll have to get a nurse for the kid, that's all I ask. Stop crying now. I can't bear to see it. Come on, chin up. I'll stand by you, Nellie.'

Nellie could not look at him for the shame of it. Her face burned, and she wrung her hands together.

'Thank you, Henry.'

'Don't thank me. I don't give a whore's gin ration what you and George get up to, but people have to know the child is mine. Nobody must ever think otherwise. For the child's sake as much as for my own. We'll have it fostered out when the time comes.'

'Understood,' said George, crossing the room and reaching for the rum bottle. 'I'll pick up the tab for that one. Leave it to me.'

'You're a good man, Henry,' said Nellie. 'I'll carry the truth of this to the grave. I promise.'

Henry raised no further objections. When the baby was born he reminded them of the need to find a foster home, and when Birdie was two months old George saw to it that a Mrs White took the child.

For a year, Birdie lived three streets away. Mrs White had been born in Glasgow, and though she'd lived in London most of her life, her accent was full of her hometown. She had half a dozen children in her care. She was an elderly nurse, thin-faced and humourless. The tendons in her wrists stood out, her hands were blue-veined and over-scrubbed, the nails cut so short the skin around them was red and sore-looking. Nellie wasn't sure she wanted to hand her daughter over to her.

'Now then,' Mrs White said, 'certain things about bairns. Condensed milk is best. Cow's milk must be sweetened with sugar. Never breastfeed. A wee tot raised on the diddy will have a common, weak character in later life.

'Never pick up your baby unless it is to feed or to change its nappies. Teach them there are rules. Avoid hugging. If you must, a kiss on the top of the head will suffice. Do not ruin children with gifts and sentimental nonsense.'

Mrs White waved Nellie away when she tried to talk about her daughter's likes and dislikes.

'She is a baby, Mrs Farr,' the woman said, 'and thus quite incapable of having likes and dislikes.'

At home, without the presence of Birdie constantly reminding them of their private arrangements, Nellie was relieved to find she and Henry and George slipped back into the easy way they had had before. They worked, ate, sat together, drank together, all their words slipping into the unanchored time between day and night when it didn't seem to matter whose baby Birdie was, just that it was a surprising thing to have a daughter between them.

Nellie visited Birdie on Sundays and brought her home one weekend a month. One Sunday morning she turned up and found the babies in Mrs White's nursery all bawling and screaming in their cots. Nellie picked up Birdie and the child cried even more. She clung to Nellie's neck, smelling viciously of dirty nappies.

Mrs White was in her study, eating a plate of rollmop herrings.

'The babies are crying.'

'And I am eating! Your daughter is a naughty little minx who is playing on your heartstrings, Mrs Farr. This is my dinner time and these children know it.'

'But why is she crying?'

'Babies cry. They do it for attention. Oh, the Lord save me from weak-willed mothers. I have rules. You need to stick to them.'

Nellie looked at Birdie, who suddenly stopped crying, seized her around the neck and kissed her cheek. 'Mumma!' Birdie gurgled, and began sucking Nellie's chin.

'What about your sister?' asked Henry when Nellie arrived home with Birdie in her arms, saying she had removed her from Mrs White's care.

'Could she not live with us, Henry? I'm sure she won't cry any more.'

'I cannot have a baby in the house, Nellie. Vivian's got a big house. Didn't you say your sister always wanted kids? A life in the country would be much better for the child's health. There's my sister Lydia of course, but she's got two boys and she's a sulky creature. I wouldn't want our daughter to go to her.'

Nellie looked at him and felt a flush of pleasure. *Our daughter*, he had said. He cared about the child after all. And who was she to argue with him? He had accepted Birdie as his own. It was up to him to decide the child's future.

She wrote to Vivian, explaining that Henry was too sick to have a small child in the house. Birdie had a neat row of top teeth now, and she was affectionate and sweet. Would Vivian consider bringing up her niece? She must make sure not to spoil her and to keep to a strict routine.

Vivian wrote back immediately. She would have the child. Of course she would. They were sisters, after all. This was her niece. Nothing and no one could take that away from them. *I will love Birdie as I love you*, Vivian wrote in her sentimental way, *with all my heart.*

When Vivian walked into the pub to collect the child, carrying a bouquet of chrysanthemums and a pair of baby shoes as gifts, Nellie realized she had missed her sister. Their lives, so far apart for so long, swung back together again.

PART TWO

Eleven

Putting a photograph of her eighteen-year-old daughter in an envelope, Nellie Farr remembered a time many years ago when Birdie had been four. She had come home from Vivian's six months earlier and still acted like she did not know Nellie at all.

'She has forgotten who I am,' Nellie had said over breakfast when Birdie sat eating her porridge in silence. George, trying to find something positive in the stand-off between mother and child, said Birdie was a bright kid to know how to upset her mother so well.

'Will I be going home soon?' asked Birdie, rattling her spoon in her bowl, kicking her legs against the chair rung.

'This is home,' Nellie said.

Birdie shook her head.

'I want my real home.' She frowned, as if she thought Nellie was having problems understanding her. She was a small, elfin child. Her voice sounded uncannily like Vivian's.

'I want Auntie Vivian,' she said. 'Please. Please may I have Auntie Vivian?' She threw her spoon across the room.

How could a four-year-old child with a pursed mouth and a way of folding her arms make Nellie, a grown-up, feel this wounded? Nellie picked up the spoon and put it in the sink. A giant and a flea. She was the giantess, lumbering, unhappy, and here was Birdie, this little red-haired flea jumping around, biting her black and blue.

George had said it would pass. Henry said the child had spirit. He liked her contrary nature.

'Two years she spent with your sister,' he said as they watched Birdie playing with a skipping rope in the backyard. 'She's bound to take a bit of time to settle in here. Mothers and daughters are always at each other's throats. I remember Lydia was furious with our mother when we were growing up. I could never understand it. Mother was such a mild woman, God rest her soul. So quiet I used to forget she was there. In fact,' he said, warming to his memories, 'I only noticed her when she wasn't there, if you see what I mean. Like one only notices a clock in a room when its ticking winds down and stops.'

Nellie tried being mild. She bore Birdie's tempers and furies as if they were light breezes and she a steady sailing ship. When the mildness infuriated both of them, Nellie tried spoiling the child. She bought her roller skates and took her to the circus, she fed her doughnuts and bagels and gave her sherbet sweets to suck.

One afternoon a few months later, a sticky, airless day in September, Nellie took her swimming at the lido. The sun was hidden behind clouds, but the heat of the day was leaden. Birdie had red cheeks. Her head was as hot as a boiler plate.

'This will cool us both down,' Nellie told her daughter. She still hadn't got used to having the child around all the time; was still surprised that this sulky-faced creature was her child. That it had come out of her.

'I don't want to swim. It's too hot.'

'That's why we need to swim. To cool down.'

Nellie felt her patience leaving her. She picked up Birdie, which was easy as she was still a tiny creature.

'Come on,' she said, and descended the steps into the water, Birdie under one arm, struggling like a cat in a sack to get free. She let go and Birdie swam away from her.

She got to the other side of the pool, far away from Nellie, and then screamed and cried, whirling her arms like washing-machine paddles. People stared. A swimmer tried to help the child, but she screamed even more.

Nellie swam over to her and slapped her.

'That's enough!'

She put her arms around Birdie and carried her out of the water, ignoring the pity and scorn in the eyes of the skinny-hipped girls that lounged on the grass in bathing costumes, smoothing their short bobbed hairstyles.

'I don't like swimming,' Birdie said in between sobs. 'I want to go home.'

It seemed such a simple request that, finally, Nellie thought it was time to give in.

'All right. But it's a very long train journey. It will take us he rest of the day to get there. I will have to send a telegram to Vivian.'

'I want to play the piano.'

'In the pub? That home?'

Nellie sat on the grassy banks of the lido with the child wrapped in a towel. She had been holding her tight in it, the way you might hold down a large wild bird, pinning its muscled wings with the cloth.

She loosened the towel, feeling her daughter's limbs relax too.

Big drops of rain began to fall. Though it could not possibly have had anything to do with a woman in a black swimsuit and rubber bathing cap, Nellie felt as if the weather was sympathetic to her and her miserable child. She tipped her face to the sky, feeling a cool breeze pick up.

'We'd better go home then,' she said.

It seemed incredible that all that had happened nearly fourteen years ago. That Birdie had forgotten her time spent with her aunt and had also, it seemed to Nellie, forgotten those difficult days.

Nellie put the photograph in an envelope. A recent one of Birdie standing outside the pub. She wrote very carefully on the back in pencil. *Bertha 'Birdie' Farr. 1939, aged eighteen years.*

For many years, since Nellie took Birdie back, she had sent Vivian photographs and school reports. It was, she always felt, the least she could do.

Vivian's latest letter to Nellie lay on the bar top. Nellie had read it with interest. A farmer called Charles Bell had been coming into Vivian's tea room for some time now. She had discovered he had built a farmhouse on the site of their old cottage.

Five years ago, in 1934, the Langhams' farm had been divided up and sold off as parcels of land, and Charles Bell had bought 100 acres at auction. More precisely, and Vivian was always precise in her letters, he had paid two pounds an acre for some scrubby land and water meadows that had been left fallow for years. With the land came their old ruined cottage, which had given the farm its name. Poplar Farm. He was a pleasant man who knew little of the region. He had come from Exeter because farming land was cheaper to buy in East Anglia.

He was only briefly interested to find I had lived in the cottage. Our lives are just ancient history to others, she wrote.

Her letter went on for several pages. She had fallen in love with cats and bought herself two blue Persians she intended to breed from. She talked of the charity work she did with her doctor friend, helping young women who had got themselves into trouble. A whole page was devoted to whether or not she would marry Dr Harding if he proposed to her. She was sure he was going to ask any day soon. She was forty-nine years old now. She had been waiting for the man to make up his mind for nearly twenty years. Was she being terribly foolish? Nellie thought that if the doctor had wanted to marry her, he would have asked her years ago. Vivian's desire for him was unfathomable, except that her sister might like the idea of being a small-town doctor's wife. That she would be taking another step up in her social world.

Vivian's letter had come with a package. Several pink cotton handkerchiefs with a silk-embroidered B, for Birdie, and wrapped within them the hagstone. Vivian believed Nellie should keep it now. She thought it was the stone that had led this Mr Bell to her, reacquainting her with their old home. She was still afraid that her baby's grave might be discovered one day, perhaps if there was a drought and the river dried up. Or equally a flood might leave the remains of that tiny life on the riverbank for somebody to discover. Vivian could not bear the idea of this. She believed the stone should be with the sister furthest away from the Little River.

Nellie held it in her hand, cool and brown as a fish's belly with a cream colour swirling through the round hole in its side. Between them the stone had taken on a deep importance. They had given it a place in their lives by keeping it. The stone was the only link they had to each other, apart from her daughter. She would keep it safe. That didn't seem too difficult a thing to do.

Over the years she had thought to take Birdie back to see Vivian. She'd imagined her spending summers with her aunt, but always there was the worry that it might upset them all. Birdie had forgotten entirely the time she had spent with Vivian. It was best to keep it like that. Too complicated to explain the giving away and taking back of a child.

You know how it is, Nellie wrote, and hoped Vivian could understand how it was to see a child grow into a young woman.

> *Time goes by and you don't see anything changing. Children seem as though they will stay children for ever. That they will always need their hair setting in ringlets and will forever wear pinafore dresses. And then suddenly here I am sending you pictures of Birdie and she's eighteen years old. A young woman who will no doubt soon enough meet a man, marry and have her own family. I want no spinster life for my daughter, Vivian. I want her to be happy. I know too well that years and years have gone by, but still, it seems like yesterday she was just a child. Just like yesterday too, Vivian, when I last saw you and yet that was many years ago now. One day soon, we must find the time to see each other again. And I will keep the hagstone safe, you can be sure of that.*

Twelve

Birdie lit a cigarette and threw the match down on the cobblestones. She sat on a beer barrel in the backyard under the soot-covered elder tree, its white blossoms flecked with dirt. Ancient hopscotch chalk marks she had made as a child, playing for endless hours out here on her own, were still visible at her feet. A train rattled past above her, and she wondered if any of the passengers were looking down onto her backyard. What might they see? A young woman with red-blonde hair waiting for a lover? Oh, the thrill of that idea. She longed to be in love. Perhaps the passengers saw her as a woman already married. A housewife taking a moment for herself. Or perhaps they saw her as she was. Just a skinny, eighteen-year-old barmaid avoiding a family gathering inside.

She stubbed out the cigarette on the brick wall and picked up a pebble, lobbing it onto the hopscotch grid. She hopped and skipped over the squares. Her wedge-heeled sandals threatened to turn her ankle over if she carried on. There wasn't time for old childhood games anyway. Her cousins and Aunt Lydia were here, and she should go and say hello.

'Birdie, there you are,' said Uncle George when she stepped into the kitchen at the back of the pub. He looked relieved to see her. Aunt Lydia and her cousins Roger and Malcolm were sitting at the long wooden table, drinking tea with her mother.

'Hello, dear,' said her aunt. Birdie tried to look pleased to see her. None of them was very fond of Aunt Lydia, but there was an unspoken belief that she had been treated shoddily by life and they forgave her time and again, her clumsy comments and judgemental ways. She wore a dark blue velvet dress with a high lace collar and a string of pearls. Aunt Lydia liked to say she was a psychic, compelled to seek out truths. She studied horoscopes and palmistry. Birdie's mother said the woman knew nothing but a load of hokum gathered from the silly journals she subscribed to.

'So now,' her aunt said. 'Have you seen my boys? Don't they look handsome?'

Birdie's cousins nodded hello. It had been a year since she had seen Roger and Malcolm. They were a couple of years older than she was and, growing up, she had always found their visits once a year in the summer months a kind of torture. Much as she had longed for brothers and sisters, Malcolm was dull and Roger was spiteful. She still remembered him stamping on her woodlouse farm, a project she and her schoolfriend Joan had nurtured one summer, building small barns out of wooden lolly sticks and the discarded sardine cans they'd dug up from the loose soil under the elder tree.

Aunt Lydia began lamenting the times they lived in. She was going to lose her boys to war. She couldn't sleep at night for thinking about it. But men had to be men. They were going to serve their country, and wasn't that the downside of having boys? 'Men have the weight of the world on their shoulders,' she said. 'And only mothers of sons understand this. Our mother knew it, didn't she, George? Having sons is a way of building nations.'

'I don't know I built many nations,' said George. 'And what about Walter? Where's the man who's covering Great Britain in linoleum?'

'He is away working,' said Lydia, and Birdie noticed how her aunt coloured slightly. 'He's in the north of England at a trade fair this week.'

'What a surprise,' said Roger sarcastically, playing with a square metal lighter in his hand. 'Our absent father is still absent.'

Aunt Lydia's husband, Walter, was always away. Birdie had only met him once, at her father's funeral. George had said one time that Walter probably had another family somewhere. Birdie's pa used to joke that Lydia had buried Walter under the floorboards years ago.

Birdie felt a stab of loss, thinking about her father. The funeral had been over a year ago, but she still woke most days with a horrible start, remembering all over again that Pa was gone.

Aunt Lydia finished her cup of tea and asked if she might have another. Birdie could see her mother losing patience. She didn't like people getting under her feet. She was chatty and friendly in the pub, but it was an act really. Her mother was a solitary, private kind of woman. She knew everybody around here, but she didn't have close friends. She'd never needed them with Pa and Uncle George around. She'd never really needed a daughter either, it seemed to her.

Birdie looked out at the backyard. That was where her childhood had been spent, out there among the beer barrels, an only child playing hopscotch on her own, or turning skipping ropes with Joan while her mother, in her own eccentric way, washed the leaves of the elder tree so that they shone green and bright.

Uncle George put some cash in Birdie's hand.

'Take your cousins out and show them around,' he said. 'Poor beggars are going off to training camp soon. Give 'em a tour of the city. Get them out from under your mother's feet, heh?'

Birdie took the brothers greyhound racing at Walthamstow. She won on the tote, backing a handsome black dog whose name, Bed of Roses, appealed to her. Roger won too and bought them fish and chips, which they ate sitting on a bench, celebrating their winnings with a bottle of R. White's lemonade.

Later that afternoon they saw a Gracie Fields film in the local fleapit, a story of a rags-to-riches factory girl. Roger talked through it, leaning against Birdie, whispering into her ear, making jokes and acting the fool. Birdie tried to concentrate on the film. Roger rested his hand on her knee, his fingers squeezing. She slapped his hand away and he looked pleased with himself.

'Little wild cat,' he said, grinning. 'I like a girl who acts hard to get.'

It was only the thought of dancing that made her agree to go out with her cousins on their last night before they left for training camps. Roger was plain awful. He'd tried to kiss her after the cinema, coming outside with his arm clamped around her waist as if they were courting. When she told him to lay off her, he'd laughed and set off up the street with his hands in his pockets, whistling. He was quite maddening.

Birdie invited her best friend, Joan, to come along. Then, at the last minute, Roger said a friend of his was coming too. A chap called Peter he had met at the army recruiting centre a few days earlier.

That rather threw the numbers. Now there was no time to find another girl to accompany this Peter chap. It was just so typical of Roger to ruin everything.

Birdie set her hair in waves with her curling iron. She put on a green satin dress she'd made herself and matching shoes, and hoped the evening would be a success. She spent a long time over her make-up. Face powder. Red lipstick. A black mascara. Her mother didn't like her wearing too much make-up, but her complaints were half-hearted. All the girls wore make-up these days. Birdie adored powders and creams and cheek blusher. They made her feel nice and pretty, and with everybody made miserable by all the talk of war, she felt it her duty to make an effort. Uncle George always said a pretty girl cheered everybody's spirits. He often took her side against her mother, though he made her swear not to say a word.

Joan came upstairs and sat on the bed. She picked a bit of lint off her black checked trousers. Birdie wished Joan would not wear trousers. Trousers were eccentric. Joan's long mousy hair was in two plaits wound tightly around her head. She took off her glasses and cleaned them on her sleeve.

'So which one is for me then?'

'You can have all three,' said Birdie, pouting into her compact mirror, drawing a Cupid's bow with a red lipstick. 'Well, you can have both my cousins anyway. Especially Roger. He's touched in the head, if you want my opinion. I'm waiting to see what Peter looks like.'

Neither of them had ever had a boyfriend, but they liked to talk like the girls they knew, the ones who were full of chat and cheeky with men.

'Let's get our hearts broken at least a dozen times tonight,' said Birdie grandly as they went downstairs arm in arm.

Joan danced them down the last couple of steps.

'And we don't come home until we can say we're ruined by music, men and too many gin and its.'

Peter, it turned out, was quite nice to look at. He had curly brown hair and a neatly trimmed moustache. His eyes were a dark brown. They had a sparkle to them. Birdie always liked to look at a person's eyes. She believed you could tell a lot about someone from their eyes. He was slim and tall, and she thought he was the sort who probably played a bit of football and liked cycling out into the country at the weekends.

The dance hall was near the cinema. The five of them paid for their tickets, put their coats in the cloakrooms and went through double doors into a big hall, which was warm and noisy. The band was loud, and already there were dancers and a lovely thick movement of people. Birdie slipped through the crowds and found a space up at the bar.

'What a dump,' said Roger.

'I like it here. I come every Saturday if I can. They have the best bands this side of the river. I want to audition to sing for one of them some day. Uncle George says I could be a professional.'

'No end to your talents, is there?' said Roger, sneering at her.

'What sort of thing do you sing?' asked Peter.

Birdie blushed. She hadn't actually sung with a band yet.

'Well, I'm quite jazz minded,' she said in what she hoped was a knowledgeable voice, leaning towards him so he could hear her. 'And I like the crooners. I read the *Melody Maker* every week. There's always auditions in the back pages. I've been to a few now and I haven't had any luck yet, but I know it'll happen soon. I can play piano too.'

'Good for you. I wish you the best of luck. I'm sure they'll want a good-looking girl like you.'

The music got too loud to talk without shouting, and they stood side by side, watching an auburn-haired woman in a white satin dress that clung to her hips singing 'The Lambeth Walk'. Birdie wondered if Peter might ask her to dance. She crossed her fingers behind her back and made a small wish that he would. The music grew louder. More dancers took to the floor. She saw the chap from the electricity shop dancing with a girl. The other week he'd asked Birdie to dance and said she had the nicest eyes he'd ever seen. She'd acted haughty with him, showing she wasn't impressed, but still, he had drawn her in with the comment and she hoped he'd ask her again tonight.

'I'm off to powder my nose,' she said, and crossed the dance floor. She walked past the man and gave him a smile, but he didn't notice her.

'Having fun?' a woman asked Birdie as she touched up her lipstick in the ladies' toilets. It was the singer. Birdie could see she'd had a few drinks. Working behind a bar, she recognized drunks easily. The woman must be in her thirties, a long way past her prime, yet she was still beautiful. Her auburn hair was waved and held off her face by a diamanté hair slide, curled in the style of the day. Her clinging satin dress was sleeveless, and her slender shoulders were pale and powdered. Birdie's mother would have said she was the wrong sort.

'You were wonderful tonight,' she said to the singer. 'I thought you were outstanding, really.'

'Did you? Well, thanks, kiddo.'

'I want to be a singer like you one day.'

'Is that right? My name's Kay. Kay Kelly. Let me guess. You're a telephonist out with the girls, or a typist maybe?'

'I'm a barmaid. I sing in the pub on Friday nights.'

'Well, you follow your dreams while you can, love. You'll meet a nice boring man one day and have to settle down and forget all about singing then. It's what most of us want, isn't it? A bit of security and a nice home. A couple of kiddies. But meet some wrong 'uns before all that. Bad men are more my kind of style. Got to have a bit of fun, heh? You won't be innocent for long, dear. Men can't stop themselves.'

'A girl can always say no,' Birdie said, backing away.

'Oh, she can,' agreed Kay. 'But why should she? That's the question. Why the bloomin' hell should she? Us girls have got to have a bit of fun, heh?'

Birdie watched her sashay out of the room. 'My name is Kay,' she said to the mirror. 'You gotta have a bit of fun.' Her face stared back at her. Her grey eyes, her mouth with the slightly too full upper lip. She swung open the powder-room door, feeling the heat and the noise of the dance hall wash over her. Kay was right. A girl should enjoy herself. The chap from the electricity shop was dancing with a different woman now. A peroxide blonde who looked like a film star. Greta Garbo. They moved together with a slow, secretive kind of focus, swaying back and forth. Birdie watched them until she couldn't bear the sight of them.

'Dance with me,' Peter said when she got back to the bar.

She wasn't sure she'd heard him right, but he took her hand and pulled her through the dancers. Birdie curved her arm around his neck, the way she imagined Kay Kelly might dance with a man.

Peter was a sportsman, he told her, his lips touching her ear. He didn't fancy going into the navy much, but he'd failed to get in with the collar-and-tie set in the RAF. He played cricket and tennis, and last year he'd hiked in Europe.

'You're a great little dancer,' he said, pulling her close.

In the shifting bodies, Birdie caught sight of Joan dancing with Malcolm and was glad. Often she and Joan ended up dancing together. Up at the bar Roger, standing on his own, radiated bad humour. He really was the most hateful man she knew.

The next time she looked, Roger was picking a fight. She saw him and then he was gone from view as Peter swung her round. Then there he was again, throwing a punch. She and Peter stopped dancing. The evening was over.

They found Roger outside in a side street, throwing up into the gutter.

'For God's sake,' said Malcolm. He had his arm around Joan's waist. 'For God's sake, Roger, you bloody fool.'

Roger looked down at the gutter.

'Fuck it. I've ruined my shoes.'

Peter laughed loudly. 'What's going on, Roger?'

'That's the problem. Nothing is going on.' Roger grabbed Birdie's arm. 'Why didn't you dance with me? Do you think you are too good for a bloke like me? Is that it? A bloody barmaid acting like Lady Muck. You make me sick.'

Malcolm pulled him away.

'You're a rotten drunk, Roger. Leave her alone.'

'She's a tease. A cheap little flirt.'

Roger lunged at Birdie, trying to kiss her. She kicked his shin and tore away from him as Malcolm grabbed his brother's collar. Malcolm turned to Birdie, apologizing. 'He's mad about you. Don't listen to him. He can't hold his drink. He's had a thing for you for years. He's jealous.'

'Birdie,' said Peter. 'Are you all right? Can I take you home?'

'Take her home? Yeah, she'll let you take her home. Like mother, like daughter.'

'What's that supposed to mean?' asked Birdie.

'Your mother lived with two men, and which one was your father, heh? Some folk have no shame.'

Malcolm groaned. 'Roger, that's enough. Why don't you shut up?'

Birdie felt tears pricking her eyes, her heart thumping.

'Ask your mother whose brat you are. You know what they say, three's company, two's a bore, isn't it?'

Malcolm grabbed Roger by the arm and began dragging him down the street.

'Get off me. She's nothing. Little slut. A tease, that's what you are.' Roger looked back over his shoulder, his voice slurring. 'You ask your mother who your father is. Go on and ask her.'

Birdie, Joan and Peter made a dejected group, walking home. They left Joan at her door, and Birdie decided to cut through the park as a short cut to the pub. There was no point in prolonging the horror of the evening. She just wanted to get home.

Peter took her hand and she felt the warmth of his fingers.

'Roger's a fool, you know. That stuff about your mother? Absolute rot, I'm sure. He's a spiteful drunk. I've seen his type before. He has a way of knowing how to get to people, that's all. It's a nasty low trick. I'd ignore everything Roger said. And anybody else who comes up with muck like that. Tell them to mind their own business.'

Birdie felt a wave of gratitude towards him. Of course Roger was a liar. A filthy liar. The way he'd gone staggering off, a one-man street brawl, his fists punching the air, had frightened her. She'd be happy if she never saw him again.

'Are you really all right?' asked Peter.

'I'll live.'

'You're beautiful, you know.'

Peter kissed the curve of her neck. An act of such tenderness, it made her feel again the hurt and the wrongness of Roger's cruel outburst. She thought of Kay, the auburn-haired singer, the way her silk dress clung to her curves, the slink of her hips as she walked. Birdie was close to tears, but crying wouldn't do any good. Peter would think she was just a silly child. And she wasn't. Not tonight.

'I'm leaving tomorrow,' whispered Peter. He took off his big wool trench coat and put it around her shoulders, pulling her to him. He kissed her nose and pressed his forehead against hers. 'I'll write to you if you let me?'

'Course you can. If you want to.'

'I think I might be falling in love with you,' he said, and kissed her.

When he suggested they sit together by the bandstand, she let him take her hand and lead her there. She barely knew him, but he had told her he loved her. Well, wasn't that what love was like? Sudden. All those songs that talked of love at first sight. Surely there was some truth in them or they wouldn't be so popular? And she wanted to be loved. To be soothed after Roger's ugly words.

'You're shivering, Birdie,' he said as they lay together. 'Let me warm you.'

The hour was late when she got home. Her clothes were damp and cold from the night air. She crept in through the kitchen and up the wooden back stairs to her bedroom. She realized she didn't know Peter's other name. Was he thinking of her? She pulled her blankets closer. She would never see him again. Birdie turned over to sleep, hoping things would be all right. That there would be nothing to regret, nothing to bind them both to this night for ever.

The summer of 1939 turned out to be the hottest in years. Throughout June, Birdie sang in the bar on Friday evenings, the windows open on to the night, sweat running down her back, her fingers slipping on the piano keys. Normally she loved the babble of gin drinkers in the public bar, their faces leaned towards her, but by the first Friday of July she had other things on her mind. The pub was busier than ever. She was tired all the time at the moment. They had the lot in that night: the dirty fascists, their black shirts always clean as a whistle. Her mother said George should ban them, but George said as long as they didn't cause trouble he'd serve them. That night Birdie sang for them all, the Reds, the cockneys, the Italians and the French, the gangs of Irish dockers; all the lovely lilting voices around her, gobbledegook and inky-pinky parlez-vous. She sang old songs, numbers from the last war jolly with nostalgia: 'Sister Susie's Sewing Shirts for Soldiers', 'Pack Up Your Troubles', 'Mademoiselle from Armentières'. Uncle George handed her a glass of ginger wine, but she couldn't face it. Normally it was her favourite tipple.

'You out of sorts?' asked George.

'Bit tired, that's all. I didn't sleep well last night. There was a cat fight right outside my window that went on all night. I'll be fine.'

The wafting smoke of Woodbines made her eyes smart. The smell of slopped beer and the scent of sawdust, as familiar over the years as the smell of her own skin, brought on nausea. Sweat prickled her forehead. Men raised their glasses to her, and women winked and told her to remember them when she was famous. She looked at the clock.

'You go off now,' said her mother. 'And come straight home after.'

'Thanks, Ma. Wish me luck.'

'There goes our girl!' said George over the noise of the bar. 'Going to be the next Gracie Fields, she is!'

In a dingy basement rehearsal room a group of musicians played, surrounded by stacked chairs and tables. Birdie sang with them. This was her chance. A chance to be a singer and not just a barmaid.

The music was wonderful, springing into life, filling the room.

Piano, drums, a double bass, trumpet and guitar. Birdie sang 'These Foolish Things' and then 'Blue Lullaby'. Afterwards the band played together. They were taken up by the music, their faces sweating, grimacing as though it was an ugly thing they were doing.

She sat and waited. Had they forgotten she was there? The trumpet player came over just as she was nodding off to sleep. He wiped his sweaty face with a towel. Yes, they'd hire her, once they replaced the bass player, who had enlisted in the navy. Did she want to go to a club with them now? Hear some black musicians? No? Well, she should learn a few new songs for next time.

She walked back slowly, letting herself in through the backyard door. The pub was quiet, the lights all off. She slipped into the bar and sat in the dark over the piano, playing chords and humming tunes. She was going to be a singer. Uncle George had wanted her to get a job in a typing pool. He reckoned that was good work for a young woman until she married. But Birdie wanted more. She wanted to be like the auburn-haired Kay Kelly. There was a pleasant calm in the shut-up pub. A dusty silence where slow cigarette smoke still wafted. A peacefulness. As if everything that needed to be said had been said, and all the punters had finally been able to go home to sleep, glad to have got another day over with. A whole new day waiting patiently for them while they slept.

The following week Birdie knew she was in trouble. She hadn't had an ounce of shut-eye for days, thinking of what hot water she had landed herself in. She was so tired, she thought she might fall asleep standing upright at the bar. She'd dropped two pint glasses that evening, and Ma had already told her to look sharp.

She leaned against the cash register, feeling its cool metal on her hot skin. Her mother swung past, swathed in widow's black, towards a customer who was leaning over the bar, waving money at her. A row of hawk-faced men stared across the bar at them. Birdie tried to smile.

'Ma?'

'Please, Birdie, I'm busy. Can you tell George he needs to change a beer barrel?'

Uncle George was at the piano, leading a sing-song. He grinned, his flattened boxer's nose shiny with sweat.

'There's my darling girl! Come on and sing us a song, Birdie!'

She shook her head and hoicked a thumb towards the bar, mimed lifting a barrel and went outside. In the backyard the air was heavy with coke fumes and soot, the smell of coffee from the flophouse across the street. She stepped past an old tin bath and a tangled heap of broken chairs. Beer barrels were piled in a corner, and she sat down on one.

She didn't want to marry Peter, and she was sure he wouldn't want to marry her. In any case, she'd have to ask Roger where he was, and she was never going to speak to him again. She didn't even know Peter's surname. Even if she did want to find him, she doubted she'd be able to.

'You all right, Birdie?'

She turned to see her mother wedging a beer barrel onto a sack barrow.

Birdie stood up and made her way across the yard. The ground seemed to shift a little. She put a hand out and her mother caught hold of her.

'Ma, I really need to talk to you.'

Birdie looked into her mother's grey eyes and thought she saw fear in them. She leaned heavily against her mother, something she had not done since she was a small child. She had been a needy child, she remembered, always shadowing her mother around the pub until she drove her mad. They'd played Grandmother's Footsteps at school. A child would turn her back and the others creep up on her as quickly as possible. Birdie had always won that game. She played it at home in earnest too, sidling up close to her mother, who complained she was like a little dog getting under her feet.

Birdie felt hot, terribly hot. Her ears were blocked, her knees weak. Her mother's face loomed and went.

'I'm sorry, Ma,' she said. 'I'm so sorry. I think I'm expecting—'

'Expecting what?'

'A baby.'

Birdie tried to grab hold of her mother before she fainted. She opened her eyes to find herself in her mother's lap, on the cobblestones.

'Who is he?'

Birdie shut her eyes again. There was no point in saying.

Nellie watched her daughter walk away into the pub. She stood outside, breathing slowly. She had never imagined having a child herself, and now that child was going to be a mother. She'd cared for Birdie the best she could, but obviously had done a useless job of it. She supposed she was like Rose. Not properly maternal. Unlike Vivian, who would have been a good mother but had never been lucky.

Nellie remembered Birdie's birth well. The speed of her labour. How she had looked down and there, between her trembling thighs, seen the baby, slick as a winkle pulled from its shell. There she had lain, neither a truth nor a lie. Nellie's baby. And again that confusing, vulnerable love had squeezed her heart.

'Nellie, are you out there?'

George was standing in the doorway, illuminated by the yellow gas lamp.

'Just coming in,' she said, and hoped that by morning she would have an idea of what to do about Birdie. She certainly wasn't going to tell George yet.

Thirteen

Vivian came to the pub because what else could she do? When she got the telegram from Nellie, she had caught the train the same morning, determined to help her sister and niece. And how long had it been since she stood here in this forlorn little street by the railway bridge, looking up at a set of pub doors, summoning the courage to go inside? Over fifteen years, she thought. Yes, it must be.

Nellie had aged a bit but so had she, and yet Vivian felt like they had never been apart. Nellie was just the same woman. Her hair was still long, though she wore it piled on her head now rather than in that tight plait she used to favour. And it was tinged with grey, of course. Didn't she look like Rose? In fact, it was startling, the resemblance.

Nellie didn't mention Birdie and ushered her inside, through the pub, into the back rooms. There she offered Vivian a seat on a hard leather couch, explaining that it was new. Bought on hire purchase from one of the modern showrooms that had opened up on the Essex Road. Nellie had seen it advertised in a magazine, and George had got it delivered.

Though she said nothing, Vivian thought the couch she was slipping about on was hideous. An awful modern thing.

'How are you?' she asked.

Nellie hugged herself.

'I'm all right. Or I was until now. You'll have to see what we're doing in the pub, Vivie. George has renamed the saloon bar "the refreshments bar". We're getting a lot of married couples coming in these days, and they want a bit of class. Some of them want cocktails, would you believe? George says these new housing estates going up everywhere are bringing in a different kind of customer.'

Vivian knew Nellie was talking too much. Her sister was near to tears. She couldn't fool her for a minute.

'Where is she, Nellie?' she asked.

'Gone shopping up west with George for the day. I'm so glad you came.'

'Of course I came. What's to be done though?'

'Birdie's a good girl. I don't want you to think she isn't.'

'Have you spoken to the boy involved? She'll have to marry him.'

'She says she met him at a dance and doesn't know his name.'

'Oh,' said Vivian, and lit a cigarette. 'I see.'

Nellie got up and began to pace. 'Shall we go out? I'm afraid George will come home and find us here. Whatever happens, he mustn't know. It would hurt him so badly.'

'But if she keeps it?'

'If she keeps it, then we'll tell him when we need to tell him.'

Nellie took Vivian to walk along the embankment and see the sights across the river. Vivian suggested Birdie stay with her. They could say she was working in her tea room and nobody would be any the wiser. Vivian could help Birdie bring the child up if she chose to keep it. Her house was big, and she still felt a great deal of affection for the girl. There was no shame in Vivian caring for relatives. But for Birdie it would be harder. Her life would be ruined.

'That's what scares me,' said Nellie. She told Vivian how in the pub just the other day she had heard a girl being described as used goods. Nobody wanted that kind of insult levelled at them. 'Used goods. It made me want to swing for the chap. What a thing to say. I think it's my fault. I've not been a good mother.'

They sat on a bench in silence. Vivian still remembered the time Birdie had lived with her. If she had stayed, if the girl had grown up in her care, perhaps this would not have happened.

When was it now? My goodness, right back in 1922. She'd come to take the child home with her. She had felt rather heroic, turning up at the public house. Henry had suggested he give her some money for the child's keep. That had been typical of him, she felt. Turning a family matter into a businesslike arrangement. She didn't want a penny from him, she'd told him.

Vivian had taken the little girl home. The walk back from the train station was a strong memory. She had finally got what she wanted so badly. A child to care for. Birdie in her pram sat up smiling at passers-by. How marvellous it had been. Up Riverside she'd gone, over the bridge where below the ducks paddled in the clear waters of the river. People said hello. Men lifted their hats to her. Several women made little clucking noises and waggled their fingers at Birdie.

'A girl, is it? Niece, you say? You've got your hands full there,' they said. 'She looks like trouble. Oh, what a cheeky face!'

Vivian had never had so many strangers talk to her before. The way other women looked at her as she walked through the town centre – it was as if she had joined a secret club of motherhood. As she neared the guest house, images of the Virgin Mary and her child had circled in her mind. She'd been a vast flowing river of warm motherly love that day. The child in the pram could have floated for ever on the golden currents of her well-being. She had smiled all the way home, thinking of gold-leaf statues of Mary and pink-painted plaster-of-Paris babies. A nursery with a rocking horse. Ribbons and bows.

'Here we are, my little darling,' she had said as she bounced the pram up the cobbled street to the guest house. 'We're home.'

For two years she had cared for Birdie, and it hadn't been easy, though she would never tell Nellie that. She would let her sister think Birdie had been well behaved, because she suspected Nellie had found it difficult to raise the child afterwards. She had been glad to think she struggled with Birdie. It hurt when Nellie took her back. She had wanted Nellie to understand that.

Birdie had been a wild little child when she arrived at the guest house, and she left pretty much the same. She only ever ran. It was as if she did not understand walking. She darted around and was never still except when she slept, which was not very often. Most of the day she threw herself about with a frenzied energy. Vivian was fond of these memories now. What a pleasure to look back upon the daily struggle with a buttonhook to get Birdie's leggings in place over her black boots while she fidgeted and wriggled. The child had refused to have her copper hair brushed out. Vivian remembered it had taken on a fuzzy look, as if Birdie had a sweep of autumn leaves dancing on her head. She had three words which she liked to shout as she careered around the guest house. *No! Cat! Enough!*

When Nellie sent a telegram saying she was coming to get her daughter back, Vivian cut Birdie's hair. She was frightened Nellie would see it tangled up and think she hadn't cared for her properly. She and the child had both cried to see those skeins of copper-coloured hair all over the floor.

'You shouldn't have cut her hair,' Nellie said when she saw her daughter. 'You should have asked me first.'

That had been the beginning of the argument. Vivian said the child's hair had been knotted and in a dreadful state, and it had been the only solution. In any case, the fashion for little girl's hair had been to keep it short. Nellie was terribly old-fashioned, always insisting on Birdie having ringlets like they'd had as children.

She had presented Nellie with a brooch. Inside it was a lock of Birdie's curls. That had silenced her sister.

Nellie sent a telegram a few weeks after she took Birdie back. Birdie was crying for Vivian. What should she do? After a brief moment of triumph – *Yes, the child wants me!* – Vivian had consulted Dr Harding and he said Vivian must not see the child until she had completely forgotten living with her. Otherwise there was a risk of personality disorder in a child split in her love for two mothers.

So that's what they did. They stopped seeing each other. Over the years Nellie, who was not much of a letter writer, sent photographs of Birdie and then, when she went to school, her school reports. A milk tooth was put in a gold clasp and sent on a necklace, and a small drawing of a black cat done by Birdie was sent in a brown wooden frame.

Vivian looked across the wide River Thames where barges passed by on the lead-coloured water. Down on the mudbanks below them a group of boys was throwing sticks for a dog to retrieve in the water. The dog splashed in and out obligingly, brown as a river rat and not much bigger.

Nellie cleared her throat.

'I'm sorry I hurt you when I took Birdie back. I know it's a long time ago now, but I still think about it. I didn't mean to upset you.'

'I wasn't upset in the least,' said Vivian, laughing as if the idea was ridiculous. 'Not at all. I was glad Henry said his daughter could come home.'

The brown dog the boys were playing with belted along the narrow shoreline and up a set of concrete steps onto the Embankment.

'Perhaps it's best if she gives the baby up for adoption,' said Nellie. 'I cannot think of what else she could do. How can she keep it? People would be cruel. I will not have anyone looking down on Birdie.'

Vivian watched the dog disappear along the path, its tail wagging as it rounded the corner and was gone.

'The child too. It would be an unlucky creature before it even took its first breath. We must think of the child.'

'There's a foundling hospital near the pub. They call it something else these days. An institution of some sort. I see girls taking their babies in there, and each time it makes my heart go cold. People look at those girls like they're bad all the way through. I've seen a group of women spit at a young girl coming out of that place. I don't want anyone ever treating Birdie like that.'

Nobody must hurt Birdie, agreed Vivian. The child could be adopted. Birdie would be able to make a good marriage afterwards.

'I could talk to Dr Harding and see if he can help.'

The sisters linked arms, and for the first time in too long the years fell away. They both loved Birdie. They hugged and cried and were twins again, the sisters who lived by the river and who spoke another language nobody else could understand. They thought the same thoughts, their eyes filled with the same salty tears. *There's no choice for Birdie*, their hearts said. *No choice but to give up the child.*

Fourteen

Vivian didn't like the heat. Sometimes, at moments like this, when she had just had to deal with the second infestation of ants in the kitchen in a week, she thought she'd like to move to one of those Nordic countries where it snowed a lot. It was the first week in August and the heat was unbearable. She took a handkerchief and wiped a small trickle of perspiration from her brow. She adjusted her hairnet and put on her new straw hat bought for the occasion. She pulled on her gloves and explained to Matilda once again how she must put down salt around the doorway to stop the ants.

She stepped outside and, yes, there was the taxi coming up the cobbled road.

On the back seat, Vivian took off her hat and cradled it in her hands. It was a hat for a much younger woman. White Italian straw with red silk fuchsias around the brim. The more she thought about it, the more convinced she was that the shop assistant had made a fool of her. Would Mrs Williams think badly of her if she turned up hatless? It had been expensive too. She would give it to Matilda, she decided. And yet the hat was rather modern for Matilda. Perhaps Birdie might like it.

Mrs Williams was going to adopt Birdie's baby. Vivian had sent Nellie a telegram to say Bernard Harding had found a couple to adopt the child when it was born. Right now, Birdie would be getting a train. Everything had been arranged as quickly as possible. In just two weeks, she reflected, so much had been achieved. Her back ached and her ankles were swollen by the heat, but she sat up straight, ignoring the desire to kick off her shoes and stretch her toes, content to endure her suffering, bolstered by the certainty of her mission.

Mrs Williams lived in a big house which sat in a slight valley. As the taxi rounded the higher country lanes, dipping down to a long gravel driveway, Vivian sat back in her seat and admired the property. It was a splendid-looking house. The lawns were mown and wide. There was a red-brick walled garden with honeysuckle and Russian vine scrambling over it. Inside the walled garden there would be espaliered fruit trees and lines of soft fruit. Raspberry canes and gooseberries. A beloved child could pick all that it wanted, choosing only the best, the softest.

Mrs Williams was a plain-looking woman. Vivian judged her to be in her late twenties. She wore a green day dress made of a soft cotton. Her brown hair was tied back loosely in a velvet bow. Vivian followed her into the hallway, the sound of their heels clicking on the polished floor. The parquet shone, though the woman immediately apologized for the scratches on it. The house had been rather badly damaged during the Great War, she explained. It had been requisitioned as a hospital. If you cared to look, there were men's names scratched into the wooden panels and etched on windows. People always wanted to leave a trace of themselves everywhere they went, she supposed.

A wide sweeping staircase led the eye upwards, and Vivian knew she was being allowed a moment to take in the size of the entrance hall; that Mrs Williams, when she apologized for the state of her home, was also drawing Vivian's attention to the grandeur of it all.

'Come on through to the drawing room, Mrs Stewart. Would you like tea? I'm afraid it's just us today. My husband is at work and Mrs . . . well, the woman who comes in from the village is not here today. Go on through and I'll be with you in a moment.'

The living room was a delight, a cool, elegant room with a white marble fireplace and a large gold-framed mirror hanging over it. Two sofas faced each other across the room, upholstered in a floral glazed cotton. A vase of flowers glowed in the hazy light, a generous display of blue and pink delphiniums and lupins. Some letters were under the white china vase. Vivian glanced at them. On a slip of blue-lined paper, poking out from an opened envelope, she read the name 'Dorothy'.

Mrs Williams brought a tray of tea in and lit a cigarette.

'So now,' she said, and gave a little shrug of her shoulders. 'When do you think . . . that is, the baby, when do you think we might . . .'

Vivian cleared her throat.

'We estimate February or late January, though one can never be sure of these things. I cannot say exactly. Before then, I suggest you stay indoors as much as possible. Make sure you tell your friends that you are resting because the doctor insists on it. Perhaps you could go away for a while? Somewhere where nobody knows you?'

'I will do that. You're so very kind. And I must tell you I am not *Mrs* Williams. That is my maiden name. My husband thought I shouldn't give you my married name.'

'Well, it doesn't matter,' said Vivian. 'All this is confidential, after all. What matters is that you have my name. Mrs Vivian Stewart, as I said earlier. Here . . .' She produced a white card. 'This is my address should you ever need to find me.'

'Mrs Stewart, thank you. I'm so glad this is all going to be handled with discretion. Can I ask about the birth certificate? My husband wants to know what will happen with that. Nobody must ever know the child is adopted, you see. My husband will not take the child unless that is the case. He's worried about the parents. They might be, I'm sorry to be so blunt, but they might be worthless sorts. You do hear of people being blackmailed over this kind of thing. At least my husband tells me he does. As a lawyer he tends to see the grim side of life.'

'A lot of new parents are worried about this kind of thing, my dear,' said Vivian. 'Dr Harding will look after all the details. He will make sure the birth mother does not feature on any adoption papers. The mother will sign a paper for the court, but she won't see your name on the paper. The court keeps an original copy of the birth certificate, and you get one which names you both as the parents. After that the baby is yours.'

'Just like that?'

Vivian nodded.

'More or less.'

'It's sudden, you see. My husband and I, we've been trying for so long and now it's really happening I wish I could meet her, the mother. I wish I could tell her how grateful I am.'

Vivian was exhausted by the hope this woman poured upon her. She reached for her cup of tea and took a sip. Her hand shook and she could feel a headache coming on. 'I happen to know the mother is a most lovely young woman,' she said. 'I'm sure she's grateful to you too.'

On the way home, Vivian thought of the large framed oil paintings hanging on the walls. Men in uniform, and women standing with children or sleek dogs at their feet. Mrs Williams had said she hated the paintings. That they were too serious. She wanted to hang something more colourful on the walls – landscapes, or perhaps some modern abstract paintings. But she had inherited the portraits with the house and she didn't feel she had the right to take them down.

The portraits stayed with Vivian. The richness of the colours. The way the people had posed, straight-backed. Full of ownership and entitlement. She could not stop thinking of a relative of hers joining them. She thought of her own baby. The memory of her was always there, close to the surface. Josephine would have been twenty-five years old now. She'd have likely been married with children of her own. But what kind of life would she have had as the daughter of an unmarried woman? Vivian hoped Birdie, when the time came, would understand what a wonderful chance in life she was giving her baby. It would be different for Birdie. She would know her baby was loved and cared for. Vivian would have given her own darling baby up for adoption without a second thought if somebody could have offered her that.

Track-side advertisement hoardings lined the route out of London. Gibbs Dentifrice, Bournville Cocoa, Bovril, and Greys cigarettes. The names huge and beckoning in bright colours. There were suburban back gardens, rows of identical brick houses and then fields and farms and woodland and silvery stretches of water and villages.

Birdie pressed her face against the window. She could not remember having been out of London before, and she wished she could get off the train and go straight back home. She'd not even had time to speak to Joan before she left. Heat hazed over cornfields and meadows. Men working in the fields stopped to stare at the train passing. The jolt of the rails rocked her back and forth, back and forth. She felt nauseous and unhappy. She had not wanted to be packed off to an aunt. She wanted only to undo this whole mess. To go back to her own life, before all this. She was ashamed and guilty. Sent away from home, she might as well be dead.

When the train pulled in and she got down onto the platform, Birdie decided not to take the bus as her aunt had suggested. She would walk. She crossed a bridge and stopped to watch ducks swimming in the narrow river below. At home they would be getting the pub ready for opening time. Nellie would be cleaning glasses with a cloth in the silent, careful way she went about all her tasks. Birdie wished she was back there, wiping down the tables, chatting to Uncle George.

She walked up a hill towards a church, a tall building made of stone and flint with a spire that rose above the rooftops. It was a hot day, but there was a breeze and nothing of the stiff heat of London. The trees that lined the road were fresh and green. Church bells rang out. There were cars and motor buses, plenty of horse-drawn carts. As she walked, she calculated the months she would be staying. She'd be able to go back to London sometime in the spring. It was this thought that carried her on, towards the guest house and whatever it was that the future held there for her.

The Unicorn Guest House was down a narrow street away from the town centre. It was in the old part of the town, where the buildings were tall and striped with black painted timbers and white plaster pargeting. Some were three storeys high, and crooked-looking. All the houses seemed to lean out into the street, bent and rickety, like puff-chested old men. The front door stood slightly ajar. A glossy black door with a polished brass knocker. A sign next to it stated the guest house had comfortable rooms at moderate terms with modern electric light and garage parking. Under it, a large black cat sat sunning itself. Birdie bent down and stroked it, and it purred and rolled its body around her legs. It trotted up the steps, pushed the front door open and went inside. Birdie followed it into a hallway. The red patterned carpet under her feet was faded. Why did the place feel so familiar? She had surely never been here before.

There was a small reception desk in the alcove under the stairs. A green-fronded fern in a glazed green pot sat on the desk, along with a small brass bell. A carved wooden cuckoo clock on the wall loudly tick-tocked.

A young woman sat dozing in a chair. She had a black dress on with a white cotton apron over it, and her grey stockings were wrinkled around her ankles. Her blonde hair was parted on the side and scraped back into a bun. Birdie cleared her throat to attract her attention.

'Hello? I'm Mrs Stewart's niece.'

The woman yawned and rubbed her face, getting to her feet.

'So you're Birdie? Matilda Dunn. Nice to meet you. I'm cook and waitress here. My grandmother did the job before me. My dad, Stan, used to be the handyman here before he upped and left us. You could say we Dunns come with the property. Come on, I'll take you through.'

Birdie followed her along a corridor and down a small set of stairs. She opened the door on to a room cluttered with figurines. Shepherdesses and blue-coated boys and white china swans filled the mantelpiece. A large gramophone cabinet stood against a wall with its doors open, revealing a stack of shiny black records. And there was Aunt Vivian. She was slim and wore a grey linen dress, pleated at the front and belted in at the waist.

'Come in and sit down, dear,' said her aunt. 'Matilda, why don't you make tea and bring it in here.'

Vivian studied the girl as she sat drinking tea. She needed feeding up a bit. She was thin-cheeked, her pale grey eyes luminous and sad. She had a full mouth, carefully painted red. Far too much make-up. She looked a bit like a shop girl. Her complexion was dull. The inside of her dress collar was grubby.

City life, Vivian supposed. Never mind, there would be plenty of time to show her how to get her clothes properly clean and help her freshen her complexion and wear less make-up. She was a pretty girl with the Marsh family eyes.

'I hope you'll enjoy staying with me,' she said, and thought how inadequate that sounded.

Birdie's room was simple but homely-looking. The single brass bed was made up with clean white sheets. Beige wool blankets with pink satin bindings had been turned down ready for her. A churchy kind of tinted sunlight poured in through the coloured glass in the fanlights of the window. There was a wooden chair with a rush matting seat. A small chest of drawers and a print on the wall. A picture of a snowy mountain range, a vivid blue sky above its craggy summits. Sheep grazing in its valleys.

Birdie sat on the bed and swung her legs, the motion of the train still running through her. She lit a cigarette and kicked off her shoes. A fly buzzed in the room. Outside, the sound of bird-song came and went. This place was only hours from London, but it felt as distant as the moon.

Fifteen

George said he wanted to do it properly. He got down on one knee in the backyard, but something in his knee bone went off like a bullet crack. He winced loudly.

'You don't have to,' Nellie began to say.

'Yes I do,' he grumbled. 'Wait up a minute. I love you, Nellie Farr,' he said, opening the box and showing her the wedding band inside it. 'I would like to ask you to do me the honour of being my legal wife.'

She heard that word *legal*. She knew what he meant. She'd been his secret wife for years now.

'Legal? Ah now.'

'It's simple, Nellie. Just say yes. Henry's been gone a couple of years. He would want us to be happy.'

When he stood up, his trousers had green moss stains on them. His knees made more cracking sounds.

'Let's do it quietly,' said Nellie. 'Just you and me. No need to tell anybody.'

'We'll do it anyhow you want. Quietly suits me too. No need to shout about it, is there?'

'A Wednesday would be best.'

'A Wednesday?'

'Don't you know the rhyme?

Monday for wealth

Tuesday for health

Wednesday the best day of all

Thursday for losses

Friday for crosses

And Saturday no luck at all.'

George rubbed his chin. 'Do you really believe that?'

'Yes, I do.'

'Well, midweek it is then.'

So Nellie became Mrs Farr for the second time in her life. There was a little joke in front of the registrar between her and George about her already knowing how to sign her name, and that was it. She went from being Mrs Henry Farr to being Mrs George Farr.

Two marriages, Nellie said to herself that night when she and George sat at the kitchen table. She had never imagined being married twice. It seemed to her she had been lucky in love. That Joe Ferier, who had broken her heart when she had been young and tender-minded, had set her life on a path that led her to this room, to this lovely man, the father of her daughter.

'Here's to Birdie,' said George. 'I hope she won't be too upset she missed the wedding. I suppose your sister might be a bit put out we didn't say anything. I know Lydia will be spitting feathers when she finds out. She can't stand being left out of things. Maybe we should have a honeymoon? Go down and stay with your sister and see Birdie?'

Nellie said she'd rather stay at home. She knew George must not see Birdie until she had the baby adopted and could start life again.

'To our daughter,' said George, and it shocked Nellie to hear him say it openly.

'To your sister, Vivian, and to my brother, Henry, who brought you to London and changed my life for good,' he continued, lifting his beer glass. 'God bless the lot of them. And us too. To you and me, girl.'

'Oh, George, you are daft,' said Nellie, blushing. But it was true that Henry had changed her life. There had been grace in the relationship between the three of them. Nellie had followed her heart, but she had also learned that the only way they could live as they had done was by keeping secrets. George and Henry had understood that. They had gone through the years happily by agreeing not to discuss what went on between them. Keeping certain things private was what life was largely about, it seemed to her. Being seen to play by the rules was what mattered. That was why Birdie had to go away. After the adoption she could have a chance of finding a man she loved, and nobody would ever know.

As long as George didn't know, he would think of Birdie as he always had, as a good girl, a girl to be proud of. There was some consolation to be found in keeping secrets if you thought about it like that.

When George went to bed, Nellie went outside, just like she had done twenty years earlier, back when she was still amazed by the city. She stood out in the yard and looked up at the night sky like she was searching for her own reflection. But no. She was nowhere to be found up there. She was here on earth, heavy as the soil, solid as rock and stone.

Aunt Vivian turned the volume up on the wireless. Chamberlain's voice sounded tired and low.

'This country is at war with Germany.'

Birdie didn't care. She had too many of her own worries. Her mother and Uncle George had got married. They had sent a letter, not to her but to her aunt, who had given it to her. It was in her pocket and she had read it many times now.

Dear Vivian

George has sold the lease on the pub, and although I know I am very late in telling you this, we got married last week. I hope you will understand that George and I have always been friends. In order to live under the same roof, as we have always done in a most respectable way, we decided we should get married. Can you explain this to Birdie for me? I hope you and Birdie will forgive me for having not mentioned this earlier. George and I so wanted you to be at the ceremony, but how could you both come? It is so important that Birdie stay hidden away until this is all over. Tell her I am sending her a parcel soon with a wedding photo and some chocolate to feed her sweet tooth.

The lease on the pub has ended and George wants to live by the sea where he and Henry grew up as boys. Please understand I am sad to be moving further away from you, Vivian, but George has worked so hard in his life, I feel he deserves to 'finally return home', as he puts it. We have found a bungalow in Hastings and will be moving there in January. My sister-in-law, Lydia, lives in the same town. She is the one who found the bungalow and showed the details to George. It is nice and modern as it was built only ten years ago and is five minutes' walk from the sea. The house is called 'Mon Repos', which is French, so George says. There is a line of shops nearby. The promenade was all rebuilt ten years ago, and there is a new outdoor bathing pool complete with diving boards (though George says I am too old to be thinking of diving boards).

There was a terrible storm over London last night and a lot of people thought it was an air raid. In the pub they were all talking about it. There are kids from round here being evacuated to the country. Tiny tots sent off to God knows where. I've told some of their mothers that, for heaven's sake, get them some proper wool socks to take with them. They'll freeze without them. Please tell Birdie I hope her health is improving and that we miss her very much. Thank you again, Vivie, for taking care of our girl.

George sends his regards.

Your loving sister, Nellie

Now her home was gone and her mother and uncle had got married. How could they do this without telling her? She was being punished again and again. And how could her mother live near Aunt Lydia? She hated her. And then another thought struck her. What if her mother told Aunt Lydia? Birdie could never look that awful woman in the face if that was the case.

There was a knock at the front door.

'That's probably Hitler,' said Matilda weakly, beginning to laugh and cry at the same time. 'Come to see about a room.'

She came back into the room with a man in corduroy trousers and a collarless shirt. He held a rough tweed cap in his hands.

'Charles, how nice to see you,' said Vivian, and Birdie noticed how she patted her hair and became girlish in his presence. Her aunt was nothing like Birdie's mother, who treated everybody in the same slightly stiff, frank way, whether they were women, children, stray dogs or handsome men. Her aunt was flirty around men. Even the bad-tempered old coal man was treated to her gay laughter.

'This is my niece, Miss Birdie Farr. Birdie, this is Mr Charles Bell. He farms in the same village your mother and I used to live in. His house is, in fact, built over our old cottage.'

'Hello,' said the man. 'I'm just checking you are all right. I wanted to know if you need help with anything . . .'

'Well, that is very good of you, Charles. So nice to have a gentleman around the place. Come and have a drink with us. I think we all need something for our nerves right now.'

'Thank you,' said the man. He smiled. 'So you are Miss Farr? The piano player? I've seen your photos.'

'Have you?' Birdie blushed. 'What photos?'

'Don't worry,' said her aunt, as if she too was embarrassed. 'I have photographs your mother sent me. Mr Bell here must have seen one or two of them. You have a very good memory, Charles, I must say. So clever of you to remember.'

'I've seen lots of photos of you,' he said in an amiable way. 'I've been coming to your aunt's tea room for years now. She's very proud of you.'

A siren sounded in the street, loud and piercing. Matilda screamed and knocked her glass off the table.

'It's a siren,' said Aunt Vivian. 'For heaven's sake, Matilda, they said it would happen. Please do calm down.'

Birdie bent to pick up the broken glass.

'Mind your fingers,' Mr Bell said. He crouched beside her and took a wet shard of glass from her. 'I've got it. You let me do this.'

He had hazel-coloured eyes. Intelligent-looking.

Another siren sounded and Matilda screamed again.

'That's the all clear, I think,' said Mr Bell. 'You'll be all right now.'

'Why don't you and Matilda walk in the garden together,' Aunt Vivian said to Mr Bell, taking the broken glass and ushering them towards the door. 'Perhaps you might see where you think we should put a shelter?'

'Such a lovely man,' said Aunt Vivian when they had gone. 'But very shy. He's been on his own too long, I think. Farmers can be such solitary creatures. Don't say a word, but I have high hopes he will marry Matilda. She doesn't seem to mind his reticence.'

Birdie watched Mr Bell walking with Matilda in the garden. How odd a feeling it was that he knew her. That he had seen photographs of her over the years. She had come here as a stranger, and Mr Bell had recognized her as someone familiar.

Her aunt put the wireless back on. An announcement was being given. Do not go out of your homes unless absolutely necessary. Do not go anywhere without your gas mask. Birdie wasn't going anywhere in any case. She had to stay indoors like a prisoner and hide her condition. Dr Harding had made it clear she was lucky. A home for fallen women would be far harder than her aunt's gentle hospitality. That was the right word. *Fallen*. Birdie saw herself stumbling, sprawled on a pavement with bloody knees, and a crowd, led by her cousin Roger, laughing at her.

The national anthem played on the wireless, slow and laborious. In the garden, Charles Bell and Matilda picked early windfalls under the apple tree. Watching them, Birdie thought it looked as if nothing in the world had changed. She wished she could feel the same way.

In October the weather turned cold. The water in the jug by Birdie's bed had a thin layer of ice upon it when she woke. And yet she didn't feel the cold. She seemed to be generating heat all by herself. Mornings were bright with the palest blue skies, and Birdie longed to go out while the day lasted. She was not supposed to leave the house in case she was seen by somebody, but she was fed up. She went downstairs and slipped out into the garden where she walked up and down, breathing the fresh air.

As she came back in through the kitchen door, she felt a sudden low pain in her belly and a dampness between her legs. A small dark stain bloomed across her skirt. She was afraid. The baby. Oh, God, the baby. She held her belly, cradling her hands across it.

'Aunt Vivian!' Birdie cried out. 'Aunt Vivian!'

Dr Harding put her to bed and raised the end of her bed on bricks so that her feet were higher than her head. She was not to move for a few days and then they'd see how things were. If she had any more scares, the best place would be an unmarried mothers' home with a hospital ward.

'You are very fortunate,' Dr Harding said, as he examined her. 'As long as the child is born without defects, there is a decent and loving couple who will take it.'

'Twins would have to be separated,' he added.

Aunt Vivian came upstairs carrying a bulky-looking gramophone and two records in paper sleeves. She set them down on the dressing table and sat on the bed to get her breath back.

'I thought this might cheer you up. I know you like music. "The Merry Widow's Waltz",' she said. 'I've always loved this.'

Birdie watched her setting up the gramophone.

'I have a letter for you too,' said her aunt. 'You try and get some rest, dear.'

Birdie waited for her to close the door behind her and then pulled the letter out of its envelope. She recognized Joan's handwriting.

Dear Birdie

I forgive you for leaving in such a hurry but I've not had one measly letter from you. I had to ask your mother repeatedly for your address. She acted like I was asking for top-secret information. It was your uncle George who passed it on to me. He said you had a good job and wanted to be safe in the country. So, have you met anybody there? Some upper-class toff who wants to take you out shooting ducks or whatever it is they do for fun out in the sticks?

I haven't been dancing since you left. With the blackout in London, no girl is safe walking the streets after dark. There are no lights on the trains or buses. The cinemas are all closed. It's too dreadful.

Latest news: have decided to move out of home. Have found a ghastly bedsit that I adore. Am also driving ambulances as a volunteer. My mother thinks I will become one of these shameful modern women who live alone from choice. I haven't told her, but I already am that woman. Independence is mine!

I hope you're enjoying your work in the guest house. Write back and I'll forgive you for being incommunicado for so long.

TTFN (ta ta for now)

Joan

Birdie got out of bed carefully. She lifted the needle from the gramophone record, letting the room fall silent. She felt homesick. She put her hand on her belly. Took it off again. Her body was a mystery to her. It went on, without her consent, growing larger and heavier. Birdie found she knew herself a little less every day.

By December, Birdie felt huge. Her breasts ached and her skin stretched like a dress two sizes too small for her. She was restless, and late one night she got out of bed. She could not stay still any longer. She walked down the back stairs, treading lightly, trying not to wake anybody. She could feel the weight of the baby pressing down between her legs, and she walked with a stumbling, wide gait that made her feel helpless and clumsy.

In the kitchen she turned the lights on and carefully shut the door. She felt driven by a need to clean the already spotless kitchen. She scrubbed the table and swept the floor, glad to find dust in a corner behind the door. From the cupboard under the stairs she pulled out the carpet cleaner and attacked the front parlour rugs. After that she unlocked the back door in the kitchen. Nobody would see her in the dark, but even so, she was afraid when she stepped outside.

The wind was cold but it felt good on her skin. She breathed in deeply. She felt everything sharply, the wind, the shiver in the trees, the damp ground under her bare feet. She put her hand on her belly and realized she longed for this all to be over. To give up the child and be free to go back to London and try to be a singer. And if that didn't work she would join the Wrens. She would be part of this war. She was tired and lonely and afraid of giving birth.

Vivian, wearing dressing gown and slippers, was in the kitchen when Birdie went back inside. Her face was pinched with tiredness. Her hair under her hairnet was flattened to her skull, her eyes blinking like a newborn creature. Her voice, though, was brisk and sure.

'Your cousin Roger has been killed in action. I'm so sorry to give you such bad news. Nellie sent a telegram yesterday. I really am so sorry, my dear.'

Birdie sat down wearily.

'I'd say you're nesting,' her aunt said, putting the kettle on for tea. 'I've seen it before, Birdie. Perfectly normal. It won't be long now. That baby wants to be born.'

*

The baby was born in the chime hours, at four in the morning, on 29 December 1939, in Dr Harding's surgery. The doctor had come to the guest house just before 10 p.m., and Aunt Vivian had hurried Birdie out into the street. Dr Harding stood holding the car door open, urging them to make haste. The sky was black and there was a smell of snow in the air, yet Birdie felt so hot she wanted to throw off her clothes. 'You said there was a month to go,' she insisted as another pain shot through her, making her gasp. 'This can't be right, Auntie. I can't be having the baby yet.'

Birdie stopped on the pavement and began to cry, while Vivian begged her to be quiet so as not to alert the neighbours.

'Up you get,' said Dr Harding when Vivian brought Birdie into his rooms.

There was a hospital bed with rubber sheets laid across it. Birdie climbed onto the bed and lay down. A lamp shone over her.

'Let's have no silly crying,' Dr Harding said. He tied her wrists to the bed and told her to put her feet into two slings that hung either side of the bed on metal posts.

'Aunt Vivian?'

'I'm here,' said Vivian. 'I'm right here. Be brave. The doctor knows what he's doing. You're very lucky. He is going to give you something to stop the pain. You just relax, dear, and you won't remember a thing, I promise.'

Did her aunt sound scared? The doctor pressed a cloth to Birdie's face and she breathed in a sweet, cloying smell. 'What if I'm sick,' she tried to say as he lifted the cloth off her face, but the words wouldn't form properly. Birdie wanted to say the room was too warm, but the cloth was on her face again and a wave of sleep dragged her down, pressing on her body. Her mother appeared in her dreams, her hands reaching out to her.

'It's a girl,' said her aunt, and her voice sounded very far away.

Birdie opened her eyes. She was a girl? Who was a girl? She slept again.

'A girl,' said Aunt Vivian, stroking Birdie's cheek. 'A little girl, Birdie. You had a girl.'

So this was her baby? Of course. She remembered nothing of the birth, but yes, this little girl with feathery blonde hair and a creased frown on her face must be her baby. Aunt Vivian opened the curtains and the crystal light of sun on thick snow filled the room. Her aunt leaned over her, and Birdie felt the woman's wet cheek press against her. Why was her aunt crying? Her face was pale. As if she had been the one who had given birth.

'You should name her,' her aunt whispered. 'Give her a name.'

Birdie sat up, leaned over and lifted the child into her arms. She would call her Kay, after the singer. She had thought she would not look at the baby when it came. She hadn't even wanted to know whether it was a boy or a girl. As her pregnancy had gone on, she had been more and more sure she was doing the right thing, giving the child up. She had yearned to get back to her old life. But now everything changed. When she had imagined a baby, she hadn't realized it would be *this* baby. This baby she loved on sight.

Sixteen

Spring brought lilacs flowering. Iris and dogwood, hyacinth and cherry blossom, and a great list of flowers Vivian named for Birdie, walking with her in the guest-house gardens, trying to encourage her to take an interest in the details of the world about her. As the sun grew stronger and higher in the sky each day, the lilac blooms turned brown and roses bloomed, the lawn was thick with dandelions. Birdie preferred the dandelions: they reminded her of the pub's backyard. She had liked sitting by the outhouse as a child, cross-legged on the cobbles, gathering bunches of the raggedy yellow flowers for her father, who, if she was very quiet, would come and sit on a beer barrel, watching her, telling her about his life as a soldier.

Birdie had been relieved when her aunt said she could stay on with her. She didn't have the energy these days to think of going anywhere. All her plans for the future meant nothing to her now. Her aunt said she could take all the time she liked. She fussed over her, worrying if she did too much housework, suggesting she go off with Matilda to the cinema and enjoy herself.

She left the garden and wandered through the streets. She supposed she had been given a chance of a new life. That was what her mother had said when they spoke on the telephone recently. Her mother was not very good with modern appliances. She preferred telegrams. 'Are you all right, Birdie?' she shouted down the line. 'I said, are you all right? Do you need anything?'

Birdie supposed she needed her child. That was what the feeling that weighed down on her was. A sense she had made a terrible mistake.

'No, Ma, I'm fine here,' she said.

It was market day, and she stopped to watch a brown-eyed calf suckling from its mother. She heard the clattering of hooves behind her and turned to see a black and white horse galloping down the cobbled road. Its nostrils flared pink, its black mane flew out in the wind, sparks flying from its metal shoes as they struck the paved road. A boy was riding the horse, arms flying, legs banging against its sides, yelling at all to clear the road.

Birdie jumped out of its path. As she did so, her beret slipped off her head. She bent to retrieve it, and two hands grabbed her around the waist. She struggled as they lifted her up and swung her to one side, just as the horse charged past, a steaming, snorting creature, a smell of sweat rising off it. The crowds were yelling furious insults at the boy, pushing this way and that to escape the horse's path. Birdie tried to see who it was that held her so tightly. As her feet touched the ground, the hands let go.

'I hope I didn't scare you.'

It was Charles Bell, Matilda's farmer.

'Mr Bell?' said Birdie. 'No. Well, a little. How are you?'

Charles Bell said he was not given to grabbing young women. He corrected himself. He had not *grabbed* her. God, what was he saying. What a word! She must think him a chump. He was sorry. What he meant was he had been attempting to save her.

'Like a knight in shining armour?' she asked, putting her hat back on. 'Like Clark Gable?'

'Sort of,' he said, grinning.

When he asked her if she might like to walk with him – he was about to look over some Irish cattle with a mind to buy them for fattening over the summer – she said yes, why not, and fell into step with him. He was a quiet man, but when he talked about his farm and discussed the animals they looked at, he became chatty and confiding with her. It was late morning when they strolled up the cobbled road. Birdie realized she had just spent the last hour without thinking of her own sadnesses. She was aware of them both slowing their walk, dawdling, as if they wanted to put off the moment of parting. They reached the guest house sooner than Birdie wanted.

'Hello?' said Matilda when Birdie and Charles walked into the guest-house kitchen. Her eyes looked them over carefully. 'What are you two doing?'

'I was nearly knocked down by a horse. Mr Bell saved me.'

'I just moved her out of its path. I was coming here in any case,' said Charles mildly. 'I wanted to ask you, Matilda, if you'd like to visit my farm.'

'Come and see where you live, you mean?'

'Matilda would love to,' said Aunt Vivian. She looked pleased.

'You could come, Mrs Stewart,' said Charles. 'Come at harvest time.'

He smiled, and for a moment Birdie imagined that his smile lingered on her. She blushed. It was ridiculous to think that. There he was now, talking to Matilda as friendly as anything, accepting a cup of tea, discussing her visit to the farm. She had imagined he looked longer at her, that was all. Like she imagined she still felt her baby move inside her some nights when she lay very still in bed. She left the room, and when she looked back through the open door she saw that nobody had even noticed her go.

A group of soldiers were billeted in the guest house for the month of June. They were working on a new airfield the other side of the town, digging up a farmer's land and laying acres of concrete for the RAF. Matilda and Birdie were suddenly busy, serving breakfasts and cleaning rooms.

'This place hasn't had paying guests for years,' said Matilda. She had on a clean apron and her shoes were polished. Her face glowed with exertion. 'They're a great bunch of blokes, aren't they?'

'Thanks for breakfast,' said one of the soldiers. He was a ginger-haired man with pink sunburn across his freckled nose. He was the last to leave, pulling on his khaki jacket in a hurry, holding a slice of toast in his mouth. The other men were calling for him in the truck outside, waiting to leave for their day's labouring. He gave Matilda a wink and she giggled.

'That's Colin,' said Matilda, leaning against the door frame as the truck pulled away. 'He's had me in stitches with his daft jokes this morning. You should listen to some of them, Birdie. He'd cheer you up a bit.'

The men returned each evening around 6 p.m., covered in dust and dirt. There were eight of them, loud and cocky and full of chat-up lines. They had pin-ups of blonde Hollywood starlets and scantily dressed girls in their rooms and talked about vamps and good-time girls. Some of them came from London. City lads who made jokes about country bumpkins and left chewing gum stuck under the tables in the dining room. They traipsed around, filling the guest house with their presence, their rapid-fire filthy jokes and banter. Aunt Vivian's cats had slunk off to live in the garages at the end of the garden, hiding under her little Austin 7 car. Birdie understood their cautious ways. She had become wary too, silent and shadowy as the cats. She had not sung for ages. Not even to herself. Sitting in bed she tried the first few bars of a song, but it died in her throat.

The soldiers left the guest house and Aunt Vivian closed the tea room. She was going to spent her annual summer holiday with Dr Harding this year. A house party at his sister's seafront home in Cromer.

Matilda's invitation to see Charles Bell's farm had been extended to a suggestion she bring a tent and help out with the harvest for a few days.

Birdie and Matilda stood on the front step and watched Vivian climb into her car.

'Well, that's it,' said Matilda as the car bounced away down the street. 'You've got the place to yourself, Birdie. Look.' She pulled a postcard from her pocket. The soldier she had liked, the red-headed man called Colin, had been writing to her.

'He wants me to send him a photo of myself. In a bathing costume, the cheeky so-and-so.'

'And are you going to?'

'Of course I am. It's for his morale. A girl I know is writing to three different soldiers. She does it to cheer them up. It's patriotic. You should do it too. It's fun.'

'Maybe I will,' Birdie said. She thought of her postcard reaching the hands of Peter. She imagined him, a vague shadowy man in uniform, holding a picture of her in a bathing costume. Would he recognize her, or had he forgotten all about her by now? Their daughter would be seven months old. What did babies do at that age? Would she be crawling? She put her hand on her belly, a gesture she found herself doing whenever she thought of her daughter.

That afternoon Charles Bell telephoned. His truck had broken down and he asked Matilda to take her bicycle. She could catch the train and cycle out to the farm. Birdie heard Matilda discussing the change of plan.

'I'll ask her,' she said, and put her hand over the mouthpiece. 'Birdie, he says would you like to come with me? Please say yes. I shall get lost cycling by myself. Please?'

Birdie shrugged. She supposed it wouldn't do any harm to go to the farm for a couple of days. Better than drifting around here on her own, thinking too much.

'It's no good confusing the enemy if you get all the locals lost too,' complained Matilda. All the road signs had been taken down, and they were not sure which way to go.

Birdie looked again at the map. 'It's that way,' she said.

They walked their bicycles along a rutted track, through

woodland where the trees gave them shade until the land opened out again and a small farmhouse could be seen.

It was surrounded by acres of flowers. A river rolled through its fields, and on the other side of it were more flowers. Birdie hadn't expected all this. Her aunt had suggested the place would be dusty and dirty. Sitting in the middle of a patchwork of colourful flowers, the house with its black corrugated-iron roof looked sturdy and true. She felt her heart shift a little, and wondered if this wasn't the loveliest place she had ever seen. And this was where her mother and her aunt had grown up. Maybe that was why she felt at home here?

'There's a shortage of flower seeds for nurseries,' said Charles, coming across the yard with a couple of black and white dogs following behind him. 'They used to come from abroad, but since the war the supply has stopped because of trade embargoes and shipping routes being diverted. We're growing sunflowers and millet for bird food too.'

He walked briskly away and waded into the field, grabbing armfuls of flowers, coming back, offering them to the women.

'Welcome to the farm,' he said.

The harvest started that afternoon, and Birdie watched the barley grain pouring from the threshing machine as the men held sacks to be filled and tied off. She narrowed her eyes against the sun, squinting as dust blew in the air, milky and sweet-smelling.

The day was heat-soaked. Dust rose in small spirals. It clung to the farm workers' faces. Birdie thought they looked like a regiment of desert soldiers, not labourers threshing the fields. In the farmhouse kitchen Birdie got herself a glass of water. Charles was proud that he had mains water on his farm. The people who lived in Ark Farm, the neighbouring farmhouse, had got their place on the mains and he'd been able to get his farm connected too. It was dark in the kitchen, and it took a moment to see clearly. There was a polished oak table and four chairs around it.

A jam jar full of large white daisies stood on the table. Birdie knew her mother would have said they were unlucky. She never had white flowers in the house. Aunt Vivian, though, had cut flowers everywhere. She favoured blue irises. Birdie liked the white daisies with their yellow centres and dusty pollen dropping on the table.

Against the far wall were piles of newspapers, almanacs and journals. The linoleum floor had recently been mopped, and a soft tideline of dirt bordered the boots and the newspapers. On the sink was a bottle of Rinso floor cleaner with its lid off. Charles had cleaned the place, perhaps for their arrival. She replaced the lid on the Rinso bottle and took a glass from a shelf. It was dusty inside and she rinsed it.

Birdie let the water run for a while and put her wrists under the tap, small rivers of dirt running down her arms. When she filled the glass and drank, the water tasted cold and earthy. She helped herself to another glassful and tried to imagine her mother and aunt here as young women. The cottage and how it must have been.

Birdie walked out into the orchard and admired the plum trees heavy with fruit. She made her way to the railway wagon at the end of the orchard. Charles had told her he'd lived in it when he first bought the farmland, before he knocked down the remaining walls of the old cottage and built his farmhouse. It was almost completely covered in a climbing vine and honeysuckle. Bees buzzed in and out of the flowers.

She sat on its step and leaned her head against the door, fanning her face with her straw hat. Poor or not, her mother and her aunt must have had a happy life out here. She stood up and walked down to the river, imagining her mother swimming in it as a child. A tall, lanky girl with long plaits, wading into the river, arms outstretched, welcoming the water. Aunt Vivian would have been small and doll-like, standing on the bank, watching her fearless sister, her skirts billowing in the breeze. Birdie envied the sisters their simple, old-fashioned childhoods. This place must have been a kind of paradise for them, far from the pressures of modern life.

Matilda was chasing chickens around the yard the next morning. Charles caught two in the shade of the elder tree by the farmhouse front door, and Christopher, one of the farm workers, was helping Birdie catch a hen too. Christopher Thomas was a tall, healthy-looking man. He had five brothers and sisters. He was the youngest.

The rest of the family still lived locally, he said. He caught a red chicken and picked it up. 'The Thomases don't move far,' he went on. 'How about you?'

Birdie told him how her mother had grown up here, in a cottage on the site of the new farmhouse.

'Ah,' Christopher said, handing her the chicken. 'So then you're already a local.'

Charles watched them together. He could see why Birdie liked Christopher. He was one of those men who made everything look easy. The sort women fell in love with.

At least like this, with Birdie so deep in conversation, Charles could watch her without her noticing. She was suntanned and freckles covered her face and her arms too, where her shirtsleeves were rolled back. When she smiled, he found he was smiling too.

He wondered what had happened to him. Where had this kind of softness come from? This weakness in him that had him checking his hair was lying flat, his collar straight? But he knew full well where it came from. Since he first saw her last summer, he hadn't been able to stop thinking of Birdie. He wanted to show her things that he had never shown anybody. The dawn rising over the river. Grey mists on a beet field in winter. He supposed this was love, finally come to him. Though what he could do about it, he didn't know. He was courting Matilda, and though the subject had not been raised by him, it was clear she thought he would be asking her to marry him at some time or other in the near future. He had believed it himself until he met Birdie.

The farm dogs ran and barked and jumped around them. By the time they had caught enough chickens, Christopher and Matilda were red-faced and weak from laughter and the dogs had gone to drink noisily from the big metal water troughs.

Charles held a hen in the brown dirt. He took a twig and pressed it against the hen's beak. He drew a short line in the ground with the twig. Slowly he took his hands off the hen. She didn't move. He took another hen and did the same thing.

Birdie squatted on her heels and held her chicken with one hand and did the same. Her chicken stared at the ground. It was as though somebody had glued it there.

'Now what?'

'Now nothing. You just have to watch.'

The farm dogs paused, ears cocked, puzzling over the stillness. The sunlight beat down, rough and insistent. Matilda was bent over, hands on her knees, watching the hens. Christopher stood beside Birdie. Charles came and stood the other side of her. He was close enough to her that he could feel the warmth of her arm next to his. Charles stepped away. He lifted his hands and clapped. Christopher and Matilda yelled and did a rain dance together. Birdie joined in, laughing. The chickens came out of their trance and ran away, squawking as if in disgust at being used as entertainment. The dogs barked. The day tripped forwards like a man stumbling out of his dreams.

Birdie washed her hair in the kitchen sink, going outside to dry it in the hot breeze. She did her make-up standing with a small compact mirror down by the poplar trees near the river. Red lipstick. Mascara. After the baby she had got skinny, and she still looked fragile, though the sun had tanned her and her nose and cheeks were covered in brown freckles.

She had brought one dress with her, a pale green cotton day dress with a pattern of hollyhocks rising from its hemline. She had on her wedge-heeled sandals with ankle straps and was bare-legged. She had rubbed her legs smooth and hairless with a pumice stone and then used the last of her cold cream on them. It was good to make an effort. To try and forget for a short while the emptiness she felt.

'There's not much to dress up for out here, I'm afraid,' said Charles, walking towards her. 'I warn you, a dance at the Parish Rooms is not going to rival London.'

Birdie said she didn't mind. She liked it here. As she spoke, she realized she was pleased to have this moment with him alone. But Charles Bell was Matilda's fiancé. He was a good ten years older than her, and a farmer. She'd been brought up in a working-class pub in London. They had nothing in common. Nothing at all. And yet, every time he stood beside her, she felt he made something right. He had a way of listening when she spoke, as if he was thinking very carefully about what she said. She saw how animals liked him. How the cows were not afraid of him and the farm dogs followed him loyally. He had a goodness that she half hoped might lend itself to her.

'I'm looking forward to it,' she said, as they walked up the grassy path towards the house. 'It's been a long time since I last danced. If you set up a gramophone out here, I'd dance on the riverbank.'

'Ah, well, we'll have to try that one day,' said Charles.

'Come on, Birdie!' yelled Matilda, standing beside her bicycle, waving at them both over the hedge up by the farm track.

'You have unusual eyes,' Charles said.

She almost didn't hear him, his voice was so quiet.

She looked back at him. 'They're plain, I think. Plain grey.'

'They remind me of stone. Granite. Or children's marbles. I'm not doing a very good job at complimenting you, but I mean to say they're lovely. I've never seen anybody with eyes like yours.'

'My aunt has the exact same colour eyes.'

Now he reddened, shoving his hands in his pockets and tipping his head on one side. 'Does she? I must admit I have never noticed.'

They stood, considering each other.

'Hurry up!' yelled Matilda, and they both walked briskly towards her.

Outside the village hall, children played in the gravel. They had skipping ropes and a group of boys played jacks, kneeling in the dust. Inside the hall was a long row of chairs against the wall where old men and women sat motionless in their black Sunday best clothes and felt hats, their hands in their laps. She wondered if some of them might have known her mother and her aunt. She could not imagine either woman sitting with these immobile old people.

There was a flurry of hopeful-looking bunting hung over trestle tables where sandwiches and tea were being served. Raffle tickets were being sold. There were prizes of eggs, butter and jam, and a bowl of bright-skinned oranges that was being admired by a group of children. Women outnumbered the men in the hall. A few soldiers played darts, and a group of local men in corduroy trousers and hobnail boots stood staring at the soldiers with a look of open mistrust.

Birdie remembered the dance halls she used to go to, the familiar smell of hair oil and sweat and the edge of urgency, the heavy smoke-filled atmosphere, men and women pressed together, their bodies filled with the beat of jazz. She imagined Joan here, peeking in the door, sneering at the quaintness of this place and suggesting they make a run for it while they could still escape.

Birdie, Matilda, Charles and Christopher stood by the bar. One of the farm lads, a boy called Jeremy, was discussing what he'd like to do with Hitler if he ever got his hands on him. Everybody talked like that. Thinking up new tortures. She had got tired, when the soldiers were billeted at her aunt's house, of hearing how many times Hitler was going to get his backside kicked. Jeremy, who was seventeen and a skinny lad who could have passed for younger, recommended drowning him in a sack down a well. 'Like my gran does with kittens,' he said triumphantly.

'You'd have to get him into the sack first, you little runt,' said Christopher, pushing him in the ribs. Christopher was going into the RAF after the harvest was finished. He was enjoying swanking it over the other men, discussing his training and where he might be posted.

'And you, Charles,' said Matilda, 'will you go and fight?'

'Farmers get to stay home,' said Christopher.

'Home Guard,' Charles said, putting down his glass. 'I'm in a reserved occupation.'

The band started up, an old-fashioned waltz, and Birdie realized she longed to dance. Several women danced together, slowly, carefully, as if a strict dance teacher was calling the steps to them.

'Birdie,' said Christopher. He held out his hand to her and they joined the dancers. He had a decent sense of rhythm and managed not to tread on her toes.

'There's a girl over there,' said Birdie. 'The one with a blue dress. She's staring at us.'

'Ah,' said Christopher. 'That's Connie, Jeremy's sister. We've known each other for ever. We used to collect snails together in the playground. I asked her to marry me when I was seven and she was six. She said she would if I gave her my catapult.'

Birdie laughed. She could imagine him as a child.

'And did you?'

'I told her I didn't love her that much. She has never forgotten it.'

'I suppose you've hypnotized chickens with her?'

'Oh, chickens, snakes, you name it. And she's staring at me, actually.' He moved away from her slightly as they danced. 'She forgave me the catapult in the end. We're getting married.

Connie has a dream of a particular wedding dress, and she's saving up coupons to get enough fabric. I was hoping we'd marry before I go away, but she is adamant that once she has the dress, we'll fix a date.'

Birdie smiled at the girl, who frowned back at her. Of course she didn't like to see another girl dancing with her boyfriend. Why should she? Birdie was a stranger in this small village. Charles and Matilda stood together, looking like a married couple already. When the song ended, Birdie sat down on a chair beside the old people. She longed to see Joan. To be home, in the city, where she understood the rules and the way of doing things. She watched Christopher talking with Connie. Matilda was dragging Charles onto the dance floor.

When Charles came over and asked her to dance, Birdie knew he was just being gallant. Matilda smiled at her. They both saw how lonely she was. Matilda had probably begged him to ask her poor wallflower friend to dance with him.

'Oh, I'm quite tired,' Birdie said, getting up. 'I think I'll cycle back to the farm.'

Joking, managing to smile, she walked out of the open doors into the moonlight.

Moths danced in front of her wheels as she cycled, fluttering white moths that moved in the odd, random way snowflakes could move. The insects were lifted back and forth by the warm air, she supposed, as snowflakes could be whipped back and forth by east winds. She felt a moth brush her face and wished she had stayed to cycle back with Charles and Matilda. The touch of the insect frightened her, though it could do no harm except to itself, leaving its wing powders on her cheek.

At the farm she walked along the riverbank, but again she felt frightened. The water at night looked dangerous. It glistened and there were small sounds everywhere, a horrid rustling in the reeds, small hiccuping noises that could have been frogs or, in her vivid imagination, dangerous animals. The trees swayed and creaked. Earlier she had stood here with Charles and felt perfectly safe. Now she was like a silly child, afraid of the dark, conjuring up ghosts in every small ripple of movement she heard in the black waters. 'Charles,' she said out loud, as if his name could protect her from her fears.

The weather broke the next day and summer rain fell. Birdie and Matilda had volunteered to whitewash the dairy walls before they left. They had buckets and wide paintbrushes and were wearing hessian sacks tied with string around their waists to keep their clothes clean. Small flecks of straw kept landing on the brushes and sticking to the walls.

'I think he's going to ask me to marry him,' said Matilda.

'Who?'

'Who? Honestly, Birdie, who do you think?'

Birdie stopped painting.

'Charles,' said Matilda. 'This morning I was telling him how I liked the rabbits he's got in that pen out the back of the house. He asked if I had ever thought of being a farmer's wife. I said yes. I thought it would be very nice.'

'And what did he say?'

'He said he thought I'd make a good farmer's wife.'

Matilda splashed whitewash onto the walls.

'And you think that was a marriage proposal?'

'Well, yes. Don't you?'

Birdie pulled off her hessian-sack apron.

'What about Colin?'

'He's a soldier. You know what they're like. They promise you everything and then ship out the next day. I've got my future to think of. I'm not getting any younger. You're young, Birdie. I'm nearly thirty. It's now or never for me.'

Birdie looked out of the dairy doors to the fields beyond. Charles was walking towards the yard with a couple of dogs at his heels. He lifted his hand and waved. She pretended she hadn't seen him. She was glad this had happened. It made up her mind for her. She had to get on with her own life. She would go back to the city.

Seventeen

Joan had cut her hair short and small curls rose up around the curved nape of her long neck. She was wearing a black beret and a wide-shouldered jacket that hung off her tall, skinny frame. She had a confident way about her that Birdie didn't remember.

'You're going to love the bedsit,' Joan said as they pushed their way through the crowds. 'I have a wireless set. A kettle, a single bed, a sagging sofa, a red rug I got from a junk shop and an armchair that was already in the room when I moved in. I also have a job in a typing pool, a thriving community of cockroaches in my flat, too many to give names to, actually. And,' she lowered her voice, 'a married lover.'

They stopped outside a dirty brick house with black railings. Joan gave Birdie a grin and searched in her bag for a key. 'You're shocked, aren't you? I knew you would be.'

They descended mossy steps, Joan pushing bottles and rubbish out of the way with the toe of her shoe. She let them into the basement flat, closed and locked the door, pulled the blackout curtains shut, pegged them in place and lit a gas lamp.

'Home, sweet home,' Joan said, and offered Birdie a place to sit on the narrow single bed. They had a cup of tea and a few slices of bread and butter. Birdie kicked off her shoes. The city had taken her back, and nobody would ever know why she had left it in the first place.

Vivian thought she should really replace the satin counterpane on her bed. The carpets were threadbare too. The cats had scratched everything over the years. Perhaps a new rug might help. A tabby cat sat on the bed, purring. It lifted its head to her and slowly closed its green eyes, a blissful expression on its face as she stroked it behind the ear. He had been the one who liked Birdie best. Now she had gone, the cat had come back to Vivian.

She slipped off the bed and opened her cupboards, looking at the rows of clothes. She was going to have a clear-out and take some of her clothes to the charity centre in town. She and a group of women were cutting up old clothes to make new nighties and pinafores and shorts for evacuee children. She pulled out a few cotton dresses and laid them on the bed. Her fur coat and the shoes and hats in boxes would stay. And there, hanging in a paper covering, was her wedding dress.

Poor Bernard Harding. He had been so angry when she had refused his proposition. She'd known he had something on his mind when he suggested they skip the bridge game organized by his sister and walk together on the beach front. Bernard surely didn't want to take off his shoes and socks, roll up his trouser legs and walk on the sands with her just for the fun of it?

Finally he had asked her to marry him, and she had said yes. At least she had not been wrong to think he would propose marriage one day. They had walked in silence along the beach, seagulls crying, the wind roaring in their ears, so wonderfully bracing and salt-edged. A fawn-haired child ran backwards, flying a small red paper kite that danced and skipped along the beach, touching the sands, lifting again, tugging against its line. Vivian had held her face up to the sky and breathed deeply, watching the kite's sudden swoop into the air high above them.

The desire to be married again had carried her along for years. It had been a project and she realized she needed projects, pilgrimages, acts of faith, whatever she wanted to call these private ambitions that gave meaning to her life. Waiting for Bernard Harding had been an act of faith.

The white-painted Georgian house he lived in would suit her well. Marriage to the doctor was to be a consolation for the loss of Joe and her daughter, a prize for the years spent being a respectable widow, doing charity work and helping others.

By the time they were nearly back at the promenade and awkwardly trying to dust the sand off their feet, Vivian had changed her mind. Bernard hopped about on one foot, trying to get grains of sand from between his toes. He could have asked for her arm or leaned against her, but instead he swayed around on the beach like a drunk, falling from one foot to the other. She began to laugh. Bernard Harding frowned at her, his polished brogues in his hand slightly down at heel, his darned socks balled up in one of them.

'I can't marry you,' she said suddenly. 'I'm sorry, Bernard. I am sure I sound very foolish, but I want to marry for love and I don't love you.'

The wind was blowing hard across the sea and it snatched Bernard's trilby off his head, throwing it onto the beach below, where it skipped and rolled into the waves. He left his shoes with her and stamped across the sands to retrieve the hat from the water.

'What is this about?' he asked when he returned, his face mottled red by the exertion of his trek down to the sea and back.

'Do you love me, Bernard?'

'Vivian, what a strange question.' He dusted sand off the brim of his hat. 'At our age, don't you think love is a little unlikely?'

Maybe it was the wind chasing around her skirts that made her feel frivolous, but she had to fight a strong impulse not to grab his blessed trilby and throw it back in the sea.

Later, in the steamy, glass-fronted conservatory of a tea room, she explained again. 'My sister married for love. Twice. I realized just now that I do not want to marry for convenience. I want love. If not, I prefer to remain single.'

Poor Bernard. He'd looked so shocked. As if he thought she had gone mad! And yet she felt very sane.

'I wonder if you are quite all right,' said Bernard as she left that afternoon. He had obviously been thinking a lot about their conversation. She saw it in his face. Heard it in his voice, that doctor's voice he put on, the one full of professional certainty that crept in when he was unsure of a situation.

'You will agree with me that over the years you have proved yourself a rather anxious female, Vivian. Let me just warn you. If you ever do find love, as you put it, don't think that it will come without risk. You are in your fifties, my dear. We know each other so well. We are fair companions, aren't we? If you want romantic love, I suggest you buy yourself some novels or go to the cinema and find it there.'

'And if you want a housekeeper, Bernard,' Vivian replied, surprised by the clarity of her words, 'I suggest you put an advertisement in the *Lady*.'

Vivian took her wedding dress out of the wardrobe. It was ivory satin with rows of satin-covered buttons. It had been a rather old-fashioned gown, even back then, but what she had wanted. Dear Frank had given her everything she desired except for a child. In retrospect, he had been what some women called a mummy's boy. Kind, but always needing to be the centre of attention. He'd wanted to be the child, she supposed. That's why he had never wanted to be a parent. Vivian lay the heavy dress down on the bed. The rippling satin spread across the counterpane, a creamy lake of fabric the colour of spilt milk. No use crying over it, either, she thought. You couldn't get the time back once it was gone. She held the dress up to her. It would still fit. She had kept her figure very well over the years. If Matilda wasn't such a big-hipped girl, she would offer the dress to her to wear when she married Charles Bell. Perhaps she still might. They could unpick it and make something new out of it. All that day, Vivian went about her chores with a sense of calm.

Joan got Birdie a job within days. She came back from work with a bottle of red wine in her handbag, a present from her lover. She'd seen a sign for a kitchen hand at a tea shop down the street.

The pay was low, just over seventeen shillings a week. She knew Birdie couldn't get somewhere to live and afford to eat on that kind of wage, but it was a start and they'd throw in a daily dinner and a cup of afternoon tea.

'We will keep this wine for when you get a promotion to waitress and we can afford to buy cream cakes for tea,' Joan said, putting the bottle under the bed.

They cooked meals on a small gas stove in the middle of the room and listened to big bands on the wireless every night at 10.30, watching the night sky from the window.

By October, the cold weather had set in and the sky was lit up by guns and searchlights. The city stank of charred buildings and broken sewers. Bombed streets were roped off and houses ripped apart; here and there walls remained, wallpaper intact, mirrors still hanging on them, piles of brick rubble full of broken furniture. Birdie discovered the pub had been bombed. Her childhood home had disappeared into a mountain of rubble and fire-damaged walls. She climbed over the bricks and piles of debris and found that the elder tree was still alive in the backyard. She took a branch of it back to the flat, telling Joan that Mother had always said it was a good plant for keeping flies off food. She had forgotten how its leaves smelled like cat's piss. Birdie had to throw it away. Joan made tea. Losing your home was a terrible thing, Joan said.

Coming back from work, Birdie met the postman, who put two letters in her hand. They were both postmarked weeks earlier. He was sorry they had taken so long to arrive.

She went inside and opened them. One was from her aunt Vivian, saying Matilda had eloped with a soldier and married him. His name was Colin Hume. He was one of the soldiers she had billeted in the summer. Did Birdie remember him? Poor Charles Bell had been let down horribly. Birdie couldn't help but feel glad. It was selfish of her, but she had always been worried that Matilda might tell Charles why she had been staying with her aunt. That she might tell the sorry story of Birdie Farr and her adopted baby. She couldn't bear the thought of Charles knowing that about her.

She sat down on the bed and opened the other letter. It was from her mother. She and George wouldn't risk coming to London, so it was up to Birdie to find some time to come and see them. Aunt Lydia's husband, Walter, had gone off with a neighbour's wife. Apparently they'd been having an affair for years. Nellie said Lydia was dealing with it all quite well now it was in the open. Malcolm had been to see them on leave. He had met a girl and married her. She was the daughter of a German woman and an Englishman. Lydia did not like the girl at all, but then Lydia didn't like anybody, did she? If Lydia could just stop judging others, she'd be a happier woman. Did Birdie remember Peter, Roger's friend? Now that was a sad story. He had been serving as a telegraphist on a warship. The ship had been sunk by gunfire in Norway.

'I'm so sorry. I thought you knew,' said Joan when Birdie read her the letter. 'Malcolm told me. It happened this summer. Actually, I saw a little bit of Malcolm after you left. We went dancing a few times.'

'Let's get drunk,' said Birdie, folding the letters up and reaching under the bed for the wine bottle Joan had put there when she'd first arrived. Peter had died never knowing he had a daughter. It felt so final. She had lost two strangers – because that was what they both were, Peter and her child. She had known them both better than anybody in her life, and yet had not had any time to know them at all. Both of them had touched her for ever, and now they were gone.

'Did you like him very much?' asked Joan gently when Birdie began to cry. 'I didn't know you knew him like that. Birdie, has something happened to you? You're different since you went away. Ghostly somehow. You cry so easily. Maybe it's this bloody war, but it's hard to know what you're thinking half the time.'

Birdie shook her head. Was she ghostly? She pressed a hand to her chest. Certainly she felt vague and her heart was a dull thing, sluggish and slow under her fingers.

'You're right. I'm sorry,' she said. 'It's the war. It wears down my nerves. I keep thinking I'll be walking along the street and a bomb will fall on my head.'

She took a swig of wine and managed a half-hearted smile.

'Let's get drunk,' she said again. 'Absolutely bloody drunk.'

In January, Joan declared 1941 would be the year of the bachelor girl. Her married lover had finished with her.

'Good riddance,' she said, waving her cigarette at Birdie for emphasis as she crouched over the gas stove, cooking cabbage and potato in a saucepan.

She brought home a book entitled *Live Alone and Like It.* She and Birdie read chapters together on etiquette for the lone female and how to live a successful life without a man. They told each other things would be all right. Friendship was what mattered. Birdie hoped that was true. She still felt empty inside. When she saw small children with their mothers, Birdie turned away from them. And yet she saw clearly she could never have brought a child up alone. She could barely afford to feed herself. She had to accept her daughter was better off without her.

Then Joan's married man turned up with a bouquet of flowers and Joan forgave him. Birdie got her coat and went walking alone.

'Please don't call him my married man,' said Joan when she got back. 'His name is Michael.'

Birdie saw a notice for a waitress in a hotel. The job came with accommodation. A tall man with a face as low-looking as the weather offered her the position. She bought a second-hand pair of flat lace-up shoes and, with Joan's dressmaking scissors, cut her hair short. Then she sent off letters to her mother and her aunt giving them her new address. Joan made a last supper for them both. She said it was for the best really. She hoped there would be no hard feelings between them.

Charles folded the newspaper shut. If a bomb or a stray bullet didn't actually kill you, then reading about the war just might make you give up the ghost. Everywhere was doom and gloom. Take this London hotel he was in. There was no hot water for a bath, and when he'd asked about it he'd been treated like an enemy spy trying to deplete the nation's riches. He'd not been to London in years. Not since his brothers and his father went to fight in the first war and he and his mother had travelled to see them off on the train to France. He'd been a child then and overwhelmed by the city. He was not much changed. The city still felt alien. His eyes were too accustomed to the colour green. All these grey buildings, the dark paved roads, the ceaseless traffic, the jostling crowds. He was a man who liked hay meadows and all the secret moments of the countryside. Seeing a kingfisher fly over the river, its flash of blue so vivid it shocked his heart. That was worth living for. The earth under his feet was what mattered to him. His fields and his animals. He'd been a child who had liked roaming across the fields more than the streets of the city he'd grown up in.

His heart lurched at the sight of Birdie coming into the room. Her neat black dress and white collar suited her. Her red lipstick made her look like a film star playing the role of maid. Her legs were slender, and the darned stockings she wore brought out a tenderness in him. He worried she might not be right for a farmer's wife. He tried to imagine her in the cow barns before dawn, helping milk the cows. Would she laugh at his suggestion that she give up her city life?

He had come to London on an impulse. He'd been walking his fields in icy rain, carrying hay to the sheep out on the high meadows. The rain slanted sideways and dripped down his neck. He pulled his hat down and walked on across his fields, carrying the bale of hay across his shoulders. Under an oak tree, noisy with the shake and pelt of rain, he dropped the hay bale and leaned against the tree in the lee of the wind. The tree creaked. The sky was dark and low. The farmhouse in the distance was all but gone in the sweeping rain clouds. He remembered the summer and, as he often did, he thought of Birdie Farr, her red-gold hair catching the sun, standing in a green dress by the river, getting ready to go to the village dance.

He split the hay bale and left it for the sheep to come and find themselves.

In his kitchen, a recent letter from Vivian Stewart was on the table. Matilda had eloped with a soldier and moved to Manchester. Mrs Stewart wanted him to know how sorry she was. She hoped he would visit her again soon.

He was embarrassed by what had happened with Matilda. There had been some vague talk of marriage and he had not known how to back out of it all. He was relieved Matilda had found herself a husband.

He told Connie Smith, Christopher's fiancée, when she called by to offer him an apple pie made from some of the apples from his orchard. She'd known Matilda wasn't the woman for him. 'That other one. The Londoner. The one with too much red lipstick. She liked you.'

Why hadn't he spoken to Birdie about how he felt when he had the chance? He made tea and sat warming himself by the stove, watching the dog sleeping at his feet, its legs moving rapidly, running away from its dreams.

When he picked up a farming magazine and saw an advertisement for a public lecture in London about the use of new artificial fertilizers and the possible increase in yield for cereal crops, he had decided to go and see Birdie.

And now Charles could not take his eyes off her. She moved around the dining room, smiling politely at the other diners, and as she neared his table he straightened his tie and swallowed hard, preparing to speak.

'Miss Farr?' he said, and she turned to the sound of her name.

'Charles? What on earth are you doing here?'

She had lipstick smudges on her teeth. Her face was tired-looking, her grey eyes questioning. His hand trembled a little when he held it out to her. She was such a pretty woman. If he had been a different kind of man, he would have kissed the back of her hand as she placed it in his.

'I'm attending a farming lecture,' he said, shaking hands with her and letting go reluctantly. 'Not exactly the best fun, but interesting enough for me.'

'But here? This hotel?'

'I saw your aunt. She said you were here. I had to stay in a hotel, so I booked this one. I hope you don't mind.'

'No, no, I don't mind. Of course not. I'm glad to see you. How are you?'

'Things are all right. The government are building an airfield nearby and ruining the roads with their heavy machinery, but other than that I have no news except that Matilda is married. Not to me. To a man named Colin.' He looked into her grey eyes. 'I came to see you, Birdie. You left so quickly. I never got a chance to say goodbye.'

He rearranged the knife and fork on the table and smoothed the tablecloth with his broad palm.

'I'm no good at this kind of thing, but I mean, look, I'm steady. Probably too steady. Boring, most likely. I'm trustworthy. I work too hard and I've two left feet when it comes to dancing. I lost my brothers in the Great War. I have very little feeling of patriotism, and I don't think war is a good or a noble thing. I don't want to fight for my country. If that makes me a coward, so be it. I just want to run my farm and live a quiet life and have a wife and maybe some children.

'My mother died of cancer. My father killed himself shortly afterwards. He went under a train and everybody said it was an accident, but I don't believe it was. I was a bank clerk, but I had always wanted to work the land. I sold my parents' home and bought some farmland at auction. It was a dream of mine. I've been on my own a long time, Birdie, and I didn't mind that until I met you. I just want to be straight about this. I want you to know everything about me, and, well, that's all there is to know.'

'Miss Farr?' The head waiter came over, crossing the room in long strides. 'Any problems here, sir?'

'Everything is fine,' said Charles, trying to read the look on Birdie's face, realizing he had talked too much. 'I was asking the waitress if she knew the best route to the Imperial College.'

'I can get you a map, sir. Miss Farr, I think there are other tables to serve,' said the head waiter, and Birdie turned so abruptly, moving away to attend to other tables, that Charles did not get a chance to see what effect his words might have had.

The head waiter watched Birdie all morning. Every time she stopped work, he had another job for her to do. She put on a white apron over her black uniform, took a broom, some dusters and a pot of wax polish, and went into the dining room to clean. In the corner of the room, the head waiter was seated, a big pile of cutlery in front of him. He said he was doing a stock inventory because he was sure somebody was stealing the knives and forks.

She left him to it and swept the brown parquet floors, working from the corner nearest the door to the kitchens across to the big bay windows that looked out on the grey street. Rain hit the windows and condensation formed on them. Birdie stopped sweeping and wiped her sleeve across the glass, looking out on brick buildings and cars and buses. She was still going over what Charles had said. Still getting over the shock of seeing him again. She finished sweeping and cleared away the dust and crumbs into a dustpan. As she emptied it into the ash bucket by the chimney, the double doors to the dining room opened.

Charles stood in the doorway. His hair was wet from the rain, and it curled and sprang up around his ears even as he pressed a hand to it, trying to make it lie flat.

Birdie looked over her shoulder. She could see the head waiter at the far end of the room. He was dozing with his legs stretched out in front of him. Charles leaned against the wall, his arms folded.

She would certainly lose her job if she stopped work to talk to him. She'd already had a warning. She decided to ignore him. She spread wax over wood and polished the furniture, her body swaying, her arm making wide arcs, rubbing back and forth. Right now the only thing that made sense was the shine coming up off the wooden tables. She moved quickly, turning chairs upside down and stacking them, dusting them as she went, thinking back to the farm, a world she often returned to in her head. She remembered the dark kitchen with the dogs sleeping under the table, a sound of creaking beams, clouds of moths dancing in the warm night air.

The tables in the dining room were glassy like mirrors; sweat was stinging her eyes. She stopped and stood, hands on hips, her breath coming in short gasps.

'What do you want, Charles?'

He opened his arms to her.

'I want you, Birdie.'

She didn't think twice. She stepped into his embrace.

He felt warm, like the summer they had shared.

Eighteen

After they married, Charles built a raised wooden verandah around the house. He said it was a lookout for their fortress. He joked about adding a drawbridge, a moat and arrow slits to the farmhouse, and though it was just silly talk between them, it pleased Birdie to know they both felt the same. The farm was isolated, but they both yearned to live out on the very edge of the world, just the two of them. At this lonely farm, memories could not reach her. She believed she could forget the child. She walked along the river every day, hoping the numbness, the sense of panic that fluttered within her when she saw other women with their children, would fade. She had a desire to have another child, and she told Charles she wanted a big family.

They were sitting under the willow trees, watching one of the farm dogs swimming to retrieve a stick Charles had thrown in the river.

'Big as in four or five, or big as in nine or ten?' he'd asked, softly stroking her neck.

'Nine or ten children. A whole rabbit litter of them.' She felt a little silly then, embarrassed by her desires. There was something not quite decent about such greedy talk of fertility. They weren't farm animals, after all. But Charles just carried on stroking her neck as if she had said nothing at all out of the ordinary.

When the verandah was finished, she and Charles started a habit of standing on it, watching the dawn, the sky ribboned with pink and white like the fat-marbled beef joints she roasted on Sundays, following a recipe book, trying to understand the cooking range, wishing she had paid more attention when her aunt had taught her how to cook. 'Do you miss the city?' he asked, but she said she had forgotten all about it.

Most of the farmers in the area worked all the hours they could, and Birdie soon realized Charles was the same. He spent his days outside, coming in late, wanting her, smelling of the earthy scent of fields, of hay and animals, the sharp odour of motor oil on his clothes. He stood behind her as she leaned over the sink peeling potatoes, putting his arms around her, lifting her skirts, dropping to his knees as she turned and pressing his sweet nuzzling face between her legs. Some days he came in and caught her dancing to big bands on the wireless in the kitchen. She insisted he dance with her, pulling off her apron, sliding her hips against him, unbuttoning his sweat-stiffened cotton shirt. Birdie knew she was still ghostly, still a person who struggled to understand her own feelings, but her desires for Charles blocked out the emptiness. And they would have children soon. The kind of love they felt for each other was bound to bring a child into the world.

They grew every kind of arable crop through the war years. Charles borrowed a caterpillar tractor from his neighbour Norman Hubbard, over at Ark Farm. He spent a week grubbing up hedgerows to make the fields bigger. With the woody copses and hedgerows gone, the landscape looked like a vast prairie and the east wind rushed across it, stirring up small dust storms.

In return for the loan of the tractor, Charles and Birdie worked scything thistles on the Hubbards' farm for a week. Norman Hubbard was a lawyer who ran his farm as a hobby. He had a farm manager, a rather taciturn man called Westfield. Norman's wife, Kathleen, bred horses, but in wartime she had given that up and helped out on the farm.

Birdie thought Kathleen a perfect English countrywoman. Just like an illustration in one of the *Country Life* magazines she looked at these days. Kathleen had clear skin and high cheekbones. Her eyes were brown and almond-shaped. Her blonde hair was tied back and fell about her shoulders in curls when she undid it. Kathleen taught Birdie how to chase rats from the hen house with the back end of a hard broom and lots of shouting.

'Never show you are afraid of them,' she said. 'Always act like you are absolutely sure you are more frightening than they are. Actually, I'd recommend having this attitude for everything. Rats, husbands, bank managers and children included.'

Kathleen had an eighteen-month-old daughter called Ella, who was looked after by a nanny. Not really a nanny, but a land girl who was supposed to work in the fields but suffered from hay fever, whereas she was good with a baby. Birdie only ever saw the child from a distance, bundled up in a pram with a large white net over the pram hood, keeping the sun off her. She was curious about the child but didn't like to ask to see her because Kathleen showed so little interest in her daughter and Birdie felt her new friend would have been surprised by the request.

When the harvest was finished, gleaners arrived on the stubble fields. Birdie watched groups of ragged women and children scratching in the dirt for grain left behind by the threshing machines. They were a strange sight, bent over, scouring the ground as if looking for things they had lost.

'They mark the end of the summer,' said Charles. 'Them and the swallows leaving.'

He worried winter on the farm might be a shock to her, and in the last months of the year, the days got shorter and a gloom descended. Connie Smith's brother Jeremy was reported missing in action, and the family had postponed Connie and Christopher's wedding.

Birdie remembered Connie as the girl who had stared at her when she'd danced with Christopher. She cycled over to see her at her parents' house.

A flush of pink tinted Connie's pale cheeks. She was a dark-haired girl with blue-veined milky skin and shadows under her brown eyes. Christopher's leave had been cancelled. They were getting married at his next leave, which might be in several months' time.

'I wish I'd never waited now,' she said. 'We could have got married when Jeremy was still here, but I wanted to save up coupons to buy enough fabric to make my own dress. Now I don't care what I wear. I just want us to be husband and wife.'

Birdie thought she understood what she meant. Connie feared Christopher wouldn't come back from the war either.

The nights grew colder and the farm dogs, always lolling in the yard, hid under the kitchen table and refused to leave the house. By mid-November, watching the sunrise on the verandah required a certain bravery. It was so cold, Birdie's cheeks felt like they'd been slapped and her fingers froze in her gloves. Her mother sent her hand-knitted socks and silk underwear, which she said was warmer than cotton. *I know what winters can be like down by the river*, she wrote.

In January, cold seemed to get under every layer of clothing Birdie wore. She'd been sure, in the honeymoon months of the summer, that she loved life in the country. Now she thought of the city again and began to miss it. At night, with the wartime blackout, the darkness in the house was total, the silence deep as a well. Sometimes Birdie woke in the early hours, eyes open, wondering where she was, dreams still turning in her mind, jumbled memories of smog and slums, noise and crowds in her uncle's pub. Then she remembered. She had married Charles. She had what she wanted. A life on the edge of the world. And still, the dark felt so boundless and confusing, the silence so thick, Birdie pressed her fingers against her face and wondered if she might be touching another person altogether.

Day after day in her first winter on the farm, there were frost and snow, cold and rain. Her mother wrote to her often, telling her about the infamous cold of the winters in East Anglia, the Siberian winds that blew straight from the USSR. She sent more socks she had knitted herself. Baggy things that Birdie and Charles made into glove puppets and laughed at.

All through February, the icy breath of the wind whistled under the door and called up the stairs like a nosy neighbour. Birdie tried to shut it out, stuffing newspapers against the doorsill, while the wind rattled the window frames and sneaked in under gaps in the corrugated-iron roof.

Charles said a farmer couldn't afford to be afraid of the weather. It was like fate. You had to bend with it, not try to fight it.

'All good things come to us slowly,' he told her. 'We just have to endure until they do.'

And then in February 1942, Birdie heard that Christopher had died when his plane was shot down.

Connie stood at her door wearing a pleated dress, a look of shock in her eyes, her dark brown hair wisping around her face.

'I'm pregnant,' she said. 'Five months along.'

'So what will you do?'

'Mum says she'll help me. Christopher's grandmother has given me her wedding ring to wear so I can hold my head up when I visit the doctor.'

'So you'll keep the baby?' Birdie felt a pang of hurt. A childish sense of unfairness.

'Of course I will.' Connie looked surprised for a moment. 'It's Christopher's. What else would I do?'

'Oh, it's the war,' said Kathleen Hubbard. The two of them were sitting in Birdie's kitchen, smoking and drinking tea and talking about Connie being an unmarried mother. Kathleen had ridden over in the rain and put her horse in a stable on the farm.

She was wearing her riding breeches and black riding boots. Her thick blonde hair was tied back severely off her face. She sat with her legs crossed, swinging her foot. Birdie knew she would not stay long. She'd be off soon, away across the fields on her dark grey horse, galloping along the edge of the winter wheat fields, her coat-tails flapping behind her.

'It's changed everything, Birdie. Even the vicar wishes Connie well. I think it's marvellous, but my God, doesn't it show up the hypocrisy in this world? Before the war, Connie would have been seen as a disgrace. Put a man in a uniform and let him die for his country, and suddenly the sweetheart he left behind is transformed into the Virgin Mary.' She looked at her intently. 'Don't you agree?'

'I just hope she's going to be all right,' Birdie said. 'I think people should mind their own business. I'm sick of the way everybody judges each other in this country.'

Kathleen shrugged. 'I suppose we all judge each other. Can't be helped. When I first saw you, I thought a lot of things. It's not often you see a woman in full make-up, red lipstick and mascara, stomping about a hay field. And then I heard you were a barmaid from the East End. Well, I'm sure you can imagine what I thought.'

'No. What did you think?'

'Well, that's the thing. I was wrong, wasn't I?' said Kathleen. 'You're a good farmer's wife.' She stubbed out her cigarette and changed the subject to whether she should be putting her best hunting mare in foal this year or not.

Birdie crossed the farmyard, leaning into the wind, her head tipped down against the horizontal rain. It was Christmas 1942. She had settled into her life as a farmer's wife. Connie had had her baby that summer. A little girl. She'd called her Judith and she was the sweetest thing, with dark hair like Connie's, and Christopher's deep-blue eyes. Connie had put Christopher's photograph over the baby's cot. She wanted her daughter to know who her father was. His name had recently been added to a wooden commemoration plaque in the church. *Christopher Thomas 1914–1942.* Kathleen, too, was having a baby. She hoped for a son, she said.

Charles had Italian prisoners of war working for him, out in the barn, repairing hessian sacks and helping him dress the seed barley. They were sifting the seeds for thistle heads and charlock. Birdie had prepared a meal for them all. She liked the men. They were hard-working and they carried something of another place with them. She was fascinated by their accents and their way of appreciating the food put before them. She knew people in the village treated them coldly, but she wasn't going to go about things like that. Recently some of the men had carved small wooden toys and given them to her, smiling, nodding their approval, holding their arms in front of them, rocking imaginary babies back and forth. '*Bambino!*' they whispered. Carved peacocks and horses, small birds and cats sat on the kitchen windowsill. Birdie thanked the men in Italian: '*Grazie tanto!*' A phrase she had picked up in her uncle's pub as a child.

The gale whipped her hair against her face and she spread her arms. Her hands came to rest on her rounded belly, and she swayed back and forth. Finally she felt completely happy. There was nobody to see her, but even if one of the men had stepped out of the barn at that moment, it would not have mattered. The rest of the world could go to hell. There was never going to be anything shameful about a married, pregnant woman dancing in a rainstorm.

Nineteen

Nellie sat in a pew at the front of the church, George one side of her and Lydia the other. It was a gloomy little building. Made of a dirty-looking stone with a dark-wood-striped alcove that she imagined the inside of a whale's ribs might look like. She disliked churches. Hatch, match and dispatch, that's all they were good for. And they were always cold. A smell of damp walls permeated the air. She knew the smell. Not just in church. You found it where? Ah yes, the smell of earth, of the damp earth where the nettles grew along the riverbank of her childhood.

It was comforting to think of Birdie living so near to the river. As if she had become the guardian of the past. Though she would never know it, she was the keeper of Josephine's resting place. And now she had a baby son, he might grow up to keep watch over her river too. Nellie thought she'd like to teach the boy to swim one day.

Malcolm in his army uniform, and his new wife, Lucy, stood at the altar. Her nephew was losing his hair. He'd be bald in later life, like his father. He looked tired and anxious and was only home on leave from the army for a few days. Lucy held their baby in a long white christening gown and a little white bonnet. Nellie glanced at Lydia. She had a pained look on her face. She was probably thinking of Roger. He'd always been her favourite.

Nellie had never wanted to live near Lydia, but after they sold the pub, George had wanted to go home, back to where he had grown up. Lydia still lived in the house their parents had owned. She was sixty years old, and frail these days. She had become untidy-looking. Her skirt hems trailed. She had butter stains on her gloves. When Nellie visited her, a duty she carried out for George's benefit, she found her sister-in-law sitting in a chair in the cluttered front room full of her late mother's ornaments, the chink of light from the closed curtains playing patterns over her ageing face. The doctor said she had mental illness. Lydia had long ago stopped talking of the importance of truth and her own psychic talents that allowed her to have a special, clearer view of the world than anybody else. She refused to talk of the war or of her ex-husband. Roger she spoke of often, but as if he were still alive and living with her.

After the baptism was over, they traipsed back to Lydia's house for tea and sandwiches. George and Malcolm stood in the kitchen, discussing selling the house. Lydia could not live alone any longer. George had found a private home for distressed gentle-folk. Nellie thought they might want to lower their voices. Sitting in Lydia's front parlour with Lucy and her parents, they could all hear their earnest discussion.

'Is this Roger's child?' Lydia asked, pointing at Malcolm's baby. Nellie watched Lucy's face cloud with upset.

'Mother,' Malcolm called wearily from the kitchen, 'he is my son. Mine and Lucy's. You know what happened to Roger.'

They managed another half-hour before Lydia ended the party.

'Of course, my brother married his brother's wife,' she announced loudly. 'Because they already had a daughter together.'

George and Malcolm stopped talking. The room fell quiet.

'That's enough, Mum,' said Malcolm.

'It's not nearly enough. The correct behaviour for families and marriage, and what they do in private, are very different things, Malcolm,' Lydia said, raising her voice. 'Look at my husband, respectable and quiet as the grave, but he was carrying on with that other woman right under my nose! To think of it! I could murder him and be happy, but he's a coward and won't come near me. And my brother with her over there, no better. I saw them once, carrying on, thinking they were alone. The two of them on the stairs. My brother Henry's wife and my brother George. Do you hear what I'm saying to you? They were carrying on. Is Birdie your daughter, George, or Henry's?'

There was a silence and Lydia began dabbing at her face with a handkerchief, as if she were exhausted by her outburst. Lucy's parents left, saying they had a train to catch, and Malcolm and Lucy left with them.

'So, are you pleased with yourself?' George asked his sister afterwards. 'Why did you have to talk like that? Why'd you have to be so bloody rotten?'

Lydia began to cry. 'Why shouldn't I call you out for what you did? It makes my skin crawl. You're just like my ex-husband, going behind people's backs.' Her voice droned on, petulant, whiny and accusing, until she fell asleep, slumped in her chair.

Nellie went outside, craving fresh air. She stood in the front garden by the low wall where yellow hollyhocks grew out of the brickwork. The wind gusted across the sea and raced inland, ruffling her clothes. Nellie could taste sea salt on her lips.

'You all right?' asked George.

'I wish Birdie could know you are her father.'

'She's Henry's girl. That's what we have to stick to.'

Seagulls soared in the sky overhead, calling loudly. Time was passing in any case. Did the truth really matter? Nellie thought Lydia was pleased to have spoken out, despite her tears, but really, what had it done for her? Lydia's son and his family hadn't cared to hear her accusations. They had been horrified by her outspokenness, turning from her words the way they might have looked away had she undressed in front of them, her outburst as shameful as dropped underskirts, slipped buttons, undone corsets. Things nobody should witness.

At the window upstairs in the farmhouse, looking out at the flat landscape and the track to the farm, Birdie watched and waited.

Any minute now, the old farm cart pulled by the grey horse would be coming into the yard, bringing her mother and Uncle George to see her son. She took a deep breath and looked in on the nursery where her baby was sleeping in his cot. He was four months old and looked like his father. Perfectly, completely like his father.

He had weighed seven pounds at birth and had lain peacefully in Birdie's arms, as if he had always been held by her. Her son made a small grumbling sound and Birdie hushed him. She was disturbing him, standing over his cot. She stared at him sleeping and wondered when she would feel love for him. All she felt was a kind of relief that he wasn't going anywhere. That she did not need to keep him a secret from anyone.

Framsden rubbed his hands against his face. His tiny fists were encased in small white mittens that the midwife had said were important because babies sometimes scratched themselves. If his fingernails needed trimming, Birdie must very gently bite them with her teeth.

'Don't cut them with scissors until he's at least two years old or they'll grow with a sharp edge.'

Birdie thought of the letter her mother had sent her after his birth. A great long list of things she must and mustn't do with a baby. In it she had given her the same advice about the baby's fingernails, except she had warned that cutting a baby's nails with scissors meant he would grow up to be a thief. Charles had laughed at the idea of it.

He really was a lovely boy. So docile and sweet-natured. He rarely cried and Charles absolutely adored him. That alone filled her heart with a deep, warm joy.

She supposed that the couple who had adopted her daughter must love her very much too.

Kay and Framsden. Her daughter and son. Kay was lucky. She had two mothers. Or was that unlucky? Twice the amount of problems that mothers could bring?

It was an odd kind of sorrow she felt over Kay. An itch, like the sense of frustration that comes from wanting something a little out of reach. With every passing hour, day, week, her daughter grew and changed yet Birdie remembered her only as a new baby. That's how she would stay in her memories for ever.

Nellie looked cheerful when she got down from the trap. She was wearing a pair of brown flannel slacks and a red-checked shirt. Birdie had never seen her in trousers. Her tall figure was just right for them. Life by the sea obviously suited her.

Birdie looked at the tea tray and the neat triangles of meat-paste sandwiches. There was a vase of cornflowers on the table. She remembered her mother didn't like flowers indoors. Quickly she ran into the kitchen and tipped the water down the sink, the flowers into the bin. She felt diminished, childishly trying to please her mother like this.

'Birdie!' said Uncle George when he stepped into the hall and she came out to meet them both. 'How's my darling girl? Where is he then? Let's see him! Where's our little lad?'

Uncle George gave her a bear hug and Birdie kissed his cheek.

'He's sleeping for the moment.'

'Babies are at their best when they are asleep,' said her mother. 'Are you going to bring him down?'

She looked so pleased, Birdie almost weakened.

'Not yet,' she said firmly. They'd have tea and then she'd get him. She had a routine and she had to keep to it. The baby had to sleep for at least another half-hour.

'Quite right,' said Uncle George. 'Mother's absolutely right.'

'Yes,' said her mother. 'Of course. Yes, let him sleep.'

They sat in the living room and her mother laid a brown paper bag on the low coffee table. Inside was a blue crocheted jacket for the baby.

'Nellie made it herself,' said George.

'I'm no good at crocheting. I don't really have the patience for it. It was something to do in the evenings while George listened to the wireless.'

'Nell, don't be modest,' said Uncle George. 'Have you seen the little buttons, Birdie? She spent ages making it for him. Lucky kid to have a grandmother like Nell.'

Birdie's mother shook her head.

'George, stop it. You know I've got two left thumbs. It's probably too small for him anyway. I made it months ago.'

The clock on the mantelpiece ticked loudly, and Birdie knew they were both waiting for the baby to be brought downstairs. Though there was still ten minutes to go before she should wake Framsden, Birdie gave in and went to get him.

'Is this my grandson?' her mother asked as she came downstairs with him. She lifted her hands, cupping them as if she were already holding the child.

Nellie took the child in her big strong hands.

'I have him safe,' she said, though she looked nervous. 'Don't worry. There. Now, shall we go outside? I want to show my grandson the orchard. I kept bees. Did I tell you, George?'

Birdie and George followed her mother out of the house and across the orchard. Then her mother took the path down towards the river.

'It's a shame your father isn't here to see the little fellow,' said George.

'Did you never want children, Uncle George?' she asked as they walked towards the river. 'I mean, I just don't know why you never married and had a family?'

'What a question!' said George. The high colour in his cheeks darkened and he quickened his pace, stumbling over the uneven ground.

'I'm sorry. I shouldn't have . . .'

'No, no, quite all right. I was always a bachelor, I'm afraid. Not now of course. Now I've got a wife, and I'm lucky to have her. Nellie and you are my family, Birdie. You're very special to me.

Like a daughter.' He began to hurry away. 'Nellie? Nellie, wait up!'

They reached her mother, and the three of them sat on the grass with Framsden between them. Birdie watched her mother and Uncle George cooing over the baby. She regretted having spoken to her uncle like she had. She should not have been so personal. The poor man had been mortified.

It was just as Aunt Vivian had said it would be. She had given up her daughter and nobody would ever know. And if, like her mother, they did know, it was clear they would never speak of it.

Aunt Vivian came a week later. She brought a hand-stitched christening gown she had made herself. A soft cotton gown with lace at the collar and cuffs, and pin pleats on the shoulders, embroidered white swans along the hem. Birdie folded it in her lap and sat smoothing the fabric.

'Did you like living here?' she asked. 'When you were a child, I mean? I saw Rose's gravestone in the churchyard the other day. I liked the inscription. *When you pass through the waters, I will be with you.* And my grandparents' headstones too. It's strange for me to come here from London and find I have family already in the churchyard.'

'Nellie and I had promised Rose we'd stay together, but so much happened to us after her death. Now you are here, I think Rose would have been pleased. We didn't even have the money to give her a proper funeral, you know. It was Mrs Langham who paid for everything. She was a good friend of your mother's. Mrs Langham was the one who gave Mother and Rose the cottage rent-free after Father died. I don't remember our parents, but Rose loved them. Their ghosts were very present in our childhood. It must be fate that brought you here, Birdie.'

'And what was Rose like? Ma doesn't like to talk about her, I think.'

'She was harsh but fair.'

'Can I ask you something?'

'Yes?'

'I know you can't tell me the names of the people who took my daughter. I know that, but can you tell me where she went? Just so that I can imagine her somewhere.'

'Rose never married,' said her aunt, as if she had not heard her. 'That was our fault. She dedicated herself to us.' She was looking intently at Framsden. 'I do think women need to be married. Whether it's for love or companionship . . .'

'My daughter.'

'Did I tell you I spoke to Matilda on the telephone the other day? She sends her regards. She has a baby son. A little lad called Andrew.'

'And my daughter?'

'You don't have a daughter.'

'I just need to know where she is.'

'Birdie, you cannot do this. I can tell you that the child went to a couple near here. They were grateful to you. I can't tell you more than that.'

'Thank you,' said Birdie softly, gently, grateful to her aunt. Hoping she could stop now with her wondering and questions.

Birdie stood in the nursery, looking out of the window. Her aunt was in the orchard, by the old railway wagon. Had it been cruel, forcing her to talk about it? She had not wanted details. Just something to help her when she imagined the little girl. Now she could think of her growing up somewhere nearby, a house somewhere in this wide landscape. There was so much space here. Huge skies and open fields, deep ditches, flint and stone churches and dispersed farmhouses. Her daughter would be part of this place. She saw her in her mind, a small blonde child running through cornfields, stopping to wait for the shadowy couple who walked behind her.

She turned to look at Framsden sleeping in his Moses basket, and carefully picked him up. She pressed her face to the window. In the orchard her aunt was picking cornflowers. She headed towards the river with armfuls of blue. Then she slipped out of view.

Birdie would tell her son he had a sister when he was twenty. Just before he reached adulthood. It sounded like the silly kind of promise made in a fairy tale, but she believed he should know. Charles too should know. But not yet. Let them get through Framsden's childhood first. By then she and Charles would have a large family. Large enough that one more child would not be all that remarkable.

After her aunt went home, Birdie took Framsden down to the water to watch the fish. Caught in the reeds were blue cornflowers. Vivian had thrown them in the river. They were beautiful, slowly sinking into the waters. She sat down on the grassy bank and made daisy chains and threw them in the water too.

They celebrated Framsden's first birthday with an iced cake and sandwiches. Charles, Connie and Judith, and Kathleen with her new son James and her daughter Ella. Birdie had found it easier not to invite her mother or her aunt. She had her own life now. She could not avoid laying the blame for what had happened on them. They could have helped her keep her child, but they had been ashamed and acted accordingly. She knew she was cruel, but really it was easier this way.

Kathleen's children danced around her legs. They had pearly pink fingernails and soft, pale faces. Both had milky-blond hair, but Ella had brown eyes and would grow out of her blondeness in time, whereas James's eyes were blue and one look at his freckled skin was enough for Birdie to know he would always be fair.

Connie's little girl, Judith, was a bright, dark-haired little toddler with big wide eyes framed by a straight fringe. She was strong-willed like her mother and sure of herself. Poor Framsden was always crying because she liked to take his toys away from him. They all stood around the kitchen table singing 'Happy Birthday' to Framsden.

Ella pulled on Birdie's skirt, and she lifted the smiling little girl into her arms.

Birdie held her tightly, the child's smock dress scrunched up around her chubby legs. Dear, sweet little Ella Hubbard. She was the same age Birdie's daughter would be and such an adoring infant. The sun poured in through the open back door. The table was covered with plates of sandwiches and bowls of jelly that Birdie had been preparing all afternoon. Green and pink balloons hung from the ceiling, bumping back and forth in the breeze.

Connie had a new Box Brownie and insisted on taking a photograph.

'Come on, Charles,' she said, gathering them together. 'Let's get you in the picture too.'

Framsden's babyish fingers were glossy with cake crumbs and butter icing. He sat in his high chair and grabbed Ella's leg as Birdie stood over him. She pushed his hand away, telling him to be a good boy. Ella leaned towards Framsden and mimicked her, pushing him away too. They all laughed. Birdie gave Ella a kiss and then bent to kiss her son. It felt like things were getting easier after all.

Two years later, in 1946, Birdie thought she might be expecting another baby. Her periods were late and she waited, ticking off each day. On the ninth day she told Charles, and they grinned at each other. They sat on the verandah and discussed names. Birdie liked Rose. Charles liked Gillian. They were sure they would have a girl this time.

Birdie was in the dairy, milking the cows, when she felt a deep, cramping ache spreading across her back and between her legs. She knew there was nothing to be done. She went to bed in tears, holding a hot-water bottle.

Charles refilled the hot-water bottle for her when it went cold. He picked cornflowers that flowered in the orchard, putting them in a vase in their bedroom. When Birdie refused to leave her bed, he took Framsden over to Connie's house. The boy stayed for a week until Birdie felt strong enough to go and get him back.

Framsden and Judith were playing in the back garden with a red tin bucket and spade in a sand pit.

'I had flu,' she said, though she knew Connie had been told.

Framsden saw her and burst into tears.

'He's missed you,' said Connie. 'He needs you, Birdie. Don't think of what might have been. Think of what you've got. That's what I do, and some days I even manage to feel lucky.'

'You go and enjoy yourself,' said Charles. A month had passed and he thought she needed to get out and see her friends. Connie came by on her bicycle, asking her to go over to Kathleen's. They were jam making together. Charles lifted Framsden into his arms, where the boy sat happily. He was three years old and stocky, with his father's straight nose and long-lashed hazel eyes. A pudgy little boy who wasn't quick to smile, but when he did, his whole face lit up. He had a way of nodding at things, as if he was taking his time to add up what might be said on different matters.

Birdie and Connie rode their bicycles up the farm track towards the village. They rode down empty lanes, on the slight downhill incline to Ark Farm. Dog roses scrambled through the trees and spikes of foxglove flowers reached as high as their shoulders. The hedgerows on the back road were filled with tall young trees forming a tunnel of green-flecked light overhead. Through this leafy canopy, Birdie could see Ark Farm. It had been pebble-dashed during the war and painted a pale pink. There was a narrow gravel drive and two dark holly trees either side of the front door. The lawns in front of the house were silky green and dotted with white daisies.

'Marvellous, isn't it?' said Connie, looking at the house. 'But

Kathleen's not as smart as you think. She's had voice training, you know. She was Norman's secretary. That's how they met.'

Three overweight black spaniels ambled across the grass, wagging stumpy tails. They pressed their soft mouths to Birdie's hands as she stooped to pat their heads. The dogs ran away as they walked across the gravel drive to the front door of the house. Only the eldest of the dogs, greying at the muzzle, with a sagging body and long, ugly, improper pink nipples that Birdie tried not to look at, stayed loyally beside her.

'Why, it's our Pearly Queen,' Norman said, opening the door. 'And Connie. Come on in. Her ladyship is expecting you.'

Kathleen's voice drifted through the house. 'Is that you, Connie? Birdie? Come on through. Ignore Norman. He thinks he is being funny.'

They stepped into the kitchen. It was the nicest room in the house, Birdie thought. The other rooms were neat and unlived in, the floors shone and the furniture gleamed, but it was in here, this room with its long refectory table and colourful rosettes won at horse shows pinned on the walls, that Kathleen spent her time. A large orange cat was curled up on a chair. There was a sweet smell of sugar and the sharp tang of cooking blackcurrants.

Kathleen stood with a wooden spoon in her hand, a flowered apron over riding trousers and a navy-blue jersey. In a big copper pot, a purple-coloured jam boiled and bubbled on the stove.

'The children are both having their afternoon nap,' she said. 'I could be out walking or riding, but instead here I am, being the perfect wife.'

Norman came in behind them, asking Kathleen where his cigarettes were. He wore a cardigan and a striped shirt with a narrow tie, wide trousers and polished brown brogues. He had bright blue eyes and a boyish smile. Birdie felt herself smiling too.

'You are always the perfect wife, my dear,' he said.

Kathleen rolled her eyes. She picked up a packet and handed it to him.

'So, how's the gang?' Kathleen asked as he shut the door. 'Cup of tea? Do you want to make it, Birdie? Only I'm watching this jam like a hawk in case it begins to burn.'

Birdie boiled water, gathering cups and the teapot, reaching up on the shelf for the tin of black tea. Kathleen had a way of expecting people to do whatever she asked. Connie was putting out jam jars. Kathleen said Norman was furious with her because she'd sacked their nanny. Now they had to find somebody else.

'I can have the children,' said Birdie. 'I'd be glad to.'

'Would you?'

'Of course,' she heard herself say. 'Framsden would be pleased to have friends to play with.'

'Wonderful. I'll take you up on that. And what about the new job?' Kathleen asked Connie. 'Do you enjoy it? I suppose you must know everything about us all in this village, working for the doctor.'

'It's good to have a bit of work. The pay's not great, but I only do three days a week. When Judith's older I'm going to train to be a nurse. And I've put my name down for one of the new council houses being built in the village. Married couples will have first pick, of course. Unmarried mothers don't count for much, according to this government.'

Kathleen said that she hoped council housing wasn't going to have a bad effect on the village. All this new building was just the kind of thing that was destroying country life. Connie shook her head.

'I'd like a council house. And there's a housing shortage, you know. People need new homes.'

Kathleen tutted. 'Well, I'm only going on what Norman says. I don't know anything about it. He thinks the countryside is under attack from urban planning and property developers.' She peered into the copper pan. 'And I think this jam is done.'

Kathleen carefully ladled out the hot jam, and Connie put waxed paper over the full jars. When they'd finished, Kathleen refilled their teacups and they took them outside onto the red-brick terrace.

The lawns were smooth and striped, and a rose arbour covered in yellow blooms gave the place an elegant look. Ella came pelting across the grass, her smocked dress billowing, James not far behind her.

'Daddy's angry,' announced James grandly in his high-pitched three-year-old's voice. Norman came across the lawn, yelling that the little menaces had pulled all the books off the bookshelves. Why could Kathleen not keep an eye on them?

'I'm going out,' he said, as if the horror of having children was forcing him from his own home. He was off to the Conservative club in town to get away from this bloody madhouse. He would have drinks with a couple of the chaps and wouldn't be home until late.

Kathleen began deadheading a red geranium in a terracotta pot, with quick deft pinches, putting the papery petals in her apron pocket.

'I should go,' said Connie, getting up.

'You don't have to.'

'Me too,' said Birdie.

'I can't believe you are deserting me,' said Kathleen crossly. 'Well, never mind. At least take some jars of jam with you.'

They went into the kitchen, and with jars of jam in their hands Kathleen insisted they take a look at what the children had done.

'Norman says I have let myself go since I had James,' she said, pushing open the door to the study. On the floor were piles of books and she began to pick them up. 'I know I should make more of an effort, but what's the point? If I spend my days polishing up my good points, wearing a dress and doing my hair, then it just makes me feel worse when he looks at other women. And he does. I can't see why I should lie to protect him. At least in my jodhpurs and old sweater I can still pretend that if I made an effort, it might change him. For heaven's sake, he actually told me the other day that I should dress Ella better. You know, ribbons in her hair, like a dolly.'

'I want a ribbon,' said Ella loudly. 'I want a new dolly and a ribbon.'

James crept round Birdie's legs and ran to his mother.

'Naughty!' he yelled, kicking a book.

'Exactly,' said Kathleen. 'What am I to do with you?'

'Throw us in the river and drown us like kittens!' yelled Ella, and Kathleen scooped her daughter into her arms.

'Ding dong bell,' she sang, turning in circles with her children. Birdie and Connie began to laugh too, all of them shaking off the embarrassment they had felt over Norman's anger. The women cleared up the books and the children sang, 'Ding dong bell, pussy's in the well,' over and over. Birdie sang with them, and then Kathleen insisted she sit at the piano, a mahogany baby grand in the drawing room, and play for them.

Birdie played nursery rhymes she had learned as a girl, hitting a few wrong notes every now and then, making a joke of it as her uncle had done whenever she made mistakes. 'You're a natural,' George had said, sat beside her at the pub's upright piano, teaching her to play 'Little Boy Blue'. She'd been five years old. Her mother and father had come into the bar to listen to her.

'Don't go,' Ella said to Birdie at the back door, as she left. The child's face was flushed from dancing.

'I'll come again,' said Birdie, smiling. She touched the child's head. 'And when I do, I'll bring you a present. What would you like?'

The girl giggled. 'I don't know. I'll ask Mummy.'

'I tell you what,' said Birdie. 'I'll bring you a red velvet ribbon for your hair.'

How nice it was to see the pleasure on the child's face.

There was a letter waiting for Birdie when she got home. She put it on the mantelpiece and started peeling potatoes for the evening meal. After tea, she washed Framsden in the kitchen sink, sitting him naked on the draining board with his feet in a tub of warm water.

'Pack up your troubles in your old kit bag,' she sang as she dried him and dressed him in pyjamas. Sometimes she wondered at her younger self, the girl who had been so sure she would be a singer in a jazz band. What a silly dream that had been. She bent to do up his buttons and Framsden wriggled away from her, laughing and giggling. She chased him up the stairs to his bedroom, still singing to him, and he bounded onto his bed. It was *Rupert Bear* at the moment. That's all he wanted, so the book was got out and the story read. She kissed him on the forehead and tucked him in.

Afterwards she sat on the top stair of the landing and opened the letter. It was from Aunt Lydia, who was in a home for the aged these days.

I will tell you straight, Birdie. Your father is not my brother Henry. It is George. You have a right to know. My husband deceived me for years and now my son, my only remaining son, has put me away in this place where they serve salt on the porridge in the mornings. I ask for cream and they pretend not to hear me. I am lonely and your mother, who visits twice a week, does not stay long. Do not tell her I wrote to you. I am afraid she and Malcolm would be angry with me. I write because I know how well you and Roger got along. He always thought you should know the truth.

Birdie joined Charles on the verandah and shared a cigarette with him. Slowly the evening sky deepened to black. The fences and trees turned to charcoal silhouettes, smudged and vague, finally disappearing into a uniform darkness. The poplars rustled and shook down by the river. She thought of her mother and her aunt living here. Of how quiet their lives must have been. She and Roger had never been friends. Where did Aunt Lydia get that idea from?

'Kathleen has sacked her nanny,' she said. 'I've offered to have the children for her.'

'I heard Norman had a bit of a liking for the girl.'

'The nanny?'

'Yes. Fool of a man.' Charles swung the kitchen door open and they went inside.

'Who was your letter from?'

'Aunt Lydia.' She had thrown the letter away. 'It was nothing. I think she's gone a bit funny in the head.'

In bed, Birdie lay curled against Charles's back. Downstairs, the jars of jam gleamed in the cupboard. They were perfect, as perfect as Kathleen's life, if you didn't know her. The clock in the room below chimed the hour. Outside, the wind rattled the windows. Birdie imagined the river, its dark waters winding past the house.

She would not talk of the letter to Charles. It was too shameful. Her mother and George betraying her poor father, all under the same roof. For the sake of her father, she would keep this secret.

Pa had been a difficult man, but he had not deserved this. How she had loved him! As a child she had been moved to tears by her father's regular tantrums of melancholy, his cheeks red as apples, the dreadful scars all livid and damp. His heavy eyes had reminded her of Jesus's martyred expression in her Sunday-school colour-illustrated Bible. Her young heart had been swollen with feeling for him. A man crying? Wasn't that the worst thing a child could see? Tears were only for women and babies, surely. Her father's misery had a religious purity to it that she had worshipped. She had admired his suffering. When she got older, a distaste for his tears and melodrama crept into her feelings. She distanced herself from him, scenting only male weakness where before she had seen strength. Now, in light of Aunt Lydia's letter, she felt wounded and angry on her father's behalf.

She would shut her mother and George out of her life. They were liars. She did not need them.

Charles turned over and kissed her. She pulled him to her.

Maybe this would be the time she conceived. Another baby was what she wanted. A daughter to replace the one she had given up. She didn't need her mother or her uncle. Birdie threw herself into lovemaking with a forcefulness that surprised them both.

Twenty

Vivian served teas and scones to an afternoon crowd in the dining room of her guest house. Her feet ached, and she thought she could do with a cup of something herself. Through the steamed-up windows she could see it was still raining outside. A silvery, wet kind of day that was bound to bring more customers in. She was putting down a tray of tea things when she saw Matilda Dunn – Vivian could never remember her married name – standing by the door. She had a baby in her arms, wearing a little wool jacket with a pointed hood. Three boys in shorts stood beside her. They all looked like Colin: freckled, ginger hair, watery blue eyes. Their macintoshes were dark with rain, and their bare legs mottled red from the cold.

'I've left him,' said Matilda.

'Go on into the kitchen,' Vivian told her, shooing them down the hall. 'Get the boys something to eat. You know where everything is.'

Vivian came back into the kitchen after she'd closed up for the day and found the boys sitting at the table eating bread and jam, Matilda feeding the baby by the stove. Around them it looked like sale day at Woolworths. There was a great heap of white and blue crockery by the sink, and cups and saucers littered the table.

'I'll have a bit of a clear-up for you,' said Matilda. 'Don't you have a maid any more?'

'Not for a while, no. I must admit, I get behind with the washing-up on rainy days. That's when I am always at my busiest with customers.'

'It'll be like old times,' said Matilda, getting up. 'I'll have this place looking shipshape in no time. Andrew? Take your brother.'

Andrew scraped his chair back and got to his feet, taking the baby with the suffering air of someone being asked to put their arms in a straitjacket.

Vivian watched Matilda bustling around the kitchen. Over the years, quite a few women had stayed with her and helped out in the kitchen in return for their keep. The last, a sharp-eyed girl called Minnie, a peroxide blonde with a tatty fur coat, six months pregnant and incapable of making toast without burning it, had left in the night, taking a whole drawerful of Vivian's satin bloomers and the petty-cash tin. She'd had the locks changed after the girl left. She might be soft-hearted, but she wasn't stupid.

For a long time now, since she had lost contact with Dr Harding, Vivian had been helping women. Ordinary women. Most of them were not like Minnie. Most were grateful to have somewhere safe to stay. She wasn't sure how the word had got around, but somehow her guest house had become known as a place of shelter. Women came to her with infants in tow. Some came with suitcases. Others appeared empty-handed, shivering at her door, coatless, hatless, looking anxiously over their shoulders. The only rule was that no men were allowed.

She offered them a room for a few days or a few weeks, until they were ready to move on. If the women were frightened of being seen, then they worked in the kitchen. If not, they put on a white apron and a white mob cap and helped in the tea room.

Some left without saying goodbye. They were the ones who arrived coatless. They moved like eels in deep water, slipping from one shadowy place to the next. One minute they were there, the next they had gone, leaving a small pile of coins on the table or a stack of clean ironing on the ironing board in thanks. They were the ones Vivian thought about the longest. The ones who wanted to be invisible. They made her heart ache most, reminding her of herself as a young woman, the intense fear she had experienced, giving birth alone.

'And Birdie?' asked Matilda. 'How's she getting on? I always knew Charles Bell had a thing for her.'

There was still a trace of jealousy in her voice. Who could blame her? It had been clear that Charles had fallen in love with Birdie the first day he saw her. Matilda had not been blind to that. Was that why she had married Colin? Simply because he had wanted her and Charles had not?

'Birdie is very well. Her son, Framsden, is a lovely boy.'

'Just the one? That's sensible. Lucky her. Colin only has to look at me and another baby comes along. I s'pose you see a lot of Birdie?'

Vivian remembered that Matilda knew about Birdie's adopted baby. She hoped she wouldn't mention it.

'Not as often as I'd like to. There's no time for anything these days.'

They listened to the boys running about upstairs, slamming doors, jumping on the beds, yelling and whooping.

Matilda said she'd go and stop them. Vivian shook her head. They were just being boys. Let them play. What harm could they do?

'Quite a lot,' said Matilda, sighing. 'You're lucky you never had kids, Mrs Stewart. Luckier than you can imagine.'

She called the boys downstairs to go and see if her father was home yet.

Matilda's father, Stan, had known Mrs Stewart on and off for years. It had always seemed to him a tragedy that she had never remarried after her husband's death at the end of the first war. Women like Mrs Stewart, with a big house and ladylike manners, didn't usually stay widows for long. Stan too was on his own. He'd retired from his job as a lathe worker and did odd jobs and window cleaning to earn himself beer money these days.

'You go and see her, Dad,' urged Matilda. 'That house is falling down round her ears. She needs a man about the place.'

He got a haircut at the barber's, polished his work boots and put on a suit and tie. Then he went to ask if the widow needed a hand around the place.

She paid him to turn the vegetable gardens back into lawns and to fix a leaking tap. There was years of leaf mould in the gutters, and he cleaned them out and scrubbed the green-stained wall at the back of the house where the water butts overflowed and silvery mosquito larvae flourished. He found it romantic, this neglected old house, the lonely lady within it, his own capacity to help her. Vivian Stewart's need of him was welcome. The house needed him too.

'Would you like to take a drive in the country?' she asked him one morning. It was raining heavily. They stood in the garage watching a blackbird taking a bath in a puddle on the bright green lawn. Vivian wore a grey dress with a full skirt, a pattern of red cherries at the hem and the cuffs. Her figure was trim for a woman of her age. He tried to imagine her as a young girl. He thought she must have been beautiful once. Water ran noisily through the cleaned gutters. He said he had planned to work in the garden. She handed him her car keys, suggesting he weed the flower beds on a drier day.

The tree-lined driveway was just as Vivian remembered it. A sweeping line of lime trees either side of a rutted gravel driveway leading to the big red-brick house. A chain was hung across the entrance, and she got out and saw it was padlocked. The driveway was at least half a mile long. They set off on foot. The rain had eased off, and clouds chased each other across a damp blue sky. The meadows, grazed by white cattle with black eyes and black-tipped horns, gleamed in the sunlight.

They stopped halfway down the drive and sat on an old wooden bench under a tree. There was a brass plaque on the back of the bench commemorating a Captain Williams of the Suffolk Regiment, '14th March 1918, Age 42'.

He'd have been a relative, she supposed.

The house was shut up. A large pile of bricks was outside the front door, along with a few piles of sand and a cement mixer. The green lawns in front of the house were bright with daisies. A yellow rose bloomed over the door. The rose beds had been freshly weeded, and a large concrete car park had been laid to one side of the house.

Stan walked off whistling, peering in the shuttered-up windows. Vivian had no clear understanding of why she had come, except that she needed to see if Birdie's daughter was still here.

'It's going to be a home for the aged,' said Stan, coming towards her from the other side of the building. 'There's some workmen out back. They said the place has been empty for years.'

It was a relief really. What on earth would she have done if the daughter had been the one to open the door?

As they drove away, Stan asked her what she had wanted to find at the house. Vivian didn't reply. What was it she wanted? Some kind of forgiveness, she supposed. But surely not from the family who had once lived in Hymes Court? She wondered what life might be like now for Birdie's daughter. What it must have been like to have grown up in that big house. To walk in the footsteps of that old family, thinking she belonged to them, loved by people who had buried all knowledge of her origins.

She looked at Stan. His face was deeply lined. He limped slightly. He thought he had found a home with her. She recognized waifs and strays very quickly these days. Their watchful ways, their desire to belong somewhere. The patience of their neediness. Stan thought her a good woman. People said it in town too. The generous widow at the old guest house.

Every day she thought about Joe Ferier. Over the years she had developed a pure sense of the power and endurance of love. Stan, she could see, was imagining a kind of love between them. And why not? He was a caring, careful kind of man. But he was not Joe. Perhaps love was not what she desired any more in any case.

Forgiveness was surely what she craved. And only Nellie and Birdie could give her that.

Nellie liked the feeling of the beach under her feet. She wore black plimsolls, but they were thin and allowed her to feel like she was barefoot. She began to jog a little and then run. She felt liberated from her age as she took long strides, skipping over shallow creeks of water. Women of her age – she was sixty-three years old now – didn't run. Her legs were still good though. Long and lean and strong-looking. She had no varicose veins and she put it down to exercise. Her legs were her vanity. She was proud of them.

The tide was an early one, and a hazy mist hung over the beach. She had already lost sight of George, who stood somewhere on the sands waiting for her with a towel, her clothes, a blanket and a flask of hot tea. For several years now this had been their routine. Rising early and going down to the sea.

The sound of the waves was delicious, a rushing and then a great pulling back, like a thirsty giant taking huge gulps of water and then sighing with delight. A foamy wave rushed towards her. Her legs were engulfed up to the knees, the sands pulled and sucked at her feet. She ran on, into the waves, up to her waist, her chest, and then, head down, she dived.

Nellie swam in a concentrated way, out to a buoy that marked a shallow channel for yachts and boats to avoid, and then back to the beach. It would take her forty minutes if she swam without stopping. An hour if she decided to tread water a while.

It was not like river swimming. In a river, fish darted away and birds saw you and took flight. The sea just rolled on and on, taking everything in its embrace. The current ran in different directions, depending on which side of the high tide she was. On an incoming tide, the current ran from west to east, but on an outgoing tide it went the other way. One of the swimming-club members, an ex-navy man, had explained it to her, citing the pull of the moon and how the water in the English Channel was connected to the Atlantic Ocean. 'Cause and effect,' he had said. 'Nothing happens in isolation.' All she had understood in his talk was that the water was dangerous. You could never trust the sea.

She swam on. Water got into her goggles and made her eyes sting. Even though she wore a thick black swim cap, the water seeped under it and turned her hair sticky with salt. She had mentioned it to Vivian in a letter, and her sister had written back suggesting beer and an egg massaged into the ends. That had helped a bit. She'd also suggested olive oil. Nellie had got some from the chemist, but it made her hair very thin-looking and was difficult to wash out. She didn't like her hair much these days in any case.

Vivian still wrote long letters about her cats, her housekeeping, the latest new cleaning product she was using. Nellie sent postcards with short messages. *Joined a swimming club. The Sea Beavers. Not the oldest one there either!*

She'd sent her sister the hagstone recently. It had been sitting on a saucer between the African violets on her windowsill, and George had accidently knocked it out of the window. Nellie found it quite by chance, almost invisible in the grass. She'd been shocked to think she might have lost it for good, and decided to send it to Vivian.

Vivian's last letter had thanked her for the stone – she had it safe in her jewellery box. Her main news was that she'd taken Framsden out for tea. Vivian said he was a nice boy and the image of his father. A rather quiet eleven-year-old who was keen on fishing and had a dreamy way about him. Nellie told George, who went out and bought a book on fly fishing to send to the boy.

Let Birdie get on with her own life. That's what Nellie told George whenever he expressed sadness over the lack of contact they had with her and Framsden. 'Do you think Charles doesn't like us?' George had asked her once, the high colour in his cheeks intensifying. He had never spoken to Birdie about it directly, and

Nellie would have told him not to. She was afraid Birdie might speak about the child she gave up.

'A love child,' George had called Birdie when she was born. 'A love child is special.'

Birdie must remain special in his eyes. Perhaps she should have been honest with him when Birdie had told her she didn't know the father of the child, but it was too late for confessions now. If this break between mother and daughter was what it took to keep Birdie special in George's eyes, then that's how it would be.

They often visited Malcolm with his two little boys. That made George happy. And Nellie saw Lydia once a month, something George found too difficult himself. He could not bear to see how diminished she had become. She did not recognize anybody from her family these days. She only remembered Roger and became upset if Nellie said he was dead.

George and Nellie had steady routines. They spent Saturday evenings at their local, a pub where Nellie sat in the snug and had a bottle of milk stout with a couple of old girls. Their next-door neighbour and his wife sometimes went with them. Jakey and Muriel both liked a drink. If George was in the mood and the crowd in the bar was older people – the younger folk tended to want music from the jukebox in the corner – George played the upright piano and they had a singalong like the old days.

Oh yes, they had plenty to do. The bungalow had a back garden where Nellie kept a couple of hens and a vegetable patch, and she still made jam every summer, though she gave most of it away. She and George liked going to the pictures. They saw a lot of westerns, mostly. And they both liked walking on the beach.

The buoy was in sight. The water moved differently around it, slapping at its sides as if the big green metal marker was a mosquito that needed smacking away. If she got too close to it, the waves would smack at her too. She trod water and then began her swim back to shore.

She had been with the swimming club for a year before she

decided to leave and swim on her own. She didn't really like being part of a club. She swam because she could be alone in the water. If she needed company, she had George. She imagined him on the beach, looking at his watch now, expecting to see her.

The sun was burning off the sea mist and the seafront began to materialize, rows of restaurants and shops and then houses, climbing up the hills, white with red roofs. The castle, on the top of a grassy hill, stood out against the sky. And there on the beach was a figure, waiting.

She thought of Anna Moats and the charm she had given her to protect her heart. The glass bottle they had floated down the river. A charm to shut her heart up tight like a walnut in its shell. Nellie had tried hard to keep that woody shell closed all her life and had never quite succeeded.

'Nellie!' called George as she strode out of the water. He looked relieved to see her. 'You're ten minutes over time, love! I thought a sea monster had got hold of you.'

He rubbed her shoulders with the towel. She pulled her bathing cap off and her hair stuck out stiffly.

'The only monster out there is me,' she said cheerfully.

The summer of 1954 was hot and humid, and Vivian and Stan drove to the East Anglian coast every Sunday, looking for sea breezes and freshness away from the heat of town. Down on the pebble beach, Stan took off his shoes and rolled his trouser legs up. He paddled in the waves and did a knock-kneed dance in the shallows. Vivian stood on the pavement above the beach, her orange fox-fur collar flapping in the breeze. She held her hat with one hand to stop it blowing away and watched Stan, sunlight warming her face, laughing at his antics.

In the afternoon they sat in striped deckchairs, looking at the sea and the families on the beach, small children running to and fro, seagulls circling in the thermals. The blue sky was full of wispy white clouds.

On the changing tide, they walked to the harbour and saw the shrimp boats coming in, the shrimps being sorted and boiled up on deck. A seaplane landed on the water, and a crowd gathered to watch it. Barefoot young women in colourful cotton dresses walked by, the sea breeze blowing their long hair, pressing their full skirts against their legs. Vivian remarked on the brightness of the light. The wide skies. She might like to live by the sea one day.

'Would you ever consider marrying again?' asked Stan.

She pretended not to hear him, pointing out instead the black cormorants on the rocks.

Why would she marry again? At sixty-four she was far too old to hope for children now. Her body had ceased to be fertile a long time ago, and thankfully she had lost the awful longing for a baby that had plagued her younger years. But her sense of romance had not diminished. She knew she was a foolish old woman, but all her life she had been waiting for Joe Ferier to return. That hope was as woven into her body as the wrinkles and lines that etched her face now. She had been the mother of his child. She'd had his daughter. She considered herself his wife.

The weeks passed pleasantly with Stan. He put a Formica breakfast bar in the kitchen for her, and a new metal sink. In the evenings they tended to stay in their own rooms. Stan often listened to the wireless and she heard it drifting through the house, the distant sound of it like a conversation going on. Several times she stood at the bottom of the stairs listening, thinking perhaps Stan had come back from the pub and brought people with him.

Vivian climbed the stairs, looking in on the bathroom. There were his shaving brushes and razors. He'd left a towel on the floor. She picked it up and folded it over the bath. Then she changed her mind and dropped it on the floor. She would not look after him. She was not his wife. She would not pick up after him.

'Vivian?' Stan stood at the door to his room. He wore black

trousers and a white vest, his braces hanging around his hips. He looked like he had been sleeping. He opened the door wider. 'About what I said. Marriage? I meant it. I swear you've got an old man feeling like a young 'un again.'

'Oh, Stan, no,' she said. The house creaked. The clock in the hall downstairs struck the hour. She saw the anxiety in his eyes. 'I was in love once, and perhaps that was enough for me.'

'I reckon you're the lucky one then,' he said, leaning against the doorpost, his face earnest and sad. 'I was too busy having a good time to think about love. And now here I am, finally found the girl of my dreams, and I'm a couple of decades too late.'

They spent hours in the garden together that summer. They put in new flower beds and Stan pruned the apple tree and planted raspberry canes, wanting to taste the raspberry blancmange Vivian had told him she used to make as a young woman in the cottage by the river.

When she looked up from weeding one day, catching sight of him putting down slug pellets, she felt dizzy with confusion, imagining not this town garden with its high brick wall and the sound of traffic beyond it, but a garden lost in time. A childhood miles from here with Rose, tall and lanky as a man, bent over, picking pea pods, and a brown-haired girl, stubborn, big-hearted Nellie, working beside her. She felt old and tearful suddenly. Why had she wasted all her years on a man she would never see again?

She'd imagined a life for Joe Ferier. She had envisaged him travelling the world, drawing, painting, that swaggering walk of his, crossing continents and oceans. Nobody sensible spent their life missing a man, did they? Yet she had, and she found solace in this. She could not change how she felt.

'Everything all right?' Stan asked, getting stiffly to his feet, taking his hat off, rubbing his head and then replacing the hat. 'Shall I get us a cup of tea, old girl?'

Vivian put her gardening gloves in her lap and watched him walk towards the kitchen, his hand brushing the lavender bushes.

'Thank you,' she murmured, and for just an instant he was Joe Ferier. Handsome Joe, walking away from her in the black hat she remembered so well, striding up the path to the house, to prepare tea for them both.

Twenty-one

White sheets and working overalls danced in the breeze. Birdie's dresses hung beside them, and then Fram's shirts and shorts, socks and vests. She stood back to admire the wet clothes. There was a whole story to them, like a family gathered together. A small gathering, but still a family. She would have liked to be gazing at long lines of girls' and boys' clothes, flapping from pegs like those paper-cut dancing maids she used to make for Ella Hubbard when she was small.

Well, there was still time. Birdie dropped the peg bag into the wash basket. She hadn't given up hope, even after all these years. She shook out the creases in a pair of grey flannel trousers. They were Framsden's. He was eleven years old, a fact that shocked Birdie. It seemed lately that she had no need of calendars and diaries to mark the fast progress of the years. Her time was measured in Framsden's shirtsleeves and shoe sizes. He grew out of both at an alarming rate. His collars got too tight, his shorts too short, his toes pressed against barely worn shoe leather. They bought new shoes so often the woman in Clarks shoe shop in town treated her like an old friend and Charles laughingly threatened to bind his son's feet.

Their boy was sprouting like a beautiful plant in her care. He openly adored her. When he fell over, which was often as he was growing so fast he had a tendency to be clumsy, he brought his wounds to her as if she alone could heal him. She washed grit from grazes and put cooling witch hazel on purple bruises. Only his mother would do.

Birdie understood how Framsden felt when, without warning, he flung his arms around her waist and pressed his face to her skirts. Charles said the boy was getting too old for that kind of behaviour, but Birdie remembered she had felt the same desire when she'd been a child. Unlike Framsden, she had never dared throw her arms around her mother. That generation had not been demonstrative with their children.

The Hubbard children, too, openly adored Birdie. Even Judith, Connie's daughter – always so independent, just like her mother – leaned against Birdie when she read to them. Over the years the four children had crashed happily about the house. They'd stumbled up and down stairs, making dens with blankets and the dining-room chairs. Framsden and James made Airfix aeroplanes with heady-smelling glues and played cowboys and Indians. Ella and Judith spanked their Sarah Jane dolls for wetting themselves, swinging them by their arms at the top of the stairs, then hugging the dolls tightly, all forgiven, proclaiming them their darlings. What kinds of mothers would those girls make one day?

Birdie's life was her son and the children. It was seasons with them. Conkers in autumn, rose-hip syrup and cod-liver oil to see off winter colds. Skating on the river when it froze, the girls in their best coats and red tam-o'-shanters. The pretty ribbons she bought Ella for birthdays and Christmases, a small joke between them over the years. Ella had a box of them.

She squinted up at the blue sky. Bees buzzed around the purple buddleia bushes. The dogs were flat out in the shade, snoring. A pink rose tumbled over the old privy at the bottom of the garden. She'd pick some of the blooms and put a vase of them on the hall table. She went to get a pair of secateurs and a garden trug and saw the Hubbard children swinging into view, the two of them on their bicycles, Ella's blonde hair flying in the sunlight.

She gave them glasses of orange squash and pulled a biscuit tin from the cupboard. This evening she might make them all dinner. Some boiled potatoes and slices of ham and salad and hard-boiled eggs. Then a treat of tinned peaches with Tip Top cream for dessert. Perhaps she would telephone Kathleen and say Ella and James could stay the night. After all, Kathleen was always delighted when she took the children off her hands.

The boys headed off to the barns together, and Birdie took Ella to pick roses. Ella, at fourteen, was too old to play with James and Framsden now. In September she was finally going away to boarding school. Now James was due to start boarding, Kathleen had insisted Ella must go away to school too.

'How is your mother?' Birdie asked.

'She got a new horse yesterday,' said Ella, pulling the petals off a rose.

'Another horse? What a lovely present. Your father is very thoughtful.'

'Oh no. Mummy bought it without asking. Daddy was very angry with her. She used his money without permission. He says she doesn't need another horse when she can't even look after us.'

Birdie cut a pink rose on a long stem and pinched off the thorns and leaves. 'I'm sure he didn't mean that.'

'He did.' Ella's face looked tight and angry. 'He's right. Mummy is bored with looking after us. She prefers her horses. Can I live with you, Mrs Bell? I don't want to go to boarding school.'

'Oh, Ella, my dear girl.'

Birdie thought she might cry. She stood with the roses in the trug, wanting to drop it and pull the girl into her arms – to tell her she didn't belong with Kathleen, in any case. 'We'll put these roses in a vase,' she said, not knowing how to respond, fearing she might voice her dangerous thoughts. 'Chin up. Come on. Let's get your face washed and stop these tears. Your mummy and daddy love you very much, I'm sure.'

In the afternoon, they turned windrows of hay, filling their lungs with the smell of sun-warmed grass. Ella worked with Birdie behind the tractor, tow-headed, her limbs brown against the white cotton of her dress, while the boys chased the farm dogs and found nests of mice in the cut hay. Birdie wondered why Framsden and James delighted in exposing those helpless pink babies. The boys were filled with such quickly changing energies. Depending on their mood, they might carry a nest of mice home in the hope of saving them, or let the farm cats feast upon them. Charles allowed the children to do what they wanted. He said they would only learn justice by being free themselves. A country upbringing would teach them all they needed for adult life.

'Boys,' said Ella to Birdie, as if she knew what Birdie had been thinking. Her voice sounded grown up and she gave Birdie an understanding smile. Birdie smiled back.

At the end of the afternoon, when they were all dusty and tired and Birdie was only thinking about the quantity of sharp thistles that had cut her arms, Charles said they should swim in the river.

Ella wore a red seersucker bathing suit. The boys were skinny in their underpants, hugging themselves as they waded into the cold water. Charles wore a pair of old trousers rolled up to the knees. His farmer's tan cut his lean upper body into shapes. His outstretched arms were russet-tanned to the elbow, his neck a deep V of colour, the rest of his naked torso sunless and pale, his watery shadow spilling over the children as they splashed around him. Birdie sat on the shore, watching them all.

Framsden did a handstand in the water, surfacing in a rush, coughing, wiping his face.

'Did you see me?' he shouted. 'Were my legs straight? Did I do it?'

'Watch me,' Ella yelled, and dived under the water. Her legs swung up, straight, toes pointed. She surfaced, grinning, hands above her head. 'Ta-dah!'

Birdie surprised them then, wading out into the water, swimming to the other bank and then coming back, circling Ella and doing a handstand herself. As the Hubbard children swam round her excitedly, she saw Charles further away in the middle of the river. Framsden was next to him, the two of them treading water. Onlookers, they seemed to Birdie, and she swam to them, aware that she had been disloyal in some way, wondering if they felt this too. She put her arm around Framsden, pretending not to have noticed.

The sun dropped slowly in the sky, but the day was still hot. Dragonflies like emeralds flashed back and forth. Birdie and Ella sat on the bank, rubbing themselves with striped terry towels. In the shallows, Framsden and James held an old pickle jar and a shrimping net on a bamboo cane. Serious as scientists, they captured jet-black beetles, and mottled newts that moved like wet silk ribbons in the water. They held the jar up to the magnifying purity of the sun, fingers splayed on warm glass, squinting at their treasures, then submerged the jar again, watching the river creatures wriggle down into the mud-stirred water.

In the mirage of late afternoon the children appeared softly blurred to Birdie. Lovely dancing limbs and sunburnt faces, freckled shoulders, polished cheekbones, their teeth white in their grinning faces.

Weren't they sweetness itself, these carefree water babies? Birdie looked down the river path and hoped someone might pass by, a stranger, a walker out with a dog. A witness to come upon them; that they might see them and think they were a family, two adults and three children. 'Now, isn't she the spit of her mother,' the stranger might innocently say, comparing Birdie and Ella.

And why not? Over the years there had been too many coincidences. Ella's birthday was the same day as her daughter's. She looked nothing like Kathleen or Norman. Kathleen, when Birdie had asked several times, was vague about the child's birth. She couldn't remember it very well. She hated talking about that kind of thing. Kathleen and Norman had been married for years before they had children. Why shouldn't they have adopted Ella? They had a large house and lived locally. Aunt Vivian had said her baby had gone to a local couple. And yet Birdie's thoughts were madness, surely?

There was a cacophony, and Birdie looked up to see the sky filled with swans. She stood up, shading her eyes from the sun. They landed one after the other on the river. White feathers drifted down as though a dozen pillowcases had been torn apart and shaken out. Birdie and Ella joined Charles and the boys, watching them. There were as many as fifty of the big white birds. They squabbled joyfully, their long necks moving back and forth, their wings beating the air. The orchestra continued as the birds sailed past them. Charles put his arms around Birdie, whispering in her ear.

'You know what they say about a swan chorus like that? If a woman hears the swans calling, she'll be welcoming a new baby in the coming year.'

Birdie stiffened. This was the kind of thing her mother might have come out with. Like suggesting she find a woman who was expecting a baby and borrow her shoes. That if she walked in them for a fortnight, she would be expecting by the end of the month.

Charles hugged her and she relaxed. He had meant no harm. He, too, wanted more children. And he had never blamed her. She agreed with him, she said. The birds were beautiful and there were so many of them it was possible to see why people might believe they heralded some kind of magic.

The swans' calls became distant. Feathers settled on the water. The children watched them drift away and then they too began moving, picking up clothes and towels and dusty sandals. Birdie wished she could hold on to the afternoon. That it might go on for ever.

Next month Ella would be starting boarding school. It would change her. Birdie knew it. She'd be different when she came back. Swimming in a muddy, weed-strewn river would not interest her any more. She would want her own kind: young ladies destined for good middle-class lives. And wasn't that something to be proud of? To strive for better things?

'Do you want to stay over?' she asked Ella and James. 'Shall I telephone your mother and ask if you can?'

She was gratified when the children all cheered together and ran off up the path, towards the house. She had been lucky to have had these years with them all. Lucky to have had Ella for this long.

My daughter, she said to herself, just to hear how it sounded.

Twenty-two

The farmhouse was always dark. Sometimes, coming in from outside in the sun, Framsden believed he had gone blind. Shapes blurred in front of his eyes. Slowly, his sight returned and he stood in the long shard of light that shone through the open door. He could make out the pattern on the lino floor, the wooden dresser with the chipped blue plates, the horse brasses dangling from a beam. The pile of boots and wellingtons by the kitchen door. Newspapers on the table were full of stories about the Suez Crisis. His father talked of that and nothing else at the moment. His mother came into focus at last, her curved shape over the sink where she was peeling potatoes.

'Go and play,' she said, looking over her shoulder, wiping her hands on her apron. 'I've got a million things to do before we leave.'

He studied her a while longer, wondering if he should console her in some way. Grandpa George had had a stroke ten days earlier and his mother had gone to stay with his grandmother. He'd been alone with his father. It had been strange, just the two of them here. Now she was back home, her presence re-instated, preparing for them all to go to Hastings.

'Will you please go on out and play,' she said to Framsden.

He was too old to be spoken to like that. He was thirteen and at the new grammar school in town. It meant an hour-and-a-half bus ride there and back each day, and just that amount of journeying made him feel he already knew more of the world than his parents. They never left the farm, unless it was to go to the village or the livestock market in town. When he showed them his homework, they looked alarmed. 'Latin?' his mother whispered. She had learned sewing and home economics at school. At his age, she'd been getting ready to leave education for good.

Framsden heard the farm dogs barking and wandered outside. His father had driven into the yard with his aunt. Visitors, even an old aunt, were a novelty out here, so far from the village. The Hubbards never came over now they were both at boarding school. Judith and he still went for long cycle rides, but not as often as before. Now she preferred the company of her girl cousins in the village. She had a hula hoop she would not be separated from.

His great-aunt was wrinkled, her cheeks dusty with face powder. Her little brown hat had a pheasant feather in it. They saw her once every couple of years, and she never changed. Small, neat, nervous of the farm dogs. She liked to bring him toffees in a paper bag. They were always covered in cat hairs. His mother wouldn't let him eat them. 'Please just call her auntie,' his mother had once said. 'It's not polite to call her "great-aunt". It makes her feel old.'

He slouched towards the car, head down, hands shoved deep in his pockets.

'How's my nephew?' Vivian asked. 'In long trousers now? What a big boy you are.'

'I'm thirteen, Auntie.'

'Already? Are you sure?' she said, and strode off, calling his mother.

The Bell family drove through the village in their large flatbed truck, all of them squashed up in the cab. Charles and Framsden were wearing black suits and moved like people who were afraid there might still be dressmaker's pins left in the seams.

'I married your mother in this suit,' Charles told Framsden as they climbed into the cab. 'A good suit lasts a lifetime. They'll probably bury me in it one day.'

His mother pushed a hat pin into the black pillbox hat she

wore. 'Charles, that's an awful thing to say.' She had on a tight pencil skirt with a waisted black jacket. Her cheeks were rouged and her lips red. 'Sateen,' she told Vivian, who was touching the sleeve of her jacket. 'I made it myself.'

Framsden was at the window seat. His aunt sat swaying beside him, grimacing as they bumped over potholes in the road.

'Have a sweet,' she said once they were on the main road, producing a creased paper bag, peeling cat hairs off a chunk of honey-coloured toffee.

Framsden pressed his face to the truck window. They travelled along roads he knew nothing of. He had never been to Sussex. He looked at his parents, his father bent over the steering wheel, his mother with a map on her lap, tracing the route with a gloved finger. He had never been this far from home.

There was a crowd in his grandmother's house. A plump woman in a black velvet coat pulled him into a rattle of amber necklaces that hung across her chest, and kissed him with blubbery lips. He tried to be polite and bear it. He gave his grandmother a pleading look and she came to his rescue.

'This is your great-aunt Lydia,' his grandmother told him.

'Come and sit on my knee, Roger,' said the woman. She smiled and patted her knees.

Framsden moved away. 'I'm not Roger,' he said. She had no teeth and he had no idea who Roger was anyway.

His mother's cousin, a balding man called Malcolm, and his stocky blonde wife said hello and shook hands with him. They had two sons at home. One day they hoped he might meet them. They wanted to know about grammar school. Would he try for university?

Framsden lolled against the open back door. An old man in a charcoal pinstriped suit arrived with a brown and white terrier he called Whisky. He was a neighbour. He was telling Framsden's father how he had recently lost his wife. 'A tragedy the way we lose people in life,' he said. 'A tragedy. George was a marvellous man. A marvellous man.'

'Have another glass of sherry, Jakey,' his grandmother said. 'Does Whisky want a biscuit?'

Framsden bent down and patted the furry little dog.

'Take him for a walk,' said Jakey. 'Go on, lad, he won't hurt you.'

Framsden shook his head politely. He was too interested in watching these people.

He stayed behind when they left for the funeral and watched horse racing on the television set. They didn't have one at home.

In the evening, the family sat in the sitting room and played Monopoly. His mother said it had been a very nice service. Grandma Farr put a metal urn on the mantelpiece. She would have to think what to do with George's ashes. She still had Henry's urn in the wardrobe. She wanted to mix the two together, but she feared spilling them.

Framsden eyed the metal jar. It had dates in neat writing on one side: 1885–1956. He hoped she would take it away with her. He didn't fancy sleeping on the sofa with that looking down on him.

His mother rolled up the sleeves of her cardigan and sat at the piano. She began to play a syncopated, lively tune, banging out the notes.

'Birdie performed in the pub every Friday night,' his grandmother told him. 'She had the voice of an angel. She could have been a professional.'

'These foolish things,' his mother sang, her voice sweet and strong.

When she sang 'Sister Susie's Sewing Shirts for Soldiers', Aunt Vivian came in wearing a pink dressing gown buttoned up to her chin and a hairnet over her curlers. She sang along too, sitting next to his grandmother, waving her hands back and forth, giggling like a girl.

'You must take the piano home,' said Grandma Farr. 'George wanted you to have it.'

She began to cry, and so did his mother. Aunt Vivian said she'd make them cocoa.

The adults talked of the pub and the old days. The King's death, Queen Elizabeth's coronation, the scandal of Princess Margaret and the divorced Peter Townsend. England beating Australia at cricket and retaining the Ashes.

Aunt Vivian remembered the end of the Great War and the influenza epidemic that took her husband. Framsden's parents talked of the end of the Second World War. They had not seen any of the celebrations in the village, but they'd gone down to the river and Charles had taken Framsden swimming.

'Nellie is a great swimmer,' said Vivian.

'What about Framsden?' said his grandmother.

'He's a good swimmer,' said his mother. 'Charles taught him.'

'He's lucky to have a father. We never had one, did we, Nellie? Our sister Rose brought us up. Of course, she never married. She didn't want us to either, truth be told. Our parents passed away when we were babies, and Rose took their place.'

'I don't think Rose ever went far from the cottage in her lifetime.'

'She didn't even like going into the village, I remember.'

'So you were orphans?' Framsden blurted out. He had never thought about where his grandmother and great-aunt came from. They were just there. Permanent and old as churches, the pair of them. It hadn't entered his head that they must have had parents and been children.

'Framsden, don't be nosy,' said his mother.

Vivian waved her hand at her. The boy could know a bit about his family, after all.

'Our father worked as a coprolite miner. He was hurt and died of his injuries. We didn't have the medicine you have today. He got a bad cut in his leg and it went nasty. Blood poisoning. And then mother was taken by diphtheria. We'd have been sent off to the poorhouse and split up if it hadn't been for our sister Rose. She was a mother to us.'

'I wouldn't say she was like a mother,' said his grandmother. 'She was loyal, but I don't think she expected her life to turn out like it did. Now, Framsden, is that a wart on your thumb?'

She told him to get string from the kitchen drawer. He fetched it and a pair of scissors and came back. She cut a short length, wrapped it around his thumb and closed her eyes for a moment.

'Right,' she said, unwinding the string. 'You go outside and you bury that nice and deep. The time the string takes to rot down in the ground is the time that wart will take to fall off. You've got to believe in the magic and it will do its job.'

'But it's dark out.' He looked to his parents, imagining they might say something.

'Come on, boy. I've never been afraid of the dark. Do you want me to go out there and do it myself? At my age?'

Framsden crouched in the garden and dug a hole with a kitchen fork. The fork wasn't really up to the job, and its handle bent in his hand. He dropped the string into the hole, covering it up. He could see his family at the window with the curtains open, the light from the house spilling across the grass.

The next morning his grandmother asked to be left alone, so they went into town and ate potted shrimps and bread and butter in a café. Aunt Vivian bought him a stick of pink rock and a gob-stopper the size of a hen's egg. He and his father climbed the steep hill to the castle and went on the dodgem cars at the funfair. His mother bought postcards of the East Hill funicular and sent one to Connie and Judith and another one to Ella Hubbard at her boarding school.

'Do you want to write a note?' she asked Framsden.

He shook his head. He wished his mother wasn't sending Ella a postcard. It was a stupid thing to do. The Hubbards' farm was much bigger than theirs. They had new machinery. Huge fields of wheat. Norman Hubbard thought their little farm was a joke. He could imagine Ella laughing at the postcard, explaining to her schoolfriends that it came from her old nanny, a farmer's wife who wore too much make-up for a woman of her age. Who would want a postcard from somebody else's mother?

Nellie saw the family off that afternoon. She watched the noisy farm truck, its exhaust belching black smoke, disappear from sight, then she went in and sat in George's chair by the fire. The mantel clock tick-tocked, steady as a dripping tap. Time dragged. Perhaps she should have asked Vivian to stay on with her? But Vivian had her gentleman friend now.

Nellie thought she had done a good job of looking happy when they all left. Charles had been desperate to get back to his farm. They all had their own lives. Even the boy. She would have liked to have kept the boy with her. They could have gone to the beach every day. She had yet to see him swim.

All right, old girl? she heard George's voice ask her.

'George?'

Fancy a port and lemon? I could do with a beer myself after all we've been through today. What a cracking grandson we have. Framsden's a fine-looking boy.

When the door knocker rapped loudly and she saw the shadow of Jakey through the half-closed venetian blinds, she sat very still and waited for him to go away. She wanted to keep the silence in the house. Only then could she hear George's voice.

Framsden thought it odd that the only holiday they had ever taken was to go to his grandfather's funeral. Other families went camping or hop picking together. Why couldn't they be more like other families? Why couldn't they go to Butlin's, like Connie and Judith did? And Connie didn't even have a husband to go with.

Now, after a few days back at the farm, it was as if they had never been away. He wandered down to the river and stood by the water, staring at the wart on his thumb. It was definitely getting smaller. His grandmother's charm was working.

The poplar trees rustled loudly and then fell silent. He gazed into the water. Shadowy fish swam past. A newt dived down into the depths. Beside him a gang of sparrows flew out of the bushes, taking their quarrelling chatter with them, and he watched them tumble in the air. What if his gran was a witch? It was quite an exciting thought.

A fish leapt for a fly, and he was spooked by the sudden movement. He saw a rippling flicker of silver rising up into the air. The fish snatched at the fly, twisting, flopping back into the river. It was gone from view, the mirror surface of the water settling again to a pure reflection of the sky and the clouds and the trees. Framsden was filled with a sense of magic. It shocked him to see a fish leaping, defying its watery life, plunging upwards into his world.

Moments later, a brown hare ran across the fields on the other side of the river. It paused, crouching, flicking its great ears back and forth. He saw its amber eyes, the dark inky tips of its ears. Then it bounded away. Had it stared at him? His grandmother would have said it had. She had been born here, like he had been.

'You and me, we share our beginnings,' she'd told him, a secretive finger pressed to her lips. 'We're river children.'

Twenty-three

The days over Christmas 1963 were wet and grey, merging into each other, short hours of gloomy daylight. There was a smell of woodsmoke coming from the chimney. The corrugated-iron roof of the house was shiny with rainwater. Birdie, in a waterproof cape over her good clothes, sang a line of a song under her breath as she cycled out of the yard and up the farm track. Charles had recently covered the track in concrete and she picked up speed, cycling easily over the smooth surface. She lifted her voice and sang out loud to the dripping hedgerows.

She had told Charles the other day that she regretted never having a career as a singer. Charles said her part-time job playing the piano and singing at Hymes Court for the old folk there meant she did have a career as a singer.

'I mean a *real* singer,' she said, irritated by his lack of understanding. 'In a dance hall with a band.'

She reached the road and a car sped past her, sending a spray of rainwater towards her. It wasn't fair to be angry with Charles: he had not stopped her being a singer; she had done it to herself. In any case, she and Charles both knew the dance halls she'd once gone to were a thing of the past. Kay Kelly, the beautiful auburn-haired singer she had named her daughter after, would be an old lady by now. Birdie cycled with her head down against the rain. It was too late for regret. She was a farmer's wife. For twenty-two years she had started her mornings before dawn, going out to milk cows in a draughty barn. The same barn whose walls she had whitewashed the summer she met Charles.

Her daughter would be a young woman now. And Framsden

was twenty. The age she had promised herself she would tell him about his sister.

She cycled fast, feeling slanting rain sting her cheeks, her eyes watering. This was always a harsh time of year. Charles thought she hated Christmas. He jokingly called her Scrooge, and he and Framsden liked to make much of her apathy towards the festive season, pulling low faces and saying 'Bah! Humbug!' to her as they opened their presents under the tree.

The old people at Hymes Court would be wearing paper hats today. They had Christmas crackers with their lunch every day over the festive season, right up to New Year's Day. She liked entertaining the old folk, and Charles was right: she did get to sing to an audience, even if some of them fell asleep.

Her daughter had been born on the 29th of December. That's what made Christmas difficult. It threw up the past at her, and she allowed herself to be sentimental. And truly, she was getting worse the older she got. Nostalgia attacked her on every side. All the children she had known in the village were grown up now. Some of them were married. Ella Hubbard was dating a county cricketer whose father owned a seed merchant's business. She, too, would be married soon, no doubt.

She'd sent Ella a pale blue ribbon for her birthday. Another December baby born on the last breath of the year. Ella used to complain about having a birthday at this time of year. People always forgot it. Birdie had promised she would never forget. And she hadn't. She'd bought ribbons for Ella every year when she was small and had seen no reason to stop. Now of course it was just a little joke. Something slipped into a Christmas card. There was nothing wrong with that. And if Ella only waved when she saw her in the village these days, it was still a sign that the girl remembered her. That perhaps she thought of the days when she had wanted to live at Poplar Farm. The days she wanted Birdie as her mother.

Birdie stopped by the council houses, wheeling her bicycle up the path of one of them and leaning it against the wall. Connie came out of the green-painted door, waving a set of car keys. She looked matronly in her nurse's uniform, a blue wool cape over her shoulders. Judith, home for the holidays, back from her job as a nanny in London, stood at the door looking skinny and leggy in tight black trousers and a roll-neck sweater, smoking a cigarette. She reminded Birdie of Connie as a young woman. She had the same determined expression on her face, the same searching brown eyes.

'How's things?' asked Connie as they climbed into her car. 'All well at home?'

'We had a quiet Christmas,' said Birdie. 'Just us. Framsden has finished making his boat. I don't know how many coats of varnish he gave it. He says he's going to row us all the way into town in the summer. He's keen to take us up to where the new flats have been built on the site of the old tannery. You can fish for eels there. He reckons he's going to set up a little smokehouse at home and smoke his own.'

'Well, that sounds enterprising,' said Connie. 'He's a good lad, your son. Judith was thrilled with the carved bookends he made her for Christmas.'

'He's very clever,' said Birdie, and wished she didn't feel she had to defend her son's interest in woodworking. When Framsden passed his eleven-plus and went to grammar school, his teachers had talked of university. In the end, Framsden had not done much at school besides being in a skiffle band and the cricket team. Woodwork had been his best subject, and everyone knew you didn't need a grammar-school education to do a craftsman's job.

Framsden surprised them last year, saying he wanted to be an apprentice to a furniture maker. Charles had been disappointed enough to say so. The farm was Charles's life. He had imagined it would be Framsden's too. Father and son had fallen out for the first time ever. Framsden stormed about, talking of leaving home. Then the harvest had started, the busiest few weeks on the farm.

By the time they had finished, somehow or other the conversation about furniture makers and apprenticeships had been forgotten.

Connie slowed down at a junction and pulled out onto the main road.

'Charles is still smarting about Norman Hubbard's offer to buy up the water meadows,' Birdie said, wanting to change the subject. She looked out of the car window at the flat landscape of sugar-beet fields, the road cutting through them. She wondered if he should have accepted. And if Framsden didn't take on the farm, what would the future hold for them when they were too old to work?

At the mention of Norman Hubbard they drifted, as they often did, on to the subject of Kathleen. Was she going to divorce Norman? There was gossip in the village that he was seeing another woman. Connie, who knew everything that happened in the village, said the rumours were true. The woman had been seen taking the train to London. 'She was expecting a baby,' Connie said, driving carefully round a pothole in the road. 'Norman took her to a private clinic to get rid of it.'

'Does Kathleen know?'

Connie glanced at her. 'I'd say she was the one who insisted Norman take her there.'

Neither of them saw Kathleen any more. She was off at horse shows in the summer, and in the winter she went hunting with the Quorn in Leicestershire. The family were rarely together. Ella had a bedsit in town, and James had gone to university. During the holidays he lived at a friend's house.

'It's Ella that bothers me,' said Connie. 'She is such an unhappy young woman.'

Birdie hated to think of Ella being unhappy. She was sorry she couldn't talk more openly with Connie. To have a secret, to keep a part of yourself hidden, was exhausting. All her life she seemed to have had secrets that kept her watchful and distant from those she should have been open with. You couldn't keep secrets from yourself. You could try to push them to the back of your mind, but they revealed themselves over and over, and always when you least expected them.

'Poor Kathleen,' said Connie. 'But she's tough. She keeps Norman under her thumb most of the time.'

Birdie didn't answer. Poor Ella, she thought as they turned down the long tree-lined drive to Hymes Court. Ella was a secret too.

Hymes Court was a lovely old house. It had a grand entrance hall with a sweeping staircase to one side of it. A large rosewood table, circular and highly polished, stood in the hallway, a red poinsettia in a pot upon it. The parquet flooring had a freshly waxed smell. Old-fashioned family portraits lined the stairs.

The first time Birdie worked there, Connie had insisted on showing her the paintings. There was one she thought uncanny. A woman and a girl. In a small gold badge in the lower part of the wood frame was a painted inscription: *Dorothy and her daughter Amelia, aged six. 1946.*

'Every time I walk past this painting I think of you, Birdie. The girl looks just like how I imagine you must have looked as a child.'

The woman wore a green evening dress with pearls around her neck. The little girl stood in front of her in a ruched pale blue dress, holding her mother's hand. The child had a calm gaze, the same straight-backed pose as her mother. She had brown curly hair, grey eyes and a delicate, elfin face, with a small chin and high cheekbones.

'She doesn't really,' said Birdie, laughing. 'At that age I was a ginger-haired street urchin, charging round on roller skates.'

Birdie played the piano and sang for an hour, then had tea and sandwiches with the residents. She liked the old people. They were like children, all of them needing coaxing in different ways.

Music was the key. When she played the opening chords to a tune they knew, she could almost see memories flying around the room. There was an unguarded enthusiasm in the old people's voices as they sang together. Sometimes she too was overcome with her own memories. She remembered the noise of the pub, her mother at the bar, her father watching through the door. She played a music-hall number and imagined Uncle George beside her, telling her to budge up and let him play something risqué. A bit naughty! 'Don't have any more, Mrs Moore,' she sang, and there was laughter and handclapping.

'Look at your hair,' said an old lady when Birdie sat down with them after the 'show', as Connie called it. 'You want to get a brush through that.'

Birdie touched her head. Mrs Livet was a plump old woman, her features sunk in doughy cheeks and a row of double chins. She knew the words to most of the songs.

'You're right, Mrs Livet. The rain makes it curly. What about you? Did the hairdresser come this week?'

'She comes every week. I like to look nice, I do. I'm right as a mailer after she's been. I've been watching you, Miss, and you remind me of somebody from round here.'

Birdie smiled.

'I'm city-born, dear. A Londoner. I told you already.'

A man leaned towards them, his blue-veined hand reaching out for a biscuit.

'Louisa doesn't listen to anybody.'

'Do you have a sister, Mrs Bell?'

The old man coughed and thumped his fist on the table. 'You know she doesn't, Lou! She told you last week. And the week before that.'

'And I know you don't have sisters, Mrs Livet,' said Birdie. 'Because you told me so.'

'Did I? Oh, I forget. I was a holy trouble, my mother always said.'

'I'm sure you were,' said the old man. 'I bet you had all the fellas after you.'

Birdie smiled and got up to leave. It was dusk outside already. The days were so short in winter. Connie would be waiting for her. She waved to Mrs Livet as she reached the door, but the old woman was still deep in conversation and had forgotten all about her. As she stepped out into the damp afternoon, the sound of rain greeted her, promising stormy days ahead.

A month later, Mrs Livet sought Birdie out after the old people's sing-song was over. Birdie settled in an armchair beside her. She didn't mind taking time to chat. The past interested her, and everybody here talked of nothing else.

'My mother was the village midwife,' Mrs Livet told Birdie. 'An old witch, some people said. I remember there were three sisters who lived nearby, Mrs Bell, and my mother always kept an eye on them. They lived a bit of a way from here. I was quite jealous of the youngest one because my mother thought she was the bee's knees.'

'I'm sure she thought you were too,' said Birdie. She stared out of the window and wondered what she might make for tea tonight.

'They had plenty to hide, those sisters. Plenty to hide.'

Birdie smiled.

'Oh, really? Like what?'

'Well, for one thing, the eldest one was not a sister.'

Birdie turned her head. 'The eldest who? Your mother? Is this a riddle?'

'The sisters. The eldest was the *mother* of the two younger sisters. Do you see? Do you understand? That kind of thing happened all the time. Girls were so innocent when I was young. Nobody knew nothing. Some chap would find you on your own in a field with not a soul about. He'd have his way with you, give you a shilling and send you home, telling you to keep your mouth shut.

'My mother delivered the babies. She knew the truth, but she never said a word. She only told me years later.'

'I'm sorry,' Birdie said, trying to keep track of the story. 'Your mother delivered whose babies?'

'Keep up, can't you? The eldest sister was the mother of the other two. Barely fifteen years old when she had the first one, a child herself. She kept those little mites and brought them up. Never told a soul. As far as anybody knew, they were all sisters. She could have abandoned those kiddies or dropped 'em down a well or something. Women did things like that in my day. There was a lot of shame for a girl caught out by a man. People could be right nasty. I do not wholly know who the father or fathers of the children was. That is something I cannot rightly tell you. In the old days we had travelling salesmen come round the villages, and they had a reputation for being ladies' men. My guess is they had different daddies. My mother never said. Funny what comes back to you. I haven't thought about those women for years. You made me think of them. They might be dead now, I suppose. There was a fellow they liked. Oh yes, they liked him all right. Handsome as a summer's day, he was.'

Birdie got up to leave. 'That's a sad story, Mrs Livet. You'll have to tell me more next time I come. I have to be getting home now.'

She was shocked when the old woman leaned across and grabbed her hand, pulling her towards her. 'You're hiding something, en't you? That's why you pretend to be all friendly when you en't really. Cold as dead fish, you are. I bet your husband don't even know who you really are.'

'You should keep your distance,' said Connie when they drove home. 'Some of our residents never have visitors. They latch on to people. One of the old men asked me to marry him the other day. He said he was doing me a favour. That he didn't like to see an attractive woman like me living like an old maid. Cheeky sod! And then when I got home and told Judith, she said that while she didn't see me marrying an old-aged pensioner, she did think it was a shame I hadn't met anybody. I mean, really. I've done perfectly well on my own, haven't I?'

'Well, yes, you have,' Birdie said. 'You're braver than most, I suppose.'

'Don't know if it's bravery or that I'm too stuck in my ways. I'm sorry, Birdie. I'm talking about myself when you're upset. Mrs Louisa Livet is known for being a tricky old girl. She drives some of the nurses mad, following them round, telling them her stories all the time. Actually, we're having a chap come and interview some of the old folk for a book he's writing. A history professor from a university. I bet she's rehearsing for him. She loves a bit of attention, that one.'

Birdie cycled back from Connie's in the dark. She saw the yellow glow of lights from the farmhouse and was glad to be home. She decided she would take her tea in the staffroom next time she played the piano for the residents at Hymes Court.

It rained heavily all through February and there was talk of flooding. Birdie's mother sent a smelly frond of seaweed in the post, suggesting she hang it by the back door to predict the weather. It was bright with salt and grains of sand. Birdie threw it away. She didn't need anything to predict the weather. You just had to look out of the window. The rain hadn't stopped in days.

Framsden and his father traipsed across the meadows. They had moved the sheep into the barns, and now the farm dogs were herding the cows back home. The animals would not waver from the path they knew across the fields, the churned-up track that was a sea of liquid mud.

'They say the river floods every fifty years or so,' said his father, calling a dog to heel. 'I was talking to an old boy in the pub and he tells me they had terrific floods round here in 1913.'

That evening, after they'd eaten, the electricity went out. The fire was lit in the sitting room and Framsden's father sat in his armchair beside it, trying to read a farming magazine by candlelight. His mother sat on the sofa, knitting. She wore no make-up, and Framsden thought she looked younger without her mascara and red lipstick. The fire crackled. They were unworldly, his parents. His father hadn't even fought in the war. He was a pacifist who didn't dare stand up and say what he was. And what did his mother believe in? A clean kitchen. Volunteering for flower duty in the church. Singing old songs to old people. There was a world beyond the farm that neither knew anything of.

Framsden woke late the next morning to the sound of running water. The drainpipes were overflowing, the rain slanting across the landscape, shutting down the view across the fields.

The breakfast plates were still out on the kitchen table when he went downstairs. His mother's tea-coloured stockings hung on a line above the cooking range. His father's socks dangled beside them, their heels darned and mended. It surprised him to see such a messy kitchen. He made some toast and ate it. He was washing up his plate when his mother came in through the front door, soaking wet, pulling off her coat and headscarf.

'Are you OK?' Framsden asked. 'Did you fall in the river?'

She stood looking at him as if she didn't know him. Her clothes were soaked through, her hair plastered to her head.

'Mum?'

'I went to see Connie over the back fields and got caught up in flooding.'

'You look like you've been swimming,' said Framsden. 'Are you sure you're all right?'

'I'm fine,' she answered, clearing the breakfast bowls. 'But the floods are terrible. Nobody is going anywhere today. We need to stay home. This rain is not letting up. Go and see if your father needs a hand with the sandbags.'

Birdie turned away from him, unhappy to be lying to her son. And yet she had done what she did for him. She had faced up to things for him. That had been the promise she'd made him when she first held him in her arms. A promise she knew she could not go back on now. That woman at the nursing home, Mrs Louisa

Livet, had made her realize she had to act on that promise. If Birdie was a cold fish, then it was only because her secrets had made her that way. And the secrets were gone now. She felt a sick fear over what she had done. A panic that crept up her spine and swam around in her chest. She had got things very wrong. She put a hand to the wall and tried to breathe calmly but still couldn't catch her breath. Her chest heaved and her head spun.

She climbed the stairs and went into her bedroom, pulling off her soaked clothes, thinking of Kathleen. How cruel the woman had been. Birdie had just tried to explain that she hadn't wanted to give up her daughter. She had been young and had no money or any way of supporting herself. Back then, you didn't have a choice.

Kathleen had been polite at first. Ella was too, when she came into the kitchen. She looked so grown up. It had shocked Birdie to see how she'd changed. Made her feel unsure of what she was doing suddenly.

'Ella? I hardly recognized you,' she said, the first thing that came into her head. Kathleen had already hardened herself against Birdie; was already wondering how to get rid of her, Birdie knew.

'Hello, Mrs Bell,' said Ella. She wore a navy-blue mini-dress with a white Peter Pan collar. Her blonde hair was shoulder length, an Alice band holding it off her face. Such a pretty young woman with her dark eye make-up and pale frosted lipstick. All the confidence in the world. Ella lit a cigarette. 'I thought I heard voices. Do you need something?'

The three of them stood in Kathleen's kitchen, the red horse rosettes dangling on the beams, moving slightly in the warm air coming off the stove. Kathleen leaned against the cooking range.

'Just tell me the truth,' Birdie asked. 'I know this is difficult, but I have been sure of something for years. I think you know what I am talking about.'

'I'm afraid I haven't a clue. But do go on.'

'She's my daughter, isn't she? You felt it too, didn't you, Ella?

Do you remember when you were small, how you wanted me to be your mother? I don't want to cause trouble; I don't want to claim Ella. I just want to know for sure. I gave her up and you adopted her. I know this is hard, but, Kathleen, you just have to say. You adopted her, didn't you? I have no right to her. I'll leave you alone, but I need to know because my son has a sister and he deserves to know the truth.'

A car horn sounded in the backyard at the cottage and Birdie jumped, imagining it might be Kathleen or, worse, Norman, coming to tell Charles his wife was insane. That's what Kathleen had called her. *Insane*. She'd threatened to telephone the police if Birdie didn't get out.

Birdie went to the window and saw a Land Rover splashing through the yard. She recognized the new garage owner in the village. Alan Jacobs. Charles and Framsden crossed the yard towards him, heads down against the rain.

'I've been driving round helping motorists,' she heard Alan Jacobs say when they came into the house, shaking their hats and coats in the hallway. 'There's a grey car stuck in the floods. I was worried there might be somebody in it. Nearly drowned myself wading out to check.'

Birdie sat on the top stair, hugging herself. A grey car? Ella had driven her mother's grey car.

'For God's sake, Mrs Bell,' the girl had said. 'For God's sake, Mother, tell her to go.'

Ella had driven past Birdie on the flooded road. She had not even looked at her.

'The Hubbards have a grey Morris Minor,' Framsden was saying.

Alan said he'd seen the keys still in the ignition. He thought the owner must have parked it up somewhere and then the floods floated the car away.

'They'll have a shock when they come back for it. Perhaps I'll call by the Hubbards' farm and see.'

'I'll come over with you while it's still possible to get there,' Charles said. 'They've got a generator they might lend me. We've no electricity here.'

Birdie went back into her bedroom and watched Charles and Alan leaving in the Land Rover. It was over. Soon Charles would know. Framsden was heaving sandbags into place at the doors of the wooden barns. He looked small, crouching down in dark clothes, vaguely discernible against the black-soaked clapboard building, his body turning to rain, slipping through her fingers. If it wasn't for the love of him, she would have gone out into the floods and let the river take her.

By late afternoon the river, so swollen and full of itself, had burst across the fields and encircled the house. Water started coming in under the back door. It washed in so fast that boots and shoes floated around the room, and Framsden and his mother went upstairs, taking food and flasks filled with hot soup. The farm dogs bounded up the stairs after them.

Framsden hadn't been in his parents' bedroom since he was a child. It was a bare-looking room. Wooden floors. A chest of drawers and a dark wardrobe. A faded red rug and a pale green bedspread. The new Teasmade his parents had bought at Christmas was on a table, a crocheted doily underneath it, the edges hanging like heavy cobwebs. A pile of books was on the floor: his father's reading matter – *The Scarlet Pimpernel*, *Moonfleet*, a book of Tennyson's poetry. A vase filled with snowdrops from the garden on top of the chest of drawers.

His mother was convinced they'd be rescued and that he should look clean for their rescuers. She'd insisted he put clean clothes on. He'd been in his work jeans and old sweater, which smelled of sheep. He could see she was frightened by the floods. He'd given up arguing with her. Now he sat on her bed, knees up, in his best suit and tie. Bought at Burton's in town for his eighteenth birthday. 'Every man needs one good suit,' his father had said.

There was a sudden loud bang downstairs. The dogs, who had settled under the bed, barked and growled. Framsden took the lamp and went on to the landing. He heard the sound of water rushing and swung the lamp to the stairs. The flood waters had broken a window. Water swirled halfway up the stairs now. The front door had burst open and an icy wind rushed towards him. Something large and dark slammed into the open doorway. For a second he thought it was a huge fish. A whale, a kind of monster trying to get into the house. He thought of his grandmother and her stories of river monsters. The tale of the giant pike that had come in through the door. He swung the lamp forwards and went down another step. Through the doorway the wind screamed and roared up the stairs.

'It's my boat!' he yelled up to his mother. 'I can see it. It's caught on the verandah. Come here, take the lamp. I'm going to see if I can grab hold of it.'

He waded until he was chest-deep in water and the boat whacked his shoulder, sending him under, gulping dirty water, scrabbling to get a foothold somewhere. He rose to the surface and grabbed the side of it. His mother came down the stairs towards him.

'We're going to die,' she was saying. 'We're going to die.'

'Get in the boat!' he yelled, and grabbed her hand as she stepped blindly down into the waters.

They sat together with the farm dogs at their feet. The boat rocked on the water. The rain had stopped, but the waters were still moving fast in the darkness of the night. The oars had been lost. As long as they floated in the open, they would be all right. If they hit a tree or got tangled up in the submerged hedgerows, then they might be tipped out. His mother clung to him.

'I have done something terrible,' she said into his ear, and he bent to her, putting his arms around her. 'I saw Kathleen and Ella this morning,' she said. 'I told them I thought Ella was my daughter.'

Framsden wasn't sure he'd heard her right.

'You're old enough now. It's time you knew. You have a sister. I had a child before I met your father. She was adopted by a couple who lived locally. I always believed it was Ella. I told her. Kathleen threw me out of the house. Now I can see I have made a mistake. I've been so stupid. I've ruined everything. I've made a terrible, terrible mistake.'

A sister? Framsden wished he could get out of the boat. His mother was making no sense.

'Ella Hubbard is my sister?'

'No, no. Not her.'

She talked about a man called Peter. He tried to understand.

'I have made so many mistakes,' she told him. 'I think I want to die.'

'We might bloody die,' Framsden said, 'if this boat hits a tree.' He told her to be quiet. He couldn't bear to listen to her.

At dawn they floated up the village high street, passing a red pillar box. His mother was ashen-faced, lips blue with cold. Policemen waded out to the boat. The river left its silted mud everywhere; mud and shallow lakes of water, the wind rippling its surface. Framsden saw James Hubbard helping the rescue workers in the village. They both pretended not to know each other.

His father arrived at mid-morning. The waters around the farm were already going down, he said. He and Alan had put on waders and got to the farm on foot that morning. He'd found the house with the doors and windows smashed open and thought they'd been swept away.

'And Ella?' Framsden asked.

She was fine. She had left her mother's car on the road and got a lift to town. She was safe.

'Framsden, are you coming? I have to get back to the farm,' said his father. He walked away with Alan.

'Mum?'

'You go,' she said, and turned her face away from him.

Framsden saw Alan put his arm around his father's shoulders, as if he needed consoling. When Framsden looked back, Connie was sitting beside his mother. He stood still for a moment, unsure of what to do. But Connie shook her head and waved him away. He turned and followed his father.

At home, Framsden's father worked day and night, cleaning out the rooms, stripping the wallpaper off the flood-damaged walls, setting bonfires of spoilt hay and straw that sent thick, billowing clouds of smoke across the yard. A generator was set up in a barn and they had electricity again. An abattoir lorry came for the dead farm animals. Framsden's mother did not come home, and neither of them spoke of her or of the sister Framsden was meant to have.

A fortnight later, Framsden put on wading boots and made his way across the fields. Where the river looped around the house, down where his boat used to be moored, the land was muddy. The field opposite was still flooded, a wide lake as grey as a milk churn, with the reflections of clouds and trees and pale sky mirrored across its surface. Framsden stood on the riverbank. If it wasn't so awful, all this might be beautiful to behold.

His mother had given up a daughter. He had a sister. His mother had believed Ella Hubbard was her daughter. There was no sense to it, only a bruised hurt that made his shoulders ache. He hung his head and kicked the ground with the toe of his boot. At his feet something caught his eye, and he bent down, picking up a smooth fragment of what looked like bone. It was very thin, curved like an eggshell, and green staining patterned its fissured surface. He cupped it in his hand. It was bone. Part of a skull, he thought. A small animal, perhaps. He wasn't sure. He was sure, though, that it had been in the river for a long time. The flood must have thrown it up on the bank here.

A flock of wild geese descended and landed nearby, pecking at the blades of grass. Framsden turned the bone over in his hand and considered keeping it. As a child he had liked collecting things: feathers, sloughed snake skins, oak apples. But he wasn't a child now and he had nowhere to put found objects in any case. All that was behind him. He took a step forwards and dropped the scrap of bone into the river, back where it had come from, back where he thought it belonged.

'There you are,' his father said, when he went into the house. He had a tall bottle balanced on a table made from lambing crates. His father never drank.

'I found it floating in a cupboard,' he said. 'It's a bottle of port your late grandfather sent me for Christmas years ago.'

'When is Mum coming back?'

'She's not coming back.'

'So you didn't know either? She lied to you too?'

'You're young,' his father said, staring at the glass in his hand. 'Everybody has things . . . things that don't need talking about. That's not having secrets, son, that's life.'

He finished his drink and poured himself another.

'Are you drunk, Dad?'

'Not yet. But I will be. I'm going to sell up. I'm selling the farm at auction. That's how I bought it. That's how I'll sell it.'

'You don't mean that.'

'I do,' his father said, slapping his knee with his free hand, as if he were sealing the deal right there and then.

Early next morning, Framsden heard him go out, calling the dogs, the front door banging shut. He realized he would always connect his father with the vague half-light of early mornings. Framsden watched him trek across the yard, the familiar hunched shoulders, the long, loping walk that covered miles each day. His father would never sell the farm. It was his life.

Framsden walked to the end of the farm track. The water had blocked the road in places, but he jumped over it and with dry feet caught a bus. If he could have chosen, he would have gone to his grandmother's house, but he didn't have enough money for the coach ticket all the way to Hastings. On the bus, he realized how easy leaving was. The thought of it had seemed impossible before. He had believed he was deeply rooted here. A river child, as his grandmother had once said. But he wasn't. He could go anywhere.

He got off the bus at the station and walked over the bridge, up the hill, past the church and up the cobbled road where the stones were dark after a fresh shower of rain, wet and shiny as eels.

The guest-house windows had net curtains covering them, and the sign beside the door advertising electricity in all guest rooms was flaked and faded. He wondered why it was still there when his aunt had not run the property as a guest house for years. He knocked on the door.

'Come in, my dear boy,' his aunt Vivian said, as if he often called to see her.

Twenty-four

Nellie stood in the doorway to the spare bedroom, watching her daughter sleeping. Birdie was such a tiny woman. Nellie could never understand how she had given birth to such a delicate person. She'd not been the right mother for Birdie. She should have been Vivian's child. Nellie left her to sleep, shutting the door behind her.

That first day that Birdie arrived, straight off the coach with not even an overnight case in her hand, no hat or gloves, her eyes red from crying, she slept for hours. She woke briefly to drink the hot milk and brandy Nellie insisted would do her good. She slept through Nellie's neighbour popping by for a cup of tea, and she slept through the evening when Nellie made herself sardines on toast, eating it on a tray in front of the television, wondering what had happened to her estranged daughter.

In the morning, just before dawn, they were both up, yawning and crumpled-looking.

'Women in this family have always been early risers,' said Nellie. She set a bowl of warm water on the kitchen table and put out a flannel, soap and two clean towels. Birdie made a pot of tea while Nellie stripped down to her vest and washed, flannelling her arms and her neck and face. 'Do you want me to boil the kettle?' she asked, blinking water from her eyes. 'Or will you use the bathroom? I can never get used to having one. I always wash here. I hope that doesn't bother you. That's a new bar of Imperial Leather. I only just took the wrapper off it.'

'I'll use the bathroom later,' said Birdie.

She drank tea and smoked cigarettes and went back to bed again.

*

'Come down to the beach with me,' said Nellie a few days later. She thought Birdie must have caught up on her sleep by now. 'I need to swim.'

Birdie looked out of the window.

'You swim in this weather?'

'I have to find somebody who will stand on the shore and watch me. George made me promise I'd never swim alone.'

At around eight the next morning, Nellie changed into her black swimsuit and put on a pair of elasticated slacks and a blouse and pullover. She handed Birdie a bag with towels, a flask of hot soup, a bar of Kendal Mint Cake and a blanket. 'Don't fall asleep on the beach,' she instructed her daughter. 'You have to watch out for me.'

Nellie headed down to the sea, wading out into the waves, feeling the shock of the cold water washing over her shins, the surprise of it flooding between her legs, probing at her. Then she was in over her stomach, the worst was done with and she swam. A numbness covered her, and she knew she would have to swim hard to warm herself. She felt as though she didn't have any body parts. She was seventy-two years old, she reminded herself. She had to be careful not to get too cold.

She turned to check Birdie was still there. She was a lonely figure on the deserted beach. Something had happened with her husband, Nellie was sure. She suspected Birdie had told him what she should never have told anyone. Didn't her daughter understand that some secrets were not to be shared? When she got back to the shore, Birdie was curled up on the beach, asleep again.

Nellie insisted Birdie come out shopping with her. She didn't like her sleeping all the time. There was a long list of things to buy. Nellie had been surviving on snacks – tinned food, cheese and crackers – but with Birdie there she decided to get into the habit of cooking meals again.

Nellie prepared the kind of food they'd eaten when Birdie was a child: tripe and onions, liver and mash, eggs in aspic, beef tea, calves' foot broth, stewed rabbit in milk, oxtail stew, sardines on toast with plenty of butter and pepper. She spent long hours in the steamy little kitchen. Birdie didn't eat much. She sat at the table, looking out on the small back garden, her face still and pensive.

'This is good food,' said Nellie. 'Eat.' She was exasperated by Birdie's silence, but she didn't know how to break it.

In the afternoons they played Monopoly and Sorry and watched horse racing on the television while the March wind outside whistled and wailed. Birdie talked about things that were in front of them. The Monopoly board. Whether she preferred being the iron or the top hat. How long it would take to walk to the newsagent's to get another packet of cigarettes.

At the end of March, Birdie got a letter from her husband. She read the letter, handed it to her mother and went to bed again.

'Everything has fallen apart,' she said as she slipped out of the room.

Nellie read the letter. So the child had been a girl. Nellie sat down heavily. She had never asked Birdie or Vivian what the sex of the baby had been. She hadn't dared. All these years she'd felt she should act like the whole experience had never happened to any of them.

The decision she and Vivian had made loomed in front of her again. A simple decision made from a belief that it would be best for Birdie and for the child. What else could they have done? And yet there was so much regret. Birdie's daughter, a young woman who knew nothing of them, had been a leading character in all their lives.

From the cupboard in the bathroom, Nellie took a dark blue glass bottle and emptied the Milk of Magnesia from it down the sink. She couldn't quite remember what Anna Moats had used in her charms except that possibly mare's urine had been part of the main ingredients. Birdie would probably object to that, so Nellie filled the bottle with olive oil, which was medicinal after all and would have to do. She put pins in the bottle and presented Birdie with it.

'We need a lock of your hair to chase away your bad luck.'

Birdie laughed wearily. 'Mother, this is ridiculous.' She sat up on the bed. 'You're not a witch, you know. Oh, all right. Go on then. What harm can it do?'

In the morning, they woke late to a calm day. The wind had dropped and the sky was a hopeful pale blue.

'March comes in like a lion and goes out like a lamb,' said Nellie. They would get breakfast later. The bottle needed to be floated away first. Then Birdie's luck would change. Nellie was going to swim out and drop the bottle in the sea. She would make everything all right.

Nellie trod water, looking back at her daughter standing on the shore. She was wearing one of George's old waterproof capes. She looked like a fisherman who had misplaced his boat.

When Nellie reached the big metal buoy, she let the bottle go, her heart filled with hope for her daughter. A wave rolled over her and knocked her against the metal buoy. She trod water, trying to calm the panic that rose in her chest. Nellie was not given to panicking. It surprised her, this feeling of anxiety. Another wave hit her hard in the face and she swallowed salty water, coughing and choking. She set off swimming, head down, kicking hard, and a wave hit her again, pulling her back out to sea. The cross-currents were too strong for her. She heard a baby crying. A high-pitched screaming sound. Another wave hit her and rolled her under the water again.

She struggled to the surface and took a breath as fast as she could before another wave hit her in the back of the head and sucked her under. She was washed forwards and she struck out, under the curve of its roll, swimming through it.

The strength was going from her legs and arms. Down she went, like she was weighted by stones. And still the sound of a baby screamed in her ears. She was sinking. Wrapped in velvet and stones, cold granite, river pebbles, a body of shingle and sand and broken shells. The water wanted her. She heard a woman calling her name. If she could just follow the voice, then she'd be safe. Another wave pulled her under and she realized the voice was gone.

Birdie stood watching her mother, far out in the water. She remembered days as a child, the lido they swam in together. Her mother plunging into the water and swimming lengths while Birdie doggy-paddled behind her. She'd never been a swimmer like Nellie.

Nellie in a black bathing costume was still surprising to see. There was something majestic about her long back and strong limbs. The way she held her head high, as if she were listening to a sound nobody else could hear.

This morning she had pushed away Birdie's doubts about swimming at this time of year, when the weather could change so quickly. Her face was pinched by her bathing cap, her eyes pulled up.

'I'll be fine,' she'd said briskly, rubbing the goosebumps on her pale arms and hopping from foot to foot. She picked up the blue glass bottle and ran into the sea without a backward glance.

Birdie walked towards the tideline. Her mother was swimming back to shore. She was there and then she was not. She came into view and then disappeared silently, like a bottle bobbing in the waves. Something was not right. Birdie called out, running to the tideline, yelling. Her mother didn't respond. She was gone again, under a wave.

Birdie threw off the waterproof cape. She kicked off her shoes, pulled off her cardigan, her blouse, her skirt, dropping them on the yellow sand.

She was not a swimmer, but her mother was in trouble. She

waded into the sea. The waves were up to her waist now, and it dawned on Birdie that she might drown. That they might both be lost. There was sand and grit in the waves. She felt it scrape her skin as it churned around her. The ground went from under her and her feet floated free. She sank, her hair covering her face like weeds, and then up she came, eyes closed, kicking and struggling with the taste of salt in her mouth, burning her nostrils. Gagging and spluttering, Birdie swam towards her mother, the fear of losing her pushing strength into her limbs.

Birdie caught hold of Nellie's arm and hung on. They were carried towards the shore by a wave and finally Birdie felt sand again under her feet. She pulled her mother forwards. Nellie was so much bigger than her, a solid, exhausted weight. They made it to the beach on all fours, crawling, pulling each other onto dry land.

Nellie woke in a panic. She turned the bedside lamp on. It was four in the morning. She shifted her weight in bed. Her hip hurt. The bedsprings squeaked. Yesterday she had nearly drowned. Birdie had saved her life. Her daughter had rescued her.

What was her life now, without George, here on her own? Her sister was far away; her two husbands were lost to memories. She'd muddled through, one way or another. She'd been a great crow-scarer as a child. A fast runner. Leaping through the bean fields, skirts all wet with dew and bean-flower petals. A fearless girl who had turned into an uncertain mother.

Birdie was awake when she knocked on her door.

'You all right, Ma?'

'I will be. I've got things to say.'

Nellie fetched a chair from the kitchen. She sat down in the doorway.

'You were a dear thing when you were born. Tiny, and I'm not a small woman. I was surprised by you. I thought you were too delicate for me. You know I can't abide fragile things. They make me feel clumsy. I was worried you might not survive. The doctor said to feed you on condensed milk, and that's what I did.

'I thought I'd call you Evie. Or Peggy. Henry said he wanted to name you after his mother, Bertha. Henry didn't want children, on account of his health, so when he asked to call you after his mother, I was so pleased, I agreed straight away. You were such a surprise. We'd neither of us planned to have a child.'

'I knew you didn't want me,' said her daughter's voice in the darkness. 'I always knew you didn't want me.'

Nellie heard the sound of bedclothes being arranged, a pillow being plumped.

'I didn't want a child,' she said. 'I didn't want one, it's true. But when you were born, I wanted you, Birdie. I wanted you with all my heart. You were a colicky little thing, and every time you cried, Henry started shaking like the bombs were coming down on him again. We couldn't keep you. It was impossible. So we fostered you out for a year. I went to see you every Sunday. Then Henry suggested I write to Vivian and she said she'd have you. She came to London to get you.'

'You gave me to your sister?'

'She had you for two years. Then Henry said we could get you back. He wanted you, you see? So I went and got you, and we never talked about how we gave you up because it didn't matter. But you looked at me like a stranger for such a long time. You kept asking for Vivian. I was always afraid you'd hate me for taking you away from her, so Vivian and I agreed you should forget you'd ever been with her. We agreed to never tell you. But I always felt you didn't trust me after that. I always felt you believed I had let you down. Sometimes I wonder if I should have let Vivian bring you up. I wonder if it wasn't the most selfish thing I did, taking you back. But I did want you, Birdie. I wanted you with all my heart.'

'And Henry was my father?'

'Who said he wasn't?'

'Aunt Lydia wrote to me. She said I was George's child.'

Nellie shook her head. Oh, Lord. This was one story that would not be told. There were promises that had been made.

'You are Henry's daughter,' she said firmly, and knew this was what George would have wanted her to say. 'Your uncle George loved you like a daughter, but Henry Farr was my husband and your father and that's an end to it.

'I love you,' Nellie whispered, and wondered why on earth such simple words were so very hard to say.

Birdie was in the kitchen when Nellie got up the following morning. She had an apron on and was making toast.

'I think it's time I went home,' she said, sitting down at the table, reaching for the marmalade. 'I have to see Charles.'

'You don't have to. You can stay as long as you like.'

'I've been thinking about it. You're on your own here. Why don't you come back and live with us?'

'At the farm?'

'It would be like coming home, wouldn't it? I don't want to leave you here alone. We've missed out on too many years. We all have. Come home with me.'

Nellie got up and pulled the lid from a saucepan on the back of the stove and lit the gas under it. She took a jug of cream from the refrigerator and poured it into the bubbling pot of porridge. She got a tin of golden syrup from the cupboard. It was a plain dish, even with the rich syrup and the cream, but it was warming and good. They were nearly finished eating breakfast when they heard a car draw up the drive. Through the front door's frosted glass they saw Charles knocking on the door and heard him calling Birdie's name.

Twenty-five

The spring of 1964 was mild, and blowsy with daffodils and blossom. Grey clouds rushed across the sky and the sun appeared and then hid itself. Yellow cowslips filled ditches. A line of electricity pylons stretched into the distance across the farmland.

Nellie and Vivian walked through the village together. It had grown bigger, with new housing estates on its outskirts. Cars and vans were parked along its high street, and women pushed prams and children ran along its pavements. Two bus stops and a twice-daily bus route into town had brought new life to the place. With the train station, it was a commuter's paradise, Charles said. Nellie still felt it was on the edge of things, a village just out of reach of the rest of the world. She remembered too well the loneliness of the place, the summers when there wasn't an ounce of shade anywhere, and too many gloomy winters where the wind came down the street like a panic of swallows, brushing her cheeks with wingtips of ice.

The White Horse Tavern had brown carpet on the floor. Nellie peeped in the public bar. There was a jukebox playing pop music, and a pinball machine surrounded by boys in tight-fitting suits. The sisters drank port and lemon in the saloon bar where horse brasses hung from the dark beams. They had never been in the village pub before.

The local store had a sign outside, hanging over the piled-up boxes of fruit and vegetables: *Self Service.* You had to get on and do everything yourself these days.

'Ferier?' said Birdie's friend Connie when she took them in her car back to the farm. 'I don't know that name. It's unusual. Perhaps the doctor has a patient with that name. I can ask him.'

Nellie shrugged. 'Don't bother.'

'If you just had time to look,' said Vivian.

Ark Farm was sold in July, and the neighbours that Birdie had so dreaded seeing again went away. The Hubbards had bought a house in Oxfordshire. The farmhouse was sold with a few acres, and the rest of the land merged into another farm.

'Charles tells me you were too kind to those people,' Nellie said to her daughter. 'You looked after their children, and it was only normal that you felt like they were your own. Anybody with a heart would have done the same.'

Nellie wasn't sure she believed her own words, though. She didn't think she had ever fallen in love with other people's children, only with her own family.

She was wading through the long grass in the orchard when she struck upon the idea of having her own place. It wasn't that she didn't like living with Birdie, but both of them were used to having their own space. Birdie was more like her than she had realized. They liked their own company, and she knew her son-in-law wanted his wife and house to himself. She stood looking at the wooden railway carriage in the orchard. It had dusty gingham curtains in the windows and a broken step up to the door, which hung open on its hinges. She went inside. There was a bedroom to the right, with a striped mattress that the farm dogs slept on. A dead bird's feathers were scattered across the floor. The main living space had a table and three chairs. A bench ran along one side, with the window above it. Over the window was a shelf where Charles had stacked a few books. Perhaps to save them from the flood, she thought. She put her hand up and pulled one down, wiping dirt from its cover. It was a Bible. Wedged inside it was an old photograph of a woman in a wide-brimmed hat, holding hands with two little girls with ringlets and white pinafore dresses. Rose, Vivian and Nellie. It was the photograph Rose had kept by her bedside.

She nearly cried at the sight of it, those young faces from long ago, staring at her, three sepia maids in a row, eyes as dark as winter rain, paper-cut women all holding hands. She lay it down with a trembling hand. It was a sign. She would live out here in the orchard. How could the Bible and photo have got there, if not by some kind of magic?

'Oh,' said Charles, and scratched his head, frowning. 'I found that Bible when I was knocking down the old cottage. There was a baby shoe too, and an ox bone in the roof space. People used to put those things in houses to bring luck. I stuck them in here when I built the farmhouse. I had forgotten all about the Bible and the photograph. And that's you, is it?'

'Let me see,' asked Birdie. She held it up to the light. 'And that's Rose? I always wondered what she looked like. What a serious face she had. Ma, are you sure you want to live in the railway carriage? It's a bit basic.'

'I've got my beginnings in the orchard. I might as well make it the place to live out my endings. Old Anna Moats brought me into the world, and she put . . .' She didn't like to use the word *afterbirth* in front of Charles. But that was what had been buried in the orchard. Vivian's too. 'Anna said this was where I belonged,' she said.

Nellie waded through the long grass, swinging a scythe back and forth, cutting a path.

'I can do that,' said Charles, following behind her. 'The scythe is sharp, Nellie.'

'I know what I'm doing. I was a farm girl once,' she replied, watching the grass fall at her feet.

Vivian visited once a week. She'd thought of selling the guest house and moving into the railway wagon with her sister. They had always promised to live together by the river when they were old. And now they were certainly old. They were silver-haired, both of them. Vivian's hair had gone feathery and as soft as the lining of a bird's nest. Nellie's hair was thick still, a long rope of a plait hanging down her back.

Each time Vivian visited, Nellie asked her if she would be coming home soon. But with Framsden living with her, it seemed difficult for Vivian to imagine going home just yet. She was enjoying being his aunt, fussing over him. He was a good-hearted young man, and she adored him living in her house.

'So you *do* think this is home?' asked Nellie. 'You said you were not ready to come *home*.'

'This is where Josephine is, and where you are, Nell.' Vivian looked at her sister, meeting her grey eyes. 'I'm sorry,' she said. 'I'm sorry for hurting you. I loved Joe, and I was blind to the pain I caused you.'

Nellie turned her mouth down slightly. She waved a hand at Vivian, as if she was batting away a fly. *Too late*, she wanted to say. *It's far too late for this.* They sat on the swinging seat on the verandah of the farmhouse, looking out to the river beyond the vegetable gardens, the two of them silenced by their own thoughts of the past.

'Josephine might have lived if she had been born at another time,' said Nellie. 'They have medicines today that we never had.'

'We didn't even get a doctor to see her.'

'The doctor was drunk in the pub, if I remember. We did what we could.'

'And what about the hagstone?' asked Vivian. She felt it in her pocket. 'Has it really kept Josephine's grave safe all these years?'

'I believe it has,' said Nellie. She cleared her throat. 'I missed you, you know. I can't think now why we spent so much of our lives apart.'

Vivian looked away. 'Neither can I,' she said.

Vivian would not mention having cared for Birdie as a baby for two years and then the dreadful hurt, the resentment really, of giving her back to Nellie, who had never known what it was to yearn to have a child. There was no point in going over that. Or that Vivian still returned in memories to a brief moment in her life, hardly a blink of an eye, a few short days in a summer long ago when she'd been young and Joe had loved her. She had kept such faith in his declaration of love that she had managed, like a thrifty housekeeper with few ingredients, to make meal after meal out of them. She still sucked on the bones of his words and found goodness in them even now.

'Joe Ferier was a bad lot,' Nellie said, and made a tutting sound.

The farmhouse's corrugated-iron roof creaked as the day cooled. Sunlight spread across the last hours of the afternoon, a burnishing glow that made the trees look like they were full of tiny dancing flames.

'I still think of him,' said Vivian.

'I know you do,' said Nellie, reaching across to take Vivian's hand. 'I know.'

Framsden drove Vivian to the farm on Sundays. He had an apprenticeship with a furniture company and went to college one day a week. His mother suggested they clear out a barn for him to start his own business, but Framsden said he was thinking of taking a job with the furniture company after his apprenticeship had finished. When he came to the farm, he walked along the riverbank or he took his boat out, fishing for trout for a few hours until Vivian wanted driving home again. He didn't avoid his parents, but he was quiet with them. Some days he went off into the village and came slouching back, hands in his jean pockets, whistling a pop song.

Vivian said Framsden had told her he did not want to come back to live at the farm. He liked town life too much. He'd been seeing a girl, but it hadn't worked out.

'A girl?' Birdie asked. 'What girl?'

'I don't know. A girl from the village, I think.'

'A girl from here? I'll ask him.'

'No,' said Charles, who had come into the kitchen to find the three women drinking tea together. He picked up his transistor radio off the table. 'To listen to while I stack the straw in the barn,' he said, and walked out of the door. 'And leave Framsden be. Don't interfere. It's his life. If he wants us to know, he'll tell us.'

The women nodded and agreed. Here we are, thought Vivian, looking at her sister and her niece. Three women in the house by the river. Together. Just as we once promised Rose. The three Marsh women. Three women with eyes the colour of the river.

The following winter the river froze over. Just before dusk, when the sun hung red in the sky, Charles and Birdie put on skates and stepped out onto the ice. They held hands and skated slowly. Charles pulled Birdie out to the centre. They turned at the bend in the river and skated back to the wooden jetty where Framsden tied his boat. A new boat, a wooden skiff, was up in the barn, waiting for the summer. Framsden had built it in his workshop and brought it to the farm at Christmas, when he'd given it to his parents. Aunt Vivian had let him clear out her old garage and set up his tools in there.

It had been Connie's daughter that Framsden was seeing. He and Judith had shocked the family by moving in together. Aunt Vivian had shocked them all even more by saying she was delighted to have them living with her. Judith was expecting a child in the spring. They were not married, but they said they'd get round to it after the child was born. Judith thought it would be nice for the baby to be part of the ceremony.

A colour photograph of the two of them stood on the mantelpiece in the sitting room at the farm. Judith wore a silky-looking mini-dress that stretched over her belly. She was laughing, her long hair falling over her shoulders. Not so long ago, women had stayed indoors during their pregnancies. They wore large smocked dresses to cover themselves up. In the photo, Framsden stood beside Judith in jeans and a tight-fitting cotton T-shirt. His hand was resting casually on Judith's belly. He needed a haircut.

It wasn't that other people's attitudes had changed much, Charles told Birdie. There were still judgements made all the time. Even now, in the mid sixties, which were surely a time of change, he and Birdie had been shocked by the photograph. The length of his son's hair made Charles want to take a pair of sheep shears to it. He could hear the farmhands now, cracking jokes about him. But it was possible to ignore the judgements of others. That was what Birdie had never understood before. That it didn't matter what others thought of you if you had the support of loved ones. If you had people you could call family around you. Connie was proof of that. Unmarried all her life, and her family had always stuck by her and Judith. She'd married Alan Jacobs last month. He was glad for her. Jacobs had been an RAF pilot in the war. He had known Christopher's squadron, so Connie said. They'd moved into a cottage in the village together.

On the river, Charles and Birdie skated until the moon came up and the hoar frost deepened its hold on the trees and fields. Charles had not told Birdie he would have accepted her daughter as his own child. It seemed too late to say it. He wanted to tell her that he would have married her back in 1939, when it could have given them all another life, but then again, was he really being honest with himself? Perhaps, in truth, he would have hesitated to marry a girl who already had a child. And what was done was done. Birdie still believed her daughter might find them one day, and, if she did, then he'd see how things went between them.

In the shadows their breath turned silver. It was hot work, skating. All this cold and their cheeks were burning hot. Charles held Birdie's face in his hands. They would go indoors and talk of a coming grandchild, of a lost daughter who might find them one day, the danger of the ice, the coldness and how warm they had felt skating together. He would remember the sad beauty of the wind, like a child's cry. The frozen river, held fast in time. He would remember the look on his wife's face, the triumph in her eyes as she crossed the ice towards him.

Twenty-six

Sunday morning in late July and Judith was the only one awake in the old house. She was standing at the kitchen door in one of Framsden's shirts, looking out onto the garden, listening to birdsong and the distant drone of the ring road, smoking a cigarette in peace before the baby woke up, demanding to be fed.

It was going to be a hot day again. A good day to be down at the river, miles from anywhere. The house creaked as the sun began to heat up the day. Poor old house. There was so much to be done to it. It hadn't been modernized since the late thirties, when Framsden's aunt had electricity put in and redecorated the bedrooms. Aside from the rewiring that had just been done, Judith had painted a lot of the rooms white and thrown away all the awful, prim net curtains. She wanted to bring light into the place. She thought she might strip the dark stain off the stairs and take them back to the natural pine.

There was the sharp sound of a baby crying upstairs. Judith threw the cigarette away and climbed the stairs. That awful brass pot full of dusty peacock feathers by the window would have to go too. She reached the landing and the baby went quiet.

Judith sat on the stair, the sun pouring in through the window, warming her legs. They would have to have a lot of babies to fill up this house. Framsden wanted a big family. To make up for being an only child, he said.

She heard a knock at the door and went barefoot downstairs. When she opened the front door, there was nobody there. It had been happening quite a bit lately. Kids playing Knock Down Ginger, she suspected. She tried to see if there were any children hiding between the parked cars. She could smell the newly tarmacked road beginning to melt in the heat. A woman stood on the other side of the road. She was well dressed, a good-looking woman with soft brown curls and grey eyes. She stared at Judith, and for a moment it looked as though she might say something. Judith lifted her hand in greeting and the woman nodded uncertainly, then walked briskly away. Judith had seen her a couple of times now, always on a Sunday morning, standing looking at the old guest house. Framsden had suggested she might be the grown-up child of one of the women his aunt had helped over the years.

'Someone at the door?' asked Framsden, putting his arms around her.

'What? Yes. Well, no. Just kids playing again, I think.'

'Come on,' he said, kissing her neck. 'We should get going. A day on the river sounds perfect to me.'

On the long grassy bank beside the arching green willows, Birdie put out tartan blankets and umbrellas for shade. She watched the family flowing down the garden towards the river. Connie and her new husband, two of Connie's brothers and their families, along for the picnic. One of the brothers was acting the fool, throwing sticks into the river for the farm dogs. Joan and Michael were there too, picking their way through the long grass in their city clothes, having driven from London to see the new baby.

Judith and Framsden carried their daughter, Kay, in her Moses basket between them. Charles walked behind, a straw hat sitting on the back of his head, a blade of grass in his mouth, the black and white farm dogs dropping the sticks they had been thrown and racing up to him, following at his heels.

'I think Kay's a fine name,' he had said when Birdie was shocked by the choice. To her it was a secret name, a name to whisper. She could see that to Framsden it was nothing of the sort. It was a name to be taken up and given to a child, a name his daughter would carry into the future, where one day she would be told that Kay was a name with a history to it: that of her father's sister. A woman they never knew.

'It's a gift to you,' Charles said. 'You should see it that way.'

Birdie's mother and aunt sat in deckchairs by the river, the two of them like ancient twins in their matching floral housecoats. They were gaga about the baby, always fussing over her. Nellie talked about teaching her to swim; Vivian wanted to teach her dressmaking.

'Wait a while yet, ladies. She's just a baby!' said Framsden, and the old women cackled and laughed and said wasn't he a terrible tease, and oh, but Judith was a lucky girl to have him.

The baby was passed around into each person's arms, warm kisses on her fine-boned head. Nellie held the little girl for a long time, pressing her to her shapeless bosom like a bag of shopping she didn't want to drop, while she instructed Judith to take a little salt from the kitchen as a gift to ensure the child would grow up rich and prosperous.

Birdie handed out drinks and sausage rolls. Framsden took his boat out on the river. The water sparkled. A frog croaked loudly, and grasshoppers sang in the long grass. Balsam seeds were popping in the heat, and the sound of cars on the road beyond the village was a distant hum. Finally the baby was passed on to Birdie.

The child stared at her. Her eyes were blue, but they were turning grey, everybody said. A darling child. A much-loved first-born. The baby drew her legs up, and her face creased in displeasure. She began to cry.

'Oh, give her to me,' said Judith, reaching out to take the baby.

Judith was independent, part of a new generation. Anybody could see she wanted a life of her own with Framsden. Birdie had felt the same when she gave birth to her son, though she regretted keeping him from his grandparents. She had punished them for far too many years, not letting even his aunt have a share in him. If Judith felt like keeping Kay for herself, Birdie could not reproach her for it.

'Unless you want to hold her while I fetch her bottle?'

'Can I?'

Birdie felt her heart soften in gratitude towards Judith. She trusted her with the child. And why shouldn't she? For of course Birdie had to hold this baby. What else would anyone do with a baby except hold it close and love it?

All afternoon, sun dappled through the willows and dragonflies darted back and forth over the water. Swans sailed downriver, as white as wedding gowns. Poplar seed floated on the breeze. By the small wooden jetty on the riverbank, an old woman sat on a deckchair, legs crossed at the ankle. She wore an old-fashioned straw hat and held a small stone in her hands, a creamy brown stone with a hole through it. She lifted it to her eye and squinted at it. Another woman stood beside her. She too was old, but tall and straight-backed, with a way of holding her head high as if she were listening to something far off. Together they linked arms and went to the water's edge, where the ground was dry and dusty. The river flowed on, over silt and mud and memories. The land and the sky breathed easily. The sisters dropped the stone into the river and watched it sink down, down, until it was completely gone from view.

Acknowledgements

I am indebted to so many people who have encouraged and helped me throughout the writing of this book. To all my family and friends – thank you.

Special thanks also to my agent, Rachel Calder, and my editor, Juliet Annan, for their trust and expertise. Gillian Hamer, for being on the journey with me; Lucy Floyd, for her heart-warming kindness; Emma Bird-Newton, Caroline Pretty, JJ Marsh, Catriona Troth and Chris Curran; David Barnett, for books, tea and the loan of his cottage in France; Kit Habianic, for her invaluable support; and Guy and our wonderful girls, for their love and patience.

read more 

AMANDA HODGKINSON

22 BRITANNIA ROAD

In war we sometimes lose ourselves . . .

It is 1946 and Silvana and eight-year-old Aurek board a ship that will take them from Poland to England. Silvana has not seen her husband Janusz in six years, but, they are assured, he has made them a home in Ipswich.

However, after living wild in the forests for years, carrying a terrible secret, all Silvana knows is that she and Aurek are survivors. Everything else is lost. While Janusz, a Polish soldier who has criss-crossed Europe during the war, hopes his family will help put his own dark past behind him.

But the war and the years apart will always haunt each of them unless they together confront what they were compelled to do to survive.

'So convincing, completely gripping, admirable' *Daily Mail*

'A powerful debut set in the aftermath of the second world war: a moving account of the day-to-day struggle for survival' *Sunday Times*